DREAMING SPIES

LAURIE R. KING

Allison & Busby Limited
12 Fitzroy Mews
London W1T 6DW
allisonandbusby.com

First published in Great Britain by Allison & Busby in 2015.
This paperback edition published by Allison & Busby in 2015.

Published by arrangement with Bantam Books,
an imprint of The Random House Publishing Group,
a division of Random House, Inc., New York., NY, USA.
All rights reserved.

A CIP catalogue record for this book is available from
the British Library.

10 9 8 7 6 5 4 3 2

ISBN 978-0-7490-1821-4

Typeset in 10.5/15.5 pt Adobe Garamond Pro by
Allison & Busby Ltd.

The paper used for this Allison & Busby publication
has been produced from trees that have been legally sourced
from well-managed and credibly certified forests.

Printed and bound by
CPI Group (UK) Ltd, Croydon, CR0 4YY

P R   G

'The Mary Russell series is the most sustained feat of imagination
in mystery fiction today, and this is the best instalment yet'
Lee Child

'These . . . are bestselling books because Lauri. . . . . . . es
the voice and character of Holmes as well as any of the thousand
and more pastiches that have been written in imitation of Conan
Doyle. But this is more than a mere copy. The narrative . . . is
completely absorbing and motivates the reader to
want to read the rest of the series'
Historical Novels Review

'Excellent . . . King never forgets the true spirit of Conan Doyle'
Chicago Tribune

'Outstanding examples of the Sherlock Holmes pastiche . . . the
depiction of Holmes and the addition of his partner, Mary, is
superbly done'
Mystery Women

'All [Laurie R. King books] without exception, leave me with a
feeling of immense satisfaction at the quality of the story and the
writing'
It's a Crime Blog

LAURIE R. KING lives in northern California. Her background includes such diverse interests as Old Testament theology and construction work, and she has been writing crime fiction since 1987. The winner of the Edgar, the Nero, the Macavity and the John Creasey awards, she is the author of highly praised stand-alone suspense novels and a contemporary mystery series, as well as the Mary Russell/Sherlock Holmes series.

By Laurie R. King

The Beekeeper's Apprentice

A Monstrous Regiment of Women

A Letter of Mary

The Moor

O Jerusalem

Justice Hall

The Game

Locked Rooms

The Language of Bees

The God of the Hive

Pirate King

Beekeeping for Beginners

(a novella)

Garment of Shadows

Dreaming Spies

Touchstone

The Bones of Paris

For Barbara Peters and Rob Rosenwald: travelling companions
in the Empire, and beyond

. . . that sweet city with her dreaming spires . . .
– Matthew Arnold

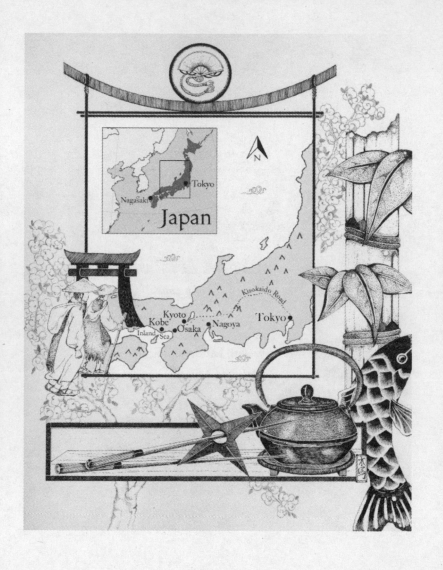

PREAMBLE

Sussex and Oxford

March 1925

CHAPTER ONE

Old grey stone travels
Moss-covered, cradled in straw,
Blinks at English spring.

'IT'S A ROCK, HOLMES.'

Sherlock Holmes raised his teacup to his lips. He swallowed absently, then glanced down in surprise, as if the homecoming drink had brought to mind the face of a long-forgotten friend. 'Is it the water from our well that makes Mrs Hudson's tea so distinctive,' he mused, 'or the milk from Mrs Philpott's cows?'

My lack of reply had no effect on his pursuit of the idea.

'It would make for an interesting monograph,' he continued. 'The significance of a society's hallmark beverage. Tea: Moroccan mint, Japanese green, English black. In America, there is – well, one can hardly call it "coffee". The Bedouin, of course . . .'

I only half-listened to his reverie. Truth to tell, I was enjoying not only the contents of my cup, but the lack of fretting waves beneath my feet and the peace of this cool spring afternoon. We had just returned, after what began as a brief, light-hearted trip to Lisbon became (need I even add the word 'inevitably'?) tumultuous months in several countries. This was far from the first time I had stood on the terrace with a cup of tea, appreciating not being elsewhere. Although it did seem that no sooner was I enjoying the peace than something would come along to shatter it: an urgent telegram, a bleeding stranger at the door. I stirred.

'Holmes, the rock.'

'You are right, it's probably best to leave America out of the matter. Although possibly—'

'Holmes!'

'Yes, Russell, it is a rock. A rather fine rock, would you not agree? An almost . . . Japanese sort of a rock?'

I turned my eyes from husband to granitic intruder.

Higher than my knee, with an interesting pattern of moss and lichen and a tracery of dark veins running through it, the stone had been planted – for 'planted' was the word – in the flower bed encircling the terrace. And not in a central position, but asymmetrically, half-concealed behind a rounded juniper. In the spring, it would almost disappear beneath Mrs Hudson's peonies.

Almost disappear. As it was *almost* Japanese. As I reflected on the massive and permanent shape, I realised that it looked as if it had risen from the Sussex earth long before juniper and peony were introduced. Before the old flint house behind me was built, for that matter – although it had definitely not been there when I left for Portugal the previous November.

'It was most peculiar.' Mrs Hudson's voice behind us sounded apologetic. 'These four Oriental gentlemen drove up in a lorry, and while the three young ones began to unpack the thing – it was wearing a sort of straw overcoat! – the older one marched back here to look at the terrace. He poked at the ground for a few minutes – hard as stone itself, it being that cold snap we had in December – and asked me what colour my peonies were. It's beyond me how he knew there were peonies at all. He was polite, you understand, but a little . . . quiet.'

We both turned sharply to look at her. 'Did he threaten you?' Holmes demanded.

'Heavens, no. I told you he was polite. Just . . . well, once or twice you've had folk here who, shall we say, give one the feeling that it's good they're on your side. If you know what I mean?'

'Dangerous.'

'I suppose. Although honestly, it was only his nature, not in the least aimed at us. In any event, Patrick was here.' A complete non-sequitur, since our farm-manager looked about as threatening as one of his draught horses. 'But the fellow clearly wasn't about to explain. So I told him – what colour they were, that is – and he said he was terribly sorry, his men would need to move one of them, but that the darker one should be fine where it was, and that's what they did. They were careful, give them that. Seemed to know what they were doing. After they left, I'd have had Patrick put Daisy into harness and drag the thing away into the orchard, but I thought it might be something you'd arranged and forgot to mention. In any event, once I'd lived with it for a few days, it grew on me, like. Peculiar ornament for an herbaceous border, but not all that bad. And I could see that the peony would be better where the Oriental gentlemen put it. So, shall I have Patrick remove it?'

'No!'

Under other circumstances, I'd have read Holmes' quick reply as an urgent need to keep her from danger, but I thought it pretty unlikely that this massive object could be hiding a bomb. Instead, I took his fast refusal to mean that this drastic addition to our accustomed view was having the same effect on him as it was on me: once the eyes had accepted the shape, the mind began to rearrange the entire garden around it. In less than the time it took to drain one cup of tea, I was beginning to suspect that, were Patrick to hitch up his horse and haul this foreign stone into the fields, our terrace would forever be a lesser place.

As Mrs Hudson said, the thing grew on a person.

'They didn't leave a message?' I asked our housekeeper.

'Not as such. Although he did say one odd thing. When they were done, the others went back to the lorry but he sat, all cross-legged and right on the paving stones, just looking at his rock. In the cold! I brought him out a travelling rug, I was that worried that he would freeze, but he took no notice.

'I went back inside, looking out at him every so often, and I was just wondering if what I needed was Constable Beckett or the doctor, when the fellow stood up again. He walked all the way around the thing, then came and knocked on the kitchen door to give me back the rug. Neatly folded, too. I offered him a cup of tea, but he said thank you, he had to be getting on. And then he said, "Tell your master he has a chrysanthemum in his garden", although how he'd know that at this time of—'

At the name of the flower, Holmes and I looked at each other, startled.

'Mrs Hudson,' I interrupted, 'what did the fellow look like? Other than being Oriental.'

'Well, I suppose he was a bit taller than usual. Certainly he was bigger than the other three.'

'With a scar on his hand?' Holmes asked.

'Yes, now that you ask. All down the back of his hand, it was—'

But we didn't wait to hear the rest of it. As one, we set our cups upon the table and strode across the terrace to the steps leading to the orchard and the Downs beyond. At the small inner gate, we turned to look. This, the more hidden side, looked as if someone had tried to carve a flower on it, a thousand years before.

Not a chrysanthemum: the Chrysanthemum.

A venerable stone we had last seen a year ago in the Emperor's garden in Tokyo.

CHAPTER TWO

Scholar-gipsy, I,
Homecoming to a strange land,
Trinity Terms mist.

THE FOLLOWING MORNING WAS wet and blustery. We took our breakfast in front of the fire, reading an accumulation of newspapers. Inevitably, the news was all about the horrors of the weather (a woman killed when a tree fell across her house), imminent threats to world peace, and the attempts at good-humoured news that convince one the human race is a lost cause. With yesterday's reminder of Japan, my eyes were caught no fewer than three times by the country's name: an art display in London, the Japanese–Russian treaty that was going into effect soon, and the results of an inquest into a drowned Japanese translator named Hirakawa. At this last, I glanced out the window at the rain-soaked rock, and closed the newspaper.

Minutes later, I abandoned Holmes to The Mystery of the Emperor's Stone (as well as a meeting he had that afternoon in London, concerning Turkey's upcoming Hat Law) to turn my face towards Oxford. I took the Morris, having tasks to do along the way, and although the drive promised to be difficult, as I passed through tiny East Dean, I found myself humming

14

in time with the pistons. When I crossed the Cuckmere, I was singing aloud – tunelessly, yes, but with modern music, who cares?

Once my business in Eastleigh was concluded (an elderly tutor, installed there and in need of good cheer and enticing reading material), I turned north. Traffic crept around an overturned wagon outside of Winchester, and again slowed out in the countryside twenty miles later, for some reason I never did see. As a result, although I'd intended to be in Oxford before teatime, I could tell that it would not be until after dark. I was glumly bent over the wheel, bleary-eyed and trying to ignore the growing headache (a bad knock in December had yet to heal completely), when a snug and ancient building rose up alongside the road ahead: grey stone, heavy vines, yellow glow from ancient windows, wood-smoke curling from a chimney dating to Elizabeth. With Japan so recently in my mind, for a brief instant I saw the building as a *ryokan* – an ancient inn, with steaming baths and a waiting masseur. A cook who had worked there his entire life, a welcoming tray of pale, scalding, deliciously bitter tea . . . But no, it was just a pub.

Still, my arms were already turning the steering wheel. The quiet of shutting down the engine made my ears tingle. I picked up my bag and, coat pinched over my head against the heavy drops, scurried for the door.

Heaven lay within, an ancient gathering space that could only be in England, every breath testifying to its centuries of smoke and beer, damp dogs, and the sweat of working men. I made for the massive stone fireplace, and stood close enough to feel the scorch of the glowing coals through the back of my coat. A placid barmaid took my order, while I continued to stand, revolving slowly, divesting myself bit by bit of the layers. Heavy gloves, woollen scarf, and fur hat migrated to a nearby chair, eventually joined by my fur-lined driving coat. When my food came, I was down to a heavy cardigan, and my bright pink fingers were restored enough to grasp fork and knife.

After a few bites, I paused to retrieve a pair of books from the bag. The first was an unlikely but colourful novel I had bought in the Gare de Lyon two days earlier, by an Englishman named Forster. It was a year since Holmes and I had watched Bombay fade behind us – almost exactly a year, come to that: seemed like a decade – and I'd bought it thinking that Forster's *Passage* might remind me of the pleasanter aspects of our trip. Instead, I was finding the plot increasingly difficult, and after another chapter I closed the covers on Dr Aziz and the criminally ridiculous Adela, to pick up the other volume, a melancholy old friend.

What is it about Oxford that puts one in a poetical state of mind? One would think that a long-time resident like me would grow inured to Oxford poetry, if for no other reason than the sheer volume of the stuff. Every undergraduate (and most tourists) who walked through one of her doors found it necessary to sit down and compose verse about the experience, all of it romantic and most of it twaddle. But still, in private moments, Matthew Arnold crept under my guard. Who would not wish to be a scholar-gipsy, leaving the safe walls – *this strange disease of modern life, with its sick hurry, its divided aims* – to learn the eternal secrets of the gipsies, like some latter-day Merlin? Which of us had not deliberately chosen to return to the city by way of Boar's Hill, in hopes of glimpsing one of the few remaining views of the city below, and thus be given an excuse to murmur Arnold's enchanting phrase:

And that sweet city with her dreaming spires,
She needs not June for beauty's heightening.

I sighed, and squinted at the pub's rain-streaked window. Not much of June's beauty-heightening today. Were it not for the pull of Oxford – less its dreaming spires than its comfortable bed and waiting fire – I would have taken a room here and ordered another pint of the man's very decent beer. Instead, warm through and well fed, I paid for my meal and dashed back through the rain, wishing I had Arnold's luck. *This winter-eve is warm, Humid the air; leafless, yet soft as spring.*

It was spring by the calendar alone, with no softness in sight. I got the wiper-blades going and turned cautiously back out onto the road, hoping the headlamps would last until I got in.

Newbury. Abingdon. *Here came I often, in old days. Too rare, too rare grow now my visits . . .*

Rare, indeed. Every time I set out with the firm intention of installing myself as a fixture amongst the stacks in Oxford's ever-blessed libraries, some figurative bomb went off under my feet and hauled me away. Once, a literal bomb.

Littlemore; Iffley. The morning's singing had long given way to groans of tedium. To keep myself awake, I recited mathematical formulae, irregular verbs and poetry. Haiku was ideal for the purpose, being both mathematical and poetic: the 5/7/5 structure was deceptively simple, which I supposed was why old Bashō came up with so many of them on his wanderings. What would the man have produced if he'd been driving through rain? Perhaps –

Sweet city of minds:
Her spires dream, wrapped in earth's folds.
June gilds the lily.

Or what about:

Dark tyres splash along,
Wanting nothing better than
A place for the night.

I snorted. Matsuo Bashō need feel no threat from me.

The tyres did indeed splash along, down the darkening road, until the edges of civilisation came down to greet me. Much more of this weather and the two Hinkseys would again be separated by swamp – despite the efforts of that other poet, Oscar Wilde, during his unlikely road-building days at Magdalen. I noticed (as Matthew Arnold had foretold) that yet more houses had been raised since I last drove this way: the dreaming spires would soon vanish beneath a tide of suburban villas.

At Folly Bridge, the heavy raindrops turned to sleet. Grandpont was all but afloat. Christchurch probably had a lake at its door instead of a meadow. Even the Scholar-Gipsy would require a roof over his head tonight. The shops on the High were shuttered, the restaurants closing, and only the drinking establishments glowed in contentment.

Dodging trams and the odd umbrella-blinded pedestrian, I wound my way through Carfax and Cornmarket, past St Michael's and the martyr's memorial, giving a tip of the hat to the Ashmolean (without actually taking my eyes from the road). At long last, more than half a day since I'd left Sussex, I turned off the many-named Banbury Road into my own lane, and my own front gate, left standing open for me.

The car tyres eased into their place for the night. The engine gave a small shudder of gratitude, and went still.

I had been blessed, three years earlier, to find a house and a housekeeper in one, when one of my aged college dons died and her lifelong companion fell on hard times. Miss Pidgeon understood the conflicting urges of comfort and privacy, and provided the first without threatening the second. She lived in what had once been the servants' quarters, separated by a small garden from the house proper, and with so much as a few hours' warning, I would arrive to find the icebox filled with milk and essentials, a fire laid (if not actually burning), newspapers beside the settee, and never more sign of an actual person than a brief note of welcome on the kitchen table. She never made the mistake of tidying my papers, and she had an unexpectedly good eye for who might be an intruder and who looked like one of the owner's odd friends.

I could, therefore, rest assured that although I should have to carry my own belongings from car to door, once inside I would find warmth, refreshment . . . and silence.

Holmes and I had been in each other's pockets for a bit too long.

The house was still, weighty with the comfort of a thousand books. The air was warm from the radiators, and fragrant with the housekeeper's lemon-scented wax. As I drew closer to the kitchen, the scent gave way to bay and onions: a soup kept warm on the back of the stove.

Tea caddy, pot and cup were on an ancient tray beside the modern electrical kettle. I checked it for water – full, of course – switched it on, and carried my bag upstairs.

I was rather longer than I anticipated, since halfway up I decided to change out of my driving clothes into more comfortable garments, and needed to dig slippers from the depths of the wardrobe. I came back down the stairway at a trot, hearing the kettle spouting furious gusts of steam into the kitchen, but even with that distraction, my head snapped up the moment I left the last step: the air from the kitchen doorway was nowhere near as warm and moist as it should have been. In fact, it felt decidedly chilly – and scented with the sharp tang of rosemary.

A rosemary bush grew outside of the back door.

One of Miss Pidgeon's estimable qualities was her horror of invading my privacy: even when she suspected the house was empty she would first knock, then ring the bell, and finally call loudly as she ventured inside. For her simply to walk in was unthinkable.

My response was automatic: I took three steps to the side, stretched for a high shelf, thumbed a latch, and wrapped my fingers around one of the house's three resident revolvers. The weight assured me it was loaded. I laid it against my thigh as I moved stealthily towards the kitchen door.

From the hallway, I could see that the door to the garden was shut. I could also see footprints marring the clean tiles: prints composed of rain, and mud, and something more brilliant than mud.

I raised the weapon. 'I am armed. Stand where I can see you.'

The sound of movement came – not from just inside the door, where an attacker would wait, but from the pantry across the room. Its light was off, but enough spilt from the kitchen to show me the dim figure inside.

A tiny woman with short black hair and the epicanthic fold of Asia about her eyes. Her muscular body was inadequately clothed, as if she had fled into the rain too fast to grab a coat. Her shoes were sodden, her trousers showed mud to the knees.

Her right arm lay across her chest, the fingers encircling the left biceps dark with blood.

'Mary-san,' she said. 'Help me.'

BOOK ONE

Bombay to Kobe

The year before: April 1924

CHAPTER THREE

Bombay: oppressive
Harsh sky pounds the land below.
Faint breeze thrills the spine.

THE ONLY THING THAT made Bombay's heat anywhere near bearable was a faint breeze off the sea, stirring the back of my neck. To think that when we'd first come down from the Himalayan foothills the week before, I had actually welcomed the balmy tropical climate! Now, with clothing that scraped my skin's prickly heat and spectacles that slipped continually down my nose, any change from this torpid steam room would be for the better. If someone had handed me a razor, I'd have shaved off what little hair I possessed.

'Why aren't we leaving?' I complained. 'Three days, and it's been one delay after another.' A diabolical conspiracy of bureaucracy, inefficiency, and the traditional bland face of the subcontinent had put us here, on just about the last ship Holmes and I would have chosen: one designed not for the brisk transport of goods, mail and the occasional paying passenger, but an actual cruising steamer, with all the social life and interaction that entailed. Holmes had suggested the alternative of aeroplane journeys, but with a nearly catastrophic one still trembling in our bones, it was a relief to discover the lack of anything resembling commercial air flight in this part of the globe. As a compromise, we had taken the berths offered, but intended to transfer away as soon as one of the touristic pauses coincided with a nice quick freighter heading for Japan without the tedium of society.

At the moment, I was not the only one to be questioning the delay. Half the population of the *Thomas Carlyle* were leaning on the rails, sweating into their flimsiest garments and glaring down at terra firma, while the great engines throbbed and the sun bellowed its way up the eastern sky.

'There.' Holmes nodded up the docks, past the nearly completed Gateway, physical assertion of the British Empire's claim to the lands beyond. A carriage bearing three passengers drove hard towards us, its horse dripping lather. When they were below us, the poor animal was allowed to stagger to a halt. I thought the creature would collapse then and there, but it managed to brace itself, head down and legs splayed, while two Englishmen (they could only be English) descended to the rough boards.

The first was a vigorous, bare-headed, blonde-haired fellow in his early twenties whose first act was that apparent impossibility of looking down his nose at people looming far above. As if the ship had been placed there for his entertainment, then caused to wait for his convenience. My prickly heat burst into fresh life as I reacted instantaneously to his aristocratic priggery: my face took on its own expression of amused scorn, my mind instantly classifying his taxonomic rank: Phylum: *Priapulida*; Class: *upper*; Order: *giving of*; Family: *not mine, thank God*—

I caught myself, and felt a flush of embarrassment rise over that of the heat. *Don't be a child, Russell! It's been a very long time since you've felt inferior to a boor.*

I shot Holmes a glance, finding him blessedly unaware of this vestige of my adolescence, then went back to watching the arrivals. The young man was probably only trying hard to conceal his own chagrin.

The second man was a large, once-muscular figure in his late fifties, who turned to help the remaining passenger down from the carriage: a woman, not as old as he. A daughter? The prig's wife? (Heaven help her.) But the younger generation made no effort to assist, merely marched around to the bags strapped to the rear of the carriage and, pompously and predictably, began to tell the ship's men how to do their jobs.

Meanwhile, the woman took the older man's hand – no girl, this, but with a womanly shape and a gleam of chestnut hair beneath the wide brim of her hat – to descend gracefully to the boards. Once there, she straightened her hat, tucked her gloved hand through her companion's arm – gloves, in this heat! – and strolled towards the gangway, ignoring the figures swarming around their bags as blithely as she ignored the rows of disapproving, downturned faces. Seeing the possessive tuck of his arm against her, I decided that this was neither daughter nor daughter-in-law. This was the older man's wife. His second wife.

'Good thing they caught us,' I remarked to the man at my side. 'Their trunks must be loaded already.' A woman that polished would be furious to watch her belongings sail away down the coast of India. But Holmes was not looking at them, nor was he taking any note of the young man, bullying the stevedores towards the gangway.

He was squinting through the sun at another fast-approaching passenger, inadvertent beneficiary of the trio's tardiness. The others were halfway up the ramp when a tiny black-haired figure trotted out from behind the quayside sheds, slipping around stevedores,

26

carts, carriages, and one exhausted horse in the direction of the gangway, a valise in one hand. Its gait was not that of a child – but only when the figure raised its head to thank the purser's steward at the base of the ramp did I see that it was a woman.

The English couple came to a halt on the one remaining gangway, immediately below us. I thought for a moment that they were hesitant about committing their exalted feet to the *Thomas Carlyle*'s admittedly mature decking, but then a brilliant white sleeve came into view. Leaning out a bit, I confirmed that it was attached to our Captain. The great man had descended from the heights for this greeting.

Hat brims concealed the newcomers' faces, but the lady's voice was quite clear as she withdrew her gloved fingers from her husband's sleeve and held them languidly out. 'I can't *think* what the Viceroy's man was up to!' she pronounced. 'Ludicrous, simply ludicrous. However, Captain, it is good to see you again.'

The Captain bowed over the lady's hand before straightening to shake the man's.

'Terribly sorry,' the husband told him. 'Idiot boy the Viceroy sent, some peculiar business with forms. Typical of Isaacs. I'll be having a word with the PM when I get back. Never would have happened under Baldwin.'

His words were less an apology than a means of venting irritation. Clearly, there had been no question but that the boat would be held for them. And steamship captains being as politically savvy as any Prime Minister, this one took care not to rebuke the latecomers, or even cast a meaningful glance at the queue of bag-laden men piling up behind them. He merely stepped onto the gangway to offer the lady his elbow. She slipped her arm through his, and allowed herself to be drawn onboard. Her husband paused to remove his hat, running a hand through a thick head of greying hair before glancing upwards. His ruddy skin indicated some weeks in the tropics, but not months. He had the son's same aristocratic manner of simultaneously expecting, surveying, and discounting his audience, with features that were handsome at fifty but would sag into petulance by seventy. In other words, a face that warned of that most dangerous of personality flaws: charm.

There was a sudden commotion among the passengers farther along the rails. A tall woman with dramatically cropped brown hair hurried for the ship's interior, losing a sudden wave of fellow passengers, their contemplation broken by the advent of progress. Below, the train of baggage-handlers was filing rapidly on, the son herding them before him. The tiny black-haired girl slipped onboard in his wake, ungreeted and unwelcomed.

With a ship-wide sigh of relief, the gangway was pulled in, the great hawsers went slack, and the throb of the engines deepened.

'I wonder who those people are we waited for?' I mused aloud. Important, wealthy: probably minor aristocrats, accustomed to the bows of captains and the scattering of crowds. Just what we had hoped to avoid. I glanced at my wristwatch. 'Only three hours late. I think I'll go sort out my things, and then take a book onto the deck. What do you—good heavens, Holmes, you look as if you've bitten into something rotten. What is it?'

'"Rotten" is the word. *That* was the Earl of Darley.'

'Sorry, do I know Lord Darley?'

'I hope for your sake you do not.'

'Holmes . . .'

'He is what might be termed an amateur blackmailer.'

I shied away from the main classification. '*Amateur?* What would be the point of that?'

The objects of his dagger look having disappeared from the deck below, Holmes turned his scowl to the receding Gateway. 'Perhaps "occasional" rather than "amateur". James Darley is a famous clubman, an amiable aristocrat long on social connections and short on cash. I am fairly certain that he acted as informant for a French blackmailer by the name of Émile Paget. I was assisting the Surété with a case of extortion in early 1914, just before I went back to America in pursuit of Von Bork.[1] Since German spies took priority over French extortionists, I was forced to abandon the investigation. In any event, they told me in June that they were closing in on Paget. Once War was declared, they lost sight of him. Permanently. They eventually decided he had been killed on the Front.'

'Do you agree?'

'I've yet to catch wind of him, so perhaps that is the case.'

'And you're fairly certain the blackmailer wasn't actually Lord Darley?'

Reluctantly, Holmes shook his head. 'I never thought he had the brains for independent planning.'

'Well, have you any reason to think Darley is still active? Either on his own or working for some other blackmailer?'

'Again, not that I've heard.'

'I should think you would have.' For both personal and professional reasons, Holmes detested blackmailers with a passion reserved for no other wrongdoer: he had witnessed, first hand and at an impressionable age, the devastation that can be wrought when a good person fears public shame. There was no doubt in my mind that any rumour of Darley's continuing activities would have caught his attention.

[1.] Arthur Conan Doyle, 'His Last Bow'.

'It is possible,' he admitted.

'This is all the more reason to make certain we're not seated at the Captain's table,' I said.

'What if they are only going as far as Colombo?'

I prayed they would be. But then I realised what that would mean. 'Oh, please don't tell me you want to follow them off,' I pleaded.

'I shall ask the purser.'

'Do that.' That should give me time to come up with a good reason why we couldn't hie off through Ceylon in pursuit of a gentleman crook.

'Perhaps if we were at the Captain's table, we might have the opportunity to—'

'Holmes, no! Surely you can find something better to do for the next three weeks than listen in on a clubman's inane conversation in hopes of catching him at something.'

To my relief, he did not persist. However, I would not leave it to chance, that we might be honoured by seats alongside the Captain and his most revered guests. Table assignments are what shipboard bribes are designed for.

We watched Bombay recede, then went below to arrange our possessions, and our bribes.

We had been in India since the middle of January, working on a case for Holmes' brother Mycroft, recently concluded.[2] Rather than turn back for England, we were now heading for California, where the pressure of my long-neglected family business could no longer be ignored.

It was also, truth be known, something of a holiday. Not that Holmes or I took holidays, but a change of focus can refresh the

---

[2.] Details given in *The Game*.

mind, and we intended to break our journey for a few days in southern Japan. As I unpacked my possessions in the sweltering cabin, I was aware of a distinct glow of satisfaction: for once, we were heading to a place as foreign to Holmes as it was to me. I would not be following in his footsteps, racing to catch up with skills he had mastered before I was even born.

While I arranged on a shelf the half-dozen books I had brought with me from England and never opened, then reached back into my case for the toiletries, Holmes flung a few odds and ends into a drawer, kicked his trunk under the bed, patted his pockets, drew out his cigarette case, and found it empty. With a grumble, he bent to drag the trunk back out from under the bunk. I sighed. It was going to be a long twenty-three days. Normally, we had more to keep us occupied during ocean voyages.

Perhaps I should turn him loose on Darley, after all? No, things would have to be desperate for that.

'It is going to feel odd,' I remarked, 'to be on a ship without having a new language beaten into me.'

His voice came, rendered hollow by the lid of his trunk. 'I thought I'd put the cigarettes in here. I don't suppose they're in your bags?'

'No. You probably put them into the "trunks not wanted".' He rarely used the middle option of 'wanted on journey', being convinced he knew his own mind, and his own possessions.

'Drat. Would it be cheaper to bribe the purser for access to the hold, or to buy onboard tobacco?' he wondered aloud. 'And, I've never beaten you.'

'Metaphorically.'

He began to wrestle the trunk away. 'You do not enjoy our intense language tutorials?'

'Oh, I'll admit they have their satisfactions' – (chief among them: survival) – 'but I don't know that I'm masochist enough to use the word "enjoy".'

'I do wish I knew more than a few words of Japanese,' he complained.

'Perhaps there's a phrasebook in the ship's library.'

'There isn't.'

'Well, there's sure to be a native speaker onboard. Maybe down in third class – or in the engine room?'

'I wonder where that girl went to.'

'Which girl?'

'The one who followed on the Darleys' heels.'

'You think she was Japanese?'

'Certainly.'

'Sorry, I find the various Oriental faces hard to distinguish.'

'The Japanese tend to be longer in face and sharper in feature than the inhabitants of China or Korea. However, it's more the way she held her body and that little bow she gave as she ducked around them.'

'Well, if she's in first she may have better things to do than give language lessons. You'd have better luck in second or third.' I latched my trunk and slid it smoothly out of the way, then rose, brushing off my hands and reaching for a book. 'I'm going for a nice peaceful read. You are welcome to borrow one of my books, but you are not to go through my trunk looking for something you imagine might be there.'

'I shall let you know if I find a tutor.'

'Holmes, I'm very happy to make use of a native guide, just this once.' And so saying, I picked up my wide-brimmed hat and left the cabin, ignoring the disapproving glare against the back of my head.

A quick survey of the *Thomas Carlyle* gave me its layout: main deck below, promenade deck with our staterooms and first-class dining, boat deck above us with saloon bar, smoking room, and a few more elaborate staterooms. Above that was the sun deck, from which rose the ship's bridge, wireless rooms, and the like. I claimed a relatively peaceful deckchair on the shaded promenade. Tropical coastline glided past. The damp pages turned. For two hours, absolutely nothing happened: no shots rang out, no tusked boars rampaged down the decks, no flimsy aeroplanes beckoned.

Normal life can be extraordinarily restful.

I came to the end of a chapter, and let myself surface. I had been aware of activity around me, voices bemoaning cabins and climate, exclaiming over chance-met friends, embarking on those preliminary conversations found among those who intend to engage fully in the compulsory social life of a sea voyage. But the racket had faded as I read, and now, closing the book, I found the area around me nearly devoid of passengers.

That indicated it was lunchtime. I stretched, luxuriously anticipating twenty-three days of enforced leisure, and – 'You did not hear the bell, miss, I think?'

I jumped, completely unaware of any person so close behind me. I spun around on the cushions and found myself beneath the dark gaze of the small Japanese girl we had seen board.

Her features were, as Holmes had described, more angular than those of the Chinese people I had grown up around in San Francisco. She was wearing ordinary Western clothing, although her frock must have been made for her diminutive frame: put her in a frilly dress and bonnet and she'd pass for a child of ten. Even with her pleated skirt and pearls, she looked no more than fifteen –

until she opened her mouth, and the urge to ask if her parents were onboard faded.

I realised that she'd asked me a question, and gave her a smile. 'No, I don't tend to spend much time below decks on a ship.'

'Keezy?'

I listened to the word in my memory: *queasy*.

'Fresh air is better,' I agreed.

'I feel right at home/Lazily drifting asleep/In my house of air.' I raised my eyebrows politely.

'Bashō,' she told me. 'One of my country's greatest poets.'

I'd heard the name. I reflected on his words: finding comfort in a house made of air. I smiled, then climbed out of the deckchair and approached her, hand out. 'Mary Russell. Headed for Nagasaki.'

Standing, she barely came to my chin. 'Haruki Sato,' she said, giving a slight emphasis to the *Ha*. 'I go to Kobe.' Her handshake was practised, although I vaguely recalled that hands were not much shaken in her country.

'Am I right in thinking that in Japan you would be known as Sato Haruki?'

Her face lit up. 'That is correct. Easier to turn names around than say to every European that no, I not "Miss Haruki".' She had a charming little gap between her front teeth, and she worked hard to push the *R* sound to the back of her tongue, away from the *L*. 'Correct' came out closer to *collect*, and 'European' – well, perhaps I could provide her with a synonym.

'What about you?' I asked Haruki-san. 'Does the sea make you queasy as well?'

'Western food make me kee—*queasy*,' she said, giving it three syllables in an attempt at the *W* sound. 'If I wait until all are finished, I can go talk the cook into some rice and vegetables.'

'But you sound as if you'd spent time among Westerners.' Beneath the accent, her English was more American than British, and too colloquial for language school. New York, my ear told me.

'Over one year,' she replied. 'My father think that Japan's future lies in its relations with the West.'

'So, he sent you to school?'

'NYU.'

Not school: university. 'What did you read?'

Her eyebrows drew together. 'Read? I read many—'

'Sorry – I meant, what was your major field of study?'

'Ah, so. Economic.'

Economics. 'Does your family run a business? Sorry, that was nosey.'

'Not at all. Economic is useful, yes, but not immediately to my family's . . . "business".'

I waited, not about to be caught out twice in the intrusive queries endemic to shipboard society. If she wanted to tell me, fine, but I would not enquire further.

To my surprise, she grinned, as if she'd read my thoughts. 'I do not think you would ever guess the nature of my family's emproyment.'

'You're probably right.' The possibilities were extensive, given what little I knew of Japanese society: rickshaw runners, bamboo farmers, ninja assassins, pearl divers. Octopus fishermen.

She leant towards me a little. 'If I say, will you promise not to tell the others? If it become known, it would be . . . distracting for me.'

Oh, heavens: she was from a long line of geisha? 'Very well.'

'We have been acrobats. For generations, my family performed for the royalty of Japan. Juggling, tightrope walking, gymnastics.

35

My grandmother was the Emperor Meiji's favourite contortionist.'

I was delighted: I'd never met a professional acrobat before. 'How superb! What is your speciality?'

'Oh, sorry, all that is the past. You see, when I was small, my father fell. From a wire. He was famous jester, you understand? Like – you know Harold Lloyd?' It took me a moment to identify the name with its transposed *R*s and *L*s, but who didn't know Harold Lloyd's character with the round glasses, dangling from extraordinary situations and snatching victory from precarious perches? I nodded. 'Father would fool on the high wire and do silly jokes.'

'Stunts?'

'Stunts, yes. His Majesty the Meiji Emperor laugh very hard at him. Father was so proud.

'And then he fell. He near to died, but His Majesty sent his own doctors and he did not die, and then His Majesty sent his . . . *anma*. Massage man?'

'Masseur.'

'Yes, masseur. With them, Father learn to – *learnt* again to walk. But he could not work. And more, it made him look at what he wished for his children. He decided to move us away from the, um, uncertainties of life as an acrobat. He retired to the family ryokan – inn, of the traditional sort, with hot springs. When his uncle died, Father became its owner. Some years ago, he saw that the future of Japan lies in its relations with the West. He think, perhaps English-speaking tourists would be most happy to come to traditional inn, but one where their language is spoken, their food and customs understood. And so five year ago, Father send my cousin to university in London. Next, he send me – *sent* me – to America for one year. My younger brother will go to New York for school as well.'

I studied her exotic features, a question mark bubbling up on the heels of my initial delight. Shipboard life was conducive to self-invention. In the course of too many sea voyages, I'd met a 'professional gambler' who disembarked wearing a priest's collar; a self-proclaimed dowager countess whom Holmes recognised as a brothel-owner; two remarkably indiscreet 'secret agents'; seventeen married couples who weren't; eight American retired Congressmen, three Senators, and a Vice President, only two of whom appeared in the Congressional Record; and enough superfluous Royals to fill a supplemental volume of Debrett's. My approach to all was the same I gave Miss Sato now: a face of willing belief.

'Fascinating. So you are on your way home?'

'I am. Although not by a direct route – I decided to see something of the world on my way. But I will be very glad to get back to proper food. And an actual bath.'

'I've heard about Japanese baths. They sound . . . interesting.' They sounded like giant cannibal pots in which the sexes casually simmered shoulder to shoulder, but 'interesting' would do to begin with.

She was traditional enough to cover her mouth when she laughed. 'Westerners do find them a puzzling side of Japan, it is true.' The word 'puzzling' coming from her mouth made me want to pinch her cheeks.

'As the Japanese no doubt find our beef pies and boiled vegetables. Although I agree, one disadvantage in travel is how it makes one crave certain foods.'

'Wrapping her dumplings/In bamboo leaves, the girl's hand/ Tidies a stray lock.'

'Bashō again?'

'Bashō spent most of his life wandering; how he must have

37

missed his mother's cooking!' She glanced down at her wristwatch. 'I shall now go and smile at the cooks. Can I bring you something?'

'No, thanks. They'll come by with tea in a while.'

She gave a little grimace. 'English tea, with milk: another thing I never learn to enjoy.'

She dipped her torso at me and walked away.

I watched her go, with two thoughts in my mind. First, that my chances of getting through the coming days without 'intense tutorials' had suddenly taken a turn for the worse. And two, for someone who was not being groomed as a gymnast, the slim figure disappearing down the steps possessed a lot of hard muscle.

CHAPTER FOUR

Pert gaze, quick sure flight.
What brings this lady sparrow
Onboard a great ship?

A SHORT TIME LATER, HOLMES found me, to deliver the news that the Darleys were not scheduled to abandon ship in Colombo. To the contrary, they planned to sail all the way to Japan. 'Oh, good,' I said gloomily.

'You don't sound too pleased, Russell.'

'Holmes, I have several printed means of keeping the boredom at bay. I have no wish to hound the footsteps of a man who may or may not have had a criminal past, ten years ago. If you want something to do, why don't you keep an eye on his son? He looks the sort who cheats at cards.'

Holmes paused in the act of lighting a cigarette. 'Cards. Excellent idea, Russell. Thank you.' He strode happily away. I sighed, and went back to my book. I would let the purser know that there was a hefty tip in it for him if he managed to transfer us onto a faster ship to Japan. Perhaps I could convince Holmes that Darley had recognised him?

I did not tell Holmes about Miss Sato, not then. I wanted to see what she would do next.

Were it not for the muscle, and the sharp intelligence in those black eyes, I would more readily have accepted her as nothing more than a fellow passenger. After all, a sea voyage goes more quickly if one has sympathetic company, and a woman on her own might be expected to seek out another of her kind, even if not of her race.

But there were other possible reasons for a stranger to seek me out. Yes, Sherlock Holmes was currently travelling under the name 'Robert Russell,' but neither of us was unknown, and this oh-so-casual meeting could be the preamble to any number of things. So I anticipated a second approach.

It did not come. She did emerge back on the deck after a time, carrying a book of her own, but merely nodded in a friendly fashion before settling into a shaded corner to read. A glance at the cover showed it to be a volume of Shakespeare's plays, heavy going for someone to whom modern English was a foreign country. From the corner of my eye, I watched her struggles, and waited for her to put forward a question.

She did not. Two hours later, when she closed the book and stood up, I expected her to 'notice' me and resume our conversation. Instead, she briefly joined a group of fellow passengers exclaiming at a pod of dolphins riding our bow-wake, then went below without so much as a glance.

When the sun was hovering at the horizon, with the sea reassuringly calm, I went to the cabin to get ready for dinner – for which, it being the first night, formal dress was not required. In any event, I needed to survey the options for table companions. We had followed our standard shipboard survival plan of booking an entire table with the purser, telling him that we would provide the names later. Over the course of the day, I had identified a handful of candidates for the remaining seats: two solitary schoolteachers, a young wife travelling alone (but for a pair of small children and their omnipresent nanny), an elderly woman artist gone contentedly deaf, and a professor of botany from an American agricultural college. During pre-dinner cocktails in the Palm Lounge, each of these proved almost pathetically grateful to be invited to join us, and I was about to take the list of names to the purser (and tell him firmly that we would begin such arrangements tonight) when I spotted Miss Sato in the doorway.

She did not look fifteen years old now. Paint emphasised her mouth and eyes, heels brought her up to a more adult height, and her dress made the most of her boyish figure. Again I waited for an overture. Again, she gave me a friendly dip of the upper torso, then began threading her way through the crowded room towards another young Japanese woman a couple of inches taller than Miss Sato. The two greeted each other with bows rather than embraces, and their expressions seemed to contain the reserve of near-strangers. As I watched their apparently brittle conversation, I reflected that the vocabulary of non-verbal interactions was at times more foreign than a language: I could not tell if these two had recently met, or were long-time friends – or long-lost sisters. The two accepted drinks from the tray of a passing waiter. Within seconds, a pair of young American men came up, drawn like wasps around a picnic, causing shy giggles and knowing glances. Before long, several other Westerners, male and female, had joined them.

I felt almost jilted.

'Whom are you studying so intently, Russell?'

I turned away from the social gathering with a wry smile. 'A perfect innocent whom I suspected of hidden plots. Holmes, your misanthropy is contagious.'

'The alert young lady with the muscles of a gymnast?'

'Precisely! What gave her away?'

'Less the build than the balance. A typhoon wouldn't tip her over.'

'Well, now she juggles books rather than clubs. She lingered on deck earlier, and I feared she might be playing up to me. It would appear that she was merely being friendly.' I glanced at his fingernails, wrapped around a glass. He'd scrubbed away the engine-room grime, leaving the skin a bit raw: I for one had no intention of joining him for lessons from that instructor. 'If you're interested in language tutorials that don't involve smothering heat and asphyxiating smoke, Miss Sato might be worth asking.'

Thus, from being a suspicious character, Miss Sato became a resource. We were too late to claim her for our table, but she dutifully introduced us to her friend, Fumiko Katagawa, and once I had reciprocated with my husband, 'Mr Russell,' the names began to run past us. The Americans were Clifford Adair from New York, dressed in a blinding white linen suit; Edward Blankenship from Iowa, whose evening wear looked borrowed from an elder brother; and Virginia and Harold Wilton, a shy brother and sister from Utah. There were two Australians, nearly identical brothers named John and James Arthur in rumpled tropical suits, who laughed loud and often and who both answered to the nickname of 'Jack'.

Then came the five English travellers in my fellow group of under-thirties. Two of them knew no one onboard: an ebony-haired woman in her late twenties with a knowing look and the unlikely name of Lady Lucy Awlwright, and Harold Mitchell, a very young man headed for a job at an uncle's business in Hong Kong, whose pronounced northern accent, spotty face and off-the-rack suit suggested he would find friendship here an ill fit. Two of the others were travelling together, an extended version of the Grand Tour that signalled their families' enthusiasm to have them safely out from underfoot for a long time: Reginald Townsman and the Honourable Percy Perdue ('I'm Reggie' 'Call me Percy'), both of whom were Eton and King's College. They were acquainted with the other man, Thomas, Viscount Darley, the fair-haired snob who had so absurdly set my hackles on edge the moment he stepped down from the carriage in Bombay. I resolved to be friendly to him, to make up for the slight.

On a simple Atlantic crossing, the numbers of young and unattached passengers would have been much higher, but this was the end of the world when it came to wealthy Westerners, thus the population of the *Thomas Carlyle* was more heavily weighted to married couples in Colonial service, retired Europeans and Americans, and Asians from Subcontinental to Chinese.

No doubt there were more Westerners onboard, attached or otherwise, but on this first night out of Bombay, nine young men and two women drew together like nervous cattle, pulling into their sphere a pair of Japanese women, a delicate lad from Singapore, a stunning Parsee girl whose husband was abed with a sore tooth – and one Mary Russell.

With a murmur in my ear – 'You "young things" are better without me' – Holmes faded away. And it was true: once he had left, the younger men relaxed, their voices growing louder as they began to crow before the women and jostle for superiority.

In no time at all, aided by the emptying of glasses, the competition had sorted itself out on national lines, with the Australian brothers on one side, the four British men on the other, and the Americans undecided between them.

Talk veered, perhaps inevitably, into sport: specifically, the kind of football – or as the Americans called it, soccer – they had witnessed in India. At that point, Thomas Darley lifted his glass and said, 'To the Colonies, long may they take our cast-offs.'

American and Australian eyes met, and a common loyalty was declared.

His indiscreet words, added to the slow and deliberate blink of his eyes, pointed to his being well on the way to drunkenness – which surprised me, as he did not seem to be drinking very rapidly. I kept an eye on him as I listened to the conversation, nodding at random points, and saw the deft way in which he stepped aside to take a drink from a passing tray, then reinserted himself into the circle next to Miss Sato. He sipped from his glass and made a remark that brought a gust of laughter. A few minutes later, he raised his hand to make another comment. When he lowered it again, somehow it ended up across Miss Sato's shoulder.

She gave Miss Katagawa an uncomfortable little smile and tittered into her hand, but the arm remained heavily in place. After a while, he lowered his head to say something into her ear. She replied, he said something else – but at her next response, his grin locked. He drew back slightly. A few moments later, his possessive hand dropped from her shoulder and slid with feigned nonchalance into his pocket.

What had she said? He was charming (that sinister word again) and educated and clearly had money at his command: if he hadn't emerged as the leader of the ship's rich, bored and unattached populace by mid-day tomorrow, I would eat my cloche. He looked about my age – twenty-four – which meant that either he had not seen active service during the War, or if he had, it was limited to the final months. He also looked to be exaggerating his drunkenness as an excuse for misbehaviour.

A few minutes later, he repeated the ritual of freshening his glass, using it to end up beside the Awlwright girl. No: perhaps I would not reconsider my initial impression of young Darley. But as his absence created a space beside Miss Sato, I moved into it.

'Mrs Russell,' she said, with that charming little half-bow. 'Not so queasy now?'

'Much better, thank you. But I have to ask. What did you tell the viscount that put him off?'

The look she gave me was wide-eyed and oh-so-demure. 'He ask me where I live in Japan. I tell him, Kobe, where my father is big manufacture of guns. Also my four brothers.'

I laughed; she raised her glass, and her dark eyes sparkled at me over the rim. 'Well, for fear of inviting a similar rebuke, my husband and I have a rather different kind of proposal for you. We wondered if you might be interested in teaching two foreigners a bit of Japanese, both language and customs?'

She demurred, on the grounds that she was a poor teacher.

'I can understand if you're not interested, but we would be happy to pay you.'

At that, she turned pink and tittered through her fingers. 'Oh, no, I could not take your money!'

'Still, think about it. We'd be grateful for any time you could give us, paid or not.'

'But I would be most happy to meet with you and talk about Japan, teach you useful phrases. Many people in America did such for me. This would repay some kindness.'

'Say, I'd like to learn a little Jap-talk – er, that is, Japan-talk, too.' This from the corn-fed Iowan, Mr Blankenship.

I realised belatedly that I should not have made my request in such a public venue, since every young man in earshot chimed in to say they'd love Japanese lessons, too, followed (with a degree less enthusiasm) by the women. I started to object, then thought the better of it. Instead, I extended my hand to my petite neighbour. 'That is most generous of you, Miss Sato. Shall we say seven o'clock tomorrow morning, in the library?'

The early hour rather deflated the interest of the others, which was what I'd had in mind, but Miss Sato gave a little bob and said she would see us then.

When the dinner bell sounded, Holmes collected me for our stroll down the grand stairway to the first-class dining room, and our chosen table. He claimed a chair with a clear view of the Captain's table: I did not comment, merely greeted our invited fellows as they arrived, making introductions all the while. A few deft questions dispelled any awkwardness, and soon the table was launched into the discovery of shared enthusiasms. When the purser came by with his seating chart, halfway through the fish course, none at our table indicated that they might be moving elsewhere.

The two schoolteachers – a man and a woman – discovered a mutual passion for Greek mythology. The deaf artist, when she'd had the topic shouted into her ear, happily turned the page on her small sketchbook and began to punctuate the conversation with a series of witty (and occasionally risqué) interpretations of Olympus, with Zeus bearing a striking resemblance to our Captain and Athena wearing a pair of spectacles remarkably like mine. Even the botany professor chimed in, with his opinion that the rites of Dionysius were fuelled not by wine but by a particular mountain herb, and that led to a merry debate on poisonous plants and the difficulties of determining cause of death. All in all, an auspicious beginning for a lengthy voyage.

Holmes, in between comments and food consumption, kept his eye on the Captain's table. I, too, glanced that way from time to time, but all I could tell was that Lady Darley and her stepson were (as happened, when inheritances were on the line) barely on speaking terms, and that she was more quick-witted than her husband. Still, even in his slowness, Darley possessed a certain easygoing attraction. The Captain seemed honestly to enjoy him, and certainly the rest of the table laughed at his remarks. Granted, one might expect a blackmailer to have mastered the art of easy banter, as a tool to disarm the unwary, but easygoing conversation did not a villain make. Some men just liked to talk.

We came to the meal's end. The schoolteachers shyly agreed to risk an attempt at the after-dinner dancing. The artist tore off a few sketches and handed them around. While the botany professor went off to examine the contents of one of the large flower arrangements, the young mother said in a wistful voice that she ought to go and see if her children needed her – then rapidly allowed the two schoolteachers to talk her into just a few minutes of dancing.

I watched the Captain's table disband, and was relieved to see the two elder Darleys head for their cabins rather than the Palm-Lounge-turned-ballroom.

Holmes had been hoping to draw both male Darleys into a card game, but not even Holmes would try to follow a man into his private quarters.

CHAPTER FIVE

Cups of morning tea:
Clear, clean, Japanese for me –
Or cool English murk?

THAT FIRST NIGHT OF dancing went on until late. At seven the next morning, there was not a young man to be seen.

I had not slept terribly well myself. First came the racket of late-goers to their bunks, then a vivid and dread-filled dream about a flying deck of playing cards – no doubt born of an overheard conversation between an earnest child and her bored nanny, and the dawning horror that I was trapped for three weeks with a juvenile whose devotion to *Alice in Wonderland* knew no bounds. Eventually, I pushed the dream away, but in no time at all, the rush of hoses and clatter of mop buckets and holystones on the deck outside wrenched me into a still-dark day.

At seven sharp, Miss Sato appeared at the door of the library, fresh as a spring flower. Holmes rose as she came across the room.

'You are here,' she noted.

'You were in some doubt?' Holmes replied.

She gave a complex little motion of the head to indicate that she would not have been entirely surprised if some more important activity had claimed us. We shook hands as Westerners, copied her bow as students of Japan, and sat down again.

She looked at the table, and her eyes went wide. 'Tea!'

Two trays sat on the library table, and two pots. One had all the paraphernalia of the English tea set, with porcelain cups, silver spoons, a silver strainer, sugar and milk.

But the other held a small earthenware pot, no spoons or extraneous substances, and little cups without handles. She reached for the pot, tentatively poured a dribble of pale liquid into the diminutive bowl, then held it to her face to breathe in the aroma. Her face glowed with pleasure.

'Where did you find proper tea?' she exclaimed.

'Between the ship's seventeen Japanese passengers,' Holmes said, 'and six of the ship's personnel, I knew that at least one of them would have something you would consider drinkable.'

She took a sip with the reverence of a Catholic at a Vatican mass, then set down the cup and stood. The bow she gave Holmes was several degrees lower than the one she'd used earlier, and held for longer. The eloquence of respect.

She resumed her seat, and her back straightened in the attitude of every schoolmaster I'd ever had. She touched her cup and pronounced a slow string of syllables, then pointed at my cup with its beverage of milky brown, shook the finger from side to side in admonition, and repeated the syllables, with a small difference: *Korē wa ocha des'; sorē wa ocha de wa nai des':* This is tea; that is *not* tea. Our lessons had begun.

That first morning we learnt a nice collection of nouns and a few key constructions: This is . . . Where is . . . ? I am . . . She had clearly already decided that, given the few days at our disposal, we should concentrate on the spoken word rather than attempt a conquest of the writing.

One tends to think of Japanese women as timid, even submissive, but Miss Sato disabused me of that notion in no time. Once convinced that we were in fact interested in both language and customs, she assumed the role of a merciless instructor.

Only later did it occur to me that this was the first time I'd actually watched Holmes devour an extended course of information. To be honest, I had to stretch myself to the utmost to keep up with him – whoever coined the phrase about old dogs and new tricks never watched Sherlock Holmes truly apply himself. That first morning, the gears of my brain were on the verge of slipping when came a fortuitous interruption. The library door banged open and in crowded a herd of young men, nervously eyeing the books on the wall, loudly greeting Miss Sato: two Brits, three Yanks and the matched pair of Aussies – Thomas Darley not among them. One of the Americans asked the steward if he had read all those books. The man smiled politely, and didn't bother rising from behind his desk to help them.

There were only seven, but with the collective mass of several more. Three of them looked like football players (American football) and two like amateur boxers with their noses still intact. None was older than twenty-three, thus a shade younger than I, and they tumbled across the room like a litter of alarmingly oversized puppies.

'Howdy, Haruki,' said Clifford Adair, clearly the self-appointed wit of the group. 'Class starting?'

'You have missed the first lesson,' she told him, friendly but firm. 'Mr and Mrs Russell already have their vocabulary assignments.'

'Yeah, well, about that. We were talking, the guys and me, and we thought maybe you could just give us some tips about the other things. Like, the food and the . . . the baths and things.'

'Japanese customs, not Japanese language?'

'Sure. The kinds of things that, you know, might keep us from putting a foot wrong when we get there.'

It was a surprisingly sensible request. I was relieved when he went on to explain where it had come from.

'Me and Ed here, we were talking to the purser about maybe spending a few days seeing your country, but we've heard, well, you do things pretty different there. And we're willing to give it a go, but the more we hear, the more it seems that we ought to learn the playbook first. The rules, you get it? One of the old guys at dinner last night, he was saying what an almighty uproar there was in his hotel when he took his bar of soap into the bathtub and started scrubbing his back. Ended up having to pay a fine – well, not a fine exactly, but an apology, even though it seemed to him that's what a bath was for. So anyway, the purser said we should talk to you, and we were wondering if you could maybe give us a few, well, lessons, like, on what to eat and how to take a bath and—'

'And taking off your shoes!' Edward Blankenship contributed.

'– and that. And, and . . . bars and stuff.'

'Bars?'

I bent to murmur into Miss Sato's ear. She looked up at the young giant in surprise. 'Do you mean geisha house?'

All seven males turned bright red and examined their fingernails. She managed to keep control of her mouth, and nodded solemnly. 'I see.'

The purser's suggestion had no doubt been twofold: he not only wished to provide a service (indeed, his income went up when his passengers were kept satisfied), but pursers and stewards were always looking for some means of keeping boredom at bay for the civilians – particularly those large and energetic near-boys apt to work off excess energy by launching into a ship-wide game of tag or blind-man's bluff, oblivious of any small children and aged ladies in the vicinity. And if he could offer an informal shipboard course with no cost to the ship, so much the better.

Miss Sato had no doubt intended the voyage to be a time of quiet before a busy homecoming. Instead, she was in danger of becoming the centre of an impromptu, three-week-long Japanese university.

'I don't know that Miss Sato needs to spend her days doing what a decent guidebook could accomplish,' I said repressively, and began to clear away the bits of paper that had accumulated, to illustrate just how much work she had already put in that morning.

But Miss Sato would not be protected. 'I do not mind in the least,' she said. 'Perhaps we could arrange for use of the library in the afternoon.'

The library steward, whose job seemed to be reading his way through the books on his shelves, stirred, and not from an abundance of enthusiasm. Without missing a beat, Miss Sato continued. 'Or perhaps the Palm Lounge would be better. That would give us more room, if others were interested.'

The young hearties looked as relieved as the steward, if for different reasons. A time was arranged, and the pack eagerly fled the disapproving gaze of a thousand book spines. Miss Sato's smile was amused.

'Sorry,' I told her. 'I don't imagine you'd intended to spend your whole voyage teaching Westerners.'

'It will help the time to pass quickly.'

The purser proved happy to host Miss Sato's Lectures for Young Men. In fact, so happy was he that, following the boat-wide lifeboat drill, a notice was posted on the boards beneath the day's news headlines, directing the passengers' attention to a talk by Miss Haruki Sato on the topic of Japanese Customs, in the Palm Lounge at 2.30.

When Holmes and I walked in, we found potted palms shoved back to the walls, rows of chairs arrayed before the band's stage, and a surprisingly large portion of the first class eager for enlightenment, or at least entertainment. While the purser's men were bringing more chairs up from the dining room, he bent his head to consult with Miss Sato. Behind them on the low stage stood a half-circle of older Japanese persons, two women and a man. The two older women were snugly wrapped in bright native dress. The man wore a suit and high collar. All held fans.

At 2.31, with sufficient chairs added, the purser and Miss Sato turned to the room. On her face was the firm, expectant look of an experienced schoolteacher. Chatter quieted, attention was paid. She gave the room a bow of approval, bowed more deeply to the purser, then took a little step back to grant him the floor.

'Good afternoon,' he said, a vestigial Australian accent emerging as he raised his voice. 'You know why you're here, so I won't delay matters, but before Miss Sato begins, I'd like to know if anyone here has seen the occupant of cabin 312? Her name is—yes?'

His attention had been caught by a stir at the back of the room. After a minute, Clifford Adair spoke up. 'Oh, it was nothing – just that Tommy here has the next room.'

'Sorry, I didn't see her,' Tommy replied: Thomas, Viscount Darley. The purser craned his head a bit to see the second speaker, who was considerably shorter than his hulking fellows.

'Did you hear her at all? Moving around?'

'I probably had the gramophone going,' young Darley said.

'Ah, yes.' The purser might have added, *So, you're the one the complaints have been about.* But he did not voice his rebuke, merely returned to the question at hand. 'The young lady's name is Miss, er, Roland – Wilma Roland? An American lady, travelling by herself. Did anyone see her? No? Well, no matter,' he said by way of reassurance. 'Miss Roland seems to have got left behind, so we'll ship her cases back to Bombay once we reach Colombo. With no further ado, Miss Haruki Sato.'

Neither Holmes nor I joined in the polite applause, Holmes because he was unconscious of it, and me because I was watching him with growing consternation. He wore his hunting-dog look, as if the purser had just sounded the horn.

'Holmes, what—' But he was up and away, following the purser through the side door.

I half-rose, then sank back: whatever was on his mind, he couldn't very well leave the ship without me.

At the front of the room, Miss Sato and her fellows were straightening from a group bow. She then turned and bowed to them, a salutation they returned, before all four Japanese citizens sank gracefully to the floor, settling onto their heels, backs straight and hands in their laps. Their fans began to move the sultry air. Heads craned side to side as fifty-some Westerners wondered how on earth two grey-haired women could look so comfortable with their knees on hard boards.

'This is how we sit,' Miss Sato told the room. 'In Western-style hotels and restaurants, you will find chairs, but we Japanese live simply, on the floor. Those floors are fitted with soft, clean mats called "tatami", very thick, woven from a kind of grass. Tatami are quite uniform. Our houses are built around them, so they fit together to keep out draughts from below. Every year, we take each house to pieces and clean it, from attic to foundation: this is required, by our government. Even then, so sorry, you will often find fleas. All—' She broke off, confused by the chuckles. With a glance at her fellows, she waited until the response subsided, then she resumed. 'All year, we sit on the tatami. We take our meals from low tables set on tatami, which also serve our children for doing homework. At night, the tables are moved aside and bedding is brought out from cupboards, and we sleep on the tatami.

'I begin with tatami so you will understand why taking off one's shoes is so basic to everything in Japan. Think of them not as carpeting, but upholstery. A muddy pair of boots will ruin the house.'

She paused, allowing every mind's eye to picture the catastrophe of footprints across pristine woven grass. Then she went on.

'But why do we not have floorboards, tiles and carpeting, like you have in the West? It is not, as you may have heard, because we are a primitive people. Yes, we lived behind locked doors until seventy years ago – but picture, please, what your country would look like if your grandparents had been born into the technology of Elizabethan times.

'However, it is not simply our long isolation. Tell me, how many of you have experienced an earthquake?' Another stir ran through the room, fed by the images that had dominated newspapers for weeks, the previous September. The two largest cities in Japan had been flattened by a huge tremor. Those buildings that survived the shaking later burnt in the terrible firestorms. Few of us had been through such a thing ourselves – I had spent part of my childhood in San Francisco, where the 1906 earthquake was an omnipresent memory – but we all nodded our understanding. 'Please allow me to warn you: if you find yourself in a brick building when the earth begins to shake, get away from it as quickly as you can. Brick and stone collapse. In Yokohama, half of all the brick buildings fell. Hundreds died. I lost friends, in Tokyo.'

A low murmur of sympathy ran through the room, which she did not acknowledge.

'In Japan, the earth moves often. In a Japanese house, roof tiles may fall, cups and plates may smash, but the house itself is soon repaired. It is built of wooden beams that lock together and move.' She held up her intertwined fingers, by way of illustration. 'Traditional Japanese house not even – *does* not even have windows. If an earthquake destroys a house – or a city – in Japan, it is because of the fire, not the shaking. In September, the earthquake came at a terrible time: at noon, when all the cooking fires were lit. Mr Yamaguchi here is an architect, and he will talk to you about the way the house is made.'

Low bows were exchanged – his not quite so deep as hers – and he began to speak. Mr Yamaguchi's English was more heavily accented than hers, but clear, and at the end of ten minutes, even the native brick-dwellers in his audience had a glimmer of how this utterly foreign style of house was created. Miss Sato bowed, and then she and the others talked about their homes, not only as machines of shelter but as places of comfort and welcome.

At the end of an hour they rose – rocking back onto their heels and flowing upright as gracefully as they had knelt – and bowed to our applause.

As a lecture, it had been quite impressive, not only leaving fifty strangers with a sense of how the cities they would see functioned, but the inevitability of the choices made by the country's traditional builders – and why such things as removable shoes and sliding walls were necessary. I had little doubt that even the muscular young men, who had come with little more in mind than lessons in colourful customs, had received instead a degree of insight into how the land, the houses, and the lives that went on inside them were as interlocked as the joints of post and beam, mortise and tenon.

The day was heating up, the Palm Lounge temperature becoming uncomfortable. Many of the audience made for the doors. However, quite a few moved in the other direction, towards the front, to have words with the speakers – or, in the case of the women, to have a closer look at the kimonos. One of those who moved forward had come in towards the end: Lady Darley.

CHAPTER SIX

Tiny thread of moon.
Vast bright cavalcade of stars.
Dark water beckons.

I WAS, AS ONE MIGHT imagine, interested in the wife of a blackmailing earl. Charlotte Bridgeford Darley – the name on the printed passenger list – was in her early thirties, with no sign of grey in her shining chestnut hair. She was of medium height and curvaceous enough to look faintly ridiculous in modern fashion geared towards those with my own stick-like torso. Fortunately, she made no such attempt, but chose soft fabrics that draped and complemented, cut in a way that made the young women around her look childish. The rest of her matched: hair short enough for fashion while avoiding the extremes, hands manicured but not showy, necklace and earrings tasteful, solid and comfortable.

The countess looked expensive, but the money had been well spent. My estimation of the earl went up a notch: this was not the wife a complete fool would choose.

I had drifted forward to join the group. Lady Darley stood patiently, with no attempt to push to the fore, yet her very presence made others fall back a little at her approach. She moved smoothly into the series of empty spaces until she stood in the front rank. She bent to admire the complex garments the older women wore, then turned to Miss Sato with a smile.

'That was a terribly interesting talk, thank you so much.' Her accent was a rich amalgam of London and Europe overlaying a Yorkshire childhood.

Miss Sato and the others all bobbed down in bows, and thanked Lady Darley in return.

'May I ask – my husband and I plan to be some weeks in Japan, where, among other things, he will be representing a friend's business. Hosting social events and the like. Do you feel I shall need a kimono?'

Miss Sato and the others assured her that it was by no means necessary, although if she was interested, any good hotel would have tailors who could make up a costume for her, as well as maids who could assist her in wearing it. This led to questions about the wide belt that held the loose garment in place – the *obi* – and soon there was a gathering of women exclaiming over the way it all worked. One of the other English women, a Kent native of about Lady Darley's age if not her rank, asked what kind of business it was that Lord Darley was representing.

'Porcelain china.' The lady gave a small laugh. 'I know – coals to Newcastle. But I believe the thought was that, considering how much destruction the earthquake caused, this could be a good time to move into the Asian marketplace. Our friend plans a trip out himself later in the year, but since we were coming through Japan on our world tour, my husband offered to, as it were, pave the way. Now, this one is made of silk, is it not? And that one of cotton?'

Talk turned to details, and thence to the undergarments. The men made haste to move away, although we did not get so far as to begin unwrapping the two kimono-clad ladies. Miss Sato kept up a stream of two-way translation, and after a few minutes, one of the older ladies had a question of her own. Miss Sato answered, and the three ladies erupted into a stream of Japanese and polite giggles, until Lady Darley broke in.

'May one ask, what so amuses the ladies?'

Miss Sato immediately turned and gave her an apologetic bow. 'So sorry, the question was what Western women wear, and I was telling Onoko-san that I would be happy to demonstrate later.'

'A ladies' salon!'

'Japanese people have as many questions about Western customs as you have about ours.'

The Kentish woman spoke up. 'Maybe we could make the afternoon lectures work in both directions? There aren't very many Japanese passengers, but it only seems fair.'

Miss Sato's eyebrows came up. 'There are more, but mostly in second class.'

'You think anyone would mind if they were invited up? I for one would enjoy meeting a few more of your people.'

'The purser . . .' Miss Sato said.

'I shall speak with the purser,' Lady Darley told her, leaving no doubt as to the result of that conversation.

Miss Sato turned to the other two for a brief explanation. One of them nodded in approval, but the other made a face and said something that caused the others to raise their hands and laugh.

Miss Sato turned back to us, eyes twinkling. 'It is proposed that the first topic of mutual explanation needs to be this substance you English call "tea".'

A storm of other possibilities flew, but since the stewards were moving into the edges of the room to prepare it for precisely that, the gathering broke up with a flurry of bows.

I found myself moving towards the door beside Lady Darley. She noticed me, and stopped, holding out her hand. 'Good afternoon,' she said, with that slight lilt of enquiry that I replied to with my name.

'That was very interesting, wasn't it?' I asked.

'Quite. I think I shall need to explore the possibilities of the kimono,' she said with an almost girlish gleam in her eye.

'They are lovely. Although I don't know that I'd be able to stand up that smoothly – certainly not after I'd been on my knees for an hour.'

As I spoke, I watched Lady Darley perform that automatic mental sorting that was ingrained in any member of English society: accent; attitude; expensive shirt slightly out of date; careless haircut; cropped nails; and no make-up. Conclusion: wealthy bohemian. Which in fact was a fair category for me.

'You're married to that older man, aren't you?' she asked.

Holmes was not an 'older man'; he was . . . well, Holmes. However, I admitted to the relationship. 'And you're travelling with your husband's son as well, aren't you?' I asked.

A tiny reaction, instantly brought under control. The countess gave me a cool smile. 'Yes, Thomas. Some people found it odd that we should take him on what is, after all, a honeymoon, but this is also by way of a business trip, seeing friends. My husband is very fond of Tommy. And perhaps he wished to keep an eye on him, just a little.'

'Indeed,' I said, and was rewarded by a slightly warmer version of the smile.

I found my 'older man' standing at the rail with a cigarette, scowling at the waves. I planted my backside against the railing. 'You missed a fascinating talk.' He said nothing. 'About the implications of tatami mats. I also spoke with Lady Darley. I get the distinct feeling that she's led an unorthodox life. Not as completely sure of herself, socially speaking, as she appears to be. I'd say an earldom is a big step up from where she started. I wonder if that's why she's travelling without maids? Servants can be so intimidating.' His reply was a grunt. I sighed.

'Are you going to tell me who Wilma Roland is?'

'I have no idea.'

'Then why did you sprint out after the purser?'

'I did not sprint.'

'Holmes.'

'I am considering revealing my identity, that I might look at her things before they are packed away.'

'Oh, Lord, please don't do that.' Invoking the name of Sherlock Holmes to the purser would spread it across the ship in no time flat, condemning him – and worse, me – to three weeks of sidling away from earnest passengers with the most *interesting* problems, or three weeks in our cabin.

'A woman disappears from the ship a blackmailer is on. And do not tell me that coincidences have been known to occur.'

'Although they do happen. You think the purser will hurry to clear her cabin?'

'They're sending her trunks back from Colombo.'

'Then we'll have to break in. If I provide a distraction, how long would you need?'

'Six or seven minutes should do it.'

'Most everyone is busy with tea, including the purser's men. If it were done . . .'

He flicked the end of his cigarette into the wind. '. . . 'twere well it were done quickly.'

On our way, I caught up a large flower arrangement from a meeting-place of the hallways, and stood with it outside the door to 312. Holmes tried the handle, tapped gently at the door, then dropped to his heels to work his picklocks. He paused.

'Scratches.'

'Every lock on the ship is scratched, Holmes.' Keys were not easy to aim when the seas were up.

'Recent.'

'Just get on with it, please.'

The laden vase was heavy. Flowers tickled my nose. I was just about to offer to trade places when I heard a *click*. He stepped inside, shut the door – and two uniformed men walked around the corner.

The vase did not break when it hit the carpeting, although I'd tried hard, but it did vomit flowers in all directions. Water glugged across the corridor, soaking the wool, and the exclamations of the men mingled with my own cries of horror and loud apologies and . . .

And it was well more than seven minutes before the catastrophe was cleared and the last apology given, along with a fervent promise that, yes, next time one of the old ladies wanted a bouquet of flowers I'd tell her to order it from the ship's florist.

Fortunately, cabin 312 had a generous porthole, and Holmes was gone when the two men went inside. Back on deck, the state of his buttons told me how close the fit had been, while the set of his shoulders testified that our bit of chicanery had not given him much.

'Did you find any further signs that someone broke in?' I asked him.

'Nothing obvious.'

No hastily scrubbed bloodstains, no upturned mattresses, then. 'Tell me I didn't spoil that nice bit of carpet for nothing?'

'Oh, Miss Roland was definitely onboard at some point.'

'Could she have got off again in Bombay?' We'd been sitting at the docks long enough for the entire passenger list to march up and down the gangways ten times.

'There were three hairs on the bedcover, but none on the pillowcase beneath. The imprint of a body, less the shoes.'

'As if she'd lain down for a time on top of the bed.'

'Also, it won't take the steward long to pack up her goods. Most of it remains in her trunk or her handbag.'

'Perhaps she's secreted away with a lover?'

'The purser said that no other passenger has failed to appear for at least one of the meals.'

'He could be down in second class? Or she,' I amended, then amended further. 'Or third.'

'This purser is an old hand. He'd have asked the stewards before he put it before the passengers.'

'It might help if we had a photograph.'

Obligingly, he removed an envelope from his breast pocket.

I took it. 'What else did you find? Or, not find, for that matter?'

'Wallet, passport, money, an expensive wristwatch, all there. She'd used her fountain pen quite recently, since it was on the top of her handbag's contents. No journal or stationery, other than a box of paper in the trunk beneath her bunk. But, no key.'

'You mean, to the trunk?'

'I mean, to her cabin door.'

Interesting.

The envelope contained four snapshots, all taken in India. Only one face appeared in all four, a tall, thin, tentative-looking woman in her thirties with a modern haircut and friendly eyes.

I studied the face: she smiled like someone coming back to

life after a long illness, not fully trusting her health. Her clothing did not look new, unlike the modern cut of her hair. I wondered which of her friends had talked her into that exaggeratedly sharp cut. Possibly the one whose blonde hair had a similar shape? Hmm. I'd seen that head before, though not from the front. Where . . . ?

I suddenly had it. 'She *was* onboard, when we cast off. I saw her in that crowd about fifty feet down the railings from us. As the gangway came in, she turned to go inside.'

Holmes thought for a moment, recalling the sequence. 'As we cast off? Or as Lord and Lady Darley passed beneath us?'

The earl's hands had come up, removing his hat, smoothing his hair. Revealing his face.

My eyes came up to meet his. 'What, so this woman recognised him and panicked? Why?'

'We know his methods.'

'You're suggesting that Darley was blackmailing Miss Roland? Ten years ago?'

'Few criminals reform without reason. Darley was never even accused.'

'You think he's still active? More than that – you think he's moved on from merely providing information to active blackmail.'

'I think it a possibility.'

'But that it was a coincidence that she found herself on the same ship with him?'

'That remains to be seen.' Holmes did not readily concede to chance. 'And she was trapped because the ship cast off the instant Darley came on.'

'Yes.'

'If she's not hiding out in her room, for fear that he knows she's here, then she's hiding somewhere else. Ships are big. And she only needs to stay out of his way until we reach Colombo. She'd probably figure that her things would be taken off there, too.'

'That is one possibility.'

'You have a more likely one?'

'She lay on her bunk waiting for the dark, then stepped overboard.'

'What? Holmes, I . . .' I stopped, considering my words. 'Holmes, not everyone commits suicide when threatened with exposure.'

He pushed aside what I was saying for an earlier concern. 'Say it was a coincidence. Would she have believed it? Blackmail oozes into every corner of the victim's life, colours every surface, weaves a thread of terror through every innocent happenstance. Those photographs were taken over a period of three or four weeks. They show her progress from a haunted creature unable to eat to a young woman with a new haircut and a tentative interest in make-up. She's gained several pounds, despite it being the tropics.'

I fanned out the pictures, arranging them in the sequence he had in mind, then reversed them. 'They could as well go the other way around.'

He jabbed an impatient finger at the one with the healthiest-looking woman, standing in a marketplace. 'Russell: the background. What fruit is that?'

Mangoes. Which had only just begun to appear our last week in the city. 'All right, let's go with your theory. Was Darley in fact following her?'

'Much as I dislike the idea of coincidence, blackmailers do not generally hound victims to their deaths.'

'What if it wasn't blackmail? Perhaps they'd had an affair, and she broke it off, but he didn't accept that.'

'Does she look the sort to rouse a man like Darley to passion?'

I thumbed through the four pictures again. Her friends were younger, with careful make-up and clothing chosen to emphasise their youth: the 'fishing fleet', sailing to India in hopes of catching a young officer. Miss Roland, on the other hand, looked like an intelligent woman with more on her mind than hooking a husband. Still . . .

'Stranger things have happened.' I handed him the photos. 'But in truth, I can't see Lady Darley giving him that much free rein. She doesn't seem like a woman who misses much.'

I told him then about the salon gathering. He waited with small patience through the substance of Miss Sato's presentation, then showed more interest when I told him what Lady Darley had said.

He grunted, and took out his tobacco.

'Their being here does sound reasonable,' I mused. 'I'd guess there is a growing market for fancy English goods in Japan, especially after their Prince Regent visited Britain three years ago. As for Darley, there could be money in it for him, if he provided his friend with any likely contacts.' It was one of the few jobs for which impoverished nobles were qualified: converting the Old Boys' Network into hard cash. And if the wife had money of her own, well, the wife didn't have to know about the transfer of pounds sterling from one old boy to another.

Holmes scowled, but he did not argue.

CHAPTER SEVEN

Black from their shovels,
White with their pure thoughts and prayers,
Red runs through the veins.

WE DOCKED AT COLOMBO early the next morning, after a
night in which my card dreams turned to earthquakes,
no doubt inspired by Miss Sato's lecture and underscored by the
nauseating roll of heavy seas. I'd spent the latter portion of the
night seeking fresh air on the topmost deck, trying to count the
blessings of a rolling ship: an absence of competing musical airs
wafting from the staterooms (the skip of needles being hard on
gramophone records); no midnight shuffleboard or deck-tennis
games; less danger of being set upon by the profoundly intoxicated
(who were kept gently but firmly behind doors by the stewards
whenever the seas were rough).

Not that counting had led to much sleep. However, the day's
lesson with Miss Sato was to be delayed, as she wished to go ashore
with her admirers during our half-day in port. I intended to take
advantage of her absence, and the motionless decks, to sleep.

Once, that is, the tumult had died down. While the
Colombo-bound passengers and day trippers jostled noisily
down one set of gangways and the coal and coconuts streamed

up another, I retired to a deckchair with my book. Holmes glowered down at the teeming dockside below. I pointedly kept my eyes on the pages.

'What do you make of her, Russell?'

He was not asking about Lady Darley. 'Miss Sato? She seems both intelligent and competent.'

'Yes.' He drew out the word. I was not surprised when it was followed by the sound of his cigarette case clicking open.

I sighed, and let the book fall. There are drawbacks to having a husband with a restless mind. 'Too competent, you think?'

'Your initial impulse was suspicion,' he reminded me. 'Your instincts have been well honed.'

'"Instinct" is hardly the word. More like "reflex". I see nothing in Miss Sato to make me doubt that she is what she said, unlikely as it sounds.'

'The daughter of an acrobatic dynasty, sent for education to an American university.'

'No more dubious than half the people we come across. What are you—' I stopped. Oh, for heaven's sake: were blackmailers not sufficient challenge for a simple sea voyage? Now we had to add espionage to the mix? 'You think Miss Sato is a Japanese spy? Or do you mean she's working for Mycroft?' It was true that if anyone could envision Haruki Sato as a secret agent, it would be Mycroft Holmes. My brother-in-law's complex, imaginative, and apparently ubiquitous information-gathering machinery left the official Intelligence of any nation in the dust. If Japan's secret police were up to that level of creativity, I was prepared to be impressed.

'Why would one of my brother's agents not have identified herself?'

'Because it's your brother.'

'Hmm. And if she's not his?'

'Who else – oh. Your blackmailer?' I felt a headache coming on. 'Because she came aboard just after he and his wife did?'

'Because two unusual events are often linked.'

'Oh, Holmes. Do you have any reason whatsoever to suspect that the Earl of Darley is a crook? Any evidence that he ever was, for that matter? Or that Haruki Sato is not what she appears?'

'None,' he replied serenely.

I rested my head back against the deckchair and closed my eyes. I was well accustomed to my husband's need to manufacture work for himself, but doing so two days into what might be considered a holiday did not bode well for the coming weeks. 'Do you want to stop the lessons?'

'I see no reason to do so,' he said. 'She is a more effective teacher than the stoker.'

'And lessons with her won't leave you black with coal dust.'

Neither of us needed to add the additional reason: keeping her close kept her under observation.

I attempted to push the conversation past this random assortment of criminal suspicions. 'Do you think we'll have enough of the language to stumble through on our own?'

'I imagine we shall find schoolboys in every village, following us about, eager to practise their English.'

'Yes, I don't suppose there's much point in trying to go incognito.'

'Not unless you're willing to act the hunchback day in and day out.'

He and I would have to lose six or eight inches to pass for even a tall Japanese – to say nothing of arduous make-up. 'I'm too young to begin a lifetime of back problems, thank you. We'll have to resign ourselves to attracting attention wherever we go.'

'Perhaps not.'

'You have an alternative? Other than amputating our legs?'

'We will be conspicuous no matter what. The trick is to be easily dismissed thereafter.' He had something in mind: I waited for it. 'Russell, I propose we become Buddhist pilgrims.'

I snorted at the picture of Sherlock Holmes in pilgrim garb, chanting his rosary.

'You believe me uninterested in Nirvana?' he asked.

'I was thinking more about the Buddhist tenet that all things are illusion.'

'That is one doctrine I might have difficulty espousing,' he admitted.

'Surely we'd stand out even more in those white pilgrim robes? Do they wear robes?'

'A short jacket and trousers, white, plus a hat and staff. In which we would no doubt attract notice. But once the locals had marvelled over us, their minds would be at rest.'

'English Buddhists?'

'Mad Westerners are all over.'

With that, I had to agree. And having just left India, where to be a foreigner is to become a magnet for every beggar, cab-driver and tout for miles, I had no wish to repeat the role. 'If we don't want to go as ordinary tourists, I'd guess pilgrim is worth a try. Surely it won't be difficult to memorise a few prayers and hymns.'

'There is a group of touring American Buddhists down in third class, robes and all.'

'*Third* class?'

'Practising humility, one supposes.'

Inwardly, I sighed. Outwardly, I put on an attempt at enthusiasm. 'Oh, good.'

Abruptly, he stepped away from the railing and made for the companionway. 'You're going down now?' I asked him in surprise.

'Miss Sato has just left the ship. The Darleys went twelve minutes ago.'

Oh, dear. I called out at his back, 'Holmes, there may be servants.'

'I enquired. The earl, his wife and his son are all doing without on this voyage.'

'Really?'

'So I am told.'

'Well, would you like me to stand by with another vase of flowers?' He did not reply. As the top of his head vanished down the steps, I muttered under my breath, 'Please don't get caught.'

He did not get caught breaking into the cabins – not quite. His search of the Darley staterooms was briefer than he'd have liked, since the cleaners were working their inexorable way down the line of rooms, but he managed to overturn all the relevant parts of the suite. However, he found nothing to support his suspicions. When it came to the Darleys, the most incriminating evidence he discovered was the earl's collection of outré books and photographs, and even those would have been legal in some of the countries we put into. Lady Darley's shelves testified to an intense interest in Oriental art, including two what he termed 'sprightly' volumes of erotica. Her clothing was expensive, her jewellery extensive, and she appeared to spend an inordinate amount of time before her dressing table mirror.

Miss Sato's rooms were the very opposite: her clothing and personal goods were sparse enough to cause speculation. Were the first-class accommodations a gift from someone with greater means? When I pointed out that her hasty arrival might have prevented her trunks from joining her, and that in any event, the few clothes she did have were far from cheap, Holmes reluctantly agreed that even the pyjamas he had seen beneath her pillow were made of heavy silk.

'There's your answer,' I told him. 'Even if her trunks did make it on, she has the sense to limit what she exposes to the trials of sea travel.' Between smuts, sticky salt air and the occasional burning ember from the stacks, the experienced traveller locked away the bulk of her wardrobe.

His search left Holmes, as one might expect, unconvinced.

The daytrippers began to trickle back as lunch was being cleared. When Miss Sato had refreshed herself and washed away the grime of the city, we met for a brief language tutorial. As she was writing down the words we were to commit to memory before the next day, the purser came in to ask if she still wished for the salon that afternoon, considering the lateness of the hour.

'Not if it is inconvenient,' she told him. 'Or if you like, we could take afternoon tea along with conversation. Japanese tea as well as the English? I bought some in Colombo, for the purpose,' she added.

'What about those special cups?' he asked. 'They might be harder to duplicate.'

'Western teacups would do nicely.'

After a few more questions, and after Miss Sato's polite but firm reminder that he had agreed to welcome those of her countrymen who were in second class, he retreated.

Her eyes lingered on the empty doorway. 'He is very helpful, considering the extra work.'

'A purser's job is to keep people happy,' I replied mildly. Indeed, the man was probably overjoyed to be given the means of entertaining those passengers who could be even more of a handful than energetic young males – namely, wealthy older women. Yes, he'd been reluctant to encourage the mixing of the classes, but he could see that bringing up a few more Japanese passengers – guest lecturers, as it were – would more than compensate for any complaints from their excluded Caucasian fellows.

The afternoon's demonstration of *o-cha* – honourable tea – included comments on the taste, the equipment and the ceremonial aspects of both Japanese and English tea. The more or less captive audience guaranteed that curiosity was roused for the remainder of the voyage. As the days went on, the informal lecture series expanded to include food, flower arranging, calligraphy, furniture (or the lack thereof), games, the disinclination of Japanese to shake hands and the subtleties of the bow (and especially the matter of how to perform the tricky simultaneous bow-handshake with a Japanese businessman without cracking into his skull), and the best methods of stepping out of shoes and into slippers. I doubted that most of the assembled would remember to give and to take with both hands, and I could not imagine any of them would replace their handkerchiefs with slips of Japanese tissue; however, the salon was packed to the windows with the eagerly attentive on the days given over to those two all-important questions the young men had first requested: communal bathing and what a geisha was for.

But all that came later.

Colombo marked the beginning of the greater voyage. The temporary residents of the *Thomas Carlyle* disembarked, with new passengers bound for Manila, Hong Kong, Kobe and beyond. Seating at dinner and on the decks was reshuffled, groups reformed, conversations were repeated, new friendships begun. And old friendships rekindled.

In the salon that night before dinner, amidst a mixture of evening wear (the continuing passengers) and not (the freshly boarded and therefore unironed), all eyes surveyed the room for the new and interesting. Having lost the professor of botany, our table was so sparsely populated that we risked being assigned random passengers by the purser. Rather than face that danger, Holmes and I were watching for one or two likely replacements. I had proposed an old lady with a wicked gleam to her eyes, a tall man with weathered skin and the scar of frostbite on one ear, and a duo of lesbians. Holmes had countered with a nervous-looking scientific woman with acid stains on her fingers, a too-smooth man with the manners of a gigolo, and two stocky individuals who could only be a criminal and his bodyguard.

Our debate over these options was interrupted by a loud drawl coming from the scrum behind me.

'By God, is that Pike-Elton? Monty, old man, what are you doing in these parts?'

Everyone there who was not completely deaf turned to watch Thomas Darley make his way to the entrance and exchange handshakes with a slim young fellow with sharp-looking teeth and sleek black hair.

'Tommy, my good chap, I could ask the same of you!'

The talk rose around us again as people turned back to their interrupted conversations. Holmes and I kept one eye on the pair now making their way towards the cluster of the viscount's particular friends, which included, unlikely as that seemed, Haruki Sato.

(Our table picks, by the way, were Holmes' nervous lady scientist and my mountain-climber. As it turned out, his was by far the more interesting choice – but there is a story for another time.)

After dinner Holmes and I divided forces: he to the smoking room where the men gathered over cards, and me to the cocktail lounge with the Young Things. I settled with my lurid drink into a seat between two middle-aged owners of Ceylonese tea plantations. They looked at me in surprise, but I gave them a bright and slightly tipsy smile and asked them how things were in Ceylon. That took care of conversation for the next half hour. I pretended to sip and feigned interest, but my ears and brain were entirely taken up with the conversation going on behind my shoulders.

'Sorry to see your time among the Babus has ruined your palate, old man.' Thomas Darley's drawl, answered by Monty Pike-Elton's nasal honk.

'What's wrong with gin, you snob?'

'Mother's ruin.'

'It does the job. But speaking of mothers, that new one you've picked up – good work, man!'

'What, the Pater's wife? Not bad.'

'A toasty crumpet, my man. How'd the old codger—'

'Monty, for God's sake, can't you at least pretend at civilised manners?'

'Touchy, eh? When'd they get hitched?'

'Last summer. They've known each other for yonks – she was married to some bloke the Pater knew in the War. After Mama died, he said the house felt empty, and when they came across each other at some tedious party, she was at something of a loose end as well. They hit it off.'

'So, what, this is their honeymoon?'

'More like a world tour. They both have old friends, here and there.'

'And they brought Tommy-the-Lad on the honeymoon?' Monty's laugh was goose-like.

'Not sure she was all that keen on it, but I guess she wanted to show that she didn't intend to push him around. Fitting in with the family, you know?'

'I'd be happy to fit in, too, if there's room.' His meaning was so unmistakeable, even Lady Darley's unwilling stepson had to object.

His drawl became more marked. 'Monty, have some respect, she is the Pater's wife. She's . . . well, she's not a bad sort, really. Had a tough time of it, for a while.'

'What, your old man married an adventuress?'

'Monty, in another minute I'm going to have to stand up and hit you.'

'Ah, you know I'm just digging at you. Seriously, chap, I'm happy for your Pa. Nice enough bloke.'

'Thank you. How's your family?'

'Don't think Ceylon is doing what they'd hoped for the family fortunes. Father's drinking himself to death. The Mother has herself a poodle-faker she drags around to garden parties.' I snorted into my mauve liquid, startling my tea-planters into silence. When I had them going again, my ears swivelled back to the two men behind me. They were talking about cards, a technical and complicit conversation that had me making a mental note: warn Holmes against playing with these two.

Chapter Eight

Madness and love are
The playwright's favourite themes.
Are they so different?

Once we had left Colombo and set out across the Bay of Bengal, the hard-driving tutorials – courses whose absence I had so happily anticipated – descended in force. My chief pleasure in the programme, apart from the benefits of knowledge, was to see Holmes forced to labour beside me rather than wielding the whip.

Our initial intention, to abandon ship at the earliest opportunity, was rendered less urgent by this unexpected series of challenges. Holmes, happy enough to cram a new language into his brain, was even happier to be given a second chance at a perceived villain he had let slip through his fingers. I, for my part, found an investigation of my own: that of Miss Sato herself.

Invariably, we were thrown together outside of our actual lesson times. This was true for pretty much every first-class passenger, but when one shared an interest in books and a lack of interest in other onboard amusements, certain conversations were inevitable.

A few mornings into the trip, I came onto my preferred section of deck (the furthest from the shuffleboard courts) and found Miss Sato tucked into one of the deckchairs, a book in her hand and a charming frown-line between her eyebrows. She glanced up, we exchanged greetings, and then both of us settled to our reading.

She was still working her way through the Shakespeare plays, although her bookmark had not made much progress. She was taking notes. A lot of notes.

So I wasn't particularly surprised when, after I let my own library book fall shut (Sinclair Lewis: I should have chosen the Mary Roberts Rinehart), she stirred.

'Mrs Russell?'

I stopped rubbing my eyes and replaced my spectacles. 'Yes, Miss Sato, what can I do for you?'

'Do you understand Shakespeare?'

Did Shakespeare understand Shakespeare? 'Not entirely. What are you reading?'

'*Henry IV.*'

'You know,' I said, 'the plays really need to be read aloud. Just following the words on the page, one loses a lot.' The rhythm of the language, the passion behind it. The meaning. There was a reason the Rabbis insisted that the Torah be read in full voice, that the whole body might participate in the learning.

'This one I did see, in New York. And I think I follow all the war and revolting things.' I stifled a smile at her English. 'But Falstaff, him I do not understand. Why is he there?'

Greater literary minds than mine have wrestled with that question. Why, indeed, keep breaking into the drama of war with the continuous buffoonery of Prince Henry's sotted companion? And why give that future King such an inappropriate companion in the first place? 'I know. They might as well be called *Falstaff Parts One and Two.*'

'Prince Henry say – fays – Prince Henry says he is only friends

79

to make himself look better, later. This does not seem to me a noble thing to do.'

'No. I think Shakespeare was far more interested in Falstaff than he was in either of the kings, but he was working his way through the kings of England, so he had to let the Henrys come forward.'

'He would rather have been writing a comedy?'

'*The Merry Wives of Windsor* does seem a more comfortable setting for the old drunkard.'

'But Shakespeare put him into the Henry plays.'

'Most of his dramas have comic touches.'

She did not seem satisfied. Then again, neither was I. There was no way around it: Sir John Falstaff got a bum deal from his Prince, and his creator.

'I think maybe Falstaff is the hero,' she said after a time.

'Oh, I agree that Shakespeare probably wanted to write a comedy here, but at the time found himself stuck with dramas.'

'No, I mean, he *is* the hero. Prince and Falstaff both not what they appear: Harry says he is pretending to be young and irresponsible – an act, so everyone will be very impressed when he suddenly grows up, becomes noble. Silly reason. But Falstaff also act the fool, only he stay there, to force Harry to choose – really choose. Where does noble behaviour get a man? Forced to behave, made to marry a stranger for his country, having to lead men he loves into death? Who would want that? But with Falstaff, Harry is forced not just to look noble, but to *be* noble, and turn his back on the old friend for the bigger cause.'

She frowned at the book, looking for words that fit her thoughts. 'I think maybe, secretly, Shakespeare make Falstaff not just the fool, but his hero. In the end, Falstaff teaches Harry all. About loyalty, about how very, very hard it is to be king. In the end, Falstaff give his – *gives* his life, his honour, to his new King. When Harry refuses his foolish old friend, that is when he is marked as a king.'

I stared at her delicate and unlined face, frowning at the mysterious volume in her hands as if it was conveying some personal message to her alone. I'd never thought of the character that way, merely regarded him as a problematic artefact of a playwright working too fast for reflection.

'That's an . . . interesting interpretation.'

She looked up then. 'Ah, sorry, is only my silly thoughts.'

'Absolutely not. It's . . . Well, certainly that's what the playwright did with Lear's fool. Have you got to *King Lear* yet?' Lear's nameless man-boy wields neither power nor fear. He is a despised servant who is yet the King's only friend, a non-son who brutally mocks his master but remains loyal when everyone else has betrayed him. The Fool spends all his energies trying to goad Lear from his madness, and at the end – with an enigmatic, *I'll go to bed at noon* – he disappears. Theologically speaking, the Fool is an Old Testament prophet with pratfalls. I shook my head. 'I admit, I'd never seen Falstaff as a hero. I will have to read those plays again.'

'Aloud?' Her dark eyes had a twinkle.

'Yes. You know,' I said, 'that's not a bad idea. We might ask a few of the others to join in, and we could do group readings.' Long ago, my teacher Miss Sim had done that with me, revealing an invaluable dimension to the text.

This entailed another approach to the purser, who was looking a bit bemused at the seaborne university taking shape around Miss Sato. However, he agreed, and half a dozen of us were soon launched on the *Henry* plays.

All of which meant that between the stern linguistic demands of Miss Sato, earnest lessons from the devout American Buddhists, the group readings, and her public lecture series on customs of all kinds (followed by the enthusiastic discussions those lectures set off amongst the passengers), Holmes and I were well occupied. He made no further mention of a rapid disembarking at the next large port.

Plus, there remained the question of blackmailers and card sharks.

Three weeks of enforced intimacy made it difficult to hide matters from one's fellow travellers. Only the most gifted and inexhaustible of actors could maintain a role that whole time. Some did not try. Lady Darley and her stepson, Thomas, for example, avoided expressing their mutual distaste by the simple means of coming together as rarely as two people could within a floating village: the viscount dined with his friends, participating in vigorous sport on the sun deck during the day and raucous entertainments and card games during the night, while the earl's wife kept to the shaded promenade deck, sat with her husband at the Captain's table, and turned in early. The only times they were in a room together was during Miss Sato's afternoon salons, and even then, the two occupied opposite sides of the room, each pointedly taking no notice of the other.

Similarly, one always knew if two passengers had a falling-out: when Tommy made amorous advances on Virginia Wilton three days before Manila, her brother, Harold, bristled every time the viscount appeared. But the ship's relief when the two siblings disembarked for their missionary work in the Philippines was short-lived, for Tommy then turned his eyes on Lucy Awlwright, and the good-natured competition for that young woman's affections that had been brewing between the two Australian brothers erupted overnight into open fury. For two days, we all awaited outright fisticuffs or a midnight cry of 'Viscount overboard!' Intervention came from an unexpected direction: I was up on the rolling deck one evening, dinner having started and the decks being nearly deserted, when my eye was caught by motion. I craned my neck, then went still at the sight of Lady Darley – and her stepson.

They kept their voices low, but one could see the intensity of their manner. Facing each other, the two stood as rigid as the deck-post behind them. She was delivering a lecture – and although he protested, even reaching out a hand to her, she took a step back and crisply delivered his marching orders. She left. He watched her go. Then he took out his cigarette case and smoked furiously, crushing the butt out on the wooden boards before he followed her down to the dining room.

That night over cards, Tommy withdrew his flirtations from Lucy Awlwright, leaving the field to the Arthur brothers. The rest of the ship breathed a sigh of relief.

CHAPTER NINE

Questions on the seas:
When is a fool not a Fool?
When his blood runs blue.

IF I WAS INTERESTED in Lady Darley, it was doubly true when it came to her titled husband. I might claim that I was merely being loyal to my own husband's endeavours, like a golfer's wife who learns to knock the gutta-percha ball into a hole. That was certainly true to a degree. But beyond wifely reinforcement, our relationship always had something in the order of a contest about it: who could claim the correct answer first?

As the days went by, Holmes had contrived an excuse to visit the ship's safe, even succeeding in a quick survey of the purser's list of its contents, and he was forced to acknowledge that nothing of Darley's appeared to be therein. Not that a clever (or at any rate, experienced) blackmailer didn't have a dozen ways to summon a needed item of extortion, from onboard confederates to a friend back home willing to drop an envelope into the Royal Post.

Short of physical evidence, we needed to watch for slips of behaviour. Thus, although I did not actively pursue testimony against Darley – or indeed, for him – neither did I avoid the man's presence as studiously as I might have under other circumstances.

However, despite the enforced intimacy of shipboard life, it proved surprisingly difficult to engage the man in casual conversation. For one thing, despite his apparently robust physique, he seemed often unwell, keeping to his cabin and missing several of the port stops (although his wife and son took advantage of the touristic opportunities – separately, of course). And when he did participate in communal events, he was often surrounded by his fellows – an entirely masculine community – and wrapped up in the minutiae of shared enthusiasms: hunting, horses, and guns chiefly among them. Holmes might get away with lingering on the edge of those conversations, but not I.

The first time he appeared at Miss Sato's afternoon salon was when the posted topic was 'sports'. Naturally, her talk focused largely on sports exclusive to Japan – sumo wrestling, archery, falconry and the martial arts – but the discussion that followed was wide-ranging, and took us into baseball, cricket, motorcar racing and beyond. Then Lord Darley spoke up.

'What about horses? You do have them, don't you?'

'Yes, we have horses in Japan. Not, I think, as many as you have in England, because we have little free land, but we do have them.'

'What about a hunt?'

Miss Sato exchanged glances with the Japanese man seated nearby. He stood and faced the room. 'Certainly we hunt. If you are interested in a day out, I have a friend near Tokyo who hunts. What kind of falcon do you have, sir?'

Confusion reigned for a time, until the difference between hunting-with-falcons and hunting-on-horseback was straightened out. Lord Darley, it seemed, was an enthusiastic huntsman, and wished to arrange for some horseback riding once dry land was achieved. His monologue concerning the difference between his home mounts and those of the Colonies – Kenya and India, for the most part – would have gone on for some time, had not the purser gently moved to rescue Miss Sato, suggesting that she might continue this conversation elsewhere while the room was cleared for tea.

It turned out that Miss Sato was to some degree familiar with both horses and riding equipment, and amiably set about describing the differences between the traditional Japanese saddle and those of the English and Western schools. However, when it came to details of the horses themselves, she regretfully shook her head and admitted that she knew nothing about the angle of pasterns. The earl was taken aback at this woeful ignorance, but his reproach was soothed when she offered to locate a stable near Tokyo for his entertainment.

He reluctantly let her be pulled away by a couple of adolescent boys who were interested in jujitsu, a martial art about which she protested that she knew little, but I slipped in beside the earl.

'I'd be very interested to know of a good public stable near Tokyo, if you hear of one,' I said earnestly.

He looked at me in surprise, running an eye down my length as if judging the angle of my pasterns. I did not, it would seem, have the appearance of a great lover of horses. Still, he replied with no apparent disbelief. 'Oh, you don't want public stables, Mrs Russell. Not unless they're a whole lot better than those you find in other countries. Ill-tempered nags with no wind, for the most part. See if the gel there can find some people with their own place.'

Before one of the others could interrupt, I asked him what he thought about the saddles that Miss Sato had described, then agreed with his opinion that they sounded more like the saddles in museums than those he used.

'I suppose that makes sense,' I said thoughtfully. 'The Samurai were fighters, they'd need something secure to brace against as they were aiming their bows or swinging a weapon.'

A second, more appraising glance, this time at my unexpected sensibility. We were soon launched into a rather more technical discussion than I was qualified for, but in those situations, I generally fall back on an open declaration of ignorance followed by a series of admiring questions. Most men read this as self-deprecating expertise, although there is always the danger that the man will be astute enough to see past the performance and suspect coquetry.

Lord Darley did not appear astute. Amiable, yes. August and self-absorbed and well pleased with his own appeal, yes – but not astute. He was the sort of aristocrat in whom generations of inbreeding and privilege led to a belief that his ermine robes were not only deserved, but proof of the rightness of the universe.

I left his presence feeling the need of a good cold, invigorating bath, to clear away the honeyed assumptions of wealth. Later, I informed Holmes that as far as I was concerned, if Darley had provided Society secrets to a blackmailer, he probably hadn't realised it – and if he had, nothing would convince the man he was wrong to use whatever resources he had to produce whatever money he needed.

In any event, I wished nothing more to do with the man on this voyage, and was happy to leave the investigation entirely in Holmes' hands.

The ship drove east: across the Bay of Bengal, beneath the end of the Andaman chain, down the Straits of Malacca. Since the combination of motion and enclosure was anathema to my well-being, I spent much of the time on one deck or another, either in my native first class or with the Americans in third. Not only were the two sets of lessons demanding – locking both Japanese grammar and Buddhist prayers onto our tongues, fitting Japanese customs and Buddhist attitudes into our minds – but we were forced to negotiate all these lessons amidst a constant stream of interruptions, from children, the other passengers and the world past the railings.

Too, my nocturnal disturbances continued, with recurring variations on the dream of flying objects and a new and more ominous image of an anonymous haunting figure. Disturbing dreams had not been a problem for many years, and I was not at all pleased with this new development.

Afterwards I wondered if, but for these distractions, I might have caught word of the ship's poltergeist earlier. Instead, it required a trio of overheard conversations.

CHAPTER TEN

Boys will play rude games.
Ship's light sparkles on the waves.
Life goes on unseen.

SHIPBOARD TRAVEL IS ALWAYS a compromise, even for those fortunate souls immune to gastric distress. Deck cabins have a window, permitting fresh air and a minimum of smells from the engine and kitchen, and even in rough weather the window can be left open (unlike the poor benighted souls below, whose portholes must be screwed shut when the seas rise). On the other hand, having the promenade deck just outside one's room inflicts the constant noises of travellers at play: strolling, playing quoits or cards, scolding children or – worst by far – carrying on shipboard flirtations. I have, at times, fallen back on the suites designed for the very rich, but the nerve-grating habits of the neighbours tend to drive me back down to the realms of the lower classes. In any event, our neighbours this time would have been the Darleys, who in such close quarters could not have failed to notice Holmes' glowers.

The solution is bribery. Lavish applications of cash can shift one's quarters to the cooler side, arrange for table-mates who are interesting (or, lacking that, taciturn), and even lead to the rearrangement of the deck's fixtures to create an obstacle outside of one's windows. Once or twice I've managed to shut the deck outside my rooms entirely, ensuring a degree of peace while forcing promenaders to bounce back and forth and back again, frustrated from completion of their endless circuits.

We didn't manage that this time, although we did (thanks to a combination of cold cash and a fulsome letter from A High-Ranking Indian Authority) ruthlessly supplant a previous reservation and take over a large, airy, relatively quiet promenade-deck suite, with a more or less functional electrical fan, located precisely halfway along the ship's length to assure optimal steadiness.

Although I still spent most daylight hours out of doors, the seas were generally calm enough that most nights, I could retreat to my bunk for a few hours. This was the case as we worked our way down the Malacca Straits. I brushed my teeth, made sure the window was as wide open as it got, directed the fan, and stripped the bedclothes down to a single sheet. Having checked that my thermos jug had been filled with ice water, and that my clock, torch, water glass and throwing knife were on the little table, I climbed into bed. After a few pages, I switched out the light.

It was one of the blessed nights when I succeeded in convincing my central organs that the gentle motion all around was a soothing thing, maternal as a grandmother's arms. I relaxed. I felt fine. I slipped down, softly, to sleep . . .

'Did you ask the Chips?' blared an English voice inches from my ear.

Answered by a drawl. 'He said he was busy with some dashed job for the Captain and couldn't help us.'

'What about Sparks?'

'Seemed to think it might be too dangerous. What about you? Did you talk to the chappie in the smoking room?' *Chips* was the ship's carpenter; *Sparks*, the radio man; and my ears instantly identified the drawler: Thomas Darley. Which made the correspondent Monty Pike-Elton.

'I rather got the impression that several others got there before us,' Pike-Elton bleated.

'There's the bath steward – nobody'd expect us to hide it in the baths.'

'Yes, but we wanted to open the hunt to girls as well, and they'd complain we weren't playing cricket. They can't very well go poking around the men's baths.'

'Some of them would,' said Darley.

'And how! Did you see what the Wilson girl was wearing? Don't know that you'd need to get *her* into a game of strip poker!'

'How about the engineer?'

Were it not for the vague puzzle of what 'it' might be, I'd have long since emptied my iced water out the porthole onto the pair of them. Holmes' change of breathing told me that he was listening, too.

They dismissed the Chief Engineer as being the standard humourless Scot, the Chief Steward as being unbribable, and the boots steward as being the opposite – all too willing to sell information to anyone. Neither, I noted, brought up the library steward. Possibly unaware that such a person existed.

'So we're back to the purser,' Pike-Elton said.

'He's such an obvious choice.'

'Precisely! Nobody would expect the two of us to go for the obvious.'

Somehow, I doubted that.

A low voice came from the other bunk. 'Russell, would you object to a spot of target practice from my Webley?'

'Have you any idea what they're talking about?'

'The tone of their remarks indicates some sporting entertainment.'

It was true: had they been planning a bomb or a burglary, even these two might have tried to keep their voices down a touch.

'The purser's office isn't very large,' Darley complained.

'Big enough to hide a lady's hat.'

Ah.

'Not with that ruddy great feather on it.'

'Cut the feather off.' There was a pause as they considered the denuded headgear, then burst into ill-stifled guffaws. 'Still,' Pike-Elton continued, 'we'll have to convince the fellow that we're not his below-decks ghost.'

'Yes, what d'you suppose he meant by that? You suppose the Americans are up to something?'

'Getting the drop on us? I don't know, those places the purser was asking about don't sound like their style. I can see the Americans poking around the bridge, but way down in the bilges? Never.' It was clear that Montgomerie Pike-Elton would never be caught dead that far below decks.

'That New Yorker's white suit would never be the same, true. Well, ships have ghosts, and any rumours of odd noises in the night will just make it all the harder for people to sort out the clues. We can see the purser tomorrow, ask if he's got a drawer we could stash the hat in.'

'Got a smoke? I gave that girl my last one.'

'The ugly one? Why'd you do that?'

'She asked me.'

'Ooh, ever the gentleman! Lord, Tommy, she reminds me of my mother's favourite hunter.'

'She does rather whinny, doesn't she? But in the dark, I'd—'

I hadn't heard Holmes swing out of bed, but his voice now snarled out from the window. 'If you two are not gone in ten seconds, you will be feeding the sharks!'

Silence, followed by the sound of retreating heels.

That night's dream was a variation on the earthquake-and-*Alice* cards: a sinuous black cat crept along the back of some shelves, its progress marked by a steady rain of fallen knick-knacks.

The second overheard conversation came the next day. We had succeeded in clearing the Straits without being set upon by pirates, but had failed to make up the time lost due to winds across the Bay of Bengal. Therefore our scheduled day-long stop in Singapore would be cut to a few hours.

We spent the morning with vocabulary drills and halting conversations based on the clothing and characteristics of our fellow passengers. Then, as the engines changed their timbre with the approach of the docks, our tutrix rose, saying that she had promised her new friends that she would go into the city with them.

'Why not come?' she asked. 'You would learn many new words.'

In fact, once onboard a ship, I rarely ventured off before the journey's end, since as the tedium dragged on and the decks shrank down to claustrophobic proportions, I found it more and more difficult to force my feet back up the gangway into a world of unremitting noise and bone-deep throbbing, with human beings at every turn, corridors that curved upwards in both directions, and air that stank of burning coal. In any event, this day I was happy to trade five hours of hurried sightseeing for the chance of a nap, while Holmes wanted a conversation with the Chief Engineer – who, since the ship's primary activity during the next few hours would be the taking in of coal and perishables, could permit his engines to fall silent. This was good, considering that most engineers were half-deaf by the time they reached forty, and this one was a solid decade past that age. Holmes went hoarse, after a long conversation below.

Passengers departed amidst loud plans for the botanic gardens and tea at Raffles, the Darleys and Miss Sato among them. Holmes changed into his oldest shirt and headed for the depths; I switched on the fan without electrocuting myself and settled onto my bunk with a nice soporific book from the ship's library.

Voices came from the deck outside, one of them very young. It was an adenoidal voice I had heard a number of times, a plump male creature of perhaps ten years who was fiercely determined to master the skills of proper tennis, despite an ocean steamer being one of the world's least congenial settings for the game: an exposed mountaintop might be a trifle worse – or a typhoon. Decktennis was the game of choice among the athletic shipboard set, with most big ships squeezing a court into some odd corner, but the game was played with quoits – rings of rope or rubber, which neither bounced nor rolled.

However, this valiant youth had his own apparently bottomless supply of tennis balls. Our very first day out, he had begun by using the section of bulkhead outside our cabin, until we thwarted him by the transfer of some potted palms. His current passion was learning to bounce the tennis ball from his child-sized racquet, as he had seen adult tennis players do back in Delhi (although to my knowledge, he'd never got past half a dozen repetitions). I applauded his change of focus, and had come grudgingly to admire the creature's tenacity, but it didn't actually reduce the noise much, merely replacing the *pok . . . pok . . . pok* of rubber on metal with fifteen seconds of concentrated silence ending in juvenile shouts and scrambling noises as the ball made its inevitable dash for the water below. We'd left a trail of balls floating in our wake, a trail of aquatic breadcrumbs.

The lad's parents had no doubt gone ashore to sample the gin slings of the Raffles Hotel, leaving their offspring in the care of his lugubrious nanny.

'But you *must* have taken it!' the young hellion exclaimed.

'Roderick, I hope you are not accusing me of lying. I promise you, I did not move your tennis racquet.'

'But it wasn't *there*!'

'You must have left it somewhere.'

'You *know* I didn't leave it up here! Why would I leave it up here?'

'You might have been distracted,' the poor woman offered.

The boy was outraged. 'I'd *never* leave my racquet lying around! *Richard Sears* gave me that racquet!'

'Well, it will no doubt show up. In the meantime, maybe the purser has one you can borrow.'

'He won't!'

'Come to think of it, when I was down in the hold yesterday fetching something for your mother I saw that one of the women had hers stored down there. Do you want me to see if she'll lend it to you?'

'A *girl's* racquet!' The governess might as well have suggested he dress in Suzanne Lenglen's skirt. Shocked silence fell. They must have moved off eventually, because after a few more paragraphs, sleep wrapped its fingers around me and gently tugged.

Loud and adult conversation woke me: returning passengers heading for their cabins to dress for cocktails and dinner. A while later, the great engines rumbled into life. Soon, Holmes slipped up from the depths, looking as if the Chief Engineer had seized on this long, thin Englishman as a convenient way to swab out some duct-work. By the time he came up the companionway, I was sitting on the deck outside our cabin. Holmes raised his greasy cap to a horrified neighbour dressed in pale blue silk (a newcomer to sea travel, clearly: the dress already had smuts on it) who shrank back to let him enter the hatch. I remained where I was – no reason to get too near the man in his current state – until the aroma of filthy grease joined the saltwater steam vented out of the bathroom, indicating that the bath steward had taken one look at Holmes and ushered him in, regardless of where his name stood on the bath schedule.

Holmes came into our cabin slicked down, smooth-faced and glowing.

As he dressed, I admired the state of his fingers (it would have taken me a week to prise that grease out of my cuticles) and asked about the ship's haunt.

'I take it you didn't see the viscount's "below-decks ghost" while you were down in the depths of the ship?'

'The ghost was not actually in the bilges then.'

'Good heavens. They did see something, then?'

'Apparently. The second night out.'

'As we were approaching Colombo.' Progress had been leisurely, so as not to inflict a midnight arrival on well-paying passengers.

'Yes. Although it should be noted that the engineer is a phlegmatic individual who accepts ghosts as a regular part of shipboard life. He even had a candidate for the wraith's identity: a lad named Mick, killed by a falling beam in the ship's building. Says the lad's a regular visitor.'

'So, not our missing passenger?'

'It would appear not.'

'Hmm. I don't suppose young Mick liked to play tennis?'

He raised one eyebrow, so I told him about the loss of Master Roderick's racquet. He grunted, adjusted his tie in the looking glass, and glanced over at me.

'Is that a new frock?'

I looked down. 'Yes. I was at the ship's tailor, making arrangements for our Buddhist pilgrim costumes, and he had some fabric samples out, things he'd just bought in Colombo. I rather liked this one.'

'Handsome,' Holmes said, to my astonishment. 'Shall we go?'

CHAPTER ELEVEN

Hand-glass and child's toy.
Moonlight blankets the dead with
A touch in the night.

THE NEXT DAY, WE rounded the end of Malaysia and turned north. Cabins formerly shaded in the mornings were now exposed, while those that had been slightly cooler in the evenings now took until midnight to become habitable. At both ends of the day, the faces of the habitués changed, grumpy at the unaccustomed hour.

Our cabin was among those now exposed in the afternoon, and although the purser assured us (after more bribes) that he could provide cooler rooms (though perhaps not a suite) it would not be until Hong Kong (in twelve days). In the meantime, I slept fitfully, one night joining those on mattresses the stewards had dragged onto the decks, although I was loath to inflict the effects of my dreams on the other refugees.

Miss Sato, on the other hand, seemed to be sleeping just fine. Every morning she appeared on the dot of seven, chipper and sharp-eyed as a sparrow, pecking at our grammar like a bird after crumbs. Every afternoon she would stand before her growing crowd of admirers, wait for silence, give us a bow, and launch into the day's topics. Following the stop in Singapore, she produced a heap of bulging string bags filled with exotic foodstuffs. She talked about seaweed, rice, the scarcity of meat and the many products derived from the soya bean – then handed us each a pair of chopsticks and invited us to try them. When the ensuing hilarity had run its course, four women – two British, one American, and a New Zealander – talked about their native cuisines. It would be difficult to judge who was the more off-put: the Japanese at the idea of calves' brains, or the Americans faced with dried seaweed and amorphous blobs of bean curd.

The next afternoon's topic was both less demanding and more sparsely attended: in tropical heat, the temptation of Our Classic Literatures was less of a pull than a swim in the boat-deck's canvas pool. Or, in Holmes' case, a session with the engineers.

I, however, did go.

Miss Sato was as punctual as ever, and seemed unaware that the numbers were less than half the usual. She bowed, thanked us for coming, and said that she hoped to introduce the English speakers to the pleasures of Japanese literature, then do the same in reverse to the residents of Japan, dividing the English side into two: America and England itself. In each case, the brief look would include both poetry and prose writers. Not that we would be able to so much as touch upon the riches, she noted, but completeness was not the goal here, merely formal introductions.

This time, in the interest of fairness, Miss Sato chose to begin with English literature – or rather, American, with one of my schoolteacher table-mates called upon to talk about Mark Twain and Walt Whitman. I had vivid memories of Mr Clemens, whom I had met when I was small, although I admit his writing never caught my attention. Nor did it that day, with the lady earnestly reading small bits from both men.

An elderly woman behind me began to snore.

Miss Sato then spoke about two Japanese writers. One was an aristocratic lady of the eleventh century named Murasaki, credited with writing the world's first novel, a tale of secret aristocracy and forbidden love. She read a few passages from an ongoing English translation, then turned to Matsuo Bashō, a seventeenth-century itinerant poet and master of the form called 'haiku'. Miss Sato did get a bit bogged down in her explanation – that the form was at the poet's time known as *hokku*, that what he had mastered was more the linked *renko* than the haiku itself, that the classic 5/7/5 syllable arrangement of haiku did not really mean syllables – but then she put aside the lecture and thought for a moment, oblivious of the stir and coughs.

'The haiku captures a fleeting moment. Of great beauty, or heartbreak. A moment that, hmm . . . *encapsulates* the essence of a season. Such as the fragrance of blossoming cherries, or the sound of snow, or the feel of hot summer wind blowing the bamboo. I am sorry, my words are not sufficient. I will read.'

So she read us a few. Those of us not peacefully drowsing in our chairs agreed that they were charming, and thought-provoking, although the intensity of their imagery perhaps failed to translate into English.

She ended with what she said was Bashō's most famous haiku. First, the original Japanese:

Furuike ya
Kawazu tobikomu
Mizu no oto.

Then, a crude translation of the words alone:

Old pond—
Frog leaps in:
Water noise!

She then reshaped it to carry the classical haiku 5/7/5 arrangement into English:

Dark, mossy old pond—
Lively frog leaps from the bank:
The sound of water.

When she bowed and sat down, the room gave a stir. I was not the only one to consider the doorway with longing – until I saw Miss Sato's choice of expert for English literature: Lady Darley.

She was wearing white – a frock that on me would guarantee instant collision with a child and a chocolate bar. It was of a conservative cut, with loose, elbow-length sleeves, a reasonable neckline and a waist at the upper hip, rather than the exaggerated drooping torso that only the thinnest girls could get away with. There were more expensive dresses in the room, but none that looked it.

The countess gazed down at her notes until the shuffling stopped. 'Thank you. When I was asked to speak about the glories of English literature, my first impulse was to decline the honour, in favour of someone more qualified. However, I have been thinking of late about a cousin, who was like a brother. He was killed on the Somme, eight years ago. I . . .' Lady Darley paused, her eyes going back to the notes until the inevitable stir of sympathy died down. 'I have been remembering Edward, and how much literature meant to him. So with your permission, I should like to make a few remarks on two writers who sustained him in the trenches. I apologise that both are poets, strictly speaking, rather than one writing pure prose, but I would contend that a playwright produces prose of a sort.

'One cannot talk about English literature without mentioning William Shakespeare, and he is indeed one of my choices. The other is Matthew Arnold, a poet who captures, not a Romantic vision of England, but one in which intellect wrestles with doubt and faith.'

She spoke for a quarter of an hour, and although she kept her eyes on the pages before her for much of the time, when she looked up, it was mostly towards the side of the room where our Japanese passengers sat. I was not sure if this was good manners, or for fear that the sympathetic eyes of the English would loosen her composure.

She was no scholar, but nonetheless spoke quite competently on the freedom and dedication to the intellect in Arnold's 'Scholar Gipsy', glancing at Miss Sato as she made note of the similarity between Arnold's poem and the ever-wandering Bashō.

For her prose work she chose *Henry V*, probably because the shipboard reading-aloud group was working through that play. Here, her impromptu attempt to link her talk with Miss Sato's was less than successful since, unlike Murasaki's *Tales of the Genji*, the *Henry* marriage theme is little more than a tune played to the drums of war. Fortunately, she abandoned the analysis and returned to the idea of her cousin, a junior officer (and yes, how many of those had died on the Front!) who shaped his picture of being a leader of men around that one glorious prologue to action, where Henry's fearful army is buoyed by his presence:

Upon his royal face there is no note
How dread an army hath enrounded him . . .

That every wretch, pining and pale before,
Beholding him, plucks comfort from his looks;
A largess universal, like the sun
His liberal eye doth give to every one,
Thawing cold fear . . .
A little touch of Harry in the night.

She described a letter in which cousin Edward spoke of his keen desire to give his men even a pale imitation of Henry's comforting touch. Then a second letter, this one from the regimental sergeant after Edward's death, to say how good the young officer had been with his men. No one was snoring when Lady Darley finished. The applause that rang out was fervent, and her colour was high – although curiously there was no sign of tears in her eyes.

After the room had cleared, I approached Miss Sato. 'I'd like to put my name down for borrowing the Murasaki book,' I told her. It had been claimed within seconds of the talk's end.

'Certainly,' she said. 'But in the meantime, this is for you.' She handed me a small, cheaply printed booklet called *A Travel-Worn Rucksack*. 'I saw it in a stall in Singapore, and thought you might enjoy it.'

I opened it, and read:

Kono michi ya
Yuku hito nashi ni
Aki no kure.

All along the road
Not a person is walking.
Just autumn's evening.

'The first poem is one of the last Bashō wrote. The rest of the book concerns a trip he made along the Kisokaido Road, that still connects the Shogun's capital, Edo – now Tokyo – with the Imperial capital of Kyoto. For Bashō, the road was both a way of life and a . . . how you say, paradox?'

'Paradigm?' Although paradox, too, perhaps.

'Paradigm, yes. In Buddhism, the road and the Way are the same.'

'That is true in other religions as well,' I told her. 'In the Christian Bible, Jesus calls himself "The Way". Literally, the path.'

'You have an interest in religion, Mrs Russell?'

'It is my area of academic interest. Mostly Western religion, but I look forward to seeing something of the East as well.'

Miss Sato smiled. 'You will find Shinto and Buddhism difficult to miss, in Japan.'

I thanked her for the book, and went in search of my own partner on the Way.

'Lady Darley did have to explain it a bit, for the Japanese speakers,' I was telling Holmes, later that afternoon. He had been in the Marconi room catching up on the latest in wireless technology – for once, his clothes were not impregnated with coal dust. 'Although the thing that confused them most was, who is Harry? She ended up admitting she didn't know how the English get "Harry" or "Hal" out of "Henry".'

'Not being an expert in Medieval English,' Holmes commented. 'But overall, you got the impression of her distress being something by way of a performance?'

'Not performance, exactly, although eight years is a long time to mourn a cousin. I would say that the emotions themselves might be genuine, but she does not care to lay them out for the appraisal of *hoi polloi*.'

'Although she will present them in a manner suitable for her audience.'

'Many women hide behind a public face, Holmes. Particularly women who marry into a position.'

The third overheard conversation took place following tea that same afternoon, when I carried the day's grammar notes to a quiet corner where I might enfold a few more verbs into my brain. The sun deck, up at the top, tended to be less popular in the heat of the day, and even when the sun was going down, it was still too exposed for anyone who wanted to be fresh for dinner. Still, there was a shelter, and some of those chairs were free. I chose one near a trio of older women, who were sure to go down to change for dinner soon, leaving me in peace.

I greeted them politely, took the furthest away chair to indicate that I was not actually joining them, and settled down with my notes.

Their voices quieted politely for a few minutes, but it was only a matter of time before a mosquito-buzz of a voice rose above the endless grumble of the engines, the sing of the wires, and the flutter of the flags overhead, drilling itself into my ear and pushing aside the verbs.

'. . . my *dear* husband, on one of his trips to Manhattan – or was it Chicago? Or maybe Philadelphia. Oh, he took so many trips, he used to joke that it was the *only* way he could get away from my voice, what a *jester* the man was, it made him friends all over! What was I saying?'

'Your hand-mirror.'

'Of course! Silly me, the *mirror*. So anyway, Bertie used to bring me a little something after his trips – not the short ones, of course, but when ever he was gone for a night or two – and they were always *quite* lovely. Sometimes not very useful, he never could remember what size I wore, but thoughtful. And so one time it was this pretty little silver hand-mirror that he said reminded him of the silver brush he'd brought me a month or two before, which was *silly* because he'd never given me a brush, and when I teased him and said it must have been some other wife he gave it to he got *very* cross and tried to take the mirror back, but of course I just laughed at him and told him that he must have been *thinking* of buying me a brush, so of course he did so the next time he went to Manhattan, or maybe that was Atlanta, and that was *very* pretty, too, even though the bristles were really too soft for my hair, although come to think of it, maybe it's not as thick as it was then, I should give it another chance when I get home again.'

She paused for breath, and her companion obediently gave her another nudge. 'So what's happened to the mirror? Did it break?'

'The mirror? Oh, no! It isn't *there*. I mean, it *must* be somewhere, of course, but for some reason it's not on my dressing table. I sat down this morning to do my face and reached for the mirror, and I had such a start, because there on the table in place of the mirror was a little tennis racquet *instead*! Can you *imagine*?'

My eyes, which had been drifting shut under the soothing prattle, snapped open. She let loose a peal of brittle laughter that lifted the hair on my neck.

The poor woman was terrified. She thought she was losing her mind, and hastened to raise a wall of words against the fear. No doubt she'd done so all her life, using endless chatter to protect herself from the suspicion that her husband did in fact have another wife, that he travelled not for business or escape, but because something in those cities drew him. Now her nervous babble pushed back the suspicion that she had absent-mindedly exchanged two objects that shared a vague outline, and never noticed.

Her friend stoutly rejected the notion, made reassuring noises and distracted her with a cheery question about the ship's hair salon.

I folded away the pages and turned to look at the trio: the jolly one was plump and emphatically groomed; the fearful one reminded me of Miss Sim, that long-ago tutor who'd got me through the Oxford entrance examinations. The third woman, stout and younger than the others, said nothing at all, either then or later.

'I beg your pardon.' I interrupted the jolly woman's description of a disastrous permanent wave involving toxic chemicals and near-electrocution. 'I couldn't help overhearing something about a tennis racquet. Was it child-sized? With black tape on the handle?'

The frightened one's eyebrows went high. 'Yes! Is it yours?'

'No, but I overheard a boy talking about one that he'd misplaced. Perhaps he . . .' What? Went into a stranger's cabin and traded his beloved racquet for a hand-mirror? 'Perhaps one of the stewards made a mistake. Which cabin are you in?'

She looked pathetically grateful at the idea that her faculties weren't at fault, and told me at length where her cabin was, how few children there were among her neighbours, what the hand-mirror looked like, and what her husband had said upon giving it to her. I cut her off before we could get into any further detail, shook their hands, and hastened away lest things grow any more complicated.

Yes, coincidences did occur. But three overlapping puzzles in such a short time suggested more beneath the surface of shipboard life.

It was time to hunt a poltergeist.

I hurried down the aft staircase and up the corridor to our rooms. To my surprise, Holmes was already there, and moreover, almost fully dressed, although dinner was not for another hour. He preferred a solitary drink in the cabin to the sociable scrum.

'Holmes, there is something—'

'—odd going on, I know. What have you heard?'

I gave him a quick review of the troubled lady. He frowned, dubious.

'Why would anyone replace a silver looking-glass with a child's tennis racquet?'

'Exactly.' One thing Holmes had taught me well: the power of an enigmatic statement. He was not impressed, but picked up his tie and turned towards the more prosaic looking-glass bolted on the wall.

'It is more likely that your lady is indeed losing her grasp on both her possessions and reality.'

'I would agree, but for the ghost in the bilges and the lad's missing tennis racquet. Don't you think—?'

'—that it calls for a few judiciously placed questions? Yes. Hence my intention to take cocktails with the masses.'

Chapter Twelve

Birds on the high wires,
Chattering wind in the lines,
Take flight in the dark.

COCKTAIL HOUR WAS WELL under way, a wall of merriment and perspiring bodies. We split up, Holmes fixing his eye on our resident community of retired colonels while I ingratiated myself into a cluster of young wives. Both groups looked at us askance, since we were newcomers into these centres of social intercourse, but both promised to be rich sources of shipboard gossip.

My merry girls became a touch self-conscious at the addition of a person who had formerly given them wide berth, but a quick joke and a high-pitched giggle confirmed that I was nearly as tipsy as they. We were soon embarked on a hilarious conversation about the *oddest* things that can happen onboard a ship like this – honestly, one would never *think* that a possession would just *migrate* like that, or one might see a person in *such* an unlikely place, or . . .

As I maintained the mask of Young Thing, I was aware of Holmes' voice booming among the retired males: something about racing stock.

The dinner bell was rung; the cacophony poured down the staircase towards the dining room. Holmes and I met in the centre of the now-deserted lounge to compare notes. Eliminating probable duplicates, we ended up with the following:

1. A shadow seen among the lifeboat davits
2. An ape climbing to the crow's nest at midnight
3. Odd sounds down one of the air intakes
4. Turmoil in second class: single shoes going missing
5. Pictures that changed on the walls

In the normal course of events we would have discounted pretty much all of these as a combination of alcohol and the innate desire to top a neighbour's story, but we agreed on two things: there were too many odd occurrences to be discounted, and there was a pattern to them.

Most took place in the wee hours of the morning, and the majority had their source at the upper reaches of the ship.

We capped our dinner with several cups of strong coffee, then pulled out the trunks from under our beds in search of dark clothing, and spent the intervening hours tormenting each other with Japanese drills while we waited for the ship to quiet. The first wave of passengers took to their beds, followed by those who had been dancing and at cards. The deck lights dimmed, the sounds of footsteps and running water faded. Eventually, we slipped out from our cabin to make for the nearest companionway.

I'd had enough experience at this kind of thing to carry one of the lightweight but dark-coloured blankets from the bed: it was dry out tonight, but even in the tropics, an open deck can feel cool.

The outside steps, used in good weather and during the day, saw little use at night, in part because they were dark (it being difficult for those in the bridge and crow's nest to see through deck lights).

We chose the dim external treads over the brightly lit internal stairways and ascended to my perch from the afternoon, on the sun deck. Only instead of settling into chairs, we hoisted ourselves onto the shelter roof, and there we lay, facing opposite directions with the blanket tucked firmly over our legs. An hour crept past. Ninety minutes. I was wondering how much longer I could lie motionless with a single layer of light wool between me and a young typhoon, when the door from the aft staircase opened, casting a swath of light across the empty decking.

Holmes felt me stiffen.

The ship's personnel tended to keep an eye on even the darker corners of the decks. A half hour before, a man had come up the forward staircase to run his torch beam across the bolted-down chairs, over the canvas-wrapped lifeboats, inside the deck's roofed shelter. But there was no ladder onto the top of the shelter, and he had not chinned himself up to discover us.

This one strolled down the centre of the deck, casually playing his torchlight across the boats – an entire platoon of pirates could have crouched in them, unseen – before wandering to the underside of our shelter. I held my breath for the sight of a head peering over the shelter roof, but there came only the rasp of a cigarette lighter, and a flare of light from below.

We lay, breathing in his smoke and listening to his dyspepsia, until he gave a sigh, then walked over to the lee side to let the wind take his burning stub. He headed for the aft stairs, and left us to the night.

Three minutes later, the same door opened, then closed – only this time, the light that spilt out was dim and indirect, as if the bulb had blown out.

I did not think it had blown out. I gave my companion's leg

a gentle kick, and when Holmes had eased around to face in my direction, I breathed words into his ear. 'Whoever it is, they're in trousers, and they removed the light bulb before they opened the door.'

The moon was not yet full and the perpetual haze of the tropics added to the obscurity, but the combination of nature's illumination and indirect light from the bridge and radio rooms gave glimpses of the figure's progress: across to where the lifeboats were mounted, up beside them, a pause – then the figure was gone.

Holmes breathed into my ear, 'Under the canvas?'

I nodded. We waited, and saw nothing . . . nothing at all. Five minutes passed. After ten, I whispered, 'Doesn't look like an illicit liaison. Could it be a passenger looking for a quiet – wait.'

I turned my head a fraction to see what had caught the corner of my eye. There were always birds around a ship, although fewer in the middle of the China Sea than near port, but the high motion had not been that of a gull stretching its wings. I let my gaze soften, waiting . . .

My hand tightened on Holmes' arm. He let slip a muted oath.

Neither of us believed what our eyes told us.

A shadow moved high among the lines, more a dark absence than an actual figure. The Marconi wires strung between the ship's twin masts – like a washing-line between flag-poles – were higher than the smoke stacks. Even in broad daylight they looked no thicker than twine. And at night? With any sheen the wire once possessed long covered over with soot? Swaying in the wind?

'I believe Miss Sato may have misled me, when she said she was not trained in the family business,' I murmured. The chance of there being a second small, superbly athletic person onboard was minuscule enough to dismiss.

'And clearly, her area of expertise is not in juggling or gymnastics.'

'We mustn't risk distracting her.'

'A fall would kill her,' he agreed softly.

With care, we edged off of the shelter and crept forward, faces down so that from above, we would be nothing but darkness against dark decking.

At the forward-most funnel, we planted our backs against the warm metal and lifted our eyes.

It took a terrifying thirty seconds to locate a faint shape against the sky, moving with excruciating slowness. I began to wonder if the next of the periodic deck-checks would find us here, chins locked upward. As for the night watch in his crow's nest – well, sailors tended to keep their eyes out for objects in front and on the horizon; this one might not anticipate an approach at his own level.

Then without warning, she dropped. But before the oath left Holmes' lips and my fingers had fully clamped around his arm, we saw that it was not a fall, but a swing. As the wire climbed to its anchor on the mast, the increase of angle made further upright progress impossible (as if it had been 'possible' before!). Instead, the figure now shinned along the remaining twenty feet to the wood – which must have felt solid as a mountainside after one hundred fifty metres of swaying, half-inch wide, plaited metal. Certainly, she clung to the mast for a time before starting a descent.

Holmes absently prised my fingers out of his flesh and took a step to the side, the better to see her movement. I was just trying to visualise the complex arrangement of wires and ropes when I saw that she had, indeed, decided not to risk passing an arm's length away from the man in the crow's nest.

The highest of the guy-wires met the mast just below the Marconi line. When that wire's drooping flags gave a brief jerk, it was clear which way she had chosen for her return to *navis firma*. The route would take her to the top of the well-lit and always-occupied bridge, but from there, she would most likely hop down the darker aft side of the bridge to the decking around the funnel.

Precisely where we stood.

Holmes and I faded back, taking up positions on either side of the massive stack. I stood motionless, my eyes focussed on the air as I waited for movement at the edges of the bridge. It seemed a very long time before one section of dark sky assumed a greater solidity, climbing over the rail and dropping to the deck-boards with a gentle thump.

She took a step away from me, and Holmes spoke.

'I wonder if I might—'

She leapt instantly – fortunately in my direction, but moving so fast, I did not pause for thought, just launched myself at her with a hard tackle.

It was like wrapping my arms around a badger. She reacted with the fury of a trained fighter: squirming around beneath me before we'd even hit the deck, using the bounce of our weight to kick out hard, followed by a blow that would have killed me if it had landed a few inches to the side. I flew off with nothing more than a scrap of fabric in my left hand.

She was on her feet and braced for a sprint when a torch beam went on and a gun went off.

I staggered upright and looked at the crouching figure of darkness, rendered motionless by Holmes' warning shot. Her head was visible now – the cloth in my hand was a dark silken mask – but the rest of her, neck to toe and down the backs of her hands, was concealed under a matte, dark blue fabric.

I brushed myself off, relieved to find nothing broken, then looked at the man with the torch. 'You brought your *gun*?'

'A good thing I did.'

'A bit excessive, to capture an acrobat, wouldn't you say?'

'Miss Sato is no acrobat,' he said. 'Or, not merely an acrobat.'

'No?' I looked at our prisoner. Her sleek hair was tousled, but the rest of her showed no sign of distress, or even exertion. Slowly, she rose from her sprinter's crouch, giving me a glance that seemed oddly apologetic. She took a breath, let it out again.

'I am *shinobi*,' she said, then smiled. 'Ninja.'

BOOK TWO

Japan

April 1924

CHAPTER THIRTEEN

Death walks in silence.
Eyes see all, but are not seen.
Ghost walking through walls.

ONE THING ABOUT SHIPBOARD travel: there is always a public room open to welcome insomniacs, card-game addicts, or a trio seeking to remove themselves from the vicinity of a gunshot before the men in the bridge came looking.

I suppose our odd clothing looked like pyjamas – as indeed it was, in parts. But our behaviour, compared to a herd of young men galloping all over the ship in search of a feathered hat, was hardly worthy of note. We chose the cocktail bar's dimmest corner, ordered drinks to get rid of the sleepy attendant, and kept our voices low.

Miss Sato watched the man leave; I, on the other hand, had not taken my eyes off of her, or let her get too close to me, for the briefest instant. 'What do you mean, you're a ninja?' In 1924, this was not a word known to the general public, but my baritsu teacher back in Oxford had told me of the secret Medieval cult, thankfully long faded into obscurity. Still, if this crazy female envisioned herself as a ninja assassin, maybe Holmes ought to keep his gun in his hand.

'We call ourselves "shinobi",' she answered. 'Or for women,

some times, *kunoichi*. But like the arrangement of my names, I use what a Westerner might know.'

'Enough grammar. Why are you here?'

'I told you, I am going home.'

'But why else? Ninja are hired assassins. Who is your target?'

'Russell—' Holmes started, but Miss Sato held up her hand to him.

'"Ninja" means "spy",' she said carefully. 'We deal in information, not death. Yes, some of us have killed. Some of us steal, when that is necessary. And some are for hire, like *ronin* – you know the word "ronin"? Samurai without masters? But many of us are not assassins, and not for hire. Mr Holmes.'

I had thought the silence profound before she spoke his name. If she knew his name, then . . . The damnable thing was, her voice sounded so reasonable. And for certain, she knew how to fight.

I shook my head. 'The ninja died off centuries ago. They're folklore, like the Knights of the Round Table. Romantic stories of invisibility, special equipment, walking up walls – all that kind of nonsense.'

'Yes. And no. If we are invisible, it is because we are below notice. We use the tools we have at hand, and our most important skills are those of deception – to look like someone who belongs in a place. We only walk up walls if there is no easier way to get inside.' She smiled; I did not.

'Although since at times there will not be an easier way,' Holmes spoke up, 'acrobatic training can come in handy.'

I could not help a quick glance sideways. 'Holmes, surely you're not taking this person's claim seriously?'

'Our own Templars were officially disbanded in 1312, but do you imagine they actually packed their things and went meekly home? All the confusion and romantic twaddle has allowed them to hide in plain sight up to the present day. Why not the same thing in Japan?'

I thought about it for a moment, thought about the times Sherlock Holmes had openly admitted to being Sherlock Holmes precisely in order to be laughed off – then my mind snapped back to the central question here. 'Whether or not there's an organisation behind her changes nothing. If she's here to kill someone, we need to lock her up until we get to Hong Kong and can hand her over to the authorities.'

'I am not here to kill anyone,' she said.

Holmes asked, 'Then what are you after?'

She turned her gaze onto Holmes. 'Without consulting my superiors, I may not give you any details of my task. But it involves the sale of an object that could be . . . compromising.'

'The Earl of Darley,' he said. His grey eyes looked like chips of ice.

'You . . . know him? Before this?'

'We have had dealings.'

'Ah, so. I was told there were rumours about his past.'

'Who told you?'

Again, the apologetic smile, but no reply.

He came at it from a different tack. 'You knew who we were. And you knew that Russell and I would be onboard this ship.'

'I . . . Yes, I was told, but only at the last minute.'

I added a question. 'Is that why we were first delayed, then offered good cabins on a sailing two days after we'd planned to leave?'

'I do not know.'

I did, curse it. Not many were familiar with my gastric

vulnerability – and hence my willingness to wait for the chance of a deck cabin at the ship's centre. One man, however, knew me well. 'Mycroft.'

I was watching her closely, but she did not react. Either she was very, *very* good, or she did not know the name.

However, if Mycroft Holmes had wanted to nudge his brother and me towards a case of international blackmail – a case with what promised to be important players – he could easily have arranged a lack of comfortable cabins until the day he wished us to depart. And one might think Mycroft could tell us directly, but being five thousand miles away, we might prove difficult to control. In any event, Mycroft never issued orders when he could achieve his results invisibly.

At last, I took my eyes off the self-proclaimed ninja and turned them on my husband, searching for deceit. 'This is not something you and your brother arranged?'

'Russell, I have not been in touch with Mycroft since the end of the Khanpur case.'

I loved my brother-in-law, but I was growing a bit tired of his methods.

When at last I looked back at Miss Sato, she appeared puzzled, but ventured no questions.

'Well,' I told her, 'just don't call him "Holmes" in the hearing of others. And I go by "Russell" – "Miss", generally. So, what is this object you're looking for?'

'I cannot tell you that.'

'Have you searched Darley's rooms for it?'

'And his trunks in the hold. I did so before we reached Colombo.'

Holmes stirred. 'Is that why you've been acting the poltergeist?'

'The what?'

'Sneaking around the ship every night, removing things from one room and putting them in another?'

'Lord Darley looks like a man who would not notice if his rooms had been searched by a water buffalo. If that dullness is an act, then to establish a ship-wide pattern of disturbances might cause him either to dismiss the search as coincidence, or to retrieve the . . . object, to keep it close at hand. Two of those whose cabins I entered had been in brief conversation with Darley. I thought they might be associates. Also,' she added, 'the skills you call "sneaking" require constant practice. Three weeks without using them could make me dangerously clumsy.'

Her English, I noted, had become remarkably fluent. 'Did you search our rooms?'

'That, I did not think wise.'

Small favours. 'What about Miss Roland?'

'The girl who jumped from the ship the first night?'

'Jumped – how do you know that?' I demanded.

For the first time, her complacent demeanour failed. She looked down at her hands. 'I saw her.'

'You *saw* . . . and you did not stop her?'

'I was walking the railings of the sun deck. The upper decks were dark, but there was sufficient light below that a figure crossing the open part of the promenade deck caught my eye. She took off her shoes, climbed the railings, and stepped off. No hesitation, and no one nearby. I don't know why the watch didn't see her, except that she was at the very back. And she went down immediately, with only the one splash – she must have weighted her pockets. Even if I had run to the bridge and they'd put down a boat, they'd never have found her.'

'You could have thrown a lifebuoy,' I exclaimed. 'These modern ones with the magnesium flares – what if she changed her mind the moment she stepped off?'

Her dark eyes stayed down. 'She did not come up. Not even briefly.'

'Was it you who searched her cabin?' Holmes asked.

She did not reply.

'How did you know which it was?' I asked her.

'She left the key in her shoes. I took it, and threw the shoes over the side. There was also . . . a note.'

'A suicide note?'

She nodded.

'You took it?'

She looked up at last. 'I could not leave it for the purser to find. The letter named Lord Darley. Without it, Darley would hear of her disappearance, and would no doubt know that she was missing because of him, but even if he were to suspect suicide, no one else would have any reason to connect him to her. With the letter, his passage would be interrupted by controversy, and possibly an investigation. I could not risk that.'

'Where is the letter?'

'I destroyed it.'

'What?' My outrage woke the attendant from his half-doze, but I waved him away. 'You had no right to destroy the poor woman's final words!'

Her chin was up, her voice even as she replied, 'I could have hidden it, yes. Instead, I assumed responsibility for it.'

'What do you mean by that?' Holmes demanded.

She considered her reply, then came to it obliquely. 'In the West, suicide is a shameful act, one of failure and weakness. A sin. To my people, taking one's life can be the ultimate weapon against defeat.

It is the most powerful blow one can make against one's enemy, when pure honour asserts victory over the shame of compromise. For any Japanese person, but especially for a Samurai, shame is far worse than death. The stories we tell our children, the events that glorify names and that give their essence to our most moving plays, are those filled with the triumph of suicide. Of course,' she added with a wry smile, 'it helps if one believes in reincarnation.'

'But to destroy—'

She cut me off. 'This is my way of explaining that Western eyes might have seen Miss Roland's letter as a plea for forgiveness. The letter was written to her sister. In it, she named her sin, and named her blackmailer. It went on for three pages, and was both highly detailed and deeply emotional. Were the case to go to court, Darley's lawyers would not have found it difficult to create the image of a flighty and deeply troubled female. He would have walked away with nothing but some gossip to stain his garments.

'Instead, by destroying the words, I have assumed their burden.'

'What, you intend to avenge her death? A complete stranger? You said you didn't intend to kill anyone,' I pointed out.

'Miss Russell, a living enemy may be made to suffer more than a dead one.'

'So you'll just torture him.'

'Physically? No. But I promise you, I shall find a punishment that fits the crime.'

The cold edge to her words caught my attention. I did not shiver, not quite.

Holmes stepped in. 'Miss Sato, Russell and I are inadvertent participants in this case. Nonetheless, I hold a special loathing for the blackmailer as a species, and an unresolved history with this one in particular. If and when you care to reveal the details of your own involvement – namely, your master and the object you seek – we might agree to be used as consultants. However, I will not work blind.'

'The moment I receive permission, I shall tell you all. And in the meantime . . .' She glanced over at the clock on the wall. 'You ought to sleep. Our lesson begins in three and a half hours.'

I looked at Holmes; he looked at Miss Sato. She rose, waiting to see if we would object to her leaving.

Anyone else and I would say, *Leave, no matter – where will you go, on a ship in the midst of the China Sea?* But this woman could hide anywhere, then slip away in any port she chose.

Holmes nodded, and let her go.

'You're sure?' I asked before she reached the door.

'If she is working against us, it is best to know before we reach Japan.'

'The real question being, with her aboard, will we reach Japan at all?'

'It does promise a certain piquancy to the remainder of our journey.'

I wondered what he would say if I proposed that we took turns keeping watch while the other slept.

Somewhat to my surprise, and relief, only dreams disturbed my sleep, not a knife between the ribs.

Twenty-four and a half days, Bombay to Yokohama. Five hundred and eighty-six hours pressed about by humanity. One hundred and eighty hours spent sweating amongst the bed sheets; eighty-four hours in the dining room; nineteen and a half hours of language tutorials with Miss Sato; ten hours reading

Shakespeare aloud with an extremely mixed group of amateurs; and seventeen hour-long afternoon salons on topics from tea to theatre. Between my morning dunk in the cold-water swimming baths and the last flicker of light from the open-deck cinema show, I kept irritability at bay with compelling reading material or, as time went on, physical activity: some forty hours spent pacing the decks to keep from leaping off them, twenty or so hours on the cycling and rowing machines in the gymnasium, and regular matches of deck tennis and quoits – played with my right hand, lest I win too often. I even spent a cumulative two and a quarter hours playing tennis against young Roderick Farquhar before his supply of balls finally came to an end.

More happy were the forty or so hours spent in conversation with Miss Sato, in various rooms and on various decks, over topics as widespread as Shinto family gods, the centrality of shame in Japanese psychology, and the English love of dogs and mistrust of baths. We enjoyed lengthy meanders through concepts basic to our two nations: heroism (Admiral Nelson and Japan's Forty-Seven Ronin); beauty (which garden had more, Versailles or Katsura? Which tea pot, Georgian silver or 400-year-old clay?); social responsibility (*bushido* having much in common with the chivalric code); apologies (how a Westerner's apology accepts wrongdoing, whereas in Japan it may merely acknowledge a rift – and we agreed that the Englishman's habit of apologising when someone walks into him bridges this East–West divide). On a more personal level, we made mutual confession of our odd training, how Holmes would set challenges for me at unlikely moments, how her father's motives were rarely made clear until long after the event.

Those forty hours made the remaining five hundred and forty-six almost worthwhile. Were it not for a certain reluctance between us, some inexplicable but definite barrier to intimacy, I might almost have called her 'friend.'

Holmes, on the other hand, occupied many of his spare hours playing cards in the smoking room, under the premise that thwarting one criminal activity is better than none at all, and if he couldn't lay hands on the blackmailer among us, at least he could foil the card shark.

Card games being a nocturnal activity – Thomas Darley's kind of card games, that is; the earl wasn't much given to long nights over the tables – I had grown accustomed to a late-evening ritual: while I prepared for bed, Holmes prepared for cards. We stood at our mirrors, I brushing my teeth and he making subtle changes in appearance and manner. When my skin had been cleansed of the day's salt air and his hair combed to evoke a man wistful over lost youth, we wished each other a happy evening and walked in opposite directions, me for my bed and book, Holmes for his table of avaricious opponents.

As one might have expected, he spotted early on how young Darley was cheating, and how Monty Pike-Elton was assisting. His initial impulse surprised me: he wondered if he shouldn't have a quiet word with the purser about the young man's chicanery.

He decided against this approach for several reasons. First and foremost was that doing so would open a writhing can of worms in the form of humiliation and public shame, with the entire ship quite aware that 'Robert Russell' was at its root. Since an open declaration of hostilities would complicate any future advance Holmes might want to make on Lord Darley, blackmailing earl, clearly this would never do. A lesser consideration was the knowledge of how unpleasant the remainder of the voyage would be – not only for Holmes, but for me, baking under the unremitting glares of the Darley family and friends.

In the end, his deciding consideration was neither of these. Rather, it was the question of how effective exposure would be as a tool of actual reform, or whether the long-term results would be nil. Surely on the next voyage, young Darley would simply resume his fleecing of the innocent?

So instead, Holmes decided to stamp down any future impulse to card-sharkery on the part of Thomas Darley: to make the young man hesitate at the very impulse, not fully trusting his ability to pull it off. And that would take a more convoluted approach than just a murmur in the purser's ear.

It also took a good two weeks of nightly labours in the smoke-filled room over the cards, establishing Robert Russell as a wealthy man with more luck than skill, whose failure to succumb to the Darley tricks was a matter of happenstance, not cause for wariness.

Naturally, this drove the viscount to ever-greater efforts, to the extent that if he really had been playing Bobby Russell, he'd have been caught. But Holmes continued in blithe bonhomie, drinking and jesting and not quite losing.

It came to a head on a Saturday night as we approached Hong Kong. The British colony would see a longer stop than usual, with most of the ship disembarking for everything from visiting a tailor (one could order a suit and have it delivered in Tokyo) to taking a picnic up Victoria Peak to spending the day at the Happy Valley racetrack. Lord Darley (I knew from an overheard conversation) had arranged for an afternoon's riding with the Hong Kong Jockey Club, for himself and his wife.

The holiday atmosphere that prevailed whenever we were due into port affected the card players that night. The bottle of old brandy Holmes bought for the table loosened things up a bit more – and although it cost him hard to watch the lovely stuff being swigged down the throats of young men like gin from a bathtub, he had his revenge, because this night, old man Russell won, and won, and won some more. The game finally came to an end at 2.40 in the morning when the steward politely declined to subsidise the young man's further efforts.

Thomas Darley's friends had run out of ready cash some time before. Now, they kept the newly impoverished viscount from pummelling the steward, pushing Tommy back into his chair and thrusting into his hands a glass with the dregs of the brandy. Holmes just leant back, playing with the heavy gold watch that five minutes earlier had been strapped around young Darley's left wrist.

'I thought he was going to pass out,' Holmes told me the next morning. 'He was not too drunk to realise just how much he'd lost, and it came crashing down on him that he'd have to go crawling to his father if he wanted the steward's debt paid.

'I gave each of the others a few bills to compensate them for their own losses, then sent them away and had the steward bring us coffee.

'After he'd had a while to think about it, to fully meditate upon the ruin that was opening at his feet, I counted out enough to repay the steward and pushed it across the table. "Cheating at cards is a dangerous game", I told him. "There is always the chance one will come across an opponent, however unlikely, whose misspent youth has left him very good at it".'

'What did he say?'

'I feared for a moment that he would fall to the carpet and kiss my shoes.'

'Precisely how much money are we talking about?'

He told me, an eye-blinking amount that explained the cat-at-the-cream expression on his face. 'Wow.'

'Indeed. The Royal Naval Benevolent Trust will find good use for it.'

'I'd say.'

'I also gave the lad back his watch.'

'Generous of you.'

He shrugged. 'I have a watch. A very nice one.'

Which I had given him as a wedding present.

'That poor boy.' I had to laugh. How long would it be before he could look at his wrist and see only a timepiece, and not a reminder of near-catastrophe?

Holmes knew instantly what I meant. 'Yes. The rest of the voyage may prove a trifle uncomfortable for him.'

To my amusement, such was the threat of discomfort that Thomas Darley fled the ship the next day in the company of the person who, until Holmes loomed on his horizon, had been anathema to him: his stepmother.

The earl, it seemed, was ill, thus unable to escort his wife to the stables. When he requested that his son take his place, it seemed that the alternative of staying onboard and risking a confrontation with the man who had stripped him dry the previous evening was an even greater horror than riding with his father's new wife.

The viscount and the countess walked down the gangway well before noon, if not exactly arm in arm, at least together. They returned at the end of the day, looking tired but with much to tell the earl about Colonial horseflesh.

Darley himself, looking somewhat wan from a bout of *mal de mer*, had managed nothing more strenuous than his weekly attendance at the shipboard Sunday services, which (I'd noticed as I walked past in search of a book) had been populated this day chiefly by the staff of the *Thomas Carlyle*. He nodded as his wife and son described the hardships of the tropical climate on thoroughbreds, and managed one or two interested questions, but he turned in early, as did his chastened son.

'Well, Holmes,' I said that night as we resumed simultaneous preparations for bed, 'at least you seem to have healed the rift between Thomas Darley and his father's new wife.'

And I was pleased that it hadn't taken him the entire voyage to do so.

In the normal course of events, a ship such as this one would put in to Yokohama, a short train ride from the capital city of Tokyo. But last September's Kanto quake and fire had all but wiped Yokohama from the map; for the past six months, most ships putting in to the remaining ports on Japan's main island were carrying some form of relief.

The *Thomas Carlyle* would be among the first trickle of returning tourists, although even then, the ports available to us were well away from the centre of devastation. Holmes and I had originally thought to depart the ship in Nagasaki, making our way north by train through Hiroshima and Okayama to Kyoto; Miss Sato suggested that Kobe would be more . . . useful to us.

Kobe it was.

CHAPTER FOURTEEN

Sun falls to starboard.
Moths have gnawed our woollen coats.
Who knew cold would come?

WE REACHED JAPAN WITH no more fatalities.

Since leaving Colombo, we had gone for days with nothing to look at but sea and the occasional passing ship, followed by the thrill, then letdown of approaching, then departing a series of ports. But after three weeks of this routine, we put in at Nagasaki. From then on, the coastline of Japan lay permanently off the port-side rails, causing a perceptible tilt with the weight of the land-hungry gawkers.

The deck remained at a cant even when we turned through the Kii Channel into first the Inland Sea, then Osaka Bay – however, by that time the reason was more the warmth of the afternoon sun on the southern decks than any view. Limbs and shoulders disappeared beneath wool for the first time since Bombay. I bundled along with the others, although once we had land on both sides, I was happy to trade the warmth of the port-side decks for the relative quiet of the starboard. I stretched out on my deckchair and watched the landscape scroll past, studying the scores of small islands and myriad foreign coastal craft – junks and sampans and barges, fishing boats with high prow and stern, their sails like Hokusai prints.

The day had been filled with leave-taking. Most of our Japanese passengers were departing here, along with the three Darleys, Monty Pike-Elton, the two British hearties on world tour, and the pair of adventurous young Americans, Clifford Adair and Edward Blankenship. (All of the men had sat eagerly in the front row for Miss Sato's final lecture, on the etiquette of the geisha house, only to be disappointed to hear that a geisha was more artist than good-time girl. When Miss Sato then cranked the gramophone to illustrate the sort of Oriental music the young men might encounter, well, suffice it to say their eagerness was quenched. One of them used the word 'caterwauling'.)

The city that rose up on the other side of Osaka Bay spread for what looked like miles along the coast. The water grew increasingly crowded with fishing boats and steamer ferries, merchant marine and pleasure boats. Progress slowed.

When the docks were clearly visible, progress ceased altogether, as the engines fell away. Pilot, quarantine agents, newspaper men and the crème de la greeters swarmed onboard. Fishing craft and curio sellers pressed up against the ship's side. Around me, complaints arose from the passengers who were too important to be under the scrutiny of the quarantine men, but too insignificant to be sought by news reporters and official greeters. Eventually, smoke began to belch from the stacks of a docked ship. When it had parted from land, our engines picked up, and we proceeded into its berth.

With the help of Miss Sato, our passage through Customs was rendered painless. She met us on officialdom's far side, along with a group of other Japanese who had been onboard, and bowing commenced.

For the time being, my wish for a local guide was to be granted, with Miss Sato ushering us into her homeland. To my greater relief, Miss Katagawa, often her companion aboard the ship, had been claimed by the young men, and although vague plans were made for a rendezvous, it meant that Holmes and I did not have to search for an excuse to be rid of the lads. Instead, after a few dozen more bows, our diminutive companion guided us, gently but firmly, in the direction of the chaotic street.

For twenty-four days, my world had been 582 feet long with a population of little more than a thousand souls. Since my rare ventures onto terra firma threatened more disorientation than relief, Kobe was the first time I had allowed myself to become conscious of a horizon that did not either vanish into the haze or curve upwards in both directions. My eyes stuttered against the concept of *distance*, just as my legs searched for footing on the motionless docks.

Disconcertingly, all around us a sea of rickshaws surged and swelled amidst a cacophony of shouts, bells, horns, warnings and exhortations. Miss Sato took no notice, merely hopped sure-footedly up onto a low wall to make a slow revolution, less as a means of seeing over the crowd, I thought, than to show herself. Sure enough, in a minute she was exchanging bows – his lower than hers – with a whip-thin man of about forty who emerged out of the crowds. They launched into a rapid conversation that included gestures in our direction, after which he bowed, turned on his heels, and darted back into the wheeled sea, to reappear with a pair of other rickshaw runners who might have been his brothers.

Our trunks would be sent on to our eventual Tokyo destination. Here, we each brought nothing but a valise. Climbing with them into the wheeled contraptions, away we flew.

Rickshaw neophytes are readily identified by their pale faces and white knuckles. I was not new to the sensations of a flying jostle several feet above unforgiving ground, although these rickshaws were lighter than their Indian counterparts, hence faster. They were in general a superior design to the subcontinental, with actual pneumatic tyres and cushions on the wooden seats. The runner wore an official-looking blue uniform with a towel tucked into his belt. His straw hat bobbed, his fraying straw sandals flew and the brisk rhythm of the little bells lulled me into complacency.

Then we left the city behind, and the ground began to rise. Ahead, I could see a gathering of similarly clad men. Three of them got to their feet and moved to intercept us, and I was on the edge of calling to ask Holmes if he had his gun to hand when the first one trotted around behind Miss Sato's rickshaw and set his shoulder to it.

These were our secondary engines, to propel us over the hills behind the town.

The view was like the world's best crow's nest. I craned, watching the city fall away, thrilled by seeing the ocean shrink, until it became merely one feature among others. At the top of the range of hills, we paused to pay off the supplementary power sources and allow our runners to rest, squatting together and renewing their lungs with cigarettes while we followed Miss Sato to a small, low building. There we were offered noodles or tea. We chose tea – not the English milked variety, of course, but watery, pale green Japanese tea, bitter and remarkably refreshing. We slurped it down to the scum in the bottom, breathing in great lungfuls of incredibly green and living air, then resumed our wheeled perches and set off again, this time downhill.

Eventually we came to a small town of low, close-knit buildings with roofs of tile or thatch above age-blackened wood walls. The air took on an oddly metallic taste and a moisture suggestive of a steamy bathroom: Arima was a town of many *onsen*, a word that means both a large public bath filled with the naturally hot mineral water from springs all over this tumultuous countryside, and the inn built around such a bath.

Miss Sato's runner appeared to know where we were going. Our little procession wound through narrow streets lined with shops and homes and unidentifiable businesses. At last, the wheels slowed and stopped.

We climbed down from the rickshaws before the oldest, simplest building of all. The front of the *onsen* resembled a gateway, thatching on the portico and atop the side wings; its central gate opened into a courtyard with a raised veranda on three sides. There assembled a line of bowing individuals: three women dressed in bright kimonos with hair like sculptures, one man in more sombre colours. Taking our lead from Miss Sato, we returned their bows, then allowed ourselves to be ushered to the entrance.

There we ran into our first barrier: none of the soft slipper-shoes marking the transition from the out of doors were designed for enormous Western feet. The ladies went pink with shame and the man dark with fury, while Miss Sato attempted to soothe the honour of the house by a string of what were clearly abject apologies. Larger slippers were summoned, although I gathered by the continued pinkness of face that mine were intended for men.

It took several minutes for the flurry of apologies to run its course, but once this international incident had been averted, we were invited inside, and shown our rooms.

Fortunately, Miss Sato's lectures had prepared me for the accommodations: stark expanse of pristine straw mats, one wall of wooden cupboards, a niche holding a narrow vase with a single branch of cherry blossoms, and a low wooden table with round silk cushions tucked under three of its sides. We traded shoes again, and a tray of tea and little biscuits followed us in the door, with steaming cloths for our hands. At Miss Sato's invitation, we lowered ourselves onto the puffy cushions at the little table and watched one of the maids pour pale green liquid into vessels that looked like egg cups. She then withdrew, abandoning us to our sybaritic refreshment.

My hand reached out for the diminutive cup, then stopped mid-air. 'What is wrong?' Miss Sato enquired.

'It's not moving.'

Three sets of eyes watched the pale liquid. It sat, precisely as the maid had left it, completely motionless in its porcelain frame, but for the faint steam rising off its perfectly flat surface. With none of the constant trembling that had shaken our drinks and our bones for the better part of twenty-four days. With something like reverence, I disturbed the cup's repose to lift it to my mouth.

Ninety seconds later I was eyeing the single shilling-sized biscuit on the plate and reflecting on how many meals my fickle stomach had caused me to miss during the past three weeks. Holmes had other things on his mind.

'Why have you brought us here?' he asked Miss Sato.

I took advantage of her distraction to sweep up the final offering, chewing it as subtly as I could.

'I received a message from my . . . employer, who is willing to meet with you. However, he—'

'Why should we wish to meet with your employer?'

For the first time, her composure slipped. Her mouth gaped, lacking words to fill it. It was clearly beyond her comprehension that anyone might question the gift of a meeting with her boss.

Her shock only lasted for a moment. She straightened her already ramrod-straight back and smiled. 'I believe you would find it to your advantage.'

'I see.'

'However, he is a . . . proud man, and not fully accustomed to the ways of the West. I intend – that is, if you agree, I would like to spend two or three days here, helping you to become comfortable with Japanese manners, before you meet.'

Holmes appeared to think, then gave a shrug. 'I have nothing more urgent to do than learn Japan from the inside. You, Russell?'

He was deliberately prodding her dismay, but this time she had herself under control, and her face remained dispassionate.

'What, forced to spend a couple of days on solid ground in a hot-springs spa?' I said. 'I think I could manage the burden.'

Her hands relaxed. 'Very good. Let us walk through the town while it is still light, and then I will introduce you to the baths.'

We reversed our progress through the spotless corridors, changing room shoes for public shoes, then those for our abandoned outside footwear.

Arima was a village nestled into a fold in the hills. *Sakura* – the famous Japanese cherry trees – that had been blooming near the coast, here showed but the smallest touch of pink in the buds. The hills were green, the village streets narrow and charming, and the inhabitants who clacked along the cobbles on wooden *geta* sandals curious but polite. The buildings were old, tiny, pristine and magnificent.

Most blessed of all, the cool air swishing in and out of my lungs held not a trace of the sea.

For more than a thousand years, Miss Sato told us, people had come to Arima to soak in the hot springs. We wandered through the town, past the steaming pools that collected along the main street, stepping into curious shops and doll-sized alleyways, examining the painted plaster food displayed in a box at the front of a restaurant and the enormous variety of brushes and ink in the shop beside it. Many people laughed at the sight of us, but they were friendly about it, and bobbed at us in response to Miss Sato's oft-repeated explanations. We ventured a few phrases, causing more laughter and friendly bobbing, and walked on.

Above the town was a Shinto shrine. There our guide showed us how to make our offering, ringing the bell and clapping to focus our attention – or perhaps that of the *kami* spirit who lived here. Further along, past a carefully nurtured garden of bamboo and moss, we climbed up until we came to a small log polished by a thousand sitters. As we sat gazing across the closely woven rooftops, I felt as if my eyes had just been born.

Miss Sato told us stories: about the monk who founded it, the Emperors who had used it, the ills cured by its two different varieties of water – one golden, the other silver, beneficial for different ailments, external and internal. Her voice was pleasant and the sensation of limitless space after the constraints of the ship was a blessing. I could feel a tight knot begin to unclench.

Not entirely, however. Holmes was a devote of Turkish baths, but public bathing never appealed much to me, less from innate modesty than from the scars I bear: they attract first attention, then sympathy, and finally, questions.

It was with a resigned sigh, then, that I stood in the bathhouse an hour later and prepared to strip. There were some seven other women in the room, of all shapes and ages, sags and blemishes (although none had blonde hair, and not one came within a hand's breadth of my height). All were utterly lacking in inhibitions, scrubbing and towelling as if they were addressing each other from behind walls. And all were either marvellously well-mannered or selectively blind, because their conversations barely paused when I walked in with Miss Sato. When one or another did take notice of me, she would look at my face – particularly my fascinatingly blue eyes – and not at the puckered scar on my shoulder or the older scars down my arms and torso.

My companion, I was interested to see, also displayed a history of violence. In her case, the blood she had shed was not from gunshot or road accident, but sharp blades: three wounds, one of them – down the side of her right arm – from very long ago, indeed.

I left my spectacles on my folded garments, and sat where she indicated, on a low stool. The attendant began enthusiastically to scrub the accumulated soil from my skin (a ship's baths of heated seawater did not actually cleanse). When I tingled all over, Miss Sato led me – *sans* glasses, less because of the irritation of them fogging than because without them, my mind was more willing to believe that everyone else was half-blind, too – towards a steaming pool populated with chatting heads. I felt like an adolescent, awkward and embarrassed, and was relieved to find the pool of silvery water nearly opaque with effervescence. My companion descended the steps and sank to her chin, making a little noise of welcome at the sensation; I stuck one foot in and yelped.

'Whoa!' I exclaimed. 'That's hot.'

She sat upright, bringing the thin scar on her shoulder into view, and gave me a frown. 'This is the coolest of the three.'

'Do you cook lobsters in the hottest one?' I tried again, venturing one foot into the silver liquid, then the other. My behaviour was attracting the curious glances my mere epidermis had not, so I told myself that if the water was not boiling the flesh of the others, it would not harm mine. I gasped as I committed the greater part of me to the onsen, and patted around until I located a ledge to sit on, leaving my shoulders and head radiating furiously into the evening air.

Two middle-aged ladies bobbed their heads approvingly. I stretched my eyes wide and said, '*Mizu wa atsui des*!' The water is hot!

The two giggled and launched into a conversation, of which I understood about three words. But I nodded and grinned back at them, and that seemed quite sufficient for their purposes.

After what felt like a very long time, head swimming and sweat pouring down my face, I said to my companion, 'How long do you keep this up?'

'I am about finished here,' she said, then to my consternation added, 'I thought I would move to the hotter bath for a while.'

Before I could moan too loudly, she raised her voice to speak past my shoulder. I looked behind me to see one of the attendants coming to help me from the water.

'I've told her to take you for a massage. I will join you in a quarter hour or so.'

I staggered from the tub, ridiculously weak and heavy, and leant unabashedly on the tiny woman's shoulder. She helped me back to the stools, rinsed me off, then guided me to an adjoining room, where I was allowed to collapse face-down on a long, low table. She 'covered' me with a minuscule towel. I was warm, I was motionless, and in seconds, I was asleep.

When I swam back up, there were hands on me: strong, capable hands manipulating the edges of my scapula, easing out tension I did not know was there. My eyes drifted open. On the next table lay Miss Sato, eyes shut, a masseuse working on her left knee. I was vaguely aware of well-being from my shoulders down, and was faintly astonished to realise that I must have been the passive object of the hands' attentions for quite some time – long enough for them to make the journey from toes to shoulders, turning muscle to limp rag all the way.

When she'd finished with my neck and the back of my head, I never wanted to move again. I'd have been happy to melt into the table and slide away on the steaming river that ran down the middle of the village, to feed the roots of those cedar trees and bamboo groves . . .

Were it not that I felt as empty as a clean bowl.

I became aware of a presence. I opened my eyes. Miss Sato's face was inches from my own.

'Would you care for dinner, Russell-san?' The English honourific had become the Japanese, but as always, the *R* required her full attention.

'Maybe you should call me "Mary".'

The dark eyes crinkled. 'And I am Haruki.'

My eyelids drifted shut. 'What does "Haruki" mean, anyway?'

'Often means "Sunshine". But Father say means "Makes life clear".'

CHAPTER FIFTEEN

Students taking an
Examination by bear
May need the scrub-brush.

WE STAYED AT THE Arima spa for three days. All the while, Haruki-san watched our reactions – to strange clothing, stranger foods, uncomfortable customs, all the incomprehensible situations that travel brings.

That first day, after being parboiled and beaten, we were propped upright, wrapped in kimonos (mine with the woman's stiff obi belt), and led away to the dining area, where we knelt until our legs were numb, picking our way through numerous courses of unrecognisable foods, most of them either raw or pickled. We slept on hard cotton mattresses laid on the floors, our heads perched on pillows stuffed, apparently, with gravel.

Fabulous luxury. For the first time since leaving Bombay, my night was dreamless.

The second day we spent in kimonos and *tabi*, socks with divided toes, sliding our feet into high wooden geta sandals when we went onto the cobbled streets. By midday my toe was blistered and my stomach querulous at the odd demands being made on it, my head spun with the relentlessness of the language, and I'd have cut off a finger for a cup of coffee. Or even English tea. However, by sunset I was negotiating the cobbles without too much thought, I knew which of the peculiar foods were more tasty, and the attentions of the bath attendant were very nearly welcome. I walked fearlessly to the baths, threw the odd ungrammatical phrases at my companions, joined in their laughter at the attempts, and scarcely noticed that I was displaying a lot of skin.

Again, no dreams.

The third day was almost comfortable . . . until the evening. Instead of taking us through the hallways and verandas to the inn's baths, Haruki-san led us down the narrow streets to a different bathhouse.

We stood outside the doors, while attendants waited to welcome us inside. 'In modern times,' our teacher told us, 'there are few truly mixed bathhouses. Mostly they are used for families, or for . . . other forms of male entertainment. Even in old times, women who bathed with men not of their family were . . . suspect. However, there remain traditional onsen in which men and women bath together. If you wish to experience one of those, this is your opportunity.'

My immediate impulse was to say, *No thank you*, but her expression was so . . . watchful, it gave me pause. That look of scrutiny was all too familiar: the sensation that my every motion was being judged, that my reaction to every assignment, or even mild suggestion, was being weighed and set down in a mental ledger. Haruki-san wanted to see just how far we were willing to go in (so to speak) immersing ourselves in the culture.

I took a deep breath. 'Will you and I be the only women among a gathering of men?'

She turned to the attendants. After half a minute of back-and-forth, she replied, 'No, there are five men and two women in the onsen at the moment. Although the two women are both older.'

I wanted to ask how much older, but decided that even a woman of ninety must think of herself as a woman, and if Haruki-san was willing, I would keep up my side.

'Sure,' I said. 'I'll try anything once.'

I was finding that nudity could be less a personal awareness than a social convention: that if everyone else in the room agreed, bare skin was just another garment. So I took a deep breath and raised my chin, then more or less held that position for the next hour.

It may have helped that I did not have my spectacles on.

Afterwards, we were served a dinner that went similarly up on the squeamish front. However, a woman who has been asked to down nonchalantly a sheep's eyeball is not easily daunted by the tentacles of sea creatures. And at least the miniature octopuses didn't squirt as one's teeth came down.

Of course, hefty jolts of warm sake helped.

When we took to our hard beds that night, we felt like honorary members of the Nippon empire.

And when we woke the next morning, we had been abandoned.

'Holmes, I do believe we're being handed our hats.'

'So it would appear.'

There had been a sort of nervous finality in the service of breakfast, an unwillingness to meet our eyes. Also, Haruki-san did not join us, for the first time. So it was no huge surprise, when the maids came in to remove the trays, that they stayed to pack our valises.

We looked down at our two bags, bemused. 'Do you suppose the onsen has buried Haruki-san under the tatami mats?' I asked Holmes.

Holmes grunted, and picked up his valise. After a moment, I reached for mine, and saw that, unlike his, the top had not been fastened. I frowned, and dropped to my heels to pull it open. On top of my clothing lay a small cloth bag with a drawstring. I pulled it open, then poured its contents out onto the tatami.

Some coins – disconcertingly few and small – and an envelope. Inside it were two slips of printed paper, tickets of some kind, and a folded sheet of writing paper containing two brief lines of Japanese characters – not the simpler *kana*, which function as a sort of alphabet, but *kanji*, the complex system based on the Chinese. 'Do you recognise these?' I asked my companion.

'I propose that we ask the gentleman at the desk.'

The desk in the inn's entrance foyer was a low table on which lay a ledger and abacus. Holmes and I knelt on either side of it, ignoring the maids who had trailed behind us. The gentleman in question dithered for a time, then reluctantly settled down across from us.

Holmes bowed, laid the piece of paper on the table, and waited. Without knowing if the characters represented a person, place, shopping list or lines of poetry, an expectant expression seemed the best way to knock information free.

But the fellow was unknockable. Holmes put together a simple sentence asking what it said. The gentleman dutifully read it aloud: in Japanese. We sat. He sat.

No set of English knees is about to outlast Japanese legs when it comes to a sitting contest. However, our faces warned the man that we intended to try. With a sigh almost too faint to hear, he turned his head and said something to one of the maids. She scurried off, and returned with paper and pen.

Wordlessly, he set to work. I ignored the numbness in my extremities. Holmes was motionless.

146

In a minute or two, one question was answered: the message – or part of it at least – concerned a place, for the man's pen began to shape a map.

Eventually, our host put aside the instrument and turned the sheet around to face us: a rough approximation of the Japanese coast, with roads and railways depicted by lines straight and cross-hatched, respectively. The gentleman put one finger on a dot near the bottom margin of the page. 'Arima,' he said, raising his eyebrows in a question. When he was satisfied that we understood, he moved his finger up to a dot to the north of us and said, 'Kyoto.' After that came 'Nagoya,' then 'Tokyo.' Retracing his path along a faint, winding inland route between Tokyo and Kyoto, he said, 'Nakasendo.' Finally, his finger stopped beside a tiny ink dot on the inland road: 'Mojiro-joku.'

He then moved his hand to tap the first line of kanji, and repeated the village name. He then pointed to the second and longer line, and said, 'Please to arrive at three in afternoon, Thursday. Today Monday. *Wakari-masuka?* Do you understand?

'We are to arrive in the town of Mojiro-joku at three o'clock Thursday afternoon,' Holmes replied.

'That winding line is the Nakasendo Road,' I said to Holmes. 'Up the Kiso Valley. It was one of the two main highways during the Edo period.' The cheaply printed book that Miss Sato – Haruki-san – had given me was of poems Bashō had written about the Nakasendo, which had, as I remembered, sixty-nine stations along its 330-some miles.

'Kiso-kaido, *hai,*' agreed the innkeeper, looking relieved at my comprehension. 'Nakasendo,' then a stream of words that either warned us of typhoons and highwaymen, or told us that the two things meant the same road. I hoped the latter, since some of the familiar sounds might have been a bit worrying, if I thought I was understanding them correctly: rain, yes, and river, but bears? At the end, he paused, then said once more, with slow emphasis, 'Mojiro-joku.'

Holmes and I pronounced the words after him, causing him to beam in relief. He checked that the ink was dry, then folded his map up and, with both hands, delivered it into Holmes' for safekeeping. He bowed; we bowed.

We had been dismissed.

Dismissed, but not heartlessly abandoned. We were assigned a cheerful lad we had seen around the inn, whose task, it seemed, was to escort us safely onto a train – the train for which we had two tickets. His only word of English was 'hello' (or more specifically, ''*aro*) which he used at all possible occasions. He grinned at the bounce of the rickshaws, grinned at the bustle around the train station, grinned as he pushed us into the arms of the stationmaster.

I decided, rather too late for it to do me any good, that the boy was a bit lacking in wits.

We had either missed our train, or the tickets were for some other station. If not country.

The stationmaster drew himself up to his full five and a half feet, resting one white-gloved hand on the truncheon at his belt. The other thrust out our two apparently useless scraps of paper.

Reluctantly, Holmes took them. One could almost hear our brains whirring through the possibilities, but as it happened, I found an answer first, triggered by a conversation with our absent teacher and the deep, red-faced humiliation of an innkeeper with inadequate footwear.

I bowed, and assembled a sentence to use against the official. 'I am very sorry. Can you help me? I wish to save a man from shame.' And then I named the innkeeper of the onsen who had just evicted us.

The stationmaster's officiousness paused a moment. I remained in my obsequious position, and haltingly explained. Holmes caught on instantly, and bowed as well. Even more helpful, he fed me words when mine faltered: *The innkeeper gave us the tickets. The innkeeper's boy brought us here. The innkeeper was wrong. We would return to the onsen and show him the mistake. He would be most ashamed, but what could one do? Unless the honourable stationmaster could help . . . ?*

In a town the size of Arima, the two men had to know each other. It was always possible that the two were mortal enemies, but even if that were the case, we would be no worse off than we were now.

We waited, heads inclined. After a moment, the white-gloved official replied with a bow of his own. Then he plucked the tickets from Holmes' fingers and snapped out an order. We followed him across the station to the ticket office, straining our ears at the rapid-fire conversation. After a string of Hais and a lot of ducking of her head, the young ticket-seller pulled the offending tickets towards her, then hesitated.

A lot more conversation, increasingly vexed, and a great deal of bowing and sideways glances of apprehension at our persons.

'Holmes, I think our tickets may be no good.'

The woman's gaze slid in my direction. 'Tickets good,' she said, then corrected herself. 'Were good, for morning train. But this not right class, for you.'

'Ah.' Perhaps Westerners were expected to shell out for first-class seats? I dug the little bag out of my valise, offering her the coins inside.

Her face looked surprised, then uncomfortable. She looked to the stationmaster for a command decision.

The two set about debating the issue. While they were so engaged, I spotted an English-language map and brochure, printed with fare, simple map, and schedule. Holmes and I put our heads down over its creative English, and eventually determined that a first-class ticket was three times the price of a third-class, and second-class twice that of third.

Holmes broke into the ongoing debate. 'We do not need first-class. Even exchange. *Wakarimasuka?*

'*Hai*,' she said, then translated for the stationmaster. Both of them looked at us with dubious expressions. We arranged our faces with encouragement and approval. The man finally gave a small shake to his head and ordered the woman to issue us the equivalent tickets for a later train. She did so, then carefully explained the hieroglyphics they held. It was a train to Kyoto, leaving in ninety-four minutes.

We accepted the slips of paper, gave them both many appreciative bows and thanks, and made our escape out onto the street. I tucked the schedule carefully away.

I still had the cloth bag in my hand. I pulled open the top, and took out a worn copper coin. 'These appear to be almost worthless, Holmes. Our first stop needs to be a Thomas Cook. Failing that, we might get money out of a bank.'

'Russell, we have been issued with a challenge.'

'True.' I dropped the one *sen* coin onto the others and folded the bag away. 'Do we want to accept it?'

'Why not?'

Indeed.

He looked up the street, at the shops and the busy traffic, wheeled and otherwise. 'Perhaps we might begin with transformation.'

The clothing of a Buddhist pilgrim was basically that of a

Japanese peasant: short white jacket over white trousers, sturdy shoes or sandals, a rucksack on the shoulders and a cloth bag around the neck, with a conical straw hat and a sturdy walking stick. Variations and refinements are, as one might expect, legion, with stoles, prayer beads, bells, badges and all the paraphernalia under the heavens.

When I stepped out of the ladies' room in my garb and saw Holmes, it was hard not to laugh aloud. Particularly with a Bond Street valise at his feet.

By his face, he felt much the same at my appearance. 'Still,' I said, 'they're quite comfortable.'

'At least you're not required to strap yourself into a kimono and obi.'

'Shades of Palestine. But we have to get rid of these valises. For one thing, they're leather.'

With that goal and ninety minutes at our disposal, we plunged into the active street.

Our first purchase was a pair of cheap cloth squares. These were called *furoshiki*, and were used by everyone, to carry everything. There in the shop, we decanted the essentials from our valises, ruthlessly pruning away extra garments, writing implements and – hardest of all – books. I hesitated over these, and in the end, kept only Haruki-san's Bashō. We then turned to the fascinated audience that had gathered to watch these proceedings, and asked if anyone saw anything they wanted to buy.

A pen, a notebook, all our handkerchiefs, a waistcoat knit by Mrs Hudson, two silk scarves and many stockings went instantly, each sale producing a few coins. We worked our way up the street, hawking the remainder and bargaining for a few essentials along the way. When we started, we collected looks that were as close to outrage as they were to befuddlement; by the time we finished, the walking sticks we carried and straw hats we wore gave us instant identity as *henro*, pilgrims. Our height and our eyes might attract second glances, but mostly as we were already moving away.

We even found a buyer for the valises, at a shop where we purchased two sturdy cloth rucksacks. Silver in pocket, sticks in hand, we marched back to the train station.

The stationmaster's face was indescribable. Mouth hanging open, he pointed mutely towards the waiting crowd.

Holmes and I stood, two unlikely pilgrims, gazing down the tracks while thirty or so Japanese of all ages studied us from head to foot.

A train appeared, narrower in gauge than English or American trains. At the precise time we had been given, it came to a halt before the platform, stopped in a great hiss of brakes, and opened its doors.

What followed was totally unexpected. This most methodical and polite of people were seized by a daemon. As if they were facing the last escape from a raging inferno, they began instantly to shove – those onboard to push out, and those on the platform to be first in. Grim determination was the rule for the next two minutes, with Holmes and me, the largest objects in the stream, pushed aside by our lack of technique.

Gasping, we managed to gain the interior, expecting the train to lurch into life and speed away. But the doors remained open while the struggle for supremacy shifted to the car's interior.

We were so outclassed, there was no point in trying for a spot. Standing by the door, we waited for matters to settle down. Which they did, with an unexpected degree of efficiency.

The narrow car had two long, blue-covered seats beneath the

windows. Those were now occupied primarily by children, women with babies and men. The other women, old or young, began to settle in the centre, possessions strewn in all directions. Oddly, two of the men were taking up multiple spaces along the seat rather than offer it to an old woman lowering her arthritic knees to the floor. One of the men was lying outstretched, his head covered with a cloth, his *geta* tucked on the floor below. And now the other man proceeded to strip off his clothing: overcoat, shoes, suit jacket, waistcoat, necktie. Shirt. When he then reached for the fastenings of his trousers, my jaw was hanging down. No one else took any notice – no more than they did of the young woman who shrugged out of her kimono to nurse her small child. She, seeing me looking, gave me a proud display of a mouth of large gold teeth.

Holmes and I looked at each other. The train jerked, and pulled forward. Women and children settled. Half the people lit cigarettes. We were the only passengers still standing. Left to myself, I would have settled onto my rucksack there at the doorway, but Holmes had other ideas. He began to pick his way across the sprawled bodies, bags, shoes of all sorts, and lumpy furoshiki of all colours – taking particular care with what turned out to be a spittoon, sitting out in the centre of everything – and ended up where the one man was stretched out beneath his cloth. His hand hesitated only briefly, before coming down on the stranger's shoulder, and shaking.

The man's exaggerated snort made it clear that he had been faking slumber. He looked around, his eyes growing wide as they took in the two white-clad figures looming over him. He withdrew his legs and shot upright, and watched along with the rest of the carriage as Holmes and I removed our rucksacks, threaded our walking sticks among the heaps on the floor, and sat.

I removed the irritating hat, dropping it atop the furoshiki between my feet, and took a deep breath. Everyone on the train was waiting in fascination to see what we would do next. Boringly for them, I just took out the train schedule and studied the map.

'There's a train,' I told Holmes, 'all the way up the Kisokaido. It appears to run fairly regularly, and every day. It can't be more than two hundred miles altogether.'

He saw what I was getting at. 'Even assuming we miss half the trains along our path, three days seems an excessive allowance for travel.'

We sat and gazed at the document, wondering at the significance of the message. 'Could the writing actually say, "Please arrive *by* three Thursday" instead of *at* three?' I mused.

'The gentleman's English seemed adequate,' Holmes noted.

I looked around the car, all those dark and attentive gazes, until I spotted one head that was not watching us: a young man in Western dress who was reading a book. 'Give me that piece of paper she left us,' I said to Holmes. With it in hand, I picked my way through the bodies and baggage towards the reading man, my audience a-goggle. When I reached him, he looked up in surprise, then ran his eyes down my white-clad pilgrim's outfit in frank astonishment.

I bowed, then said in English, 'Pardon me, but do you speak English?'

'Yes, I do.'

'May I ask you please,' I continued, 'what do these lines of writing say?'

He took the unfolded sheet, and read the words aloud, then translated. 'Mojiro-joku, at three Thursday. I think this must be a village.'

'It is. But, does "at three" mean "precisely at three", or "no later than three"?'

His eyes went down again, and he shook his head a little. 'It says, "*mokuyobi no gogo sanji ni.*" "At three o'clock Thursday".' He laid his fingernail under a character composed of an upright line and two shorter horizontal dashes to its right. '"*Ni.*" "By three o'clock" would be, "*mokuyobi no gogo sanji <u>made</u>*".'

I accepted the paper back, bowing my thanks. He then wanted to know where I was from, and what I was doing in Japan (the unspoken portion of the question being, *What is an English woman doing in a third-class compartment?*). We spoke for a while as those nearby craned to listen. He was a university student in Kobe, headed to Kyoto for a family funeral, and went slightly pink when I complimented him on his English. After a while, I wended my way back to my seat.

'It's definitely *at* three,' I told Holmes. 'And we have an invitation to stay with that nice lad in Kyoto, if we want to play the tourist. Could that be what Haruki-san had in mind? Just giving us some leisure to make our way up the Nakasendo?'

He frowned at the page holding her writing. 'It would seem uncharacteristic.'

'She may have business that will keep her from that village until then.'

'Yes.'

'Or . . .'

'Yes?' he asked.

'As you said: a challenge. There have been a number of times, both on the ship and since we came here, that I had the impression she was setting us an examination. Seeing how we – how *I* – would handle a public bath, for example. Or a few of those . . . creatures we ate the other night. She and I had a talk one time about being your apprentice – this was after I realised she knew who we were, of course. I told her about the tests you would set me – like leaving your slippers next to the cut poppy heads with an order to find you.'

'You suggest this is by way of a final examination? To see if we can make our way to a remote village, at a precise time, armed with nothing but a pair of train tickets covering half the distance and a small handful of coins.'

'We could accept this young man's hospitality for two days and take the Thursday morning train up to Mojiro-joku. We'd arrive with two hours to spare, according to the timetable.'

He could hear the hesitation in my voice. 'Or?'

'Or we could accept her challenge, and add to it.'

'Russell, are you proposing actually to follow the precepts of the Buddhist pilgrim?'

I laughed aloud. 'Perhaps not all of them. Of course, we're going to feel a bit idiotic, having gone to all that scrupulous effort, if it turns out that she'd intended nothing of the sort.'

'Not necessarily. Our intent in coming here was to see something of the land and its people. Who would claim that travel in touristic luxury would be a superior way so to do?'

'Who indeed? Although I suspect I'm going to regret this, before we finish.'

Thus we turned our backs on the sybaritic pleasures of the Western *hoteru* for the cheap and Spartan pleasures of the native *yadoya*, flea-filled tatami and all. How difficult could it be? If we were here for adventure, surely native accommodations formed a part of it? At least we were on solid ground, which made food – any food – more appealing than haute cuisine at sea.

Chronic hunger and the exhaustion that comes from straining to understand one's surroundings were, in fact, a good thing. We chose an inn that did not look too villainous, two streets away from the Kyoto station, ignoring the reaction that made it clear we were the first Western feet that had walked therein. I swallowed the meal that was put before me, then entered the bathhouse with more concern for its heated water than for its disbelieving eyes. And once I had been both fed and boiled, I stretched out on the hard mat and rock-filled pillow, and slept like a baby in its mother's arms, equally oblivious of the fleas, the racket from our neighbours, and the eyes peering through the holes in the paper walls.

Tuesday morning we rose, scratched our flea bites, gulped bitter tea resembling well-watered mud, and donned our pilgrim outfits again. The anticipated regret was setting in.

'So, Holmes,' I said. 'It's something like a hundred and fifty miles to Mojiro-joku. We really ought to see something of Kyoto. We could stay here today, then make our way westward. We could even take the train up Thursday morning.'

'We could,' he replied.

'You have another idea.' But – Kyoto! Imperial capital of the Chrysanthemum Throne, home of temples and shrines, castles and gardens, the likes of which would not be found in the rest of the world. A month here would not be sufficient . . .

The face he lifted to me held that bright optimism I have learnt to dread. 'Russell, how would you feel about hitch-hiking?'

Chapter Sixteen

Delicate white necks
And hairy ursine backsides:
Nursing mothers all.

W E DID NOT HITCH-HIKE the entire way. If we'd been given three weeks rather than three days, Holmes might have proposed it, but even he had to agree that, as the superficial map on the railway timetable showed, the area around Nagoya, midway between us and our goal, was heavily built up. It appeared the kind of industrial concentration that would suck in any traveller attempting to circle around it for the hinterland beyond.

Instead, we submitted to the city's pull, returning to the train station to part with a few of our coins in exchange for two third-class tickets for Nagoya. This time, I had been belatedly studying the brochure's finer print.

'Something I wish we'd known back in Arima: the fare goes down as the ticket's mileage increases. The first fifty miles are two and a half sen per mile, but after that, it's just a bit more than two sen.' It went down more, to one and three-quarter sen, when one passed a hundred miles, but that would put us too near to Mojiro-joku for our sense of fair play.

We compromised, choosing a town far enough beyond Nagoya

that we would be outside the city's pull, but not close enough to threaten an early arrival on Haruki-san's doorstep.

As in the Arima station, the arrival of the narrow-gauge train in Kyoto sparked a riot of competitive shoving. And again, the passengers set about claiming space and strewing around their bags in that same exasperating manner. However, this time Holmes dedicated his bulk to the contest, and was the possessor of three linear feet of velveteen bench by the time I fought my way on.

When my possessions were stored and the train lurched away, I straightened my clothes, studying my fellow passengers with every bit as much curiosity as they were studying us. 'What is it about trains?' I asked my partner. 'These are the politest people in the world until the carriage doors open.'

He gave the question some consideration. 'Perhaps the railway, being a Western introduction, left them with no previous form of behaviour they could adapt to the occasion.'

I thought about that. 'If so, remind me never to venture into one of this country's department stores.'

Being old hands by now at the intricacies of rail travel, we were ready with coins at the next stop. The call of *O-bento! O-bento!* rose above the chaos, and I leant out of the window with a one-yen coin. The green-capped boy outside the window, seeing the foreign colour of my eyes and hair, proposed to hand over a single pair of the wooden boxes for my coin, but I had noted with care how much others paid, and I shook my head until he had parted with two meals, and twenty sen in change. Those I traded with the next seller, obtaining hot tea and a couple of tiny oranges, and we settled back onto our benches, unwrapping the chopsticks from their sealed glassine envelopes and conveying the assortment of warm titbits from box to mouth.

When we had finished, leaving little but a few grains of rice and a wizened object that experience had taught us was salty to the extreme, we gingerly placed the empty vessels at our feet as everyone else was wont to do, and sat amidst the rubbish-strewn car until the train boy came along to retrieve the bottles and containers, ready to be tossed into a passing ravine, or used again.

At last, fed and relatively secure, I turned my attention to the view out of the windows. We were passing through hill country, but unlike hills I had ever seen. The surface of these were etched with curving lines: stone, marking off the tens of thousands of small, uneven terraces; green, with diminutive tea plantations set within the terracing; brown, the water cut by small wavering lines, marking the shoots of newly planted rice.

Even the wilder places were cultivated, I saw, when I spotted three women in straw hats harvesting among the bamboo groves, children strapped to their backs.

It was a landscape that had felt the hand of man for thousands of years, and yet it appeared completely natural. The hedgerow-edged fields of England would feel artificial by comparison.

And that was without the cherries. They were in bloom here, and they were all over. Every terrace, every lane, every garden under the view of the passing train was adrift with blossom in colours ranging from near-white to delicate rose. A school's playing field was framed by a sea of pink. A cluster of rusty metal roofs was rendered beautiful by its echo of the pink. At one stop, an ancient water wheel, dripping moss, became a museum piece with the delicate arch of blossom to frame it.

How was it Haruki-san had described those odd, brief poems of which Bashō had been a master? Capturing a fleeting moment of great beauty, or heartbreak. Or moments like this, of heartbreaking beauty.

Breaking a journey
To rest beneath the cherries,
Life becomes a play.

The old woman beside me turned her back on the car, sitting with her face to the windows, and fell asleep. My arms twitched, ready to shoot out and rescue her at every uneven section of track, but she never fell, no more than did the young mother similarly resting across the way, her back turned into a hump by the small infant strapped thereon. As the car warmed, more and more of the men removed their garments. The baby woke, causing the mother to perform a series of contortions that ended up with the infant free and her shoulders and back bare. Quiet descended again.

I studied the woman's pale back, and wondered if Bashō had ever tried to describe the charm of a young woman's spine.

The train emptied at Nagoya, the incoming passengers scarcely needing to push at all. We travelled for another half hour before our tickets ran out, watching the city become country and the country become hills.

When we climbed down, we were in a small town. I admit, I felt a pulse of apprehension. What if we were set upon by thieves? What if the police decided we were spies? What if we could not make ourselves understood? What if—?

Holmes stretched his back, took up his staff, and walked through the little station towards the road. Once there, he settled his hat and put out his thumb.

An ox cart, coming back empty from the market, slowed. As did a remarkable variety of conveyances over the next forty-eight hours.

I will not say it was simple, exactly, to make our way to the designated spot at the assigned time. Nonetheless, our progress was regular, and there was no doubt that it showed us a side of Japan a tourist would never have guessed at.

As Buddhist pilgrims, we were forgiven much. Even when we mistakenly paused for prayer at wayside shrines that turned out to be Shinto, the good manners of the attendants did not waver. It would appear that we were not the only Buddhists to embrace the traditional ways, and that the shrine keepers were less surprised by our presence than by our height.

For the next two days, we would walk for a time, sooner or later (usually sooner) to be offered a ride. Astounded farmers, curious rickshaw-men, and (twice) wealthy owners of motorcars could not bear to pass us up. During the walking periods, we were rarely without an entourage of schoolboys, with one or two bicycles ticking along as the group practised their careful English. On several occasions we encountered other white-clothed pilgrims, but even if they were going in the same direction, they were too put off by our appearance to join forces.

Our meals were from wayside stalls and cafes, bowls of *udon* or *soba* noodles, breads fresh from the recessed pots they were cooked in, skewers of mysterious meat-like substances, and endless thimblefuls of tea. As night approached, we began to watch for a likely ryokan or lacking that, a yadoya. Both times we were fortunate, to find a ryokan owner who, seeing two pilgrims, offered us bed, bath and dinner at a price we could afford. No more fleas. We both craved beef (a most non-Buddhistic desire) but having been in the country for a week now, the earlier frank hunger was subsiding to a faint wistfulness, usually when confronted by another plate of dried fish and soya sauce. Our evening entertainment consisted of sitting with our feet around the room's firepit while Holmes smoked a last pipe, and then unconsciousness.

Not once did I dream – although in the wee hours of the second night I woke standing bolt upright in a pitch-black room, primed to run, heart racing for no discernible reason. Fortunately, Holmes broke my panic by clearing his throat: Holmes; bed: Japan.

'Sorry,' I said. 'I must have had a nightmare,' although I could remember nothing of the sort.

Bedclothes shifted. After the sound of a hand fumbling against the mats, our small torch went on, revealing that I had got halfway to the door before waking. I turned back towards the lumpy *futon*.

'It was probably the earthquake,' he said.

I froze. 'Earthquake.' After a moment, I pushed down the nonsensical desire to run and put myself back between the bedclothes. An earthquake: I should have expected one, spending any time at all in this volatile island country. I just . . .

'I don't like earthquakes,' I admitted.

In the morning, we woke as usual to the rhythmic pounding of rice being hulled and the coughs and grumbles of rousing travellers on the other side of the paper. Tea came, a tiny sum was paid, thanks given and received. Then, geta back on our feet and straw hats on our heads, we resume our staffs and hit the road, watching for a likely source of breakfast along the way.

That was the pattern (less the earthquakes) for our pilgrim time in Japan: four days on an unlikely adventure. We walked until our feet ached, the clatter of our geta gradually becoming as brisk and sure as all the geta around us. We hunkered on our heels, we slurped pale tea at roadside teahouses, we sat out rainstorms or plodded, shoulders hunched and feet sodden, beneath our oiled-paper sheets. I do not think I had a single entirely kosher meal – then, or the whole time we were in Japan – save those made up of nothing but rice and tea. But the rabbis do not demand starvation of the traveller, and I found I actually enjoyed eels, if I didn't think about it too much.

Moving intimately among the people, on foot and on their common forms of transport, we absorbed the rhythm of their lives and the structure of this tight and efficient society. And its beauty: the simple elegance of a rundown shed; the meditative quality of a waterwheel turning a stream's power into clean rice.

Along one stretch of quiet road, I walked into an adjoining grove of timber bamboo. The smooth green trunks thrusting from the mossy soil were no bigger around than my arm, yet the lacy tops had to be sixty feet over my head. All parts of the giant grass flexed with the slightest breeze, yet it would take a typhoon to flatten them.

As I stood mesmerised by the lacy green motion, the rich odour of earth, the endless susurration of the flat leaves brushing the sky, it came to me that this country embodied the Chinese doctrine of paradox: the apparently weak prevails over the overtly strong; soft and yielding will always overcome hard and rigid.

Time and again, our senses had been jarred by the hard intrusion of the West: a kimono-clad man wearing a bowler; corrugated roofing on a two-hundred-year-old wooden structure; the fizzy lemonade served with our perfectly grilled fish the day before. But even then, a vine had already begun to overgrow the metal roof, and the cloying drink had been transformed by a sprig of some unassuming herb.

On the one hand, traditional Japanese life appeared to be under threat from the habits of the West; on the other, I would no longer be willing to bet on the outcome. When one considered this country's willingness to embrace the foreign (ironic, considering its two centuries of deliberate isolation), one had also to take into account the innate industry of every citizen, from the small child gathering sticks for the fire to the ancient grandfather shooing away the birds from a fresh-planted rice paddy. There seemed to be no loungers in the land. No beggars. Even pilgrims like us were regarded as being hard at work on our prayers.

Flexibility added to deep roots, and the willingness to work: I did not think Japan would remain on the edge of the world for long.

The days might have been easier had our Japanese been a touch more fluent and we had been able to read, rather than guess at the meanings of signs. However, this was an educated land: if there was no eager school boy to hand, we needed only hold out our piece of paper to be escorted down the road in the right direction. Bows came more naturally now, as did the slurping of our food, the scrubbing of our backs in public, and the art of sitting on our heels. I caught sight of my face in a looking-glass tacked up outside a *benjo* – the toilets – and for an instant, I gaped at the woman with the weird, pale eyes.

Mojiro-joku, the place we were headed – we lacked an address, but then, Japan did not seem to have actual addresses – was a village in the hills, formerly a station on the Kisokaido road. In the days of the Shoguns, a traveller would have been guaranteed good lodging and a ready supply of bearers and horses, every three or four miles along the way. Since 1911, when the train was laid through the valley, things would have changed. As we climbed the Kiso Valley, we saw shuttered shops and ryokans in need of repair, as the cold breeze of modernisation blew the skirts of the shopkeepers' kimonos.

Wednesday night, our last on the road, we scrubbed and soaked with extra care, and gave our clothes over to be cleaned. In the morning, we bought new tabi, trimmed our fingernails, restored our rucksacks to order. Holmes submitted to a shave that left him smooth as a baby. When we set off up the road for the last time, we were remarkably presentable.

The rainstorm hit us at noon, pounding from above, throwing mud from below. We crammed into an inadequate space beneath a fallen tree and cowered under our oiled-paper sheets, watching the sky try its best to wash the Kiso Valley into the sea. Eventually it slowed. We crept out, gazing ruefully down at our formerly white garments. Even Holmes, despite his cat-like ability to avoid muss, was comprehensively spattered.

'I did not know that Japan went in for mudbaths as well,' I said.

'Perhaps we should have kept the new tabi until the last minute.'

'Do you suppose there's an inn nearby?'

'Not one that will permit us to arrive in the village precisely at three.'

'Well, at least there is plenty of water to wash in.'

The now-raging creek was nearly as brown as our garments, but we followed a smaller stream back a distance, and found a spring with a calm pool of relatively clean water.

And that is where the bears discovered us.

As I rubbed at the mud under my nails, I studied my bedraggled tabi, wondering if an honest rinse would make them any more uncomfortable. I turned to address the question to Holmes – and found myself face to face with a bear.

I admit it: I screamed. Even though I had heard they were herbivorous, even though the short-sighted creature looked more puzzled than aggressive, the noise I made could only be called a scream. I turned to flee, and a bar on the geta broke away, shooting me down the stream bank like a greased log. I banged my backside, wrenched my ankle, and ended up with mud in more orifices than I'd realised I had.

As I sat there, dripping brown and watching the tail ends of mother bear and cub rapidly crash into the undergrowth, I began to laugh. So much for impressing Miss Sato with my supreme competence.

* * *

I was limping rather badly when we trailed into the village, at 2.59 in the afternoon. News of our progress had clearly preceded our persons, for as we walked along, people gathered in shop doors and windows to watch us pass. I gingerly fished the weathered page from my furoshiki, but no one seemed to need it, simply waved us on through the village.

As the shops thinned and gardens peeped between the houses, we neared what could only be a ryokan. Ancient wood, well-maintained thatch, raked gravel and a small and perfectly spontaneous garden on either side of the entrance. Everything – thatch, gate, stones, tree bark – might have been manicured at dawn. If I'd been told that the gardener had chosen the precise arrangement of cherry blossoms drifting across the moss, I'd not have doubted it for a moment.

Beside the entranceway, half-concealed by the world's most perfect green bush, emerging from a bed of flawless green moss, was a stone about thirty inches tall. Its surface was blotched with lichen, and as one studied it, the lumps and indentations made it look remarkably like a crouched monkey. A shaggy patch of moss even gave the suggestion of a head, twisted into a sly grin.

Inside the gate was the usual welcoming committee in bright kimonos. I had to give them full points: they stifled their natural reaction to finding a mud-clotted Golem on their doorstep.

I pulled a wry face at the neatly arrayed slippers, then shook my head, saying in Japanese, 'Bath first, *neh?*'

A wave of relief swept through the committee. One of them performed the inimitable quick step-and-turn that swaps indoor shoes for outer, gave me a quick bow, and scurried along beside the high wooden wall to a gate. We startled a pair of gardeners – a tall man whose left hand was a mass of scar tissue and his short, middle-aged, half-lame assistant – who broke off their contemplation of a large rock hanging from a sling to gape at this mud-caked Western female. I gave them a nod, then hurried after the maid.

As with most ryokans, the inn was a series of pavilions linked by roofed-over walkways. This design meant that if fires were spilt by a tremor, there was a chance the whole place wouldn't burn – a floor plan used even by inns whose baths were naturally heated, as was the case with this one.

The washroom attendant scoured furiously away, toe to scalp, using many rinsing buckets before I was permitted to limp across the room and sink into the steaming water. By this point in the regime, I no longer took much note of other women, even before removing my spectacles. And on those occasions when men were present, I was learning the trick of selective blindness. This time, I was alone in the broad wooden tub. I closed my eyes and submitted to the blissful heat. The room was still, the only sound a musical drip of water and the murmur of distant voices. Somewhere, a rooster crowed. The day's tensions began to give way. The bear; the fall; the freezing water and disgusting muck: going, going . . .

I opened my eyes to find Haruki-san kneeling at the side of the bath, hands together in the lap of her simple indigo-patterned kimono. I hadn't heard so much as a whisper of cloth.

'You'll have to show me how you do that,' I said.

'What is that, Mary-san?'

I just shook my head. 'It's good to see you, Haruki-san. Do you need me to get out?'

'My father wishes to know if you and Holmes-san would like something to eat.'

I slid off the bath's low seat to submerge in the water, then came up again, running my hands back over my hair. 'I'm sure Holmes is starving. I'll come now.'

'I regret curtailing your bath, but later there will be . . . another opportunity.'

I looked at her sharply, caught by an odd depth in the statement, but I said nothing, merely worked my way up into heavy air and out of the bath. The attendant came forward with a tiny towel, but Haruki-san was looking at my ankle.

'You are hurt.'

'Just a sprain. One of your local bears took me by surprise.'

She blinked, but merely addressed the attendant, who trotted from the room, returning with a low stool and a bundle of cloth strips. I sat. Haruki-san knelt and took my ankle in her hands, weaving the bandage into a support around the joint.

When she had tucked in the ends, I stood, testing it gingerly, then with more confidence. 'You've done that before,' I remarked.

'A few times.'

'You could get a job in the best sports club in London,' I said. 'Thank you.'

She stepped back with a bow, and allowed the woman to finish wrapping me up in a simple *yukata* of the same design as Haruki-san's. There wasn't much the woman could do about my cropped hair, and I would not permit her to apply any of her powders and paints, but when I followed the maid along the walkway to our room, I looked better than I had for quite some time. I felt positively glowing.

I felt even better after the substantial afternoon snack, in which the usual rice, pickles, and unidentifiable creatures were supplemented with skewered bits of chicken roasted over the coals in the low firepit. Haruki-san joined us, and the questions that followed were like any other *viva voce* exam: starting with the general, closing in on the specific. How had we spent the last four days? gradually narrowed in to, How well did you sleep in the noisy yadoya? and finally, How much did we pay for the tabi that morning?

At the last question, I laid down my implements and stood – rising as smoothly as I could off my heels – to go to the cupboard where our rucksacks had been stored. I came back with the small cloth bag, laying it on the tatami beside her knee.

I resumed my seat, and my meal. She took up the bag, pulling open the top.

'We are returning your loan,' I told her.

'Along with the cost of the tickets,' Holmes added.

Her expression, which had gone from curious to bemused, now relaxed. She wore a faint smile as I carried on a rudimentary conversation with the maid. The smile broadened as we managed to transport boiled quail's eggs from plates to mouths without sending them skittering across the tatami. We were qualifying with at least second-class honours.

Qualifying for what, I did not know.

We ate, we drank our tea, we chatted about the journey while Holmes smoked a cigarette. The dishes were cleared away, the hibachi coals were going cool, and Haruki-san prepared to stand.

'Perhaps this is a good time for a longer bath.'

Holmes and I exchanged a glance. I was, I admit, a little apprehensive. I could tell she had something planned, something that honed a nervy edge on her imperturbable nature. Another test – but why did this one have her worried?

My mind sorted through a hundred possibilities. A mid-bath snack of tiny live octopus? A horde of ninja crashing through the shoji, knives drawn? I thought it was more likely that she would present us with mixed bathing, although it had to be more than just that.

We went to our respective stools, divided by screens, and submitted again to the scrub-brush. Haruki-san was judged clean first, and off she went towards the bath. Holmes and I were released, and I heard him speak to his attendant, then heard his bare feet patting across the washing-room floor.

We reached the onsen at the same time. Haruki-san was in the water, up to her neck. To her right, at the other side of the large square bath, was a slim Japanese boy with a few silky hairs on his upper lip. His presence itself was not odd – not as odd as the other figure, fully clothed and on his knees, back to the wooden wall. His eyes snapped onto us as we appeared, in that unmistakeable attitude of a bodyguard.

There is nothing that makes one feel quite so naked as a person with clothes on.

But Haruki-san was waiting. I took a breath. Under the gaze of the two strange males, I propelled my naked body across the boards to the water.

I blame the lack of spectacles for my tardy realisation. Or perhaps my blindness was learnt Japanese habit rather than physical myopia. In any event, the water was past my shoulders before I raised my eyes to the boy – or rather, young man. It took me a moment, since he, too, was without the glasses he invariably wore in photographs.

In a flash, the entire point of the past four days – indeed, the point of the past four weeks – crashed down upon me.

Haruki-san had been preparing us for the experience of sharing a bath with the 124th Emperor of Japan.

Chapter Seventeen

Roads go ever on.
Travellers may turn away —
But the road goes on.

To be clear, this young man with the sad eyes in the controlled face was in fact the Prince Regent, since his father, the 123rd Emperor, was still alive. But Prince Hirohito had been made Regent upon his return from Europe in 1921, when His Majesty the Emperor was judged too frail (physically and, rumour had it, mentally) to conduct the business of the Empire. Two and a half years later, the Crown Prince was, in all but the seat on the Chrysanthemum Throne, the Son of Heaven.

Still, a person does not go into a London steam room expecting to see the Prince of Wales. And there was one point of etiquette Haruki-san had failed to cover: how to prostrate oneself in a tub without drowning.

My initial impulse, to leap to my feet, was instantly countermanded by the knowledge that I should be bowing deeply. Together, the impulses caused a slosh of water that set the others bobbling on their perches. Holmes, not being afflicted with weak eyes, had performed his own bow at the edge of the tub, and at the Prince's incline of the head, stepped placidly down to fold himself into the now-undulating water.

'I'm sorry,' I started – then stopped. Perhaps Japanese royalty was like England's, in that one did not speak before They did? Before I could enter further into confusion, Haruki-san stepped smoothly into the break.

'His Highness understands that you are not familiar with our ways, and he wishes you to know that he does not take offence. His Highness wishes a conversation with you. He also has a . . . favour to ask of you.' The hesitation, I thought, came when she needed to substitute 'favour' for 'command'. The idea of the Emperor – even the Prince Regent – having to ask for a favour was offensive to her.

'What service may we do His Highness?' Holmes enquired.

Before he finished the question, Haruki-san was translating his words into Japanese. Similarly, when the Prince Regent began to speak, in tones nearly as high-pitched as hers, their two voices overlapped, and not only in timing: the nuances of her intonation made her sound more than a little Imperial herself.

Still, his initial words were astonishing, coming from a person whose face wore that mask of controlled authority. 'I was pleased when I received news that Sherlock Holmes was coming to my country,' he said. 'When I visited England, I expressed a desire to meet you, and was surprised, and frankly disappointed, to be told that you did not actually exist. Yet, here you are.'

Holmes' face was indescribable. 'I . . . Your Highness, I think . . . Perhaps you will understand that a . . . fictional existence . . .' He cleared his throat, then started again. 'Allowing the world to think I am a character in some stories is the only way to obtain a degree of freedom. Fame is a sword with two edges: it permits a man to cut through the inconveniences of bureaucracy, but it also threatens to open one's life to the world. Naturally, had I known Your Highness was interested in meeting with me, I would have insisted that you be told the truth.'

I sincerely doubted that – indeed, I wouldn't have sworn that even King George knew for certain that Holmes was not Doyle's invention – but I said nothing.

The Prince Regent gave a regal little dip of the head that managed simultaneously to accept the excuse and convey his disbelief in it – a note of humility that seemed odd coming from a man who could have us disembowelled at the lift of a finger. But then, he did want something from us.

He even gave Holmes a little smile. 'Freedom is indeed a desirable state, Mr Holmes. Unfortunately, I do not believe it possible to convince my people that *I* am a storybook character.'

Holmes, a lifetime of experience with royalty and the powerful behind him, laughed freely. I, less experienced, could not entirely stifle a cough at the unexpected humour. Even Haruki-san seemed to have a bit of a crinkle next to her eyes.

Then, with the deft hand of a born politician, the prince used his disarming joke to slip in the knife. 'However, you "suspect my motives". Is that not how your Mr Doyle would put it?'

'I would never think of such a thing, Your Highness,' Holmes replied.

The Prince Regent went on as if he had not spoken. 'It is true that I wish merely to converse with Mr Sherlock Holmes – and with his wife,' he added with a glance in my direction. 'But you are correct to wait for . . .' He paused, and consulted his translator for a moment, then went on. 'To wait for the other shoe to drop.

'Miss Sato has told you already that there is an object I wish returned to me. I am informed that the two of you are my best hope for retrieving it. My ability to pay you is . . .' His voice went on, but

174

Haruki-san's did not. He turned the regal gaze on her. She bent her neck until her nose was a millimetre from the water, and spoke in their mutual tongue, her tones an odd amalgam of deference and protest. After a few moments, he cut her off with a curt syllable, but her translation did not resume. Instead, she lowered her head a fraction more. When she spoke again, it was with a note of pleading.

At his second, sharper refusal, she hunched her shoulders, then sat up in acceptance. When he spoke, her translation resumed.

'My ability to pay you is somewhat limited, which may sound odd to you, but in fact, in Japan, even an Emperor is controlled by his position. I will say merely that if you help me—' Again the simultaneous translation broke off for an exchange, capped by Haruki-san's face going pink. '—that if you *choose* to help me, I, Prince Regent and future Emperor of Japan, will be in your debt.'

The bodyguard near the wall was as outraged as Haruki-san at the idea of the Son of Heaven being in debt to a mere foreigner: the older man shifted, as if the pistol on his belt was pressing into his flesh. In an earlier age, his fist would be tightening against the grip of a long sword.

Holmes bent his neck, a gesture I duplicated. 'Your Highness, my wife and I would be honoured at the opportunity to assist the Prince Regent of Japan. That privilege would be payment enough.'

The Prince relaxed, and suddenly looked not only young, but something I would not have imagined to see on the heir of 2,500 years of divine sovereignty: he looked vulnerable. I wondered uneasily just what this 'favour' would entail.

However, I was not going to hear it from him, for the expression was fleeting, and quickly replaced by one of eagerness. 'I have recently read the case concerning the Sussex blood-drinker,' he said. 'I think it was most clever of you.'

Holmes frowned, and he looked a question at me. '"The Sussex Vampire", maybe?' I replied. 'It appeared in the *Strand* while we were on our way to India. Some of the passengers were talking about it.'

'*Vampire?*'

'The resentful adolescent who tried to murder the child?'

'Ah. Was that why Watson wrote to ask about South American poisons last autumn?'

'Probably.'

He summoned a degree of enthusiasm, and turned back to the Prince Regent.

And so we carried on a conversation, there in the steaming water with the future Emperor of Japan, about fictional vampires and the state of India, about poetry and what we had seen while moving around his country, about King George V and his place in the hearts of the British people.

We tried our utmost to give Prince Hirohito our honesty. It was not easy, with an armed and testy Samurai bodyguard ten feet away and the knowledge of an Empire pressing down on us, but he seemed to crave an open response, and we tried to give it, even when it meant admitting that all was not idyllic among the British people – or indeed, among his own. He was clever enough to see a thread of criticism beneath polite words, which made honesty easier: no need to be openly rude.

But then Holmes mentioned that I had been born in America. The Prince Regent's formal mask slipped, as he turned on me, his dark eyes flashing. 'Why does your country insult us?'

It was difficult not to cringe back from his burst of fury; I grew very conscious of the bodyguard. 'Your Highness, I'm sure I don't know what you mean.'

'Your Congress is discussing a law that would prohibit any immigration from Japan.'

'I am very sorry, Your Highness, but I have not lived in America for—'

'You must tell them to stop! Japan values American friendship. We have done so for many years. If America wishes to slow the numbers of my people entering in, we can certainly talk about it, but to simply ban us, to put us in the same category as China – that would be an intolerable insult to our good relations.'

'Your Highness, I – you understand, I do not live there and I have little authority in the country where I was born. But I will certainly write some letters and make my voice heard.'

'I fear for our countries, if this Act goes forward.'

'I see your point,' I said. I would not have before I came here, but having spent the past days in intimate contact with Japan, I now knew that a carpet decree of banishment would be a slap in the face to a proud people.

His eyes continued to bore into me, then, abruptly, the mask came down again. He turned placidly back to Holmes, with a question about bees. I was rather startled to discover the future Emperor's interest, and apparent expertise, in natural history. Although he seemed most interested in marine biology, his knowledge was wide enough to ask informed questions about beekeeping.

All in all, that hour spent in the Mojiro-joku bath was one of the most extraordinary of my life: gently boiling away, chatting with a god about Oxford, London, and the familial sensibilities of King George V. At the end of it, the Prince Regent raised his hand from the water, watching the water splash down. When he spoke next, it was in English. Hesitation made his voice go even higher.

'Mistah Holmes, I am happy for having this talk. I am pleased to find you are not a . . . fictional character,' he added with that shy smile. 'And I give you, with your honourable wife, my thanks, both for the task you have agreed to do me, and for this talking. It is rare to meet one who speak to me as man and not as god. This also why I treasure the onsen of Mojiro-joku. Its keeper is a . . . person I value.' Although he stopped short of using the word 'friend', Haruki-san still went bright pink, dropping into the aquatic form of prostration, her face brushing the water. We made haste to follow her example, and the three of us bent staring at the water while the next Emperor of Japan, the Son of Heaven and sovereign of the Land Where the Sun Was Born, His Imperial Highness the Regent of Japan, Honourary Knight Grand Cross of the Royal Victorian Order and the Order of the Bath, Honourary General of the British Army, Prince Hirohito lifted his imperial self to his feet and stepped out of the bath.

Sounds followed, as he was rinsed, dried and dressed, like any lesser mortal. The three of us stayed motionless. My head swam with the heat. An external door slid open, then shut; the air pressure seemed abruptly to drop.

Haruki-san let out a long-held breath and slumped back against the side of the big tub. I instantly wallowed up onto the highest shelf, to sit with my legs in the water and the room swaying around me, my skin working furiously to rid itself of my body's dizzying heat.

Holmes cleared his throat again. 'I begin to see the purpose of our baptism by fire.'

CHAPTER EIGHTEEN

In the book's pages
The key to a great Empire
Lies, unsuspected.

WOULD WE HAVE BEEN so much as permitted a glimpse of this Son of Heaven, had we not submitted first to Haruki-san's tutoring, then to her rigorous examinations?

'Without the past week,' I said, 'you could not be certain we wouldn't give some deadly insult.'

She opened her eyes. 'I was told that you were both remarkably clever and adaptive, but time was too short to coddle your lessons. Although I am sorry about the bear,' she added.

'Have Russell tell you about stopping a charging boar with a spear,' Holmes suggested mildly. 'What is the thing your young Emperor-to-be wants us to find?'

'More important,' I said, 'who told you about us? I'm assuming you knew, long before you got on the ship.'

She sat upright, summoning the familiar schoolmistress attitude – if one could imagine a nude schoolmistress in a public bath. 'I am not permitted to identify our informant. And I cannot say that I knew about you much before I was sent to board the *Thomas Carlyle*. But yes, our meeting was arranged. His Highness has requested that I tell you how this came about. And he told me to answer your questions. Most of them.'

She was, clearly, prepared to launch into her long explanation then and there. I interrupted. 'Must we do this here? If I spend another five minutes in this water, I'll pass out.'

We adjourned, first to the outer section of the baths to be dried and dressed in the ryokan's indigo *yukatas*, then to one of the freestanding pavilions, where tea and trays of snacks awaited us – and where, I noted, no one could approach without our seeing.

The air was cold, following the lengthy parboiling, but I pulled a padded *haori* coat over the thin cotton garments and edged closer to the glowing coals of the firepit. I cupped my tea in both hands, thinking that a long nap would have been nice. Instead, I attacked the tray's contents.

'There was much,' Haruki-san began, 'that His Highness did not say to you. It was necessary that you meet him, just as it was necessary that you be . . . trained to the proper behaviour in meeting him. His Highness wishes me to tell you about the object he requires you – that he would appreciate your retrieving for him. However, in order to do so, I told him that I would need also to tell you the background of the object, that you may understand its significance.'

We made ourselves as comfortable as we could. Holmes took out his pipe.

'You know something of the Samurai, the warrior class of Japan. Samurai are trained from birth, men and women alike, to serve. Under the Shoguns, they became an aristocracy of warriors, and although we are no longer a feudal society, Samurai influence remains powerful.

'As the Shogunate grew in power, the Samurai became more

aristocrats than warriors. There became jobs they would not do. Shinobi – ninja, if you will – came into being to fill those holes. A warrior proud of his adherence to bushido – our code of conduct, with Samurai values of loyalty, courage, humility, self-control – will die willingly in battle, or commit *seppuku* – suicide – to assert his honour. But he will hesitate to lie, steal, or sneak, even when such things are necessary to serve his master. A proud warrior is worthless, if one requires a spy.

'"Ninja" means hidden. We are invisible, because we look like something else. We may be Samurai, but we appear to be peasants, or priests or one of the *eta* – outcasts, who perform the filthiest of jobs – in order to bring our master the information he requires. Or, I admit, sometimes to gain access to a man our master requires killed.

'And then you have our Emperor, who is above all this, and yet a part of it all. For much of our history, he has wielded supreme authority, yet had little actual power.

'Of course, over two and a half thousand years, matters change. Some Emperors have commanded armies, others were mere puppets. In theory, the Shogun was the Emperor's battle commander. In practice, the Shogun's rise marked the Emperor's retreat from power. I do not say, as the radicals of my country would, that the Emperor is an empty symbol of the past. The Emperor retains enormous power in the hearts of his countrymen. He is the country's connection to the gods. The people love their Emperor. Most would die for him. A huge power, and an equally huge responsibility: the Emperor exists because the people would never permit him to be removed. At the same time, he would never act in a way that would harm the people, and his ministers know that, and use that knowledge to keep him in control.

'In the West, our Emperor is a puzzle. To us, he is the essence of who we are. The man who walked out of here is a Japanese citizen by the name of Hirohito. He will also be the manifestation of the Divine in all of Japan. Even the Japanese constitution leaves the role of the Emperor . . . ambiguous. He has every freedom – so long as his wishes do not stray from expectations. This is why he was trained from birth to control his ambitions and desires. When he was seventy days old, he was given to be raised by a man who would teach him proper behaviour and self-control. When he returned from your country with new ideas about democracy and freedom, he gave a party for his friends, permitting them too much familiarity with his person. He has not made that mistake again.

'The danger is, when a person becomes too high to dirty his hands with matters of daily rule, he is laid open to . . . manipulation. The more luxury a man is given, the fewer personal rights he may claim. You and I earn money, keep it in bank accounts, spend it as we need. The man who just walked out of here has no such needs. But as you heard, he also has no such money. What need for personal finances when all luxuries are given?

'His Highness the Prince Regent's grandfather, the Meiji Emperor, was probably the last Emperor of Japan to wield actual power, and that came about because the Americans decided to sail a battleship into our harbour. His Majesty's advisors were in a panic, with no idea what to do. So for the first time in centuries, they turned to the heart of the people: our Emperor. It is ironic that the Enlightened Age, when democratic rule began to replace that of the Shogun, was overseen by an Emperor.

'But now the new system of government has again locked the Emperor away. And as His Highness revealed to you, he is kept on tight reins indeed, even financially.

'And that is the very root of our current dilemma.

'Three years ago, as I am sure you know, His Highness became the first Crown Prince to leave the country. He was twenty-one years old. He was to spend six months on the journey, visiting England especially. He would meet your Prime Minister, Mr David Lloyd George, but more than that, he would spend some days in the Palace home of your King. His Highness regarded this, rightly, as both a state honour and a personal one. As he prepared for this momentous journey – and remember, he was barely twenty-one – he decided that the many gifts provided by the Government and the Imperial Court might be fine for the state honours, but as recognition of the personal favour King George was doing him – having Japan's Crown Prince to stay in the family home – such formal thanks were most inadequate. He wished to give your King something personal in return.

'His choice was . . . unfortunate. Had he been Prince Regent then, or had his father been well enough to tell him, His Highness would have known its importance. However, as Crown Prince, he thought it was merely a beautiful possession that, belonging as it did to his family, he had the right to give where he wished.

She frowned at the embers. 'I cannot emphasise too much, just how dangerous a position His Highness stands in. Our entire world rests upon unspoken agreements: that His Majesty represents the will of Japan; that the opinions he voices are those of his government. For him to go against the decisions of his ministers would be . . . I will not say unthinkable, but His Highness would need to override his awareness of how catastrophic overt disagreement could be for the nation.

'All of which means that, were evidence to come to light that not just one Emperor, but generations of the Sons of Heaven, had been quietly acting on their own – that they possessed their own network of spies and advisors, even a sort of private army of shinobi . . . Were that to be known, the delicate balance that holds this country together would be destroyed. The government would shatter. Revolution would be at hand. And, as a side matter important only to me, one probable result would be the arrest and execution of my entire family.'

'You are saying that there is evidence of an Imperial shadow government.' Holmes, growing weary of Haruki-san's attempts at explanation, was moving to the point.

'"Shadow government". A good description, as it would not exist without the one that stands in the light. Yes, this government of the shadows is very much a part of Japan. And yes, it leads us to what His Highness requires – *requests* that you help us find and take back.' She drew a breath, then with the attitude of a swimmer facing a very cold plunge, dove in.

'What His Highness gave to your King is a book. A folding book of illustrated poems, some eight inches tall and three and a half wide, with a slipcase to hold it. When stretched out, it forms a panorama of the very road you travelled along to get here: the Kisokaido. The poems are by Bashō. The illustrations are by Hokusai, under his name of Gakyo Rojin Manji. That means, Old Man Crazy About Art.

'The book was commissioned by a wealthy Samurai as a gift to the Ninko Emperor during the Tempo era, what would be your 1838 or 1839. Shortly after this, the artist's studio burnt and his sketches were lost, although some earlier prints survive, with waterfalls that he later painted into the Emperor's book.

'The images in the book are paintings, not prints: this book is the only one of its kind. I am told it is extraordinarily beautiful.

The poems and illustrations are innocent. The key, I am told, lies within the binding.'

'That "key" being what, exactly?'

But she shook her head. 'That, I do not know. I doubt it is an actual key. Although the binding was done in the artist's lifetime – he died in 1849 – the hidden object belonged originally to Matsuo Bashō himself. It is difficult to imagine any serious locks of his era tiny enough for its key to be concealed within the binding.'

'So it's probably a paper,' I said. 'A letter or treaty, a signed agreement of some kind. Bashō was the late seventeenth century, wasn't he?'

The poet had been born in 1644, a few years after the edicts that shuttered Japan into two hundred years of seclusion. He had died in 1694, no doubt worn out by his constant wandering. What did an itinerant haiku-master have to do with an Emperor's authority? I decided to ask.

She smiled at my question. 'The Master was born a few miles from here. He was, in fact, a distant relative of mine. And yes, Matsuo Bashō was ninja.'

CHAPTER NINETEEN

Knife slices through wind,
Butterfly floats on a breath.
Sharpen my wings, please.

Poetry was, once I thought about it, not a bad cover for an Imperial espionage agent: who would suspect a shiftless, hard-drinking poet – a seventeenth-century bohemian – of acting as eyes and ears for the Son of Heaven? And it was not without parallel: Will Somers informed on Cardinal Wolsey under Henry VIII. Minstrels wandered anywhere, fools befriended anyone. Christopher Marlowe had almost certainly spied for his Crown, and I'd long suspected that Rudyard Kipling was writing autobiography when he penned, 'Slip through his lines and learn – that is work for a spy!' Spies came in all flavours: poet, nurse, retired consulting detectives. Lady academics with an interest in the Hebrew Bible.

It did put a rather different light on some of Bashō's more enigmatic phrases and imagery.

Asleep on horseback,
The distant moon in a dream,
Steam from cooking tea.

Was the poet describing a dream during a doze on his horse? Or was this some coded message regarding local landowners or troop movements? Perhaps, like Kipling, Bashō was a spy writing about a spy's dreams . . .

I shook myself from the reverie, but before I could pursue the idea of a poet-spy, Haruki-san spoke up.

'There is another thing you need to know, and then I will return you to the bathhouse for a massage, before dinner.'

'Just one thing?'

'My family are Samurai. Most Samurai serve *daimyo*; for three centuries, we have served the Emperor – or, in the case of our first patron, the Meisho Empress. How we came to serve Their Majesties is a story for another day, but serve them we have, thirteen men – now fourteen – and two women, since 1640. During the years my family performed as acrobats, we served the Emperor; when my father returned here to run the family onsen, he served the Emperor; while I was away being educated in America, I served the Emperor. To the world, we are just another rural family with nobility in our distant past. They see the Prince Regent coming to an onsen run by his favourite juggler, and think nothing of it. They see a village with rice paddies and tea fields and a restorative hot springs, and look no further.

'But we serve the Emperor. All of us, down to the smallest child. Any outsider who comes to the village is soon given reason to leave.'

A small, uneasy thought bubbled up to the front of my mind. Holmes and I were about as 'outsider' as you could get. If we chose *not* to serve this Emperor-to-be, would we, too, be 'given reason to leave'? And if so, would we depart on our feet, or in shrouds?

As if she had seen the question on my face and wished to divert me, Haruki-san gave us bows, then rose to her feet. 'I hope you do not mind, I have instructed the maids to dress you in clothing proper for the evening, following your massage.'

'I'm not going to be strapped into one of those formal obis,' I warned her. 'I'd like to breathe.' And eat.

She laughed. 'I shall instruct your maid not to bind you too tightly.'

I might have worried more about the statement were it not for the attentions of the blind masseuse, who pummelled the aches from my tired body and replaced the binding around my ankle. When she had finished, I lay for a time, summoning the energy to raise my head and glare at the woman sitting patiently near the doorway with a heap of clothing.

There are many, many layers covering a Japanese woman, which goes far to explain the lack of heat in the houses. I doubt many women here managed without assistance, but I did not even try. I merely stood with my arms out and let the maid push me around and bundle me like a doll.

In the end, although yes, I did have the wide obi belt of a woman and yes, I submitted to a small decoration in my hair, I was at least permitted the truncated sleeves of the married woman rather than the ridiculously cumbersome wings of a young girl, and the colours were sombre enough that they wouldn't set the dogs to barking.

I was, in truth, not entirely dissatisfied with the image in the mirror – until I saw Holmes.

If the paradigm of women's clothing in Japan was the butterfly, that of men was the knife. Dark grey, crisp white, snug body, and loose around the extremities: he looked . . . dangerous.

'Oh, Holmes, that's just not fair.'

The question was, I reflected later, had the garment come first, or the lack of furniture? Haruki-san's shipboard lectures had laid the groundwork for my ongoing awareness of cultural interconnectedness, and now I was seeing it everywhere. Steam pipes and plumbing fixtures were impractical in a land where the earth was always shifting: therefore, lightweight building and portable fires. But flimsy walls and hibachi burners were inadequate for a cold country: therefore, many layers of clothing. The question then came, was kneeling the norm because of the building techniques, or because of the clothing? It was awkward enough to fold into a chair while wrapped in an obi, and it would be even more difficult when wearing a sword. So, now that men no longer stuck swords through their belts, would chairs gain transcendence? Would carpets replace tatami? Would the women adopt Flapper dress?

Such were the thoughts I used to take my mind off the fading sensation in my legs. The Western body is not accustomed to sitting with the backside tucked against the soles of the feet. We had been in position for twelve minutes, waiting for our dinner to appear, and the tingles were turning to actual pain. Experience had taught that the throb would soon die away and my legs would go numb, to stay that way until it was time to stand. That did not make this stage any easier.

I studied Haruki-san, demure beside me in a quiet brown kimono, her untouched cup of sake in her hands. She might have been carved from stone, and I was certain that she could sit motionless for hours. I was also certain that she could rise instantly into fluid motion, with no problem of dead feet.

The tiny fire burning in the sand-lined pit between us was hardly enough to warm a bird, but I was finding that the layers of cotton and silk did in fact keep the cold at bay.

Except for the nape of my neck. For some reason, all those garments did not manage to cover the back of one's neck – on me, that is, and Haruki-san: Holmes' garments came up to his hairline. I made a mental note to look for a nice thick scarf in the next shops I came to.

Perhaps Japanese women were expected to demonstrate

vulnerability at the expense of comfort? In my experience, such overt declarations were often designed to mislead. Which would suggest that the much-demonstrated fragility of the Japanese woman was but a front.

Some butterflies, I had heard, could be deadly.

This string of useless thoughts was broken with a tinkle of glass bottles outside the door, followed by a burr-*slam* of wood as the external door was thrown back in its tracks. A man lurched in – the gardener's lame assistant, his worn blue clothing replaced with a motley collection of garments, including a green and black kimono with brown *hakata* pants and a sort of grey obi. From one meaty hand dangled a wooden bucket, of the kind used for everything from transporting fresh fish to scooping night soil from the benjo. I hoped this had not been used for that last purpose, because at the moment, it held bottles of beer.

The fellow appeared to have emptied a few of them along the way. He ignored the door he had flung open, and his progress across the spotless tatami was more of a stagger. I was just beginning to wonder why one of the maids had not intercepted him to take charge of the delivery, when his tabi-clad foot caught one edge of the tatami and he fell.

The beer bottles launched into the air in all directions, followed by the assistant gardener, who tumbled head over heels across the room. We all reacted fast to get out of the way of his flying heels –

And he came to a halt at the very edge of the firepit, controlled, perfectly balanced on one knee, a bottle in his right hand.

He looked from one to the next of the remaining three bottles, one in Holmes' hand, one in Haruki-san's and the last in mine. His mouth twitched, then he threw back his head to laugh.

Thus we met our tutor's father, the jester-assassin.

CHAPTER TWENTY

Bamboo softly bends
In the wind over the grove
But not soft on flesh.

THE MAN SITTING WITH his bottle of Sapporo looked like any of a thousand other Japanese men I had seen in the past week. Stocky, balding, perhaps a bit fitter than the suited men on the trains; perhaps with marginally deeper laugh-lines beside his eyes – nothing that betrayed his nature to a casual viewer.

But a non-casual viewer noticed how the intelligent eyes missed nothing, and how every motion was precisely calculated. Studying him across the firepit, I also perceived a faint discrepancy in the angle of his body, as if legs and torso were put together wrong.

He wasn't lame, although the hitch in his gait was not entirely feigned. According to his daughter, a broken spine had ended the family tradition of acrobatics and turned him into an innkeeper. Looking at his face, I wondered just how much chronic pain he held at bay, day in and day out.

Had you told me the man was a professional entertainer forced to abandon his chosen life, I'd have seen that face alone: a pool of merriment over a rocky past.

On the other hand, if you'd told me this man was a professional assassin, I'd have seen that, too: a faint disappointment at the failures of the world, but no regret.

Because I knew – or at any rate, thought I knew – both sides to the man, I saw the two faces overlaid: a man with a long history of living a secret, who had long since reconciled himself to the state of his world.

His dramatic entrance had been immediately followed by a line of maids carrying small tables laden with food. An informal meal, there by the fire, but blessedly plentiful. To my dual pleasure, they arranged more coal on the fire to cook the skewered meats, and coincidentally to push back the night air.

Haruki-san had greeted her father by setting down the bottle she had snatched from mid-air and giving him *dogeza*, a low bow with both hands on the tatami. The smile he gave her was both loving and serene – and the thought came from nowhere that although the laughter of many Japanese, male or female, was an expression of discomfort, when this man laughed, he meant it.

Head still down, Haruki-san introduced us, then sat up. 'My honourable father speaks English,' she told us, her eyes on the hands of the middle-aged maid arranging the plates.

'Like a child,' Sato-san added. 'Good not to use big words.' His voice was calm, his accent clear. He handed his bottle to one of the maids. She held it over the firepit, gingerly popping free the cap. When the foam began to stay inside the bottle, she returned it to him, performing the same ritual with ours, then tucking the opener into the bucket.

'I imagine we will understand each other well enough,' Holmes said drily.

I'd been right about the laughter: Sato-san's belly strained at the front of his kimono as he chuckled, like the laughing Buddhas in a curio shop.

'I think we will, yes,' he agreed. 'As I think you want to know why you here. All the things my daughter could not tell you.' He glanced at Haruki-san.

The attendants finished, the oldest of them pausing to adjust the tray of rice rolls before Sato-san, then bowed their way out of the door, sliding it shut behind them.

'She has told you that "shinobi", or as you call it, "ninja", means hidden. We began as a tool of war, going to a place and not being seen, listening to talk and not being noticed. Silent, invisible. In the background, neh?

'And then the time of war ended, and all of Japan was under the Shogun. The West was locked out, Emperor embraced Shogun, peace fell. Sometimes uneasy, but for three hundred years, it held. Emperor, Shogun, daimyo, Samurai, and peasant, resting on each other's shoulders.

'But the tools of peace can be used for war. Ninja know this, and practise other—' He paused to consult with his daughter, then resumed. 'We practise *alternative* uses for sickles and garden knives and lengths of chain. The most useful tools are those that make no one look twice. Just as most useful ninja are those that look stupid but have big ears.'

We chuckled, having used this method of invisibility ourselves. He took a swallow of beer before going on.

'Samurai are proud; ninja not. Samurai treasure honour above all. Rather die than fail. Ninja happy to fail at one thing if the bigger job is a success. Sacrifice, neh? Honour, life, family – all second to getting the job done. We become office-workers and ticket-sellers, to understand the modern world. We even become entertainers. No one takes those seriously. We send our children to school in America, so they can walk unseen in the West. Many tools, ready to be used.'

Haruki-san had said she was being educated for the family business – meaning all aspects of the family business.

'Two hundred eighty-four years ago, the head of my family was honoured to have a—' He paused again to consult. 'A private audience with Her Majesty the Meisho Empress. My ancestor had been fortunate enough to overhear a plot against Her Majesty and take it to her advisors. They offered a reward, but my ancestor said he wished only one thing: a private audience with Her Majesty. Five minutes only. Everyone most surprised when Her Majesty, instead of having his head, laughed. Then granted his wish. The only other person present was a deaf bodyguard.

'My ancestor bowed to Empress. He thank her for the honour she was doing to his entire line. And he tell her that if ever she or one of her descendants needed a man who could pass unseen and hear whispered secrets, she, or they, had only to send word.

'I do not suppose he thought anything would come of it. Like an elephant and an ant, Emperors are far too powerful to require the services of a small and unimportant clan of Samurai.

'But the Empress did remember. And somehow, she passed the word to her son, and he to his, that there is a family in Mojiro-joku waiting to serve. A family that looks near to peasants, but has useful skills. Perhaps once a generation, in the three centuries since then, a quiet message has been received, and a Sato is honoured to do a task for a Son – or Daughter – of Heaven.

'It is, for us, what you might call a sacred promise, that we might be there when needed. Not only be there, but be able. We train, that when we are called upon, we may serve.'

His broad face broke into a grin. 'Crazy, neh? Three hundred years we play with our thumbs and wait for a message that may never come? On to now, a time of telephones and cameras and aeroplanes?'

He allowed silence to fall, so we could think about what he

had told us. The charcoal in the fire whispered. Voices came from outside. Holmes stirred.

'It is not only your family, is it?'

'Our family is broad,' Sato-san replied. 'With ears in many places. Such as Bombay.'

'Some ears are family. Others are paid for. The English are not always as . . . circumspect, is that the word?'

'Yes.'

'—as circumspect as their superiors might wish. So.' He drained the last of his beer, and put the bottle down by his knee. 'One winter day last year, message comes. His Highness the Prince Regent will visit my humble onsen. I first met His Highness many year ago, when he was a child. Five, maybe six. I was called to perform at a festival for Meiji Emperor, and Prince Hirohito there, he laugh at my tricks. After my accident, Meiji Emperor help – send doctors, little gifts. Four years later, Meiji Emperor die. His Majesty become Emperor, but little Prince still remember his grandfather's acrobat, old man with funny tricks. Prince grow up, send little gifts, too, even come here, two, three times. To see tricks – old man can still juggle, but you guess that, I think, *neh*? – but also likes waters. And talk. Hard for Son of Heaven to find someone just for talk.

'So. Message come last winter from Prince Regent, want to come for the baths. Roads bad, cold and rain, but he coming, so we fast-fast buy new tatami and beds. He take bath, have massage, eat my simple foods. Walk through hills. And on second morning, His Highness send for me. When he told guards to leave, I knew what was coming.

'Yes: he need my help. There was a book, very pretty, of poems and pictures. His Highness took it to the King of England as a gift. One crown to another, *neh*? Was in His Majesty's private rooms, I guess. No one notice it gone, the Palace so full of beautiful things.

'But now – this is . . .' He paused to consult with his daughter. 'November.'

'November, last year. His Majesty get letters, many letters, but His Majesty not well, and His Highness doing more and more answers of letters. So here is one, it say, "Your Honoured Majesty, I have come into possession of a book of poetry by Matsuo Bashō, containing hidden truths, which I am offering to sell to you for so many English pounds." More words, but that is sense of it. His Highness first thinks, I must write the King of England and tell him someone has stolen his book. But then he see that "hidden truths". He wonder about that, and think, Maybe I go to my Honourable Father and ask if something I not know about this pretty book. His Majesty not well, you know this? Last four, five year, he has no official duties?'

Holmes and I assured him that we were aware of the erratic behaviour of the Emperor of Japan, who had once famously stood before the Japanese parliament, rolled up his speech, and held it to his eye like a spyglass. 'England, too, has had rulers who were . . . unwell,' Holmes said.

'This just short time after earthquake. Two, three month, neh? Important that His Highness be in Tokyo, helping hard. It take some time before he can get free to see His Majesty. And when he does, His Majesty ill. So His Highness think, I cannot ask my Honourable Father a thing that will disturb him. Instead, he talk, about this and about that. Childhood, *neh*? And he say, "We have so many beautiful things, so lucky to have. I remember one book, poems and pictures, in a case. Was anything very special about that book?"

'But Honourable Father His Majesty get very—' He paused for another consultation. 'Very agitated. Wants to go looking immediately, go to Tokyo and see if the book safe. His Highness have to call in doctor to calm him. Pill, you know? But then sent doctor away again, and say to Honourable Father, book very safe, locked away in personal vault, fire not harm it, nobody possibly steal it, absolutely secure where it is. Much better to leave it there than to travel with it across the roads to show it to His Majesty, *neh*? And His Majesty agree, and feel less agitated – drugs, *neh*? But before he go to sleep, he tell His Highness a story about this book. About how Ninko Emperor see the gift and think it a good place to hide away a document. Tempo era very filled with unrest, rebellion, famine. Only thirty, forty years after French revolters cut off King's head. Dangerous to have a document like this that can be discovered. So hid it away inside the book.

'There it stay. Ninkō to Komei, Komei to Meiji, and now His Majesty. Hidden secrets, as letter say. I do not know what those secrets are. Not even sure if His Highness know – even His Majesty himself. All I know is, Emperor's book first given by accident, then stolen. Have to get it back.'

'This letter,' Holmes said. 'The one received in November. Who was it from?'

'English Lord Darley.'

'Really? Darley put his name to an open demand for ransom?'

'Ah, so – not open. Only say: here is book with hidden truths. You want it back? It for sale. Here how much.'

I spoke up. 'Is it possible that Darley doesn't know what the secret is, either? That he only heard a rumour about the book, indicating that the Emperor of Japan might not wish the thing to become public?'

'Possible,' Sato-san agreed. 'But how he know?'

One tended not to criticise the ruling families of host countries, so neither Holmes nor I voiced aloud the main scenario that came to mind: that their somewhat erratic Emperor had carried on a conversation he should not have done, which was overheard by someone who sold secrets. Three years was plenty of time for that conversation to work its way to England, there to find a man who could figure out how to lay hands on a pretty artefact in a cluttered palace.

'Letter say that this lord was coming to Japan, and he want to sell the book back to His Highness.

'Very, very fortunately, the Prince Regent knew how to find Sato clan. One week after talk with Honourable Emperor Father, His Highness permitted himself a visit to the baths of Mojiro-joku, to the onsen run by the old man whose tricks made him laugh as a child. A man his grandfather had helped after a fall ended his career as acrobat.

'And so, the Sato machine begins to turn. We have friends with ears in England, yes? They find the earl and his wife already left England, sailing here. Other friends find them in Bombay. I telegraph to my daughter: hurry to Bombay by any way she can, money no matter. We wait to hear: has she made it? Or will she go on to meet their ship later, in Singapore, Manila? While we wait, another word reaches us. Two other English travellers, also an older man and younger woman, are about to sail for America.

'I have heard, long ago, about these other two people. One has a brother in the British government. They interest me. If my daughter can make friends with them, they could be help. To delay them for a day, even three, is no great problem. And as it happens, my daughter does reach India in time to join the English lord and his wife.'

He shook his head ruefully. 'Between bribes and aeroplanes, my daughter's travel cost me more than raising my three children. However, my ancestor who asked the Meisho Empress for nothing but a private audience, two hundred and eighty-four years ago? He was given the money as well. Turned out good at investing.'

He smiled. After a time, Holmes spoke.

'It's more than the money. You went to huge effort to bring us into contact with your daughter. She spent weeks drilling us in Japanese language and customs. At the end of it, you arranged for His Highness the Prince Regent to tell us himself that you are to be trusted. So, what is it you want of us?'

Our host leant back like a fisherman who's just managed to hook a wily trout. He shot a quick glance at Haruki-san, eyes sparkling.

'My daughter will tell you, sometimes I tell her to do a thing that seems strange, then later say, "an exercise". Perhaps this an exercise for her. Perhaps is to sharpen a tool, for use one day. Or perhaps,' he said more deliberately, 'old Sato-san look into his future. Perhaps he see that there will come a day when my country and yours need a private friend behind a public face.'

Slowly, Holmes nodded. 'The tides of international pressures being as they are.'

'American law against Japanese immigration, plus our earthquake stopping most Western visitors, together make for a perilous time. Time for thoughts of isolation and resentment. And if it comes to choice, England will choose America, not Asia.'

I thought it was time to bring things down a bit closer to earth. 'All that is far off, and the future can change a dozen times. Today, in this village, your English guests want to know: why are we here?'

He gave Holmes a wide grin. 'Your wife is a fine woman, Mistah Holmes.'

'She has a knack for getting to the point,' Holmes agreed.

Sato-san turned his sparkling eyes on me. 'A party, Miss Lussell. I wish you to go to a party.'

Something told me I was not going to like this. I sighed. 'You'd better call me Mary.'

Chapter Twenty-One

Sleek black too-large car
Slips down the ancient post road.
Time to speak of death.

THE PARTY WOULD NOT be Sato-san's affair. It was to be hosted by Lord and Lady Darley, on behalf of the friend's porcelain-ware company that the earl had agreed to represent, with a guest list that included the highest-ranking financiers and aristocrats in the country – and the Prince Regent. It was the sort of thing that Prince Hirohito would find difficult to attend once the golden bars of the Emperor's Palace rose up around him, but as Prince Regent, he still had a degree of freedom, to attend the theatre, travel for a soak at his favourite hot springs along the Kisokaido, or stand with a drink in his hand while Westerners vied for his attention.

There would be few Japanese there. Even many of the servants would be British, since the event was intended to be a showcase of the best England had to offer, down to the gloved hands on the silver trays. It would, Sato-san declared, be little problem for two English people to obtain invitations, particularly when they had shared a recent voyage with the host. Western visitors were thin on the ground, these days.

'And you believe Lord Darley intends to exchange his stolen object at this soirée?' Holmes asked.

'His Highness has been . . . instructed to bring money.' Sato-san's genial features turned stony at the thought of a foreigner issuing instructions to Japan's Prince Regent. '"Bearer bond",' he spat.

'For how much?'

'Twenty thousand pound sterling.'

The number dropped into the room and sat there for a while. On the one hand, it was a considerable sum for a picture book, even one with its unique provenance. On the other, if one accepted that the future of the Emperor – if not the Empire – rested on it . . .

'One does wonder if Darley knows just what he has,' Holmes mused.

'I only care that the English lord has the book.'

'And I suppose there is no plan to have him arrested afterwards?'

Sato-san left it to his daughter to reply. 'There can be no question of scandal touching His Highness,' Haruki-san said.

'Particularly,' I ventured, 'since questions would be asked regarding the book itself.'

'Is shameful enough that His Highness will have contact with this man.'

Incredulity slowly dawned. I looked from daughter to father. 'You do not intend for Darley to walk away from this!'

'His Highness would find the memory . . . unpleasant,' Sato-san replied.

My eyes sought out Holmes. He looked almost as troubled as I felt. It was one thing to detest a blackmailer, but to condone cold-blooded murder . . .

'We will find an alternative,' he said in the end, his voice tight.

* * *

Sato-san excused himself shortly after that, limping away to join the Prince Regent while Haruki-san supervised the conversion of dining room into bedroom. We walked down the hall to the communal facilities and brushed our teeth, then down the outdoor walkway to visit the benjo. We succeeded in changing our footwear the correct number of times, and stepped back into our quarters without hearing the suck of embarrassed breath that came when one of the maids was witness to some major faux pas.

Holmes and I settled beneath the bedclothes, and blew out the lamp. After a time, I became aware of a play of light on the roof, a stone lamp reflecting off one of the garden pools. I could hear voices, too: once, the laughter of Haruki-san's father. Later, a different voice raised in anger, followed by a slamming screen and footsteps in the courtyard.

Holmes was not asleep, no more than I was. 'How much of today's talk are we to believe?' I asked.

'Rather a lot of it, I should think.'

'But not all.'

'Verisimilitude may be woven from lies.'

'So what if we just say we're not going to help them?' I said.

'Do you want to refuse?' Holmes asked in surprise.

'Not necessarily. But one can't help thinking that Westerners who are privy to a dangerous secret are not in the most secure of positions.'

'You think Sato-san would pull out his sword and behead us if we turned him down?'

'I think he could. Don't you?'

'I know he could.'

'Reassuring.'

'My dear Russell, our host is not about to leap in and murder us before we've had a chance to refuse him.'

And with that, Holmes turned on his side and was soon snoring. Sleep took somewhat longer, for me.

The next morning, His Highness left the village, climbing into a gleaming Rolls Royce that I would have thought too large for the roads. His guards closed in around the frail, stooped figure with the dark suit and the mask of obedience. The entire staff of the inn lined up in deep obeisance, including the inn's two English visitors, but His Highness walked past as if we were not there. He seemed oblivious of anything but his motor – or, was his neck stiffer than it had been, his lack of a parting glance deliberate? Had last night's angry voice been his?

When the sounds of the engine had faded to nothing, Sato-san eased back onto his heels; with the sound of a breeze through standing wheat, the others rose to scatter in all directions. Haruki-san put her hand on his arm, but the innkeeper shrugged her off, turning his dark gaze on Holmes and me. The previous night's good cheer was gone: the man appeared to be aching, although whether the pain was from his back or from drink, I could not have said.

'The time has come, for me to ask.'

'We will help you,' said Holmes.

'Why?'

Holmes raised an eyebrow. 'Do you need to know why?'

'A man must understand the tool in his hand, before he trusts it not to break.'

Holmes nodded, not in the least offended at being compared to a tool. 'I am sure your Emperor and his Prince Regent are fine men; however, I have less interest in helping them than I do in stopping a wicked man.'

'So you do not see this ransom as mere business?' Sato-san asked.

'Until we are certain that Lord Darley is unaware of the book's hidden contents, we need to regard this as extortion. Blackmail, not merely fencing stolen goods. The earl has a history of blackmail, and to my mind, there is nothing more evil. Such a man preys on the vulnerable. He turns morality back on itself. To rid the world of one such, I will take your case.'

Our host's eyes shifted to follow a small naked child, wandering down the road in pursuit of a chicken. Then he stood – allowing us to follow his example, to my relief. 'My daughter tells me that you understand honour. This has not always been my experience with outsiders.'

'The English gentleman's code of conduct is little different from bushido,' Holmes replied.

'Although in all fairness,' I pointed out, 'one can't assume that all Englishmen are gentlemen.'

'Granted,' Holmes said. 'But in this case, Russell and I understand the duties one has to a client.'

I clarified: 'We will do all that we can for your Emperor.'

'Would you die for him?'

Holmes answered this one. 'We'd prefer not to. However, that is a part of one's commitment to a client.'

'Would you make a fool of yourself?'

Holmes laughed. 'It would not be the first time.'

Haruki-san spoke up. 'Would you kill?'

Three sets of eyes converged on me, but when it came to that question, I was far from untried. '*My* hand will not hesitate. What about yours?'

I might have touched a live wire to the young woman. Her chin snapped up, her face went dark, but her father merely looked amused.

204

'There comes a time to test one's tool,' he said. 'That time is now.' He added something to Haruki-san, and walked off.

'Come,' she told us.

We had seen something of the village the previous afternoon, since the onsen was at the northern end of it. It was busier now, either because it was earlier in the day or because it was drier. Businesses lined the road, with greengrocers' displays of the familiar and the unknown, shops with pots, shops with rolls of bright fabric, shops with farm implements. The women's clothing was more subdued than in the city, and fewer men wore Western dress, although even here, a number of them had bowler hat and brogues above and below their traditional garb.

The village shrine lay on a narrow street behind the main thoroughfare, a small, simple wooden structure that appeared to have grown from the earth. In typical Japanese fashion, it was an easygoing composite of Shinto and Buddhist, with a *torii* gate rather in need of paint, an upright slab of mossy granite carved with flowing characters, and half a dozen statues of local kami spirits and Buddhas in the lotus position.

Next door to the shrine stood a wooden building that might have been built at the same time, although it was considerably larger and lacked the statues. The wooden doors along its deep verandas were drawn shut, but for one. A curious glance revealed a simple rectangular expanse of rather worn tatami with no inner walls.

I recognised it, although I had not until that moment realised how pale an imitation my one in Oxford was. 'This is a *dojo*,' I said.

'Jujitsu and karate are national sports,' Haruki-san said. Two sports she had claimed, back on the *Thomas Carlyle*, to know nothing about.

Was this Sato-san's idea of testing each other's mettle? Well, there's nothing like throwing a person around to cement a friendship.

Haruki-san led us past the structure to a smaller building at the back. This one was far more heavily built than the usual Japanese posts and beams. Its walls were of closely fitted stone and its door was on hinges, rather than sliding. It had one of the few locks I'd seen in the country. She drew a key from the sleeve of her kimono and worked the mechanism. We followed her inside.

High, narrow windows revealed a storage room with stone floors, wooden cabinets covering two of the walls. The third wall was hung all over with weapons: spears, axes, vicious little sickles, maces with barbed ends. The wall on either side of the door seemed to be draped with body parts – which, on closer examination, became sections of armour, from chain-mail waistcoats to heavy leather arm protectors.

Haruki-san started pulling open the armoury's cabinets, revealing yet more objects of mayhem: wood, steel, bamboo, leather; small to massive; dull to bright. Some of them were chained together.

I stood gazing down at a drawer filled with flat metal stars possessing from three to six points, each of which resembled a double-sided razor. I had handled *shuriken* – gingerly – in my Oxford dojo, but there was no way to sheathe them, and throwing them always seemed to me a great way to lose a finger, if not a hand.

My contemplation was interrupted by a voice from the door. One of the inn's maids knelt there with an armful of dark blue clothing, very like the pyjamas Haruki-san had worn on the night we caught her walking the ship's Marconi wire. On top were tabi of

206

the same cloth, large enough for Western feet. She bowed, separated the clothes into two piles, bowed again, and left.

Haruki-san finished opening the cabinets, bowed, and went to the door.

'You have six minutes to choose your weapons and change your clothing. When you hear the knock, enter the dojo through the door directly in front of you.' She pointed towards a slid-back panel at the large room's corner. 'Your task is to walk out the door at the front.'

I narrowed my eyes at her voice, which had become a little too eager, a bit too pleased with herself. She intended to make me pay for questioning her commitment to death. Would she kill? I could hope she didn't decide to demonstrate her capabilities on me.

She paused at an odd contraption I had dismissed as a kind of Oriental decoration: a length of heavy bamboo in a frame, suspended over a wooden bucket of sand. She filled a scoop with the sand, levelling it off precisely before she poured it into the open end of the bamboo tube. When she let it go, it sank on its hinge. A dribble of sand began to leak out.

When it was empty, the length would tip and knock against a cross-bar.

'Six minutes.' She bowed, and walked away.

I looked at the trickle of sand. I could always just block the hole . . .

No, that was an unworthy thought for an English gentlewoman. Strictly speaking I was neither – but the shoes were mine to step into.

Or, the tabi. I turned to the clothing. The morning being chill and most of my wardrobe in a hotel storage room in faraway Tokyo, I had dressed by putting on a yukata over my own trousers and shirt. And really, the blue outfit the maid had given us would not be any more invisible in a dim room than my own black trousers and dark green woollen pullover. I merely replaced my white tabi with the navy blue ones, and let it go at that.

Holmes had traded his white shirt for the dark blue tunic, and was now buttoning on his own tabi. 'Holmes, what does a fight to the death have to do with retrieving an old book?'

'I shouldn't think anyone will die,' he said.

'No, just blood loss and brisk amputations.'

'Some of the armour may fit you.'

I was tempted by the massive leather breastplate with the raised neck, but I imagined it might be difficult to move in it.

'What about you?' I asked.

He bent over a metal hoop set into the wall and started pawing through the sticks it contained, like a restaurant-goer in search of his umbrella. When he found one he liked, he drew it out, practising its weight with a few jabs and swishes. His preferred weapon was a single-stick; lacking that, a riding crop. My own favourite weapon was strapped to my ankle.

I looked at him. 'Holmes, are we honestly about to go up against two trained assassins in a dark building?'

'Just think of it as an examination for your *practicum*.'

'A comforting thought when I lie on the floor with a broken leg.'

'Remember: they do not know us. To them we are merely outsiders, with few skills and little experience.'

'So, you propose that we take them by surprise.' It didn't seem to me much of a plan, but when he looked over his shoulder at me, he was grinning.

'My dear Russell, why ever not?'

I laughed. 'All right, but you may need to summon a cup of English tea to bring me out of my concussion.'

We chose a few bits from the cabinets, then crept from the armoury and across the mossy earth to the dojo's veranda. Like all such, it was sturdy and made not a creak as we eased our weight onto its boards. The sun was on the other side, so our shadows were not a concern. We took up positions on both sides of the dark opening.

I closed my eyes, so as to let my pupils expand as much as possible, and strained my ears as if I might hear the waning dribble of grains of sand through the bamboo timer. As we waited, I sought to reach that state of relaxed tension that prepares a body for sudden demands. I listened to my breath, I felt the cold spring air against my face . . .

The device gave an almost imperceptible pause of sound, then a hollow *clok*. Before the echoes died, we dove through the door, flinging aside the noisy clacking sticks we had brought as distraction and sprinting across the tatami towards the opposite corner.

We might have made it, had the building been as we had seen it. In the interim, the open space had gained a pair of shoji half-walls, effectively converting a clear room into an arena designed to confuse strangers and conceal defenders. The space was further cluttered by some odd tangle of machinery hanging from the beams and a large trunk. I dodged to my right, loath to dive through a paper wall into some unseen threat – and from behind the wall burst Haruki-san, sword raised.

She was incredibly fast; the sword slashed down while she was still mid-air. Had it been steel, I would have lost a hand – even a solid wood practise sword might have cracked bones. But it was a bamboo, and merely left me with numb fingers.

I jabbed her with my own weapon, a stick much like Holmes'. My superior reach forced her back a few steps, while I tried to think as fast as she moved.

For all the Satos had known, Holmes and I would enter the arena bristling with razor-sharp steel. That they had chosen bamboo for defence meant –

My attempt at reasoning was cut off by her instantaneous recovery and advance. Armed only with a flexible stick, her reach a foot shorter than mine, she nonetheless managed to deliver two brutal blows to my torso before I fought her off. There followed a blur of attack and counter-attack that seemed to last far longer than the few seconds of actual clock-time. I was relieved to see, when we both backed off a step, that she was panting as hard as I.

Inevitably, Holmes had been too much of a gentleman to abandon me to a sword-wielding woman. Instead of making his dash for the far corner, he had turned to do battle – which allowed the father to pounce from his position just inside the entrance.

I was aware of the two men thwacking away at each other off to my left, but my attention was locked on the small woman crouching before me. She edged sideways, watching for an opening, and I knew that her own mind was whirring as rapidly as my own. The first moments of our engagement had taught her a lot about me – if nothing else, she now knew that I was not without skills – but perhaps it did not teach her everything.

And perhaps it did not teach her about herself.

The sounds from across the room indicated that her father, too, was armed only with light bamboo. The exchange of grunts and gasps showed that the men were also gauging each other's skills, and—

Haruki-san's bamboo came at my face. I retreated: one step,

two. She followed, her sword arm adjusting to my left-handed style; I continued to fall back. Three steps, five, she was driving me with the skill of a sheepdog. Seven steps – and a flash of triumph on her face when the floor disappeared from beneath my feet.

The innocent tatami that had been laid across the room's firepit (cold, fortunately) collapsed the instant my weight hit it. I flung out my arms, the wooden sword flying away, and she leapt for the kill.

But as I went down, even as her feet were digging into the woven mats for her final attack, my body tucked and my feet stretched upwards, amplifying the speed of the fall. An instant later, my outstretched fingers dug into the firepit sand, and my every muscle thrust in an explosive movement: finger to toe, up, over – and to my astonishment, instead of a bone-cracking landing, my feet slapped onto the mats with barely a stagger.

A reverse somersault was the last thing Haruki-san anticipated. Her body was already committed to air, and although her face began to change when she saw my hand coming up from my ankle with a knife, there was little she could do about the laws of physics. She smashed into me. We tumbled hard across the tatami, my whole being focused on the razor-sharp steel in my hand. When we came to a halt, I stared desperately at the place where steel met flesh, and saw – blood.

But not much. And, a brief throb from my finger told me, not even hers.

I let out a huge breath of relief. However, I kept my hand where it was until she gave an infinitesimal nod, then I got to my feet. I watched her rise, waiting until I was certain that she had capitulated, before looking to see how far Holmes had got.

Holmes' age and relative lack of expertise were balanced by

his longer arms and his general fitness; Sato-san's greater skill was hindered by his body's infirmities. The innkeeper would have won in the end, but Holmes was making him work for it.

Until I intervened. At the *thwack* of steel in bamboo, both men stopped moving. Their eyes rose to the sliver of steel protruding from the end of Sato-san's bamboo weapon. He drew it back, pulled out the knife, and swivelled on his heel, eyes sparkling. Haruki-san climbed out of the pit, brushing sand from her clothing. Holmes lowered one end of his stick to the tatami and leant on it.

And Sato-san, his face alive with mischief, brought his other heel around, to bend his upper body into a deep and lasting bow.

CHAPTER TWENTY-TWO

Clear light twinkles from
A warrior's cedar torso.
Star from the teacher.

'YOU WERE TOO CONFIDENT,' I told Haruki-san.

Two hours after we had walked out of the dojo, when the sweat had been washed away and the sharp aches soaked in the baths, the four of us were sitting around another firepit, this one sending fragrant wisps of charcoal smoke into the rafters. Our host had asked how I had come to beat his daughter, although I was certain that he knew.

'I gave you no quarter,' she objected.

'You told me you thought us weak, the moment you came out with bamboo *shinai*.'

'We couldn't attack with actual *katana*,' she exclaimed.

'Probably not, without knowing more about us. But you did not say that *we* shouldn't use the real thing. You had no reason to think that Holmes and I would not step into the dojo with steel. You weren't even carrying wood. Either of you,' I pointed out.

Sato-san grimaced – although I thought it as much from his body's protest at the violent exercise as it was chagrin. He was on his second flask of sake.

'It is foolish to underestimate the enemy,' Holmes said.

'You are not the enemy.'

Until that moment, I had not thought of Haruki Sato as particularly young – not since our first conversation on the *Thomas Carlyle* at any rate. I gave Holmes a brief glance before frowning into my cup of tea. 'Haruki-san, I believe that your experience with enemies may be largely . . . theoretical.'

She stiffened, but before she could shape a retort – no one enjoys being accused of naiveté, not least a member of the Samurai class – her father deftly undermined her outrage. 'My daughter is trained, but not tested.'

'Well,' I said, 'testing comes soon enough.'

She wrestled with the lesson, but had to admit defeat. 'Next time, I will use the wooden sword.'

'Next time you should bring a gun.'

They thought it was a joke. I watched father and daughter relax into laughter, and hesitated, but decided to let it go. Suspicion was a theory for her, a lesson learnt, but not yet hammered home. Her innate trust for the world testified to a surprisingly gentle upbringing – like mine, until I was fourteen. There's nothing like losing one's family, or being shot by a friend, to bring wariness into a person's life.

Still, today would not be young Haruki-san's last opportunity to learn.

We stayed in the village for three days. We came to know the area quite well, wandering up into the hills with Haruki-san or one of the village children, to gather wood or stones or the long streamers of bamboo. This being a farming community, we lent hands to a number of activities, from wading in sticky mud to plant tiny shoots of rice to scooping buckets of night soil onto the rows of tea plants. Helping the fire-scarred gardener, who was Sato-san's tall and austere cousin, to pluck weeds from the courtyard garden was pleasant relaxation, after the fields.

But mostly, we collected bruises on the dojo floor. Each night, we soaked out the stink of the day's work and the aches of the day's workout in the mineral baths, then groaned under the hands of the ryokan's masseur. Our host's good humour increased and took on an element of respect, until one afternoon he requested to be taught a technique Holmes had for turning a walking stick into a lethal spear. Haruki-san was much taken with my left-handed skill with the throwing knife. In return, she went to the armoury and retrieved three of the vicious little metal stars, then whirled and, faster than the eye could follow, sent them – one, two, three – into the chest of the nearest dummy. I had to pull hard to get them out of the wood, nicking my forefinger in the process.

'Shuriken are toys,' she said, 'but very useful. It can be most distracting to get hit with one. Try them.'

As blades, they were ambidextrous, equally hazardous to either hand. Under her guidance, I rehearsed the motions of throwing several times before committing my flesh to the effort, and was pleased when the star flew from my hand without pulling streamers of blood in its wake. That it bounced off the target hardly mattered.

It took seven tries (and two more blood-lettings) before the star's point sank a fraction into the wood, but having got the technique, I improved. By the time we broke off for bath and dinner, I was sinking it in nine times out of ten, the depth increasing as my throw grew more assured.

Those days in Mojiro-joku were a gift. If our arduous trip to the village had prepared us to meet our illustrious client, the days under Sato-san's roof and in his village wrapped the case around our hearts. Before our stay, as Holmes had said, our chief interest was in thwarting a wrong-doer; after it, the case was personal.

Our last morning in the village, my breakfast tray of tea-pot, chopsticks, and small bowls of rice, pickles and stinky dried fish included a flat leather pouch. I pulled the string to look inside, then eased onto the low table a trio of throwing stars, old but freshly sharpened. Unlike the others I had seen, these bore delicate swirls of engraving. Shuriken were meant to be abandoned after use, not retrieved – but I supposed that a present from one's *sensei* was designed to be treasured.

I thanked Haruki-san and managed to get the things tucked safely away without shedding blood on the tatami. Holmes and I donned our pilgrim garb and slung our bags over our shoulders. Then we set off on the long road to Tokyo.

CHAPTER TWENTY-THREE

Escaping my death
In a cloud-girt mountain place,
To be crushed by trams?

W E STAYED THAT NIGHT in a pleasant ryokan in one of the old post-towns of the Kisokaido. In the morning, we resumed the Western clothing we had put aside in Arima. My legs felt strangely exposed in the skirt, and Holmes kept easing his collar with a finger as we made our way through the town to the train station. It was a train with only two classes, second and third. As we elbowed our way into our seats, in the luxurious quarters this time, I felt as if I'd stepped into another world – one without undressing passengers, nursing babies, and spittoons on the floor.

I wasn't sure I felt entirely comfortable.

One advantage, however: Holmes and I could carry on a conversation without people pushing their astonished faces in closer to hear our gibberish.

I stretched out my legs and looked at the landscape rushing past, the dip-and-rise of the telegraph lines, the bright splash of the cherry blossoms. There was the place I had paused to bind up a blister. And that peculiarly shaped tree – that was where we had tried to shelter from a particularly vigorous cloudburst. Several times, passing through more urban areas, I spotted large gatherings in parks, families having picnics under the glorious white cherry blossoms.

After a while, I dug Haruki-san's booklet of poems from my pack, and searched out a page – changing the last word in my mind to 'springtime':

Goodbyes are given
And received, as I set off
Through Kisos autumn.

Bashō, too, travelled light. Although Bashō, too, weighed down the practical necessities with sentimental gifts from friends.

'Do you suppose Bashō could truly have been a ninja?' I asked my companion. He had his long legs stretched out, his shoes reaching past the centre of the narrow carriage, and he did not open his eyes to reply.

'The man seems to have had friends all over. No doubt some of them were high-ranking government officials happy to get news of the provinces.'

There are times when a person craves the road, taking up one's raincoat . . . Holmes and I had been on the road since the new year, with many miles yet to come. So why did I feel as if our journey was coming to an end?

'What did you make of Sato-san?' I asked.

At that, Holmes drew in his feet and sat up, fishing out the cigarette case he had not used since donning pilgrim garb. 'I should like to have spent more time with him,' he answered eventually.

'It all feels a bit . . . fairy tale,' I said.

'The whole country has an otherworldly flavour to it.'

I looked at him in surprise. In our partnership, the airy-fairy remarks were generally left up to me. 'We should be thankful it's not the full moon. We might have stepped into the garden at night and walked into the realm of Titania and Puck.' No, not *Midsummer's Night*. There was another play – *Henry!*

Holmes' eyebrow rose. 'Russell, perhaps you should brush up on your—'

'Haruki-san was reading the *Henry* plays on the ship, and we got to talking about Falstaff. How Shakespeare seems more interested in that fat old knight than in the King himself. And she said something remarkable, about how Sir John offers up his honour, just so young Harry can refuse him, and grow into kingship. I think she was talking about her father.'

'The Samurai who offers the Emperor his most valuable possession: his pride.'

The role of a Fool was not only to entertain, but to speak the truth. Particularly dangerous truths, words that the King does not want to hear. If the angry voice that night had in fact belonged to the Prince Regent, perhaps truth-speaking was a Fool's job here, too.

Which would make Sato-san more King Lear's companion than Prince Harry's buffoon.

I smiled to myself, and resumed my reading of that poet-Fool, and possibly spy, Matsuo Bashō.

If boarding the train had felt like stepping into another world, coming to Tokyo felt like entering a whirlwind.

A universal characteristic of the Japanese people, I had discovered, was their energy. This industrious nation seemed never to pause – whether small child or ancient crone, every citizen had some task at hand, at every moment.

Multiply that devotion to labour times a million, for the population of Tokyo. In a city that had been half-levelled by quake and fire seven months before, the pitch of activity was feverish. Signs of the disaster lay on all sides, but on our ridiculously brief taxi drive from the central train station to the Imperial Hotel, every other building appeared to be either freshly repaired or currently a-boil with activity. Every pedestrian trotted, every rickshaw-puller ran, every bicycle, car, and lorry dodged and sped.

There were picnics beneath the cherries here, too, but far from languid perusal of blossoms, those were hives of activity, with children running about and every adult either eating, drinking or carrying on a vehement conversation.

'Many people are in the park,' I said to the driver in Japanese.

'*Hai*,' he agreed. '*Hanami*. You know hanami? Pickanick, *hai*? Under sakura – cherry. Every year, big parties. Much sake!' He laughed.

A picnic with a few thousand intimate friends under the flowering trees. After days spent among the bamboo-covered hills, the cacophony was dizzying. No less, the hotel.

'Good heavens.'

The taxi driver heard my astonishment, if not the reason behind it. 'Yes, yes!' he exclaimed. 'Imperial Hotel! Open day before earthquake – you know earthquake? No hurt at all. Everyone come here for help, after. American build it, light. Fank royd light.' I had grown accustomed to the inability of the Japanese tongue to distinguish between the *L* sound and an *R*, but it took me a few moments to sort out the driver's words. A name: Frank Lloyd Wright. I'd vaguely heard of him, a small man with a large ego.

And, it would appear, an imaginative view of Japanese architecture. The compound was built from an unlikely mix of yellowish brick and rugged lava-stone slabs of a peculiarly greenish tint, combining the roofline of a Japanese farm house with a right-angle Illinois sensibility and the brutality of a Mayan temple. Over this uneasy mix lay a heavy dusting of Moorish detail, apparent as we drew near, circling an enormous sunken pond. Our driver slowed so we could admire it, pointing out that the water it held was designed to fight the fires after a quake. The low, rectangular pond, half-covered with shiny new lotus leaves, somehow brought to mind a Yucatan sacrificial arena.

The foyer was a similar giddy blend of East and West, with vast Navajo-esque carpets stretching to walls made of children's stone building-blocks. When we reached the desk, I was almost disappointed not to be greeted by men in buckskin and feathers.

Dared I hope that the kitchen of this ethnic hotchpotch contained an English tea pot?

Our rooms, we were told, were ready. Our trunks had been forwarded from the ship. And yes, a tray of English tea would arrive immediately.

I was relieved to find the rooms somewhat less frenetic than the exterior. They looked out onto a Midwesterner's version of a Japanese garden, and my bones cried out in joy at the sight of an actual bed. I will say, however, that using a bar of soap inside the porcelain tub felt distinctly wrong, and my skin did not feel entirely clean as I climbed out of the murky water. Nor did the clothing I took from the trunks seem to have been designed for my body, being too loose in some places and too snug in others.

I studied the Western woman in the glass, absently trying to adjust the buttoned blouse to lie correctly. 'I need a haircut,' I told Holmes. Something on the farther edge of fashionable, like that of the late, lamented Miss Roland. 'And I'm afraid I'll have to have my nails done.'

'Stop tugging at your clothes,' he ordered.

'*Stretching out wrinkles*,' I quoted, '*I make my coat suitable/For a snow-viewing.*'

'Call down for a maid,' he suggested.

I laughed. 'Wrinkles aren't the problem.' After all my complaints to Haruki-san, my belly missed the firm grasp of the obi. Although, interestingly, I thought it would be easier to set aside the learnt habit of bowing at every greeting, introduction and encounter when I wore a frock instead of Japanese attire. *Apparel oft proclaims the man* – or rather, clothes make the manners. However, it was not just the clothes: 'I'll need to find a salon right away, if we're to make an impression.'

'While you are submitting to the womanly arts, I shall hunt down a Thomas Cook and restore our funds.'

'You might also make enquiries as to the Darleys. Shall we meet in the bar around six? I'll definitely need a drink by then.'

The Darley party was on Friday night; today was Tuesday. That left us little time to trail our skirts in front of the earl and his lady and achieve an invitation. I could do little about my wardrobe tonight, but I did have two frocks that had spent the voyage in the ship's hold, as well as an exotic, heavily embroidered silk tunic given to me in India. All of them had been ironed and hung in the wardrobe awaiting our arrival. Those clothes, along with a fresh haircut and my mother's emeralds, would catch the eyes of the fashionable set: even in a city of a million souls, I had no doubt that the Darleys' circle would be exclusive, and not given to stray travelling companions with uncontrolled hair and rice-planters' cuticles.

By six, I was a different woman – one who tossed down her lurid cocktail with aplomb. One who crossed her silk-covered ankles with little regard for the length of her hemline. One who accepted a light by cupping her much-older husband's hands against the end of her cigarette, before slumping back with a dramatic flourish of the garish enamelled holder.

Much-older husband was one of Holmes' least favourite roles, but he manfully concealed his distaste, pasting on an expression of proprietary approval.

We drank, I flirted, he beamed, all the while surveying the room. We were hoping for the Darleys, who (as Holmes had confirmed during the afternoon) were guests in the hotel. When they failed to appear, we shifted our attention to the type of person Lord Darley would have migrated towards, whether his interest lay in promoting his friend's chinawares, or in the darker realm of the blackmailer: moneyed, assured, and young enough to misbehave.

One group we discarded because the men were mostly Japanese. Another because their raucous behaviour implied sins too openly indulged for a blackmailer's attentions. There was a trio seated in the bar's most desirable corner, but they, too, were not ideal: two Japanese Flappers wearing far too much make-up and a highly polished Englishman in his thirties. As my eye surveyed the room, I found him surveying back. I gave him a polite smile over my cocktail glass, and moved on – or, was about to move on, when one of the girls at his side bounced a little and gave an exuberant wave towards the door.

Aha: Thomas, Viscount Darley and his blaring pal, Monty Pike-Elton.

They did not notice us as they went past. We gave them time to order a round of drinks, then rose to make our way towards the dining room – with a sideways loop to greet our old shipmates.

Neither recognised me, although they stood somewhat warily

to greet Holmes. Then he gestured in my direction with a faintly owlish, 'You remember my wife, Mary?' Both young men gave me a look that could only be called appraising.

'Well, well,' said Tommy. 'You've certainly polished the diamond.'

It was said in a manner that would have made a lesser woman smack him, and a lesser man than Holmes knock him down. But both of us just upped the wattage of our beams, and as I leant over the table to shake various hands, I loosed a stream of chatter.

'It's *such* a relief to be off that ship and be ourselves again, don't you find it so? (How d'you do, Kiko, Mina.) I mean, ships can be so *incredibly* tedious with the sorts of people (Eugene – oh, sorry, Gene, good to meet you.) one is trapped with, the only thing one can do is either spend the whole trip tipsy or just go grey and dull like the others. I *swear*, we haven't been completely sober since we got off – and the first thing I did was go and spend some of Bobby's money!'

Robert Russell spoke up from my side. 'One thing my Mary's good at is spending money.'

In fact, while I was submitting to torture in the salon that afternoon, it had been Holmes who rounded up half a dozen expensive sparklies. I held one of them out now, an ornate snarl of silver, pearls, jade, and enamel weighing down my right wrist. The two girls oohed over it while the three men calculated its worth. Holmes and I preened over the monstrosity for a while, then stood back.

'Well, it was lovely to see you again,' I gushed at Tommy, following it with an inclusive smile at the others. 'We're off to eat – isn't it nice to have something other than rice! Why, even Prince Chichi—'

Perfectly on beat, Holmes cut in. 'Mary, let's be a bit discreet about throwing names around.'

I made a little exclamation of mingled irritation and embarrassment, doing my best to summon a faint blush. 'Sorry, sweetie, he was just – oh, there I go again! Never mind,' I said to the others. 'I hope you've been having as grand a time here as we have. Perhaps we shall meet again, if you're staying at the Imperial?'

'Of course. Some of us, anyway,' said Tommy. 'Gene's a permanent fixture here, has a flat in the city. Say, I don't suppose you'd like to accompany us to a club, later?'

'Oh, I'd love—' I began, at the same time that Holmes let loose a repressive grumble.

'After today, I'm a bit tired,' he complained.

It was time to distance myself from the man who had humiliated the aristocratic card shark. I turned to Holmes, making my eyes wide in the fashion of Clara Bow. 'But *I'm* not, and you promised me . . . Would you mind, if I went along with them? Just for a little?'

'I want my dinner,' he stated.

'Well, me, too.' I turned to Tommy again. 'Where were you thinking of going? I could maybe catch you up, if . . .'

The polished Gene replied. 'I thought they'd like a visit to the Caramel Box. It's a new jazz club just off the Ginza, very popular with young people and foreigners.'

In the end, I said that I'd join them there for a time if my energy hadn't lagged (meaning: if my fuddy-duddy of a husband didn't stop me) and we passed on to the dining room, into a realm of tables laden with more meat than I had seen in weeks.

'Holmes, your grin is slipping,' I murmured.

'Part of the act,' he replied. He intercepted the waiter, to pull out my chair, although he did allow the fellow to drape me with the table napkin.

Wine where my palate had grown accustomed to clean tea; meat where I wished for rice and pickle; conviviality when I craved a peaceful turn through the garden, or curling up with one of the books from which I had long been separated. But we played our act to the hilt, and attracted the amused smiles of those around us, and were rewarded, just as I laid a hand on Holmes' arm to deliver a loving gaze, to see our would-be friends pass by the door: I caught the eyes of both Tommy and Gene, before withdrawing my hand and using it to raise my wine glass to Holmes.

How we both got through the meal without gagging, I do not know.

Even with a determined sleight of hand – tiny sips, tinier top-ups of the glass, a heavy meal, and three outright exchanges of my full glass for Holmes' empty one – I was fairly pie-eyed at the end of the meal. Holmes, having taken the brunt of the two bottles, had no need to feign inebriation. We walked from the room more or less holding each other upright. Once behind closed doors, he dropped heavily onto the bed and ran a hand over his face.

'I am out of training when it comes to wit . . . withstanding alcohol,' he said, his voice precise.

'You'll have a head on you tomorrow, Holmes. I'd better go, before they decide to move on. Will you be all right?'

'Shall I ask you the same question when you roll through the door in the wee hours?'

'I'll try not to wake you.' I fetched my coat, settled my good hat over my crisp hairdo, and opened the door.

'Watch your back, Russell,' he warned.

There was greater risk of him falling out of bed than in me

falling into dangerous company, but I did not say so: he was Holmes, so he would let me go. At the same time, he was Holmes, and he would worry.

I rolled in, as Holmes had it, well after three, trying to tiptoe until I tripped over a carpet and sent shoes and handbag flying from my hands. The room's snores stopped for a moment, then resumed.

In the morning, both of us were bleary with headache and hoarse from our attempts at ridding our stomachs of excess.

Tea – Japanese – and rice were all we could manage until noon.

I dug through my trunks, finally uncovering the pair of glasses with smoked lenses, and we crept down to the dining room, valiantly concealing our every wince at the noisy hotel. The day was distressingly bright. We chose the dimmest corner possible in which to nurse ourselves back to some semblance of cheer.

Holmes, having stopped his intake some hours earlier than I, was in slightly better condition, but even he passed up the noisy salad to concentrate on soup. When I had plumbed the depths of the bowl, I felt almost human. Laying down my spoon, a vague memory pushed to the surface.

'I think I may have agreed to go somewhere with those girls. Shopping, was it?' I frowned, then shook my head – stopping abruptly as it set my skull to spinning. 'Can't remember.'

'"Shopping" to them would mean dresses and make-up rather than books or art,' he noted.

'Make-up – that's it!'

'You agreed to accompany two Japanese Flappers to buy make-up?'

'Not quite. One of them – Mina, the one who speaks English' – the other one, Kiko, being merely the proud possessor of many English words – 'has a sister who works as a geisha. She thought I'd like to

227

see the process they go through, getting dressed for the evening.' A plate of food had appeared before me, although I couldn't remember having requested it. I picked up my utensils with a somewhat grim determination.

'You remember we have a meeting with Miss Sato today?' he asked.

'I do – and I did. The problem is, I must have more clothing, if we are going to spend the next few days looking fashionable. I may have to give up one meeting or the other.'

'I will have some free hours, if you wish me to order you some frocks.' My knife and fork paused. Certainly he knew my measurements down to the half-inch, but he was a man – and moreover, a man who had come of age when women wore bustles. 'You need not trust my taste,' he added. 'Any dress-shop recommended by this hotel will provide the sort of clothing you need.'

'Since it's more a matter of disguise than of taste, I'm sure that a disinterested party would come up with more suitable raiment than either of us. I'll give you a list of what I'll need. If you don't mind spending your afternoon among ladies' fashion,' I added.

'It is a new role for me,' he remarked serenely. 'That of poodle-faker.'

I nearly spewed a mouthful of peas across the tablecloth.

CHAPTER TWENTY-FOUR

How one dresses here!
Jewels and silken glitter, or
Blossoms in the hair?

BEFORE LEAVING THE VILLAGE, Holmes and I had sat down with Haruki-san and her father to design a campaign for the invasion of Lord Darley's party and a retrieval of the Prince Regent's book. Specific details would have to wait until we had compiled information – hence today's meeting with Haruki-san.

Had it been a different sort of party, other members of the Sato clan could have filtered in. However, Darley's purpose – his ostensible purpose – was to court the Imperial family and a collection of influential Japanese and Western businessmen, politicians, newspaper owners, aristocrats, and what-have-you. The owner of a small onsen in the hills and a young woman with a severely limited shipboard wardrobe held little chance of an invitation. Presentable Europeans, however, might be welcomed, to fill out the kind of amiable, Western setting Darley desired.

We followed Haruki-san's instructions to the meeting-place, making sure we were not followed. The designated shop appeared to sell nothing but jars in the shape of cats, with minor varieties of size and colour. The tiny dried-apple of a woman behind the counter bowed, sucked in her breath past toothless gums, and ushered us through a low door half-covered by fabric (also printed with cats).

The back room was marginally larger than the front, and seemed to be the living quarters for the shopkeeper and her family. The old woman's grandson was hunched before the tiny fire – but no.

'Haruki-san,' I exclaimed. 'That's a very effective disguise.'

She grinned, demonstrating the over-large front teeth beneath the thin moustache, and removed the round glasses of a caricature Oriental, leaving the slicked-back hair, dumpy black suit, and highly polished shoes so ill-fitting, they could only be hand-me-downs.

'You look like a poor student hunting for a job.'

'Would you give me one?' she asked curiously.

Frankly, I thought, as a prospective employer I would avoid a candidate with that much intelligence and mischief in her eyes. 'If I did, I would be certain that I had your loyalty for life.'

'Good. Tea?'

We knelt on the thin mats to enjoy the pale, hot drink. When she had poured our second cups, she began.

'There has been an interesting development. I had a letter from Lady Darley yesterday, asking if I might be available to translate at the party.'

'Ah,' said Holmes.

'That puts a rather different light on things,' I said, trying to hide my disappointment. The only reason Holmes and I had become involved was because of our chances of swindling invitations. If that had changed . . .

'Not necessarily,' she said, 'although it does simplify matters a little. We had intended to slip one or two of our people inside – as hotel staff of one kind or another. My being invited within means I can infiltrate openly, rather than having to take a position as a maid.'

'Are you assigned a specific person to translate for?' I asked.

'I am there for His Highness the Prince Regent.'

'Do you think that a good idea?' Holmes' tone indicated that he did not. 'You and your father wished to avoid a direct connexion with His Highness during this episode.'

'As we have. My invitation comes from Lady Darley, after two of her planned-for translators fell ill.'

'Convenient. And unnecessary.'

'I agree with my father, that one of us ought to be there. We had considered having His Highness recommend his favourite juggler to entertain the Darleys' guests, but this is not that sort of a party.'

'Nor is Darley stupid enough to allow free rein to a blackmail victim,' I noted. 'Anyone openly requested by the Prince Regent would be highly suspect. One would not want your father handed a poisoned cup the moment he appeared.'

'You have others there,' Holmes said, not a question.

She shook her head. 'If we do, it is best you not know.'

'My dear young thing, neither Russell nor I is raw enough to be caught shooting meaningful glances at co-conspirators.'

'Nonetheless, you do not need to know.'

And that was all she would tell us. We agreed to a means of delivering a message to her, if and when we achieved an invitation. Other than that, the next time we saw her would be at the party itself.

I laid down my cup. 'Well, I have an appointment with a

geisha, and Holmes intends to spend the afternoon investigating Tokyo's world of ladies' fashion. We shall see you on Friday.'

> *In fine new clothing*
> *I feel so unlike myself,*
> *I am another.*

Bashō's poem ran through my mind as I stared aghast at the cheval mirror later that evening. 'You honestly thought this frock appropriate for your wife?'

'Good Lord, no. But for the young bride of "Bobby Russell"? I fear so.'

I sighed. 'The glasses don't go with it.'

'It is not the dress of a bluestocking,' he agreed. Easy for him to say: he had perfect vision, and he could wear the same evening suit every night of the week. 'How was your afternoon with the geisha?'

I contorted myself, trying to catch a glance of the garment's back. I would have to wear shoes with heels. 'Surprisingly interesting. One almost begins to suspect that the Floating World contains the most sensible women in Japan.' Certainly the most clever conversationalists. I told him about the Flapper's sister, who had mastered the traditional arts of *samisen*, dance and waiting on drunken men, then gone on to do the same with the parallel arts of the twentieth century. 'I wouldn't have thought a person in full kimono could manage a Charleston, but she did. A somewhat constricted version of it, at any rate.' She also knew the words to many American songs, could discuss (in simple, charmingly accented English) the relative merits of Lillian Gish and Louise Brooks, and seemed to have a better understanding of the stock market than I did. She also played a mean game of poker.

'Geisha is all about entertainment, and she's expanding her realm to the Western world. She seems to be doing very well for herself, too. And that reminds me,' I added, looking around my mascara brush at him. 'I bought you a gift. It's in my handbag, there.'

With considerable suspicion – we did not, in the general course of things, buy each other gifts – he picked up the small bag and worked the clasp. The box inside bore the usual meticulous Japanese presentation, with perfectly folded wrapping paper and a decorative twine designed to complement not only the paper, but the contents and the giver as well. He tugged, unfolded, opened . . . and winced.

When it comes to evening wear, a man's options for peacockery are somewhat limited. Unless Holmes were willing to stoop to some shocking heresy – a wristwatch, say, or a cummerbund – that left the width of his lapel, the pattern of braid on his trousers, or the weave of his white silk scarf – a garment generally abandoned at the door.

However, if I were to be a flighty young thing, some degree of iconoclasm would only be expected of my escort. Therefore, my mad addition to his wardrobe.

'Cufflinks?'

'And studs.'

'One cannot wear—'

'Sherlock Holmes cannot wear cufflinks other than the standard black studs. But Robert Russell? Go wild, Holmes.'

He prised one of the objects from its box, tilting it towards the light. It was, in fact, mostly black. However, the parts that were not . . .

'I do not think I could eat my dinner, looking at these.'

'You won't be looking at your own cufflinks, Holmes, and everyone else will find them nicely daring.'

'I do not think . . .'

'Holmes, if I must wear this, you have to wear those.'

His eyes came up, and studied the dress he had . . . well, I couldn't precisely accuse him of *choosing* it, but he had approved it to the extent of exchanging money for it.

Where the garment lacked fringe, it had sequins; where it had neither, it was caked with garish embroidery and – to prove money was no object – seed pearls. It looked like an explosion in a haberdashery.

With a matching bandeau for my hair.

The cufflinks I had chosen for him were oval, and two millimetres larger than his usual studs. Their shiny black surface was circled by a pencil-thin line of red enamel, and set with a ruby approximately one millimetre across. The stone had been mounted deliberately off-centre.

He shuddered, then cast another look at my dress. Wordlessly, he proceeded to thread the offending objects through his cuffs. I resumed my work at the mirror. The bandeau resembled a fallen doll's-house chandelier.

When I had finished, I tucked my arm in his. We looked at the reflection in the glass, gave identical shakes of our heads, and turned to head for the night life.

The salon was in full swing. Mina, the geisha's sister, was there, although Kiko had been replaced by half a dozen other Japanese Flappers, wearing more expensive clothing and speaking better English.

A piano was pounding out music that I eventually decided was a string of American songs, although they were either in a different scale or the instrument needed tuning. That didn't stop the people, however, who shouted merrily over it and occasionally jittered to the beat, although the salon was both carpeted and too crowded for dancing. The cigarette smoke was heavy, the alcohol fumes positively hazardous, and we had no trouble locating our 'friends' of the night before.

And this time, their circle included the object of all this folderol: Lord Darley.

The man, as one might expect of a person with grey in his hair, looked somewhat less enchanted with his surroundings than his son did. Even his wife looked amused at the tumult.

I felt Holmes summon a deep breath very like my own. Then we both pasted on expressions of committed gaiety and moved into the crowd.

Twenty minutes or so later, the last intervening clot of individuals shifted away and we found ourselves face to face with the Darleys. The countess was flushed, the earl was drunk, and they were both astonished to see us.

'The Russells! Dear, look, it's those lovely people from the ship.'

'Old chap!' he exclaimed, sticking out a hand to Holmes, whose hesitation was imperceptible. 'Good to spot someone who isn't twelve years old among this lot!'

'Have you been in Tokyo all this time?' she asked. 'Why haven't we seen you before this?'

Most of that I got by reading her lips, then I leant forward to shout, 'No, we just arrived a couple of days ago. We've been seeing something of the country, what a fascinating place! But now we've made it here, we're certainly going to stay for a while. I had an absolutely *spellbinding* time yesterday with one of Tommy's Japanese friends, her sister is actually a *geisha*, can you believe it? And she invited us to come along and watch her sister get ready for an evening – Lord! I thought dressing for a garden party at the Palace was an ordeal!'

My voice sounded brittle to my own ears, the words too filled with naive gusto for belief. However, in a room that noisy, it is necessary in any event to over-emote, and neither of the Darleys seemed to find anything odd in my transformation from shipboard bluestocking to enthusiastic social butterfly. So I continued gushing, until Lady Darley cut in with a question about one of the shops I'd visited.

She and I talked commerce for a time, while Holmes kept Darley entertained with a largely invented tale of Japanese railways, his distaste for the man firmly tucked behind Bobby Russell's amiable facade. At last, as I was racking my memory for intriguing items to spend money on, she gave a quick exclamation and glanced at the diamond-studded wristwatch she wore.

'Oh, darling,' she exclaimed, 'we told Mr Takahashi we would meet him at eight. Time to run! So nice to meet you again, Mrs Russell, I hope we meet again.'

Oh, God, I thought: would we have to perform this charade again tomorrow night? 'It was indeed,' I told her. 'If you'd like me to arrange a visit to the geisha, I'd be happy to go along a second time. There's a lifetime of lessons there!'

'Perhaps they'd like dinner one night?' Holmes interjected. 'What about that funny little place down the Ginza?'

'It would have to be the first part of next week, I'm afraid,' Lady Darley replied. 'We're scheduled to leave on Thursday, and this week is rather heavily booked.' And just when I was having to restrain my tongue from blurting out a demand to attend her party, she turned to place a dainty hand on her husband's arm. 'In fact, darling, we could use another pair of handsome faces on Friday, couldn't we?'

'Capital idea, m'dear! Capital! By all means, do come, you two.'

'Are you by chance free, Friday evening?' Lady Darley asked us. 'It's just that we're having a little party for some rather important Japanese leaders. I can't really tell you their names – security, you know? And it seems that, although a year ago we'd have had no problem filling the room with the right kind of English people, since the earthquake, civilians to balance the officers and diplomatic staff have become rather thin on the ground. You do have evening wear?' Her eyebrows rose in concern. Or was it a sudden memory of the Bohemian figure of the *Thomas Carlyle?*

'Of course,' I told her. 'I could even dig out the old tiara, if you wish.' She looked reassured; he looked proud; Holmes looked near to boiling over.

We made our escape from the salon two minutes after the Darley heads passed through the doorway. We spent the rest of the evening in our rooms, wearing pyjama trousers and yukata kimonos, quietly turning the pages of our respective books. In addition, having achieved our invitation meant that we were now blessed with an entire thirty-six hours of freedom in which to map the battlefield, collect information, synchronise plans with our collaborator – and see something of Tokyo.

In the end, our Tokyo sightseeing was done mostly through the windows of various motorcars, although I did manage to escape across the way to the park for a stroll among the hanami parties beneath the cherries. And we did catch two or three glimpses of Fuji, when the mountain ventured out from the clouds.

CHAPTER TWENTY-FIVE

Unexpected sights:
Moon on blossoms; prince's laugh;
Fool with a silver tray.

THERE WAS ALWAYS A chance that Darley was better than we thought. A chance that he had recognised Holmes, without showing it. Not that Holmes looked much like the images set before the reading public, but Britain was a small nation, and Darley might move in the kinds of circles that actually knew Holmes the man.

However, we had been watching Darley closely from the moment we encountered him on the ship, and neither of us had caught so much as a trace of suspicion on his face. Holmes was certain of the man's ignorance. I was less sanguine, but I did not believe Darley clever enough to lay a trap that we would walk into.

The blackmailer's one unavoidable moment of vulnerability is when the exchange is made. No matter what threats he raises or how thoroughly he has locked away the object being ransomed, be it incautious love letter or key to an Empire, at some point he or a trusted representative must creep out from the dark corner to trade it for payment.

Darley's protection lay both in numbers and in the Prince Regent's reluctance to bring matters into the light. Unless the

Prince wished to risk exposure, the exchange could be made in the centre of a crowded room, with no one the wiser.

Still, Holmes and I agreed that payment was unlikely to be taken at the beginning of tonight's party. Even a business-like extortionist prizes the gloating. Forcing a Son of Heaven to stand about in a crowded room with a drink in his hand and a hundred people competing for his attentions would be a memory to treasure long after the £20,000 was spent.

The end results of the evening would not do his friend's porcelain business any good, but I doubted that knowledge would trouble the earl's sleep.

By noon Friday, we knew every nook and cranny of Mr Wright's idiosyncratic hotel. The Mayan wonderland was composed of a long central block, the ground floor containing the lobby and dining room, the upper level holding private dining rooms, a parlour, an auditorium, and a wide promenade that connected the entire block with two longer, narrower guest wings. Its footprint resembled a sturdy canoe balanced by a pair of outriggers.

Normally, a party such as that hosted by Lord Darley would be held in the private dining rooms. However, either in the interest of security, or because it was more impressive, the earl and his countess would take over the upper level of an entire wing for the night. Beds and dressing tables were moved out, potted palms and mirrors were brought in, turning the two adjoining rooms at the end of the wing into a private lounge with a dramatic view. The end rooms even had substantial balconies, if the weather permitted.

By the afternoon, decorative screens tended by bodyguards were obscuring the wing. From that point on, no one would be permitted entrance without either an invitation or a hotel uniform.

Between the party and the guard station lay the Darleys' actual rooms, on either side of the corridor. Convenient for Darley: rather than distort the fit of his evening wear with a bulky rectangle, he merely needed to slip away from his party and retrieve the book.

But not if Holmes and I found it first.

Our initial plan had been just that: slip away from the party when it was at its peak and find the book. Once Haruki-san was brought in as translator, we had another set of eyes, early warning in case one of the Darleys left the party.

My first intimation that all would not go as planned came when I walked up the corridor and into the converted guest rooms, and found myself face to face with the Emperor's Fool.

Sato-san's quizzical face rose incongruously out of a waiter's formal garb, his sword arm holding a silver platter laden with champagne flutes. The tray moved smoothly down before us. 'Champagne, Sir, Madam-san?'

Holmes recovered first. He seized two glasses, pressing one into my hand. Sato-san bowed and moved on to the next guest. Neither the bow nor the pronounced hitch in his gait (rendered more pronounced by a pair of overly-large but brilliantly shined shoes) caused the wine to shift so much as a millimetre on the tray. 'Drink your wine and stop staring, Russell,' my husband ordered.

I reflexively downed a large swig, stifling a cough. 'What does this mean?' I muttered to him, my teeth clenched behind a bright grin.

'When Miss Sato arrives, we shall ask her. Now let us say hello to our hosts.'

The earl was in his full panoply of decorations and honours, everything short of a Lord Mayor's collar. Thomas had gone in the opposite direction, with a pristine chest and the glow of youth about him; he looked like a motorcar advert. Lady Darley's dress could only have come from Paris, in an unusual shade of burnt orange that did wonderful things to her upswept chestnut hair. As one might expect, there were diamonds in her heavy necklace, long earrings, and tiara, but the stones were interspersed with lesser gems that threw off distinctly golden sparkles: topaz, perhaps, or orange sapphire.

My dress was really quite nice, my emeralds nothing to be ashamed of, but standing before this woman, I felt like an oversized schoolgirl fumbling along in her mother's patent leather shoes.

We got through the greetings, followed by two and a half minutes of inane talk and admiration. My glass emptied fast, and I was looking around for the stocky waiter with the limp when half the room came to attention, including the earl's family.

Holmes and I dropped from the Darleys' attention like used tissues, as all three of them moved towards the door. In it stood the Prince Regent, Haruki-san at his elbow and a large man with suspicious eyes at his back. The Prince wore impeccable formal garb of the European style, but Haruki-san was dressed in a stunning kimono in shades of green, an architectural wig concealing her short hair. Even next to the Prince Regent, she looked tiny.

Stillness settled over the noisy room, broken only by the rustle of silk gowns and the receding tinkle of crystal brushing crystal.

'Welcome, Your Highness,' Darley's voice boomed. 'Thank you for coming to my little party.'

The earl stopped in front of the Prince Regent and thrust out his hand. The Prince looked down, and for an instant, the room was filled with the clash of steel and the coppery reek of arterial blood. Darley's eyes stretched wide for an instant before his head parted from its shoulders, toppling to the floor while the wrath of Japan . . . but, no. The moment passed, and the 124th Emperor of the Land Where the Sun Is Born, this direct descendant of the gods,

241

this slim figure for whom every man, woman, and child in the land would willingly die, reluctantly held out his fingers and permitted the Englishman to pump them once or twice.

I shivered. How did Darley dare touch him, with those waves of godlike fury pounding the room? The bodyguard had come to sharp attention; Haruki-san almost swayed with it, and I could feel Holmes' tension from ten feet away. The very room creaked – at any rate, its occupants shifted. But not the Darleys: man, wife, and son, they merely smiled, and smiled.

Haruki-san recovered, her translation stuttering back into life. The Prince gave a brief bow to Lady Darley, and what amounted to a nod to the viscount.

'Beautiful evening, isn't it?' Darley asked. 'I saw the Palace gardens as I went past them this afternoon. Those cherry trees you have are magnificent. I was telling my wife that we'll have to take some home with us. They'd be gorgeous in our garden in London.'

It was difficult not to read a double meaning into the words, but the Prince did not so much as clench his jaw at the possessive overtures of this English enemy. Either that, or Haruki-san toned the words down in the translation. Lady Darley, who may or may not have understood the reason for the Prince's expressionless features, stepped forward and asked if His Highness cared for a glass of champagne.

I looked around, wondering uneasily what the future Emperor would do when confronted with the onsen owner of Mojiro-joku in a hotel uniform, but the thin older man who stepped forward with a tray looked nothing like him. Indeed, Sato-san was nowhere in sight.

I met Holmes' gaze: if the man was not here, we probably knew where to find him.

* * *

Our original plan had been to take turns out of the room, since the absence of both Russells at once might cause notice. However, that plan had long blown to the four winds, so as soon as the Prince Regent's entourage moved towards the viewing windows, Holmes slipped from the room, with me following a bare minute later.

The screens blocking this section of the wing made it simple. Holmes already had the door unlocked; I stepped into the suite.

Sato-san gave me a friendly nod, then bent awkwardly to resume his search of the earl's wardrobe.

I opened my mouth, but there were both too many questions and none. Instead, I turned to Holmes, head down at Lord Darley's bedside table. 'I thought the Prince was about to turn his guard loose on Darley.'

'The temptation was apparent.'

'Why didn't he?'

But Sato-san answered me from the wardrobe, his voice muffled by clothing. 'The Son of Heaven is guided by his advisors. Since he was first laid on his nursemaid's breast, the Prince has been schooled against the impulse act. Personal desire will always come second to an agreed course of action.'

I kept picturing those limp fingers in the strong grip of a foreign blackmailer. A peasant's life for me.

I tugged off my long kid gloves and got to work. We turned the suite upside-down, scrupulously returning every item to its position. Holmes started in the earl's room with Sato-san, while I moved next door to sort through Lady Darley's gowns and frocks, furs and hatboxes. I ran attentive fingers along all the edges of her furniture, lifted her mattress, opened the drawer in her bedside table. There I found a pretty blue Moroccan leather box. I was excited for a moment, and picked it up, lifting its top, staring down at the contents, wondering what . . .

I closed it hastily, trying not to picture the two Darleys making use of those objects. There had been a couple of items whose purpose I could only guess at, but with the others, it was all too clear. And sitting there in the drawer for maids to see, as if its contents were no more exotic than the tube of lavender-scented hand crème, or the violet cachous, or the ornately bound Bible! Well, that last was a bit exotic: a large volume with a spine so perfectly hinged, the inner pages did not so much as shift when I flipped open its front cover. I closed it, thumbed the latch shut, and arranged the . . . other things as they had been on its top.

Then closed the drawer and knelt to feel around the rest of the small table.

Nothing there. No slipcover book of illustrated poems, nor the document it hid, in the entire room.

We met up at the doorway between his quarters and hers.

'Could it be in Tommy's rooms across the hall?' I asked.

'Either there or in the hotel safe.'

'One of us had better get back to the party.'

'You go.'

I did not argue. Holmes was welcome to search the young man's bedside table. I worked the long gloves back up my arms, then opened the door a crack, to check that the corridor was empty. We left the suite, me for the end rooms and the two men for the son's suite across the way.

The party had grown louder as darkness approached, helped by bouncy music played by a mixed quartet of Western and Japanese men in evening wear. The Prince Regent was still by the windows, Haruki-san at his elbow.

I plucked a half-empty glass from a sideboard and edged into the room in the lee of a group of tall young men, including the inescapable Monty Pike-Elton. The group laughed at some no doubt off-colour joke, and I joined in. They heard my voice and shifted back to incorporate me into their circle. Young Pike-Elton looked at me – then looked again.

'You know, Mrs Russell, if it weren't for those glasses, I'd never have recognised you.' His smile became frankly appreciative.

I gave him a tipsy-sounding laugh, and asked how they had been enjoying Tokyo.

A bit later I glanced into the room. Lady Darley was looking in my direction, so I raised my borrowed glass at her, eyes beaming in appreciation of her party, then returned my gaze to the circle of men.

Things went on this way for an interminable ten or fifteen minutes, as the windows went dark and the quartet began to repeat itself. Finally, Lord Darley made his move – although it was not the move I anticipated.

With a hand resting on his son's shoulder, the earl clambered onto one of the chairs that had been pushed back to the wall. The band fell silent, and his voice rang out over the still-shouting voices.

'Thank you all for joining us tonight, I hope you've enjoyed the champagne, thanks to my friend hosting this little bash – and thanks to my clever wife, who put it all together. But now Lady Darley and I have a little surprise for you. Our prayers were answered by a lovely soft night, so we've had Imperial set up dinner on the roof. They even have warm wraps, for those of you who didn't arrive from outside, so pick up your garments and come up the stairs for dinner – and another surprise!'

I had about thirty seconds to warn Holmes, and did so by darting into the corridor and giving a sharp whistle. But there was no time for him and Sato-san to escape, since the first guests were on my very heels. I paused to let the excited gabble wash past me, then watched, heart in throat, as Thomas Darley marched down the hall to his room and flung open the door.

I waited for the explosion. And waited. And three minutes later, when the migration was thinning and Lord and Lady Darley were about to bring up the rear, young Darley came out, brushing a splash of water from his cuff before shrugging into his ebony overcoat.

I let out my breath, and walked past his rooms to ours, fetching my warmest shawl.

The earl's second surprise was searchlights. The party came together again on the hotel roof, where in good weather films were shown and constellations admired. Tonight, it had been transformed into a grotto of potted palms and Oriental statues, with strings of fairy lights creating a rooftop of artificial stars. When all the guests had fresh glasses, Lord Darley gave an order to one of the hotel staff. The man trotted away, and with a series of clicks, the lights went off. Darkness held for a few seconds, and then a searchlight beam split the night. The party gasped as one after another, half a dozen brilliant spotlights, mounted on the highest reaches of the hotel and on several nearby buildings, pointed down into the gardens that lay all around us, beginning at our feet and extending across to Hibiya Park and the Palace itself. The cherry trees, which in daylight were delicate clouds, burst into a sea of startling white. It was utterly unexpected, and completely spectacular.

It took me a moment to remember why we were here, and what this considerable distraction might be covering. I looked around for the Prince – but there he was, standing at a slight remove from the rest, gazing down at a city transformed into a stage set by the cheque-book of an English interloper.

I wondered what was going through his mind.

I felt Holmes at my shoulder, and murmured, 'I hope you weren't hiding in Tommy's wardrobe?'

He shook his head. 'Under the bed.'

'Good thing this isn't a ryokan. What now?'

'Now,' he said in bitter tones, 'unless we can intercept the final exchange, you and I will have the singular opportunity of watching the future Emperor of Japan pay off an English blackmailer.'

The Darleys took their places at the end table. The Prince was seated at the head, with Lady Darley at his right and the earl beside her, and Haruki-san on the Prince's left, followed by Tommy. The bodyguard merged into a potted palm.

Holmes, who had bluntly overridden seating protocol in favour of having me at his side, now spoke into my ear. 'One of those three will leave to fetch the book. If it's Lady Darley, you go after. I'll take the earl, and Sato-san can watch Tommy.'

But watch as we might, none of them slipped away. The fairy lights were lit again, the guests were seated, soup arrived. Fish, meat, endless courses of English food: bland, overcooked, tasteless.

Sato-san worked his way up and down between the tables, serving wine. Judging by his aroma and the increasing lurch to his gait, he was sampling it as well. The Prince Regent listened to Haruki-san's translations of Darley comments, looking as inscrutable as any Oriental face ever was. I could feel Holmes beside me quivering with suppressed desire to do *something*.

The last course was cleared. Next came dessert.

Holmes and I saw it at the same moment, and sat up sharply. When a platoon of white-hatted cooks appeared with carts, it could only mean the drama of crêpes Suzette. The most distracting dish in a chef's repertoire.

All eyes turned to the cart nearest them – all eyes but ours. The drama began, the chefs lit their burners in preparation, and Lord Darley raised his table napkin to his lips and set it aside. Then to our surprise, the earl bent forward, feeling under the surface of the table in front of his knees. His shoulders gave a small jerk. He then leant over to say something in his wife's ear before silently easing back his chair and striding off into the shadows.

Carrying something in his right hand.

We had failed.

Lady Darley bent to deliver her husband's message to the Prince. He sat for a moment, gazing into nothing. Then, with the expression of a young soldier determined to face his firing squad with dignity, his shoulders went forward. His chair slid back. Haruki-san looked at him. His raised hand ordered her to stay where she was. Once on his feet, he made the same gesture, with greater emphasis, to the bodyguard standing behind him.

And the future Emperor of Japan followed Lord Darley away from the mesmerised dinner guests, into the shadows at the edge of the rooftop veranda.

We could not intervene. Anything we did in this too-public venue would point back to the Prince Regent, raising questions, accusations, repercussions. So, ransom would be paid; a potential friend of England would be forever alienated. Weeks of preparation, words of promise, the love we had come to feel for this magnificent country – and all we had left was the taste of ashes in our mouths.

But the taste was more than Haruki-san could bear. She pushed back her chair to hurry in her Prince's wake. Lady Darley, looking surprised, followed her first with her eyes, then in fact. Then Tommy laid his own napkin onto the table and trailed along, with the dark figure of the bodyguard bringing up the rear.

This migration of the better part of the high table drew notice where a mere two men had not. A dozen pairs of eyes followed the green kimono and the silken gown, winking with the fairy lights and the gouts of flame from the Grand Marnier. Twenty others noticed their preoccupation, and turned to see.

What they saw was this: two men – host and honoured guest – standing at the dim reaches of the veranda. Joining them, the small Japanese woman, then the earl's wife and son. The large figure that had watched over the Prince all night went, too, pausing away from the others.

And then from stage left: the wine waiter, his face wearing the look of serenity one sees on a statue of the Buddha, or a man profoundly drunk. He was frankly weaving, pursuing the others with his tray, determined to provide them with his wine if it was the last thing he did. The clot of figures gathered around the Prince Regent, heads down in urgent conversation, did not notice.

The waiter's upraised tray flared light as his uneven progress caused it to waver first this way, then that. The dinner party held its collective breath, watching aghast as the series of would-be recoveries took their toll on the man's precarious balance. He lurched in an attempt to compensate, and that was one trial too many for the tray at the end of his fingers. One of the laden glasses teetered, tipped, nearly returned to its place, but finally gave up its argument with gravity, vaulting lightly over the side of the tray. Up it went, over it turned, and down it came, to land with unbelievable precision straight above the back of Lady Darley's gown. She shrieked at the cold champagne bath, gloved arms snapping up in reaction. One of her outflung hands hit the tray: silver, crystal, and bubbly wine exploded in all directions.

But the polished silver disk was not finished with its path of destruction. In a move a cinema crew would have laboured over for days, its fluted edge lifted the tiny translator's elaborate wig from her head, tossing it in the direction of Lord Darley's face. Reflexively, his hands jerked out. The brisk sequence of pratfalls raised stifled snorts and titters from the tables; those facing the other direction started to turn in their seats. And all might still have been well, except that the waiter's over-large shoe then caught the edge of a tile. He stumbled, his inebriated waver turning into a heavy forward stagger.

Monty Pike-Elton's bray rose up: 'That drunken fool is going—'

The wine waiter tried hard to catch his balance. Instead, he caught Lord Darley.

The object in Darley's hand shot into the air as the smaller man slammed him back into the railing, and then – beyond. Incomprehensibly, horribly, the earl and the waiter were simply . . . gone.

Embarrassed laughter strangled in fifty throats. I rose, my nails biting into Holmes' sleeve as I waited for that quizzical face to pop up over the edge again. And waited. Electrified silence stretched unbearably; hands remained frozen mid-air.

And then the first woman screamed.

The Prince Regent disappeared long before the police arrived, bundled away by his translator, leaving behind the bodyguard. Who, it turned out, had seen remarkably little of anything.

Few of the guests noticed how deftly the translator had snatched the earl's dropped object from its trajectory. None of them saw her press it into the Prince's hand, nor did they see how closely he clutched a dark rectangular shape in one hand and a white envelope in the other. She hurried him towards the stairway, but His Highness was not the only one to make a hasty and discreet exit. Those who remained were busy pushing forward to see the two figures tangled together in the garden below. The reactions of the people who rushed out to assist made it clear that both were dead. The earl's neck, it turned out, was broken, even though the waiter appeared to have landed first. One brilliantly shined shoe gleamed in the garden lights from a drift of shed blossoms, twenty feet away.

Talk ran wild through the city for a few days, particularly among the less inhibited Western community. But when the newspapers said nothing, and when it was given to understand that the Prince had in fact left some time before the accident, that it was his bodyguard everyone had seen speaking with Lord Darley, not Hirohito himself, the talk subsided.

No one could provide a name for the drunken waiter. A terrible accident. The humiliated management of the Imperial Hotel prostrated themselves in all directions, and quietly tore up the sizeable bill for the Darley stay. Three days after the incident, the two remaining members of the family quietly sailed away. In the end, Lady Darley and the new earl took the old earl's body with them: they had been mysteriously unable to obtain a Japanese burial permit.

Holmes and I moved out of the Imperial that same night, to a lovely quiet traditional ryokan just outside the geisha district. There, on Sunday morning, an invitation was delivered, by a uniformed footman who walked across our tatami in stockinged feet to deliver the ornately calligraphed missive. He bowed, took a few steps backwards, bowed again, and stood waiting. Lacking a gold-and-ivory letter opener, Holmes thrust his thumb under the flap of the suede-textured envelope. Several layers later, he came to the meat of the matter.

'We are invited to call upon the Prince Regent at his home, at two this afternoon.'

'If he tries to give us a medal I'm going to throw it in his face,' I said. The corners of my eyes kept catching on objects they imagined to be shiny black shoes.

'You will not.'

'Holmes, you go.'

His grey eyes held mine. 'Sato-san might have been the closest that young man had to a friend.'

After a minute, I sighed. 'Two o'clock is fine.'

The Palace was a short walk away, although once we had shown the guards the invitation and proved that we were neither assassins nor, worse, photographers, the walk up the long drive from the street took almost as long. The Akasaka Palace was a vast neo-Baroque monstrosity built for the Prince Regent fifteen years earlier. Together with the Imperial Hotel, Tokyo now had a complete set of lessons in the things to avoid in Western architecture.

Up the steps, through the columns, up to the door, through echoing marble and several hundredweight of gilt into a room that would have pleased that other Sun King, Louis. We were parked in a room that looked about as Japanese as I did, with painted ceiling, gilded swags on every exposed inch of plaster, and a pair of massive crystal chandeliers. I eyed them, considering the nature of earthquakes, and declined the damask-and-gilt chairs that lay beneath.

I anticipated a long wait, but to my surprise, in under a minute the door came open.

Looking very small and pale, Haruki Sato stepped in. The muted cotton fabric of her kimono instantly shifted the room from merely gaudy to frankly vulgar.

I was pleased when she led us outside, into the gardens.

The moment we turned down the manicured paths, the Palace and the city beyond faded from all awareness. Here, it was all about the shape of the patches of lawn among the trees, the descent of the tiny stream, the odour of moss, and the intense emerald and scarlet of the unfurling maple leaves.

And above all, the cherry blossoms.

'I am sorry,' I said. 'About your father.'

'You should not be. He was privileged to serve his Prince. And unless the afterlife is a cruel place, his body no longer causes him pain.'

We walked, pausing on a bridge over a pond. Haruki-san pulled a bit of rice-cake out of her sleeve's pocket and crumbled it over the water. A swirl of enormous, brilliant orange and silver carp rose from the muddy depths, all jewelled scales and wide mouths scooping up the crumbs. When the bits were gone and the fish dispersed again, we, too, went on, still in silence.

Around the next corner, Prince Hirohito was seated upon a silken carpet among a stand of blossoming cherry that would have made Hiroshige weep. To one side was a beautifully woven rectangular basket, its top shut. The Prince was wearing a kimono, rather than the Western dress he preferred; a few petals had floated onto his shoulders and hair.

His dark eyes rose to watch us approach. We stopped a distance away, and gave him formal bows.

'Please,' he said. 'Sit.'

We knelt at the far side of the carpet. Haruki-san took up a position halfway between us. He said nothing for a time, his gaze wandering to one side, where a sturdy lichen-covered rock nestled comfortably between the trunks of a pair of cherry trees. One side of its weathered surface had a slight starburst pattern beneath the lichen, as if someone, a thousand years before, had tried to carve a flower there.

After a time, he gave a small sigh, then turned to speak to Haruki-san in his soft voice. When he had finished, she bowed and turned to us.

'His Highness wonders if you have participated in our tradition of hanami?'

'Blossom-viewing?' I shook my head. 'No, although I've seen a lot of people doing so in the parks.'

'It marks spring. It is also a recognition of the transience of beauty, and of life. The blossoms quickly pass, and summer comes. You would not like a Japanese summer,' she added. 'Very hot, very humid, very hard.'

The Prince spoke up again, and after a bow, she moved obediently to open the wicker box – which was, to my surprise, the picnic basket it resembled. But a far cry from English sandwiches and thermoses of tea.

Sake, cold or hot, and tiny lacquered boxes containing a myriad of delicacies savoury and sweet. It was too lovely to eat, but our host gestured at the trays Haruki-san had laid out, so we put a few of the little gems on our plates and accepted cups of sake.

When his cup was empty, he raised his eyes. 'Thank you,' he said in English. 'For what you did Friday night.'

'We did nothing,' Holmes told him. 'We failed. A good man died because of it.'

The young man shook his head gently, and spoke, Haruki-san translating. 'A good man died achieving his highest desire, to serve his Emperor.'

'We—' Holmes started, then stopped at a tiny motion from Haruki-san's fingers. One did not argue with an Emperor. Well, most of us did not.

But as if he had heard my thought, the Prince Regent's features suddenly twisted into an expression that looked remarkably like regret. He said, in English this time, 'In Mojiro-joku, Sato-san make me angry. It is hard for a man, to make his Prince angry. It is

254

good for a prince, to have a . . . friend, who make him angry. Life will be . . . more empty, without Sato-san.'

The three of us sat stunned by this regal admission, until he went on in Japanese, Haruki-san automatically resuming her translation.

'The night before that man's party,' the Prince Regent continued, 'my old friend came to meet me here, in the garden. Sato-san always admired this rock, and told me many times that it was in the wrong place, here. 'The Chrysanthemum needs other flowers,' he would say. I think he wanted me to give it to him, for his own garden in the hills. I would tell him that he was a peasant who did not deserve an Emperor's Chrysanthemum.' The smile on his face was sad, the insult fond.

He withdrew his gaze from the mottled stone, to ask in English, 'Have you been to Kyoto?'

'Mostly the train station,' I replied.

'Take them to Kyoto,' he said to Haruki-san. 'Come back and tell me how beautiful it is.'

So she did.

Many months later, the Chrysanthemum followed us, brought halfway around the world by a ninja's cousin, from an Emperor's garden to an Englishman's flowerbed.

BOOK THREE

Oxford

April 1925

Chapter Twenty-Six

Oxford in the spring:
Tints of pale pink and yellow
But rarely scarlet.

I LAID THE REVOLVER ON the kitchen table as I hurried over to where the daughter of the Emperor's Fool stood bleeding onto my pantry floor.

'How bad is it?' I demanded.

'It looks worse than it is,' she said. I had my doubts – even in her dark blue clothing, I could tell that she was spattered with blood from shoulder to shoe – but her face was no paler than usual and her pain looked more like embarrassment than physical distress.

'Come and sit down,' I told her.

'Close your curtains first,' she said.

I started to ask questions, then shut my mouth and went to switch off the belching kettle and secure my windows – picking up the gun as I crossed the room.

When we were invisible to anyone standing on the back step, I pulled out a chair for her, stuck the gun in the back of my belt, and placed my largest pan under the hot-water tap. As the pan filled, I dug through cabinets, wondering how long it took for Japanese tea to go stale.

Not that someone in Haruki's – Haruki-san's – no, *Haruki*. This was England, and as the automatic bowing had fallen from my shoulders, so had the 'san' left my lips: not that someone in *Haruki's* condition was likely to complain at stale tea.

I placed the tea in front of my guest, shut off the tap, and went to fetch my well-stocked first-aid kit. When I came back, she had tried to get out of her shirt, but in the end, it proved not worth saving. She let me slice it open with the kit's scissors, and we looked at what lay beneath.

I'd thought it would be a knife-slice, because of all the blood, but if so, it had been a terrible blade. The injury was, as she'd said, not deep, but the skin seemed to have been savaged.

'What did this?'

'One of your British iron fences.'

Ah. For a woman of her training to fall into a fence-rail . . . No wonder she was embarrassed.

However, the physical effects of the injury had to be considerable. The metal point had jammed into her arm at a shallow angle, lifting a flap of skin the size of a child's palm. It had bled like crazy, but nothing seemed to be missing. If she could avoid infection, the edges would heal together.

'We need to—'

'No hospitals. No friendly nurses. This is a simple wound. I am sure you have a needle and thread.'

I made a face. 'Haruki, there'll be a generation of filth in there.'

'You do it. You can stitch it. I would have done it myself if I could reach it.'

She would, too. I shook my head at the source of all that blood, then lifted the kit's hidden drawer.

She watched me pinch off a small pellet of the opium paste. I thought she was going to refuse it, so I just stood, holding it out. After a minute, she took it between two bloody fingers and placed it on her tongue, washing it down with tea.

I brought the steaming pan over to let her rinse her good hand, drying it with the pristine kitchen towel Miss Pidgeon had set out on the counter. I then wrapped the towel around her lower arm to catch the ongoing dribble.

'When did you last eat?' I asked.

'This afternoon.' But the drug was already beginning to work – that testified to an empty stomach. I raised one eyebrow. 'Breakfast,' she admitted. 'Tea and rice.'

Wordlessly, I refilled her teacup, then ladled Miss Pidgeon's soup into two bowls, and sawed off some of the fresh bread in the bin. I ate mine; she ate half of hers. I took my time, eating a second slice of the bread. When I walked back from putting my bowl into the sink, her gaze had lost its focus.

To a large extent, it is easier to bear pain than to cause it. Washing the wound created as much distress – to both of us – as I had anticipated, and I was no more skilled a seamstress when it came to flesh than I was at fabric. By the time I had snipped the last length of thread and wrapped her arm in gauze, we were both drenched in sweat. My hands, I thought, were shaking more.

I constructed two fresh cups of tea, then said, 'Stay there.' I trotted upstairs for one of Holmes' old bathrobes – a man's robe being shorter than my own – then stripped her down, sponged her off, and wrapped her in the worn plaid. I led her to the ground-floor guest room, pulling the bedclothes to her chin.

'I will be here. I have a gun. You sleep.'

Back in the sitting room, I ran a hand through my hair, surveying the chairs, the low-burning fire, the calm books. It felt like days since I had brought my things through the front door: according to the clock, it was little more than an hour.

I dumped several ounces of brandy down my throat, cleaned up the carnage in the kitchen, and went through the house, checking the windows and doors. I then stirred up the fire and settled onto my favourite chair, a blanket around my shoulders. The gun was in my lap.

I dozed, on and off. No sound came from the next room; no platoon of ninjas crashed through my windows. Only the ordinary noises of an Oxford night.

At dawn, I rose. Haruki had pushed the covers from her shoulders, but I left them, for fear of waking her. In the dim room, I could see no signs of fever.

I put on the kettle, pulled back the curtains, made some telephone calls. Then I took my mug of tea out into the garden – only when I stepped down to the paving stones, I went open-mouthed with astonishment.

Over the past fifteen months, I had spent a mere handful of days in this house. During one of those rare days, last summer, I had sat with Miss Pidgeon here on my diminutive terrace and talked about the drawbacks of travel. I told her about the intense beauty of Japan, almost shyly confiding my intention to plant a Japanese cherry tree – perhaps in that corner, there. And, O blessed among women, she had heard my longing, and responded.

Japan was now blossoming in Oxford: a sapling no higher than my chin, showing a handful of rich near-white blossoms along its bare branches. Transient loveliness, they would be gone in days.

I walked across the stones and the small patch of lawn to the low rise that was now home to a *Prunus serrulata.* In twenty years, I could host a hanami picnic beneath my very own blossoming tree.

I was still looking at the tiny splashes of white against the weathered red bricks of the wall when I heard a sound behind me. Haruki's face was a lot rosier than my tree; I hoped it was merely from the warm bed.

'Good morning,' I said.

'You shouldn't have let me sleep so long.'

'Why not? It's the best medicine.'

'It is more difficult to leave a place by daylight.'

'All for the better, since you don't need to be anywhere. No one knows you are here, no one comes in. And no one overlooks the garden.'

She glanced out, her eyes lingering on the skinny blossoming twig. 'You have no servants?'

'What would I want servants for? Unless you stand in the front window, no one will see you. Now, what do you like for breakfast?'

I ignored her protestations and assembled the only meal I could cook without having to chip the remains from the skillet and air out the kitchen. I beat eggs, sliced tomatoes, carved bread – and all the while, she talked. I would never have thought her so garrulous, and could not decide if it was a remnant of the opium or the beginnings of fever.

In either case, she talked. I heard about her older brother, who had taken over the running of the inn, and her younger brother, now studying business at Princeton. Then she told me of the much-anticipated birth of the Prince Regent's first child, due in the winter, and Tokyo's progress after the great Kanto quake, and the arrival of the first telephone at the Mojiro-joku onsen. All manner of things – except those that mattered.

Plates were emptied, then moved over to the sink, while she

talked. I retrieved the first-aid box, changed the bandages (the skin was red and oozing, but not dangerously so), and fashioned a sling for her. She rambled on, and on.

Finally, I sat down in front of her, forcing her to meet my eyes.

'I was so very sorry about your father,' I told her.

At this, she fell silent.

'I'm sorry also that I didn't have a chance to know him better. He was a good man.'

She nodded.

'Now, before I put you back to bed, tell me why you're here.'

CHAPTER TWENTY-SEVEN

Proctor's bulldogs stroll
Beneath the faded blue sky,
Quick as a spring breeze.

THE YEAR BEFORE, SOON after the events at the Imperial Hotel, Holmes and I had slipped quietly away from Japan. Any news we had received of the country since then was both second hand and in general terms. Of course, if we had chosen to bring Mycroft into matters, we could have had every iota of detail imaginable, but our return to England had been first delayed, then somewhat chaotic – and when that chaos subsided, a degree of mistrust had crept into my attitude towards my brother-in-law.[3]

We simply assumed that the Prince Regent's book had gone safely back into its former hiding place, and all was well.

But, no.

Haruki did not enjoy voicing any faint criticism of her future Emperor, but in truth, the blame was his. Not the original problem – in 1921, the young Prince could hardly be blamed for not knowing that the gift he carried to King George was anything but an innocent piece

---

[3.] Details found in *The Language of Bees*, *The God of the Hive*, *Pirate King* and *Garment of Shadows*.

of Japanese history. What followed, however, was . . . less excusable.

'As you saw, His Highness received the book that very night. He took it into his own hands. He had bodyguards with him lest anyone think to steal it again. He knew its value, knew that the very future of the Son of Heaven touched upon its safety.'

'Oh, God. Who has stolen it now?'

'No one stole it. The book is where His Highness put it.'

'Then what?'

She sighed. 'It is not the correct book.'

I sank my head into my hands at the table and repressed a groan. 'I don't suppose the Emperor had a second one he didn't tell Prince Hirohito about,' I said after a time.

'Only the one. This is not it. This is a very fine forgery, but when His Highness . . . the Prince Regent . . . when—' She stopped. She cleared her throat. 'His Majesty the Emperor has been unwell – more unwell, I mean.'

'I'm sorry to hear that.'

'His – that is, His Highness the Prince Regent hesitated to bring anything before His Majesty the Emperor that could cause distress. Perhaps if he had brought the matter before His Majesty earlier – if he had not been so very occupied with his new marriage and – well. At any rate, he did not show it to the one Person in all of Japan who might have seen that it was . . . lacking.'

My heart dropped. 'Lacking what?'

'The hidden . . . key.'

'The document? Oh, Lord.'

'Yes. His Highness the Prince Regent took the book that night, carried it back to the Residence, and placed it in his personal vault. He left it there. I suppose . . .' She drew a breath; let it out again. 'He was fond of my father.'

Prince Hirohito was Japan's Regent, but he was also a young man whose only friend had died at his feet. A young man schooled from birth to hide away his emotions – or to hide away those things that provoked emotions. The book reminded him of Sato-san, and of how his own self-perceived carelessness had killed his loyal retainer.

Haruki cradled her arm in the sling, trying to find a comfortable rest for it. 'In November, His Majesty the Emperor took ill – a cold, merely, but every minor illness is a threat. His Highness the Prince Regent has assumed more and more of His Majesty's business over recent years, and at this illness, all of His Majesty's correspondence came to him.

'One of the letters, which His Highness did not see until the third week of November, was from England. It was on stationery he had seen before. The letter was the request for a donation. An enormous donation. His secretaries saw no particular importance in it, merely passing it on for approval before they sent back their polite reply turning down the request. It was fortunate His Highness even saw it. And extremely fortunate that it reached him rather than his Honourable Father.

'Because it contained this.'

Her good hand dipped into the pocket of her robe, and held out a photograph. It showed a narrow book on top of a slipcase, with an object protruding from its pages – but no, not from its pages: the rectangle of paper was sticking out from the book's front cover.

'When His Highness opened the safe to truly look at the book we had retrieved, he saw that its pages were not as worn as he remembered them, and the colours of Hokusai's blue did not seem as vibrant. To be certain, he took a knife to the covers.

'There was no document. No letter. In fact, some of the filler

266

matter used to add bulk to the covers was modern newsprint. *The Times of London.* From March and April, 1923.'

Well, at least that gave us a date for the forgery. 'So the Prince came to you.'

'He sent for us. For my older brother. However, because our father had made me the family's expert in the West, my brother brought me as well. His Highness gave us the letter, the photograph, and the remains of the book, and commanded us to set things right.'

'How big is "enormous"?'

'One hundred thousand pounds sterling.'

'Whoa!'

'Yes.'

'Does His Highness have £100,000?'

'His Highness has all the wealth of Japan. But only if he is willing to turn the matter over to his advisors.'

Which, I reflected, was precisely where we had come into this whole mess.

'So what did you do?'

'We began by replacing the response that the secretaries had composed to the "request" with a reply that was – is the word "noncommittal"? Saying that His Majesty was unwell, but that His Highness would take the donation request under advisement, and would reply in some weeks. We posted the letter the first part of December.

'Immediately, we set about learning as much as we could, as well as restoring the covers of the forged copy of the book. When it was presentable, I sailed for England.'

I thought over the sequence of events, so far as we knew. 'What was the date of Darley's original letter? The one demanding £20,000?'

'October 14, 1923.'

'So: in 1921, Prince Hirohito gives the book to King George. At some point between then and the spring of 1923, some very good forger gets his hands on it long enough to make a remarkably good copy. In October, Lord Darley writes to the Emperor demanding £20,000 for the book's return. In . . . November I think it was, Darley and his new wife and son leave on their world tour, planning to visit Tokyo on the way to pick up their money. The following April, they get to Japan. Darley dies. His wife and her stepson sail home. And six months later, in October, someone writes a second letter demanding five times the initial amount. Did it come from the House of Lords?'

'No. It was from the Darley house in London.'

Wouldn't want some Parliamentarian secretary opening the thing by mistake, I reflected.

'One has to wonder if Darley himself knew of the hidden document.

We assumed that he did, but – do you remember the wording of that first letter?'

'"*Your Royal Majesty, an item of yours has come into my possession, a book of illustrated poetry by Bashō that contains hidden truths. If you wish it back, I should be happy to exchange it for a reward when I am in Tokyo next April, and say no more about it. Yours, James Thomas Edward Darley,*" etcetera.'

'But no photograph.'

'No.'

It sounded increasingly probable that Darley knew nothing of the hidden document, but had merely caught a rumour that the Prince Regent was looking quietly to retrieve his gift to the English King.

But at some point, the secret document had come to light. And come to the hand of someone in the Darley household. The most likely person to have uncovered the document was the forger; however, forgers didn't tend to be politically sophisticated, nor did they tend to branch out into blackmail. That would suggest – I was loath to even think the term – some kind of 'Master Criminal' to link forgery and blackmail. Someone connected to Lord Darley.

I frowned a while, then shook my head and pushed it away: all investigations were a grey confusion at the start.

'And you've been sent to recover the original?' I asked Haruki.

'I brought the repaired forgery, to exchange for it.'

'Any idea where that original is?'

Her rueful smile made her look very young. 'That is proving to be a more complex question than I anticipated. It seems that in 1923, the Palace staff were facing how best to preserve what was clearly a valuable and somewhat fragile piece of art. This book, along with several others, was quietly transferred from the Palace to a place accustomed to caring for old books.'

'Ah,' I said, breathing out my relief. 'The Bodleian.'

'Yes,' she said. 'Do you know it?' Library of libraries, resting place of the Magna Carta and Shakespeare's first folio; Handel's own score and Shelley's personal letters; Tycho's *Instrumentology* and Polo's *Travels*. The Bodleian Library was the reason I was in Oxford.

'You could say that.'

'Good. Then you can help me break in.'

I had to smile. 'I'm not sure that would help much. Unless the book's in an open display case or something, you could search for weeks. The place is a labyrinth.' Light dawned. 'Does breaking into the Bodleian have something to do with that gash on your arm?'

She went a bit pink around the ears. 'It was stupidity. I arrived in England six days ago. I intended to ask for your assistance – yours and Mr Holmes' – since you had given me your addresses and telephone numbers. But when I spoke to your housekeeper in Sussex, she said you were away for another week or two. So I made my enquiries in London, and found that the book had come here. I arrived in Oxford yesterday afternoon, thinking that I would go to the library and find it.'

'The Bodleian is not a place one simply strolls into.' Indeed, those without links to recognised academic institutions found entrance a challenge.

'I discovered that. And since there was not much I could do in daylight, I walked around Oxford, and came to look over your gate, thinking that you might have come here. I saw a woman moving around inside, dusting and sweeping the front step – the sorts of things one might do when the occupant of the house was coming home.

'I returned to the Bodleian at dusk. As soon as it was dark, I went up the drainpipes. What very helpful things drainpipes are. Do all your buildings have them?'

'Pretty much.'

She shook her head in amazement. 'They are an open invitation to climb. But when I was halfway up, a gentleman in a bowler hat saw me and started shouting.'

'Bulldogs.'

'I saw no dog.'

'No, that's what those men are called. Oxford University has its own police force – small, but effective. They wear bowlers. And although in other places a patrolling constable might never look up from street level, Bulldogs are well used to the pranks of the undergraduates – who also consider drainpipes an open invitation. The Bulldogs keep an eye on the tree branches, the rooflines, the tops of passing motorcars, and the upper reaches of local statues.'

'I see. That would also explain their fleetness of foot.'

'Pretty much a requirement,' I agreed. 'Did you get that gash when you came down?' Why not just knock the Bulldog out? Someone with her skills could surely do so in seconds flat.

'My honourable father would mock my clumsiness, but I did not wish to hurt the man. I jumped, and came down a quarter of an inch too close to the fence.'

I knew that fence. She was lucky not to get its wrought iron spear through her neck.

'He whistled for reinforcements. I was soon running through the streets with two bowler-hatted men in greatcoats behind me. It took me several minutes to outdistance them. When I had bound up my arm enough to keep from leaving a trail, I made a wide circle around the town, working my way through the quieter streets to here.

'I was,' she added, 'most relieved to see you, Mary.'

I imagined she was. Even when one speaks the local tongue, a stranger in a strange land is vulnerable. She did not know about the Bodleian's limitations; she did not suspect the skills of the University police. Her father would have been right to chastise her, because she had overlooked the most basic technique of the shinobi: become invisible. Not knowing her ground, she could not help standing out.

I, however, could.

She was fatigued from her long conversation, and slumped unmoving before the fire while I changed the dressings on her arm. I threw the old ones on the flames, returned the medical kit to its place on the shelf, then went through the sun-drenched kitchen and pantry to scrub away any bloodstains overlooked the night before. I ended my circuit by opening the back door and sluicing the soapy bucket across the steps.

Then I locked the garden door behind me, closed the curtains, and took another pot of green tea into the sitting room.

She was instantly awake.

'I'm going to the Bodleian,' I told Haruki. 'You'll be safe here, and it will give your arm a chance to mend a bit before you make demands on it. I'll leave the gun with you. You may have two visitors. One is Miss Pidgeon, who lives in the other house – you saw her tidying yesterday. I'll speak with her on the way out, to let her know you're here. She is absolutely reliable. If you need anything, go through the garden and knock on her door. She will not give you away.

'The other,' I said, settling my hat over my head, 'is Holmes. I phoned him first thing. He has a meeting in London, but he'll take the train up as soon as it's finished. Anyone other than Miss Pidgeon or Holmes, feel free to shoot.'

'I need to come with—' she protested.

'It would be pointless,' I cut in. 'By the time we got you a reader's ticket, you'd be leaking all over the floor. I, on the other hand, can go anywhere, talk to anyone, and no one will think twice. If your Bashō-Hokusai book is there, I will find it. I'll be back by two or thereabouts. Do try to rest.'

I shut the door on her protests, slung my book bag over my shoulder, and walked quickly away.

CHAPTER TWENTY-EIGHT

Bodleian ladies:
Widow, geisha, bluestocking:
Duke Humfrey's welcome.

THE BODLEIAN LIBRARY IS one of the glories of the Western world – although, if the world (and the University) was a fair place, the institution would be called the 'Ball Library', after the wealthy widow Thomas Bodley had married. It was Ann Ball's money (inherited from a trader in pilchards) that restored the old library of Duke Humfrey, stripped bare in the Reformation.

However, the Duke's original room proved vastly inadequate for a library that not only purchased books and received them as gifts and bequests, but since 1602 had been allowed to claim a copy of every book published in the country. Bodley's original 2,500 volumes now numbered well over a million. The library he founded had crept out over the rest of the Schools Quadrangle, then the Radcliffe Camera, and had moved on to infiltrate neighbouring basements. Before I ever came to Oxford, the University had constructed a massive underground book store beneath Radcliffe Square with closely ranked wheeled cases, but even that was proving too little: eyes were being cast on nearby buildings.

The library pushed at its bounds in ways other than the merely physical. With its incorporation of a number of filing systems, all of which were idiosyncratic to begin with, there was quite literally nothing on earth to compare – either to its collections, or to how it managed them.

The Bodleian was no lending library. Not even Oliver Cromwell had been permitted to take a volume past its doors. Bodley guarded its treasures closely. It had much practise in making certain that its books did not wander out, depending less on the fervent Latin oath taken by its users than on the sharp eyes and incorruptible passions of the staff. Neither does one browse the stacks in Bodley: one sits in one of the reading rooms and awaits requested volumes. The further one presses into the labyrinth, the more difficult passage becomes.

But not impossible.

I was well known to the librarians, who greeted me with the sort of respect large donations engender (then searched my bag, both coming and going). There was also affection in their greetings, since I was equally well known as an appreciative and regular patron. As I went forward, I passed through a gauntlet of friendly salutations, questions as to my absence, photographs of new grandchildren, and proud news of the academic triumphs of offspring. At the far end of this happy ordeal, I eventually came before the person who knew the most about the Library's Orientalia.

Mr Parsons was, on the surface at least, what one might expect a Bodleian librarian to be: small, tidy, bespectacled and bent, as if from years searching the lower stacks. His face was wizened, and when worried, he resembled one of the New College gargoyles. Below the surface was a different matter: he was blessed with five sons; his wife was a doctor; he spent his holidays in adventurous and far-flung parts of the globe; and he had a sly and occasionally risqué sense of humour.

We greeted each other warmly, agreed that I had been gone

for some long time, and caught up on recent travels – Portugal, Morocco, and Turkey for me; St Petersburg and the Canary Islands for him. I commented on a photograph pinned to his wall, an aeroplane turned upside-down.

'Yes, that's called a "barrel roll",' he said. 'The wife wouldn't let me fly until the kiddies were finished with their schooling, but I'm making up for lost time. Haven't crashed yet. Now, Miss Russell, with what can I help you?'

I took my horrified gaze from Mr Parsons' latest hobby, and gave him the story I had prepared. 'You may remember that a year ago, I was briefly in Japan.'

'Yes, we found some nice books for you to look at, after.' Nice, indeed: woodblock prints from the seventeenth century; scrolls from the sixteenth – I'd even perused the logbook of William Adams, an English ship's pilot who had gone aground in Japan in 1600, befriended the Shogun, been made Samurai, and lived out his life in Japan.

'That's right. Well, there's another I heard of, that I don't remember you showing me. It's a folding book about the Kisokaido road, with poems by Bashō, illustrated by Hokusai.'

'Yes,' he said, nodding. 'Lovely thing. A recent acquisition. Don't think we've put it on display yet, but it should be on the shelves.'

'How recent?'

'A year, perhaps two. After Albert's wedding, at any rate. Strictly speaking, it doesn't belong to us, it's on loan from the King. Seems someone sensible was cleaning house and decided that a few of the more fragile things were better off elsewhere, before there's grandchildren tearing around the place. Didn't want some international incident caused by a boy's energies.' Mr Parsons, in addition to being an enthusiastic father of boys, was no Royalist.

'And it's been here the whole time, after that?'

He fixed me with a sharp look. 'No . . . We sent it out for minor repairs and restoration. With the approval of the Palace, mind. Why do you ask?'

'The person who mentioned it – a collector, lives in New York – said he'd seen it outside of Bodley. Which seemed unlikely. I have a feeling there may be another one out there, somewhat similar to yours.'

He frowned, and the gargoyle look returned. 'Hmm. I suppose that's possible. He might have seen it at the expert's workshop, although it is a part of our agreement that the pieces we send him are not for display.'

'But it's back now?' I asked.

'Oh yes. Shall I have it brought?'

'That, and anything else of the sort that you think I might like.' This was by way of distraction, linking the book with others of its kind. As if there were others of its kind.

But to Mr Parsons' mind, there were. He made out the slips himself and bustled away, leaving me to hunch in my coat against the chill morning. It was not the first time I had napped in my chair under that hallowed roof, awaiting books.

I was wakened, not by the arrival of dusty volumes, but by a gentle hand on my shoulder.

'Beg your pardon,' Mr Parsons murmured, 'but I've moved you around near a window, so you can see them better.'

'Very kind of you,' I said, jumping to my feet. 'Which Regius professor did you have to evict?'

'Only Moral Theology,' he said blandly.

'Upstarts,' I agreed. That particular chair had been established less than a century before: might as well have been Jazz History.

I settled to the display of masterpieces with profuse thanks, and let him go back to his work. I picked up one and glanced through the pages, then another, before laying hands upon the one I was after.

It was in a protective paper board case that bore the Bodleian's marks, and was tiny – little more than eight inches by three, and about an inch thick. Its slipcover was of a silk so dark blue, it looked black. The covers of the book itself were also silken, although they bore a pattern of tiny flowers, possibly chrysanthemums. The book more or less fell open since it was little more than a scroll, folded rather than rolled. Its pages made for a continuous image perhaps ten feet long, a meandering road with inns, farmers, pilgrims, snow-capped peaks, and intense blue streams. Threads of ink formed the calligraphed poems: riding the sky like a flock of birds, growing among the leaves of a tree, coming up in the unfurling lines behind a farmer's plough.

I wished I read Japanese. Even without, I could identify several stops along the Nakasendo – and yes! (I bent close over the page, shifting to catch the light from the window.) That could only be the Mojiro-joku onsen – yes, there was the stone that resembled a monkey! Hokusai's flexible perspective allowed the viewer to peep into the bathhouse behind the main building, and catch a glimpse of a woman's red garment across a chair. Towards the end, in a view of the road through a narrow, mountainous bend, the brilliant blue of the ocean shimmered off in the distance.

It was a beguiling piece of work. The energy of the people was vivid, the colours intense, the touches of Hokusai's earthy humour unmistakeable.

Not at all bad, for a fake.

CHAPTER TWENTY-NINE

Duke Humfrey's bookshelves:
Drowsing scholars and dust motes:
Let's not burn it down.

I DID NOT TELL MR Parsons what he had. Time enough for that, and I dared not risk the investigative machinery of others getting in my way.

Instead, I straightened the desk for the evicted Regius Professor of Moral and Pastoral Theology, tucked the Nakasendo book among the others, and went to find Mr Parsons.

'Thank you for showing me those. I'm afraid I'll have to start learning to read Japanese, in order to appreciate them properly. I hadn't seen Kitagawa Utamaro before, his images are extraordinary. When I was in Tokyo, I watched a geisha having her hair arranged. It might have been the same woman.'

He beamed. 'I have a small Utamaro print, myself. I gave it to my wife as an anniversary present last year.'

'Lucky woman.' Holmes' gifts to me mostly had edges to them, if not literally, then at least figuratively. 'I did buy some small prints when we were there – there was a pair of women so alive, one expects to see their fans move. I was so taken by them I bought both of them, even though they're not in very good shape, and –

say! Who's the restorer you use? Does he do private work, or only for institutions?'

'He's happy to have individuals bring him their pieces, although it may take him a while. Sometimes a very long while, indeed. Would you like his address?'

'I would, thanks. And after he's finished, I'll bring my two ladies by, for you to admire.'

We talked for a time, about prints and the dreadful Oxford damp, and he gave me a piece of Bodleian stationery with a name and address in his spidery librarian's handwriting. I thanked him, pushing it casually into a pocket, then asked when, oh when, the Bodleian would enter the modern era and bless its scholars with artificial lighting. This complaint was a source of continuous teasing between us, which by its familiarity might help him forget my earlier concerns.

He replied with his usual stout defence of the Library's policy, enshrined in the oath's second declaration: *item neque ignem nec flammam in bibliothecam inlaturum vel in ea accensurum*; 'not to bring into the Library, or kindle therein, any fire or flame.' He did admit that a discussion was being held as to the various forms of electrical lights, but that neither arc nor incandescent had been deemed sufficiently proven as to safety.

I had to agree, that when it came to Duke Humfrey's library, a tinder-dry piece of architecture filled with priceless and irreplaceable paper, I would probably opt for the conservative view, even though the lack of lighting made for short hours, particularly during the winter. At least by my time, there were radiators – early generations of scholars had been a hardy lot, shivering at their desks until the library had figured a way of heating the place that did not involve the kindling or bringing in of flame.

I thanked Mr Parsons again and made my way past the hunched

shoulders and straining eyes, through the comforting aroma of old paper to the stairway, and thence out of doors. In the shadow of the Sheldonian, I stepped down onto Broad Street, only to see a gentleman in a bowler hat walking in my direction, his eyes playing constantly up and down the streets and buildings. I nodded as he went past, causing him briefly to touch the brim of his bowler, and I wondered what he would say were I to congratulate him on having a colleague who had bested a trained Japanese spy-assassin, however inadvertently.

Fortunately, my smile did not reach my face until after he was past, or his constabulary suspicions would have been raised in an instant.

On the other side of Broad Street, beside the comforting portal of Blackwell's, I took the slip of paper out of my pocket. Go on, or go back? Perhaps I should check on Haruki. And if Holmes had arrived, bring him up to date on what Mr Parsons had said.

On the other hand, both of them would want to join me. And I had, after all, come prepared for this eventuality.

Mr Parsons' handwriting gave the name Bourke, with an address in Jericho, a neighbourhood just outside of the old city walls. Jericho was now a working-class area near the Oxford Canal, a short walk from the railway station, or the Covered Market – or from me.

Surely, a visit to a book restorer was something I could manage on my own?

Chapter Thirty

Innocent young man:
Indigo's face has no blue
Deep as summer dusk.

I FOUND MR BOURKE THE book restorer at the far end of a cobbled mews. His door was in need of paint and the brass nameplate had not been polished since before the War, but a light burnt in the depths of the building, so I went up the step and pushed at the door.

No bell tinkled, although a glance overhead showed that there had been a bell at one time. I was standing in a small shop front cluttered with books, a stairway leading up to the left, a half-open doorway to the right. I called a tentative greeting, waited, and called again, slightly louder.

There was a *thump*, an oath, and the sound of movement accompanied by grumbling. A man in his late sixties came through the inner door clutching a wad of damp, tea-stained rags. 'Yes?' He scowled from beneath wildly jutting white eyebrows.

'I, er, that is, I wonder if—'

'What is it, gel?'

'I have a picture,' I blurted out. 'Two pictures, in fact, but they're in rather bad condition, and I was told, that is, the Bodleian recommended—'

Again, his impatience shoved my flustering aside. 'What've you got?' He threw the rags into an overflowing bucket, wiped his hands on the sides of his trousers, and lumbered over to the equally cluttered tall wooden display cabinet, shoving aside six pens, three paper sample books, a wickedly sharp knife, and an accounts ledger that dated back to Victoria's youth.

I laid my book bag on the wood and reluctantly took out the heavy paper envelope. In it were the two prints I had told Mr Parsons about, but decided not to show him yet. I held on to the manila, reluctant to entrust my ladies to this clumsy oaf – they really were quite charming. I hoped I would not have to break his grubby wrist to keep him from smudging them with tea.

But to my astonishment, the moment the prints emerged from the envelope, he bent down and whipped out a jeweller's velvet display tray from beneath the wooden surface. Next, from somewhere about his person, he conjured up a pair of pristine white cotton gloves, tugging them on with a gesture of long practice. He separated my two ladies, holding them tenderly by their very edges, and in a series of deft moves shifted over a swivel lamp, switched it on, and summoned up a large magnifying glass.

He bent over the prints, muttering to himself. 'Eighteen hmm. Utamaro hmm mumble. Toyogrumble. Where *have* you ladies been to?'

'They were like that when I bought them,' I hastened to say, lest he think I had been responsible for the wear on one lady's collar and the little tear in the corner of the other print. 'I got them in Japan a year ago.'

He put down the glass – to one side of the prints – and fixed me with a hard look. 'They need work.'

'Can you do it?'

'I can.'

'What, er, what is it exactly, that you do?'

'Repair, restore, get them ready for your walls. Don't frame them. Don't like framing. And for God's sake, don't hang them in the sun!'

'I promise. But I wonder, do you by any chance have, well, an example of what they'll look like? Just so I can see? Because I thought I'd give them to my sister-in-law as a wedding gift, but not if they're still . . . worn.' I did not have a sister-in-law.

He glared out from under the shrubbery of his eyebrows, then wheeled to head back through the doorway from which he had come. Hesitantly, I followed – and stepped into another world, this one the spotless, tightly organised realm of a master artisan. Shelves of neatly stacked supplies, three presses ranging from petite to massive, a magnifying glass eight inches across, mounted on a hinged arm for hands-free examination. The work benches gleamed in the sunlight through the windows. Bourke stopped before a table against the wall, and lifted his chin at what lay there. 'This fellow was in worse shape than yours, when he came.'

The print showed a young man with a book and a flat Renaissance cap; its lines were as crisp as the day it had come off the press. His expression was uncertain, as if ordered to look pensive when all he could think about was breakfast. 'Francesco Bartolozzi,' the restorer said, but more than his easy expertise, it was his hands that decided me: one glove had come off, that he might touch the very edges of his work with pride and affection.

The man might be a crook and a forger, but as a restorer, I could trust him with my ladies. 'Do you do all this yourself?' I asked.

'Why?' The scowl was back.

'Oh, nothing – I just thought, there's so much here, and it's just, well, the wedding is in July.'

'Can't promise. I'll try.'

He turned to the door, our business finished. I followed slowly, my eyes probing every corner for any evidence of duplication, as opposed to restoration. Of course, anything here could be used to produce a new version of the pieces on display, nonetheless, I could see no sign of a forgery in progress.

But as I turned to go, my eye was snagged by a splash of a familiar deep indigo colour.

Prussian blue: new from Europe in the 1830s, this was the blue Hokusai used for the deep sea and deeper skies, for his giant waves and calm bays and the trim on a geisha's kimono. Here it was on a pinned-up sheet of watercolour paper, a competent but unimaginative rendering of the Round Pond in Kensington Gardens. The ships were model yachts rather than junks and exotically-sailed fishing boats. Coincidence?

Mr Bourke's head reappeared in the doorway.

'Sorry!' I said, as if his entrance had wakened me from a dream. 'I just – that's a lovely little piece, there.'

He saw where I was looking, and gave a nod. 'Not bad.'

'Did you do it?'

'No, not me. My son tries his hand, time to time.'

'Your son's an artist!'

'He'd like to think so,' Mr Bourke muttered sourly, and withdrew again into the untidy storefront.

This time, I followed.

I gave him a deposit on his work, and an address Holmes and I used when we did not want people to find us. In return, he handed me a receipt for the two prints and an estimate of the final bill. I attempted further conversation, but Mr Bourke was not forthcoming when it came to his living situation or where his son might be, so I bubbled my way out of the door and away from the mews, through the bustle of Jericho towards north Oxford.

When I opened my front door, I knew that Holmes had come. Either that or Haruki had taken up smoking.

My partner's face appeared from the kitchen door, and went from mistrusting to relieved. 'It's you,' he noted unnecessarily, and vanished again, followed by a clatter of dishes.

'Who would it have been?' I called.

'I saw your neighbour out in front.' I almost laughed at the wary edge in my husband's voice.

Not everyone held my same respect, even affection, for my combination housekeeper-guard dog. Without Miss Pidgeon, my habit of picking up and departing would become cumbersome, and my every return would be milkless, breadless and cold. Moreover, without her, my name would have to appear on land registry and telephone lists, for all the world to see.

There was a cost for this, and not simply the 'housekeeping fees' I paid her each month. Those who knew her, and knew that she and I shared closely adjoining houses behind a single gate, no doubt made amusing assumptions about our status. Those assumptions bothered Holmes less than they did most males; however, he, like most other men, had discovered that Miss Pidgeon was not a Sapphite who befriended male persons easily, and that she saved the razor edges of an already sharp wit for the male of the species.

Men walked cautiously around Miss Pidgeon, lest she take notice of them. Even Holmes drew in, just a fraction, when he saw her approach. I was grinning as I hung up my coat and book bag. 'I hope you settled the Turkish problem?'

'I made my contribution and left.'

I shut the door to the hall closet and walked back to the kitchen. Holmes had his hands in dish-water, while Haruki sat against the windows in the last patch of midday sun, clearly having decided to take my word for the invisibility of the house from outside. Her face was pink, which could mean either fever or the sun. I greeted her, and asked how her arm was.

'Healing nicely. Does the Bodleian have the book?'

'Well, it has *a* book.'

All motion in the kitchen stopped, except for mine. I was hungry, and I wasn't about to be trapped in the upcoming conversation without some bread and the wedge of Stilton Miss Pidgeon had left in the pantry.

In between mouthfuls of brown bread and butter, chunks of the Stilton with Mrs Hudson's pickle, and swigs of the tea (English) that Holmes set before me, I gave them the results of my morning.

At the end of it, Haruki looked tired, Holmes thoughtful. He examined the end of his pipe, and reached for my table knife – one of my mother's silver table knives. I snatched it away, replacing it with a metal skewer. While I was standing, I went to get the first-aid box – noting that I was going to need more gauze very soon.

'That's not necessary,' Haruki protested.

'It is, actually. We need to see what condition you are in.'

'I told you, I am fine.'

'Haruki, unless you plan on dismissing us from the case, your health is a prime consideration. You're free to walk out of here and stumble through unfamiliar ground, as you did when you first got here. You may have more success this time.'

She was not pleased, but if she didn't want medical treatment, she shouldn't have introduced her arm to a wrought iron spear. She gave a brusque nod. I rolled up her sleeve and slipped the scissors between gauze and arm.

Holmes set a steaming bowl down beside me on the table. The dressings had stuck, but not too badly, and when I eased them away, I thought that, despite my amateur efforts, she was indeed healing.

'This will probably be all right if you rest it,' I said. Holmes grunted at the likelihood of her resting. 'But there's one part of it looks nasty. Holmes, what happened to that – ah, that's the stuff.'

The pot he unearthed from the lower reaches of the medical box might have come from an Egyptian burial chamber, so encrusted with dark substances was it. The pot contained a remarkably disgusting yet equally remarkably effective poultice. Haruki winced back as the smell hit her.

'I know, it's pretty rank,' I told her. 'But it is the best thing in the world for drawing infection. Holmes gets it from the gipsies, or maybe from the lascars down at the docks. It may even be a recipe from our local witch – all I know is that if you can bear the stench, it works.'

I often suspected that Holmes actively preferred his nostrums disgusting, in a childlike belief that when it came to medicines, the nastier, the stronger. But I could not argue with the result.

The stitches themselves were holding, and most of the holes were only pink, not red and weeping. There was no sign of blood poisoning, no indication that the infected areas would make for the heart. I slopped on the gipsy goo and loosely wrapped her arm in a clean towel, and then dug out a hot-water bottle and filled it, propping it against the poulticed arm.

Later that afternoon, I renewed the poultice, reheated the

rubber bottle, and led her, only mildly protesting, to the bed in the next room. Even a ninja had to admit that rest was restorative.

She did make me promise on my very life that we would not leave without consulting her, before permitting me to shut the sturdy door.

Holmes had cleaned away the detritus of both meal and medical procedure, and replaced the tea pot with a jug of coffee. I described in more detail what I had learnt at the restorer's workshop, including the painting on his wall.

Holmes sat back in his chair and resumed his pipe. I stretched out an arm to open the window.

'You are thinking we need to look at the son,' he said after a while.

'Aren't you?'

'It would simplify matters if we could ask Lestrade about the man's criminal records.'

Chief Inspector Lestrade was one of the cleverer members of New Scotland Yard. This quality was ideal in a partnership, but could be a liability when one merely wanted to use the Inspector as a source of information.

'We can't risk it,' I decided.

'Of course, there's Mycroft.'

'No.'

'Russell—'

'Absolutely not. Once Mycroft gets his hands on a piece of information, it's his forever.'

'I would trust Mycroft with my life.'

'As would I. But would you trust him not to make use of an Emperor's secret, if the day came when he needed to manipulate Japan?'

He scowled into his pipe, and prodded it a few times. A year ago, I would not have hesitated to bring his brother into the matter. Since then, I had witnessed the scope of Mycroft's actions, and the troubling questions they raised.

'I trust my brother's decisions,' he reiterated, but there was a thread of too much protest in his voice, and no further insistence on bringing Mycroft in.

'We'll have to take a more direct approach,' I said.

'You said you thought your Misters Bourke lived over their shop?'

I smiled.

CHAPTER THIRTY-ONE

Buoyant spring flowers
In the winter of a life:
Vincent's geisha smiles.

THAT EVENING, HARUKI'S FACE was more flushed than ever, and I thought we would have to shackle her to the bed. Not that any locks would hold a woman with her skills, but they might delay her long enough to let us escape.

In the end, we made an exchange of promises: she would remain here with her hot poultices, and we would come back before acting on whatever we discovered.

And she vowed, if we were not back in four hours, she would come looking for us.

Holmes and I might have lacked the mythic passing-through-walls invisibility of the classic shinobi warrior, but our skills were adequate for Oxford. And as the ninja costume is simply that of an everyday worker and the weapons variations on farming implements, in the same way did Holmes and I dress in the modern English equivalent: old, dark suits, dark overcoats and hats, our pockets full of everyday tools. Well, the everyday tools of some professions – and in Oxford, what would be considered odd, anyway?

At the entrance to the mews, Holmes paused on the pavement

while I turned inside, edging along the walls to a pile of crates beneath the only overhead light. I waited, cobblestone hunk in hand, for the grumble of a passing lorry to echo through the enclosed yard. The tinkle of breaking glass went unnoticed, and I moved to Mr Bourke's door.

Holmes came up a minute later, and stood in growing impatience as I worked with my steel picks at the lock. It was not a complicated mechanism, and should have been easy, but with dripping rain and Holmes' breath down the back of my neck – then I had it.

He reached up as the door drifted open, but the bell was still missing. Inside, we stood, counting off ninety seconds, letting our eyes adjust and our ears listen for any surreptitious presence: few people can remain motionless and unbreathing for ninety seconds while their home is being invaded.

I took out my tiny pen-light with the red cloth around the end, and led Holmes back to the workshop. There were windows along the back, so we should have to take care with our lights.

I turned the glow on the wall where I had seen the Prussian-blue lake – and saw only plaster.

Correction: plaster and a nail, with a fragment of paper fibre, as if someone had jerked the watercolour off the wall. Interesting. I told Holmes what was not there, and felt him nod. He flicked on his own light, and we turned our attention to the workshop itself.

In half an hour, we were satisfied that no forgery was done here.

However, nor was watercolour painting done in this room – none but the minimal application of pigments necessary to the restorer. We left Mr Bourke's workshop, and made for the stairs.

The northern end of the mews had been rebuilt, its roofline raised for another level of flats, but this end still had three storeys, and looked much as it had since the days of George III. The inner stairs suggested that the upper levels were a part of the Bourke realm, not those of a different business or residence.

We had seen no lights from the upper windows, but there was a risk that Bourke and his son were asleep on the next floor up.

I went first, being both lighter and – if a door came open – faster down the stairs. I crept my way upwards, trying each step before committing my weight to it. The wood was stouter than it appeared, and the squeaks were minimal.

The landing at the top of the first flight of stairs had a locked door on one side, but the carpet on the stairs going up was just as worn as that on the first section, indicating that the living quarters were over our heads, not on this middle level. I gave Holmes a small hiss, and as he climbed the stairs, I bent again to my picklocks.

This latch, interestingly, was a lot sturdier than that on the front door. After sweating over it for a while, I deferred to the more experienced Holmes. He, too, had problems, but at last the final pin slid aside and the cylinder turned. The door began to creak when its edge was ten inches from the jamb. Holmes held it while I squeezed inside. I ran my light quickly around the space, an odd and dusty foyer, then worked spittle into the hinges to allow Holmes inside as well. When the latch had clicked shut again, I pulled the red cloth off my light and studied our surroundings.

It looked like an unused sitting room, with a thin layer of dust on the side-table, the armchair, and even on the book that lay face-down on an ancient leather ottoman before the chair. As if someone had walked away from their evening read, weeks before.

The room was the same size as the shop downstairs, but where the door to Mr Bourke's workshop was, here stood a bookshelf. A ceiling-to-floor bookshelf with a narrow track of disturbance in the floorboard dust. Either the reader habitually fetched volumes from just one section, or the reader was not interested in the books.

The latch for the hidden door was attached to an old Balzac novel I'd never heard of, but clearly Holmes recognised. The moment he spotted *Pierre Grassou*, he gave a grunt of amusement and reached for the upper edge of the spine. A click came from deep within the shelves. We shoved, and opened the door to gold – better still: gilt.

The artist's current project was a series of oil paintings. Pinned up to a wall were a dozen or so reproductions of landscapes by the Dutchman van Gogh, whose odd perspective and lively technique had, since his death a generation ago, been of growing interest to collectors. It was the ideal situation for a dealer in fakes: when an artist's work had gone unsold and uncollected during his life, who was to say how many versions of a wheat field or cypress tree he had actually produced?

Coincidentally, the piece was appropriate to our own search: a blossoming cherry tree with a geisha looking coyly out from under its branches. Three large colour photographs lay on the table beside his easel, with what I assumed were actual van Goghs: a flowering tree with Fuji in the background; a geisha with a frog; and a bearded man with a hat, seated in front of various Japanese scenes. A strong light hung overhead, and a large magnifying glass distorted the frog on the geisha scene.

Leaning against the wall were two other very fresh-looking oil paintings, signed 'Vincent'.

A brief search gave us the evidence we had come for: a file-box on one of the shelves with sketches, colour swatches, close-up photographs of every section of the Kisokaido illustrations and calligraphy, including three incomplete but full-sized versions of the book itself, discarded for various reasons including a large black drop of ink in the middle of one. There was even a trial version of the cover boards.

'He's very skilled,' I murmured.

'A wonder Mycroft hasn't adopted him.' Holmes was looking at the contents of its neighbouring box, which contained treated pages and sketches for a very old-looking will.

The one thing we did not locate was, who hired Bourke?

We spent an hour looking through every box, every file, prodding for hidden corners, but came away with nothing but dust and sore knees. Finally, we migrated back to where we had begun, and stood contemplating Vincent's geisha.

'Do you think this could be a one-man operation, from beginning to end?' I asked. 'That he comes up with ideas, constructs the forgeries, and sells them?'

'That might be so for the forgeries themselves, but the blackmail?' It was true: the son almost certainly came across the Kisokaido book in his father's workshop, awaiting restoration. From there, he might have chosen it as a candidate for a lucrative forgery – but how did one go from forgery to international blackmail? A restoration might have uncovered the hidden document, but once found, how would a forger have guessed at its meaning?

'We need to speak with him,' I said.

'You have your revolver?' he asked.

'The ladies' accessory,' I said, pulling it from my pocket.

He chose a precarious stack of paint-stained tin bowls, and prodded it with a forefinger.

The clatter was satisfying. Even more so the sudden squeak of bed springs overhead, followed by the thump of feet hitting the floor. We left the studio, closed the hidden bookcase entrance, and took up positions at the doorway.

That the man came through the door armed with nothing more deadly than a torch and a metal poker was both reassuring and informative: this was not a person who thought in terms of £100,000 extortion demands. Indeed, considering the podgy, middle-aged figure's sleep-rumpled hair and down-at-the-heels carpet slippers, he appeared at first glance someone whom £100 might impress.

Holmes flipped the light switch; at the same instant, I said in a firm whisper, 'I have a gun.'

The forger's reaction was not quite what I had expected. He took a step back, poker clattering onto the dirty carpet, and stared at me with the blood draining from his face. I spoke again before he could pass out, keeping my voice low so as not to wake the elder Bourke.

'We've been in your workshop, we see what you do. We're not the police, but if you want to avoid having us call them in, you need to talk to us about a piece of forgery you did two years ago.'

Again, his reaction was unexpected. He frowned, tilting his head a little. Was he hard of hearing? I raised my voice a fraction.

'We can see this operation is yours and not your father's. You've been working right under his nose – you even laid out this sitting room for him to see, if he happened to pass while you had the door open. We need – sit down, man!' My sharp order came as I saw him begin to sway. He did not argue, but dropped onto the ottoman and put his head in his hands, breathing deeply.

Holmes and I exchanged a glance: one might think the man had never seen a gun before. How could he have worked amongst criminals and never faced a threat of robbery and violence? Belatedly, I realised that there could be another explanation for his going weak-kneed: shell shock lasted a long time and carried a wide array of symptoms; faintness at the sight of a weapon could easily be one. I supposed I should be grateful he hadn't left his supper on my shoes.

I went on more gently. 'Mr Bourke, we don't intend to hurt you, and we're not interested in most of your work. We merely want to know about the Japanese folding book you forged in the spring of 1923. A book with prints and calligraphy.'

He held still for a while, as if letting the words sink in. When he responded, it took a couple of throat-clears before the words would come. 'The Hokusai.'

'That's right.'

He sat for a bit longer, head down. His body seemed to pull together somehow, losing its shakiness. When at last he raised his head, the extremity of his fear was gone, replaced by a look of calculation that seemed far more natural to his features. Certainly, he seemed less concerned with the gun. He looked at Holmes, studying him for a minute, then got to his feet.

'I'm sure I don't know what you're talking about. I help my father with restoration, that's all.'

'Mr Bourke, we've been through your workshop. There's enough there to keep Scotland Yard busy for a long time. And you can't tell me your fingerprints aren't all over it.'

After a moment, he gave a little shrug. 'Had to try. What was it you were interested in? That Japanese book, right? I could do you a copy of your own, if you like. I knew you were going to be trouble,' he muttered. 'When my father told me there was someone asking about my painting. Shouldn't have left it up.'

Holmes interrupted his monologue. 'How many copies did you do?'

'Just the one.'

Holmes' voice went hard. 'Young man, that is the last lie you are permitted. At the next one, you will find yourself explaining your operation to an official detective.'

Young Bourke believed him. He ran his eyes over me for a last time, then turned to Holmes. 'Look, can we go into the other room? My father might hear us, this end.'

We filed through the bookcase, keeping a sharp eye on our prisoner, but the forger made no fast move towards a weapon, merely came to a halt in the centre of his workshop, as if wondering how his tools had come to betray him.

'How many copies?' Holmes reminded him.

'There were two. One was better than the other. The best work I've ever done. Took me weeks. I even got the wear on the cover just right.'

'It was impressive,' I agreed.

'You saw it?'

'In the Bodleian.'

'You can't tell them,' he said thickly. 'The Library. They'll never hire my father again.'

He seemed actually to care – whether for his father's welfare or for his own supply of candidates for fakery, I could not tell. 'How much were you paid?'

'I . . .' His eyes shifted rapidly about the room, searching for a place to hide this secret.

'How much?' Holmes growled.

'Six hun—' He gave my gun a glance, and retreated from the lie. 'A thousand. For the two.'

'Who hired you?'

This was the question he had been dreading. He answered instantly and with fervour. 'I don't know. Honest to God, I *swear* I don't know who it was. There was a voice on the telephone, and letters, and twice a man with a scarf up around his face and his hat pulled low. He was young, and a gentleman – educated. That's all I know.'

Holmes allowed silence to fall, and to remain. Surprisingly, Bourke kept still, and eventually Holmes went over to the man's drinks cabinet and splashed a dose of whisky into a glass. He placed the drink on the work-table, shoved a stool over with his foot, and settled onto another stool. I took a chair. Young Bourke gave an unhappy sigh, and sat.

Sometimes when a witness is wrought up over some piece of his testimony, the best approach is to step well back from the sticking point. Holmes waited until the man had the drink inside him, then began.

'Tell us how you got started, forging art works.'

'Restoration, of course. I apprenticed to my father, learnt how to restore damaged paintings. I had a knack with watercolours, which aren't easy. Not that there's much money in it, even before Pa's eyes started to go.

'Anyway, one night when Pa was out, one of our regulars came to pick up a piece, and we got to talking. Nice enough fellow, so I closed the place and we went for a drink. After—'

'The man's name?'

'Collins. Bart Collins. So after a couple of pints, he said that if I ever felt like making a copy of something in the shop, he'd be happy to find a buyer. Reproductions, you know? I knew my father would never go for it, but I didn't see any harm in trying. The first one was an Italian drawing – Pisanello, was the name – that came out pretty nice. Collins took it, sold it, and gave me half. Twelve pounds! Couple months later I did another, then another. Then a year or so later, after I'd done maybe a dozen different pieces, Collins got to talking about how good they were, and how much more I could earn if I switched mine for the originals. I said absolutely not, and he said that was fine, but that I should think about it.

'So I did. And I thought that since I do most of our deliveries, it wouldn't be all that much of a risk. Sure, if my father looked, he'd know, but most times, the owners themselves haven't a clue, and they're all the happier if the thing looks new again. So that's what we've been doing, for seven, going on eight years now, in between the work I do downstairs. Most of the time it's paintings some rich American has bought: we give him my piece and send the original to someone in France or Germany. A couple of times, Hong Kong.'

'The Bodleian is a far cry from a rich American,' I pointed out.

'Yes.' He cast a wistful glance at his empty glass. Holmes renewed it, and its strength got him through the next part. 'All of my Bodleian Library copies have gone to outside collectors. Until now.'

'Tell us about the Hokusai book.'

'We got it in . . . April? May? Two years ago, any road. The Library sends things by special messenger usually, but this time it was one of the sub-librarians who brought it. I'm not sure if that was because the thing didn't actually belong to them – it was a gift from Japan's Prince to the King – or because they wanted to check that Pa could still do the work. Pa said sure, no problem. I was here, too, and I could see that it was something I could handle. I'd been doing more and more of the really delicate stuff, see. The old man's hands are getting a little shaky.

'I just wanted the job. I didn't plan on making a copy, since it wasn't Collins' kind of thing. But then he happened to come by with a couple of nice paintings some pub had been letting people blow smoke on for a century or two. I was alone at the time, so we went back into the workshop to look at them under the light.

'That's where he saw the book. Now, we'd had it a couple of weeks and I'd made some sketches and a few notes about what I'd need to do and in what order, but just that morning I'd discovered a little puzzle about it. The front cover was coming apart – that's the Japanese front, which is around the back, understand?' We nodded to indicate that yes, we were familiar with the contrary nature of

Japanese writing. 'Anyways, the cover was separating, just a little, and when I put it under the big glass, it didn't seem to be made like the others. I mean, for the most part, if you want a cover to stay together, you wrap the material – in this case, silk – around the edges and seal it on the inside. You see? And although the back cover was like that, the front cover was only that way on three sides. The fourth side, on the back where the spine would be on a normal book, it was more like a sandwich. The two pieces just pressed together?' He waited until we had nodded, then went on.

'I put it in the clamp and worked at the separation – gently, so as not to tear anything. That's when I found that my sandwich had a filling.'

'A document,' Holmes supplied. 'In Japanese writing.'

Bourke's expression went from surprise to reflection, ending up with something very like fear. 'So it *was* important, then.'

'Why do you ask?'

He rubbed his hand across his face. 'It was part of what I showed to Collins. And when he saw the book, he said he might know someone who'd be interested in a copy, but when he looked at that folded-up page, he said he'd take that then and there. I didn't want him to, but he said he just wanted to borrow it, had a friend who might be able to read the thing. But he also said to ease off working on the book, while he asked around for anyone who might like a copy of it. We took some pictures of it for him, then days went by, more than a week. When he came back, he was excited. Tried not to show it, but I could tell. He said he'd found a client who wanted me to do two copies of the book. And I'd get six hundred for the two, and maybe more work in the future, if they were really good.'

'What happened to the document?'

'He did bring it back. It was the original,' he said, the voice of expertise. 'Told me to put it back where it was, restore the cover around it, but not to bother making copies of the document inside my two fakes.

'Six hundred is a lot of money, with more where that came from, so I took my time with it. When he came to pick them up, he couldn't tell the three of them apart, not without strong light and a magnifying glass.' He paused. The pause went on, indicating that we had returned to the sticking point in his tale.

'What happened next?' Holmes pressed.

'He paid me. Said I should let the Bodleian know I had their book ready, at last.'

'And?' Holmes was getting impatient.

'And then Collins told me that he was taking the original, and I'd have to hand one of the copies over to the Library. I said absolutely not. They're not fools there, and any reader who asks for that book is going to be somebody who knows what he's looking at. I told him the chances of getting away with it were too small. I couldn't risk it.'

'But Mr Collins changed your mind?'

'Wasn't him. It was the phone calls.' He shuddered, and cast another longing look at the bottle. When Holmes made no move towards it, Bourke just wrapped his hands around the empty glass and stared into his empty future. 'Two phone calls. The first one said that if I didn't do as Collins asked, a list of my forgeries would go to the police, and my father would end up in the poorhouse, if not in prison. The next day Collins came again and I tried to explain how really impossible it would be to get away with it. That night . . . It was late. Pa had gone to bed hours before, but I had a piece I wanted to finish. And the phone rang. There was that same muffled voice, a whisper, that said, "If you did a good enough job, it won't be discovered." I started to say that it wasn't what I wanted, it was what was possible, but that damned whisper cut me off. That's why I went funny when you started in whispering,' he told me. 'Gave me a turn.'

'What did the voice say then?'

'"If you did a good enough job, we will pay you a thousand pounds. If you did a good enough job, your father will live. If you failed, or if you speak to the police, he will not. Go downstairs and look at the shop ledger." And then the earpiece went dead.'

'What did you find downstairs?'

'A dead rabbit.' He shuddered. 'Not just dead, but . . . pulled apart. Took me hours to clean it all up. Thing is, my father has a soft place for rabbits. He likes to walk down the Christchurch meadow round about dusk and feed them. Has some of 'em near to tame. So whoever left it not only broke in without leaving a sign, they knew us. They'd been watching us.'

'So you did as they asked.'

'Yes. Though I gave the Bodley the best effort, just in case. And I guess I did a good enough job, because nobody came complaining. I thought I'd got away with it.' He raised his eyes to Holmes. 'But if you turn me in, I won't tell the police what I've just told you. Not about the phone calls. I'll go to gaol first.'

There was not much more the man could tell us. The voice on the telephone had been educated, but muffled and whispering.

In the end, Holmes and I walked out to a clatter of glass, the sound of a man with uncertain hands pouring himself a much-needed drink.

Chapter Thirty-Two

Dark, shining cobbles,
A glimpse of spring's first new moon,
Through the dirty glass.

Dawn was still a long way off. Our footsteps echoed from the narrow walls, splashing in the puddles amongst the cobblestones. The rain had stopped for the moment.

We turned north on Walton Street, passing through the sleeping Jericho. 'I don't suppose you're familiar with Mr Bart Collins?' I asked Holmes.

'Not yet.' In the Baker Street days, Holmes' encyclopaedic knowledge of his country's criminals would have made it a simple matter of flipping through his memory's files – or at last resort, his actual compendium on the shelves. With the new generation, it was more a matter of knowing a man who would know Collins – or, knowing a man who knew a man who would. 'At any rate, we have the sequence. Young Bourke discovered the letter and showed it to his fence, Bart Collins. Collins recognised that it might be valuable, and took it to a client. The client kept it for several days, probably finding someone to translate it. Once he realised its importance, he came up with a means of turning it into cash.'

'Twice over,' I pointed out. 'First asking £20,000, using the counterfeit version of the book, then a second demand of £100,000 for the original. But what if the Prince had spotted that it was a fake last April?'

'I expect he would have been told that the original sum was for the book, the greater was for what the book contained.'

'Why not ask for the larger sum to begin with?'

'Human nature: once a man has agreed to extortion, you have softened him into paying again – particularly if this time he can be sure he receives the original source of the blackmail. And second, were the demand to have been that enormous to begin with, it would have invited a reply of aggression. The Prince Regent did not order troops into the Imperial Hotel over a matter of £20,000, but he might well have if confronted by five times that.'

Troops, or pet ninjas.

'Clever. Too clever for Lord Darley?'

'Darley may have been simply the middle-man.'

'Like he was with the Frenchman? A Frenchman who may not have died in the trenches, after all?'

'Darley's personality seemed to me more that of assistant than master,' Holmes mused.

'Any road, we need to talk with Bart Collins. He may even have had two separate clients – one for the book, the other for its hidden contents.'

'That rather overcomplicates matters. As you say, Russell, we shall have to ask Mr Collins himself.'

We turned up the Woodstock Road. In the distance, a horse-cart clopped along. It started to rain again, and I turned up my collar.

'I wonder if Darley just didn't realise what he had,' I mused. 'If he set out to ransom the book, but discounted the letter. We've been thinking of it as a clear document, something that might be legal in a court of law, but what if it was more . . .'

'Poetic?'

'Exactly. It's possible that the meaning would only be clear to those in the know already. Those who have eyes to see, as it were.'

'And Darley himself did not have eyes to see, but someone else now does. Someone with access to the Darley mailing address.'

'I wonder when Lady Darley and Tommy returned? One or the other of them may be in the house in London.' The house where Darley had wanted to plant Japanese cherry trees, no doubt. 'What time is it?'

He retrieved the watch from his waistcoat, and held it up to the next street lamp.

'Just going midnight.'

Too late for the trains. 'Holmes, care for a drive?'

I pretended I did not hear his sigh. In fact, I am an excellent driver.

To our relief, Haruki was curled asleep on the settee, and did not wake when I passed through to retrieve my keys. I left a note where she could not miss it:

Much news from the book restorer,
we've gone to London to follow it up
and will be back by breakfast.
– Mary

The engine starting just outside the house may have wakened her, but we were out of the gate in a matter of seconds. The London road was almost deserted, and London itself as quiet as that great mass of humanity ever got. We crossed the river and wound through the roads of Southwark, until I pulled to the kerb and shut off the engine. In the noisy silence, we peered up at the dark house. The very dark house.

I made no effort to be first out of the car.

Holmes' relationship with William Mudd had begun thirty-five years before, when the street urchin tried to pick the great detective's pocket. Holmes had promptly drafted little Billy into his Irregulars, demanded schooling of the lad, and eventually set him up in his own investigation offices. He drew the line at permitting Billy to name a son Sherlock – as if Billy's wife would have approved: Emily Mudd did not appreciate some of the scrapes Holmes got her husband into – but Billy's new daughter had been christened Mary.

Very fortunately, Billy's wife sent her husband to the door. Seeing him and him alone, I made haste to follow Holmes, and we were soon tucked into a spotless kitchen, still warm from the day's fires. Cups of powerful tea scrubbed the sleep from Billy's face, and after answering our questions as to the health of daughter and family, Billy asked what he could do for us.

'Do you know a fence name of Collins?'

His reaction was not what either of us had anticipated. He leant back in his chair, as if to put as much distance between us as possible. 'Why do you ask?'

It was not a question he would normally have put to Sherlock Holmes. Why does Holmes ask anything? Because there is some kind of crime attached, of course. Holmes merely raised an eyebrow, and in a moment, Billy realised what he was doing, and seemed deliberately to set his wariness aside.

'Sorry,' he said. 'No business of mine. Yes, I knew Collins.'

Past tense.

'What happened to him?' Holmes asked.

'He got in the way of a bullet or three, in the Isle of Dogs.'

'When?'

'Just before Christmas.'

'Any arrests?'

'Nothing. Not even any whispers, far as I know.'

'Would you know?'

'I have been keeping my ears open. Collins was on the edge of a case I was working.'

'What kind of a case?'

Billy didn't hesitate. 'House up in Essex got broken into and stripped to the walls. I traced one or two of the paintings back to him.' He went on to describe the details, complete with all names and information, but neither Holmes nor I could find any point of connexion between stolen country house paintings and an incriminating Japanese document. Eventually, Holmes cut him off.

'Doesn't sound like anything to do with us. But if you hear of any ties the man had to forgery and blackmail – particularly any of his buyers who might have been looking for useful material along those lines – let me know? And it would be good to hear any further details of the killing itself.'

Billy assured us that he would see what was available, and urged us to stay – for breakfast, for the night, for good if we wanted. I glanced involuntarily at the ceiling, and told him that we were fine, that he should go quietly back to bed, and please do give his wife our apologies.

'Before we go,' Holmes said, 'let us use your telephone.'

'Good heavens,' I said. 'Who do you want to phone at this hour?'

'I'd like to know if the Darleys are at home.'

'Shall I?' Billy offered.

Holmes looked amused at his one-time assistant's eagerness. 'By all means.'

It took Billy a little while to uncover the Darley number, but once in hand, he did not hesitate. It rang several times, but then his face changed – and his voice as well, going thick and drunken. 'Lookin' for the Darleys,' he said. 'Nah, the young one—'

'Thomas,' I provided.

'Tommy,' he said. He listened for a moment, then cut off the rising protest on the other end. 'Just lookin' fer 'im. He there? When he comin' – I unnerstan'. Thank you very much, my good man.' He replaced the earpiece.

'I didn't know we were dealing with the nobs.' He raised his nose and spoke in the exaggeratedly posh accent of a butler. '"Lord Darley and Lady Darley are at the country house for the remainder of the month. One believes they are currently visiting friends in Leicestershire."'

'Nicely done,' Holmes told him. Billy beamed, and showed us to the door, pumping hands with Holmes, then me, then Holmes again. I started the engine with as little noise as I could manage and put the car gently into gear – only to have Billy's voice ring out along the darkened street in a goodbye as we pulled away.

The information we'd got was very nice, but making our escape without having to face an outraged Mrs Mudd was the night's true prize.

Less of a prize was the drive home, compounded by an empty stomach and the loss of a potential witness.

Holmes smoked, and brooded. He only broke the long silence as we touched the outskirts of Headington. 'A question remains.'

'More than one.'

'Who has resumed the criminal activities of Lord Darley?'

'I'd say the son, Thomas, is the most likely candidate.'

'He's been to hand all the while, certainly,' he agreed.

'He's a cad and an habitual cheat, and he's bright enough to plan it all.'

'What about Lady Darley? Could she be in on the business?'

I thought back to the time on the *Thomas Carlyle*: a year later, I chiefly remembered it as long weeks of endless sea and broken sleep. 'She and Tommy didn't seem all that keen on each other.' They had exhibited the kind of stand-offish politeness one often saw between a grown son and his stepmother – to say nothing of two future rivals for a fortune.

'Although one might say the same for her and Darley himself.'

'True.' Was she one of those generally amiable and much-friended women who yet have little depth to their relationships? She'd had some show of emotion over a brother – no, a cousin, who had loved poetry. If his death in the trenches had left her timid of further blows, well, she wasn't the only woman whose heart had been hardened by War. The only one who married a wealthy older man for the protection offered. (I do not, by the way, include myself in this category: I married Holmes for the adventure of it, not from any delusion of security.) A man who already had the needed son and heir, one whose interests lay outside of the London whirl . . .

A thought darted around the back of my brain, until I managed to drag it to the light. 'Back on the ship, the earl showed up to one of Haruki's talks, on sports. Were you there that day?'

'I do not remember ever seeing him in one of her salons, no.'

Had he known Darley would be there, he would not have been absent that afternoon. 'He asked about hunting, and after some confusion about falcons as opposed to foxes, I believe he mentioned riding with the Aylesbury Hunt.'

'Which suggests that he has a house very near here – capital, Russell! A pity you have never assembled an adequate library of British life; we shall be forced to wait until your public library opens its doors.'

'Holmes, Oxford is *my* city; I have my own personal reference librarians.'

For a century and a half, the Covered Market had sheltered the many shops that fed the city. Originally exclusive to butchers, one could now buy anything from cheese to chives. But its heart was meat: sides of beef, pork haunches, hares and pheasants and hanging game in season, cut into chops and baked into pies and transformed into sausages. It smelt of death and the sawdust was not swept as often as it might be. Ardent vegetarians avoided Market Street entirely.

But it knew its meat. It knew its customers. And some of the shops had been there a long, long time.

The Market would not open to the public for hours yet, but much of the action went on long before the gates went up. Colleges, after all, could not be expected to wait until mid-morning for delivery of the day's roasts.

I had been formally introduced to this butchers' guild when I was still an undergraduate, when a matter of no great importance to anyone but the child involved led me through the forbidden doorway out of hours. Fortune had smiled on me, and on the child; ever since, the patriarch of the most noble of meat-cutters gathered beneath those glass roofs had claimed me as one of his own.

I waved to Anthony the greengrocer, arranging his baskets of spring lettuces, and paused at the stall of Nigel the fishmonger to admire his artistic display of Cornish spider crabs and early mackerel. It was distracting, and I became very aware that it was coming to breakfast time; on the other hand, the odour of blood and corruption (meat, after all, needed to be properly hanged) became more cloying as one pushed into the centre.

The king of the butchers spotted me coming down the lane (Holmes and I being the only two people in sight who were not hauling slabs of dead animal) and threw down his massive cleaver to greet me. I did not react to the slight stickiness of the hand that seized mine, merely asked after the man's daughter. His face lit up and he pulled an aged leather case from his trousers, removing a recent photograph.

I dutifully exclaimed over the image, a shy girl with large teeth but beautiful eyes wearing the soft cap of an Oxford undergraduate, then submitted to the praise and jests he pulled out every time I saw him. I introduced Holmes, and when the butcher found where Holmes lived, he instantly launched into a lecture on *thymus serpyllum*, the Sussex native herb that had given Sussex lamb its distinctive flavour but which, after Napoleon's war caused much of the countryside to be put to the plough, was largely unavailable. Before Holmes could illuminate the man on a reliable source for this succulent meat (our neighbours down the lane), I interrupted with my question.

'Darley?' he said. 'Lord Darley, yes. Died a while ago, in some heathenish place. Liked his beef, that one did. Sent me birds from time to time, when he'd had a shoot on his land that left him with more than they could use. Deer, too, couple of times. Had a conversation with him once about peacocks, his were breeding like pigeons and he thought I might like to develop a line of them. Brought me some, but they had no taste at all. Maybe if he'd fed them—'

'He lived not too far from here, didn't he? His country place, that is.'

'Up towards Bicester,' he said promptly, then scratched his head, displacing the whitish cap. 'Stratton Audley? Fringford? Somewhere in there. I'd have it in the order books, for sure. Let's see, when did he order last? Couple years ago.' He pulled out a book, prepared to hunt through its thousands of orders for an address.

'No, no,' I interrupted. 'That's plenty close enough. I'm not actually looking for the Darley place. I met him a while ago and he told me about one of his neighbours who bred a particular kind of horse that last week another friend told me he was looking for, so I thought I might see if I could find it.'

Arrant nonsense, but any tradesman who dealt with the aristocracy had a wide acceptance of nonsense, and exotic horse-breeds was well within the realm of possibilities. We thanked him, assured him again that we would be on the watch for anyone raising sheep on undisturbed pasture ('It's the native thyme, you see? Dies off under the plough but gets into the beastie's blood and waits for the oven . . .'), and made our escape from the sanguinary realms of the Market.

Turl; Broad; Magdalen; St Giles; Banbury – it takes nearly as long to name the roads as to drive them. We were back at the house before Miss Pidgeon's lights were burning, although the sky was growing pale. My bleary eyes squinted at the gates, my numb hands steered the motor through without losing either headlamp. My body craved a large meal, a gallon of coffee, and sleep.

Maybe not the coffee.

Haruki heard us come in. Before our coats were off, she was swaying a path across the sitting room, fever declaring itself in her damp hair and pink cheeks.

I reached out for her forehead but she twisted away irritably. 'Where have you been? You left hours ago. Look, it's almost morning! You must have learnt something?'

'Didn't you get the note?'

'Note? Yes,' she said, 'I found the note.' But it sounded to me as if she had forgotten it, and I wasn't at all certain I wouldn't need to catch her when she turned. She pulled Holmes' old robe around her shoulders and went back to the fire, complaining peevishly if not entirely coherently. I tossed wood on the coals, then told her I would make tea. Two minutes later, I looked into the sitting room, and found she had fallen into an uneasy sleep.

Holmes looked up as I came in. I shook my head.

'You have a pet nurse?' he asked in low voice.

'A doctor, actually. She worked at the college before she retired. But our guest will have to be unconscious before she lets me ring the woman. It'll have to be Miss Pidgeon.'

I almost laughed at the subtle shift on my husband's features.

Men might walk cautiously around Miss Pidgeon, but in our absence, the woman would watch over Haruki like a mother wolf.

CHAPTER THIRTY-THREE

Morning newspaper,
Coffee's steam curls in the sun,
Pink of wounded flesh.

WE ATE A PAIR of hastily composed sandwiches as birdsong started up in the garden. On my way up the stairs, I looked in on Haruki, finding her turning restlessly on the settee, hair damp with sweat. I pulled a rug over her tiny form, then followed Holmes up to a bed inadequately shaded by the curtains. My consciousness shut down four heartbeats after my head hit the pillow – and I slept undreaming for a solid ninety-seven minutes.

The telephone jangled like a screech of Doom. I stumbled down the stairs and snatched it from the stand, making a gargling sound that the person on the other end interpreted as a greeting.

'Morning, Miss Russell. Billy here. I have the information Mr Holmes asked me for. About Bart Collins?'

I repeated the sound, which this time he took to be encouragement. 'Collins was shot three times with an automatic pistol, and Scotland Yard recovered two of the casings. So if you come across an automatic pistol somewhere, keep that in mind.'

'Good,' I croaked.

'I also have the precise location where he was shot. You want that?'

'Just. Wait. Yes.' I stuck the corner of the pad under the telephone stand to weight it, and scribbled down the information. It meant nothing to me. No doubt Holmes would be able to picture it in an instant.

I squinted at the page to make sure the marks were actually legible, then straightened. 'Thank you, Billy, I'm not sure what—'

He interrupted me. 'Another thing. I went past the Darley house this morning, just to be sure? And looking in, all the furniture was covered over. So they are actually gone, for a bit, anyway.'

'That's very helpful, Billy. Thank you again.'

We both rang off. I yawned, and turned to face my audience of two. Holmes held out my spectacles; I traded him the scrap of paper. 'That's where Collins was found. Did you put the coffee on?'

Wordlessly, he moved towards the kitchen. I studied the remaining person, who looked surprisingly fresh and fit.

'Good morning,' I said. 'You look—'

'Did you get it?' she demanded.

'Get what?'

'You went to London for information. Wasn't that what the phone call was about?'

'May I have some coffee before the interrogation starts?' I begged.

Coffee, food and sunshine. It was going to be a glorious spring day in Oxford, although I wasn't sure I was in any shape to appreciate it.

But the brain cells began to pull themselves together, and we moved to provide Haruki with the promised information.

It does help, sometimes, to review a case aloud. As we talked, she sipped her tea and nibbled at a half piece of toast. A year ago, she'd looked fourteen years old: that morning, she looked older than I – although perhaps not older than I felt.

When we had finished, Holmes went upstairs to shave while I examined the patient's arm. The torn stitches were healing, the skin was pinkly swollen, but there was no sign of dangerous poisoning.

She was lucky not to have lost the use of her arm – if not the arm itself.

I covered it with a waterproof wrapping so she could have a bath, and later restored the bandages.

Between one thing and another, it was nearly ten o'clock when she faced me with the question. 'What do you plan next?'

'Holmes and I need to locate the Darley house.'

'Not the one in London?'

'Seems that they're both off with friends. However, the Darley country house is not far from here, and we thought we'd go and take a look. Merely a reconnaissance,' I hastened to add. My local maps had showed a hamlet by name of Darley Holt, in the general neighbourhood of the places the butcher had given us – but in England, mere name was no guarantee of a family connexion. In any event, we could hardly drive up to the door and stare openly.

'You are not going to break in?'

'During broad daylight? No.'

'You're going now?'

'Yes.'

'I will come with you.'

I had expected that. 'Your arm may be better, but you're in no shape to wander about the countryside with us. In any event, where we're going, you'd stick out like a bandaged thumb.'

'Only during the daytime.'

'Well, more so during the day,' I conceded.

She thought over what I had said. 'If you give me your word

that you will come back after your reconnaissance, I will stay. But if you go out again tonight, I shall come with you.'

'Let's see how it—'

'I will come. A team of three is better than two, for the purpose of invading a home. And if you avoid me, I will not be here when you return. I think you would rather I be with you than pursuing matters on my own, in directions you can neither control nor anticipate.'

True. The consequences could be disastrous. It was also true that having a third person keeping watch permitted the other two to devote their fuller attentions to a search. And if the house was like most of its kind, there would be a vast enough square footage to keep all three of us occupied.

I nodded in agreement. 'If you stay quiet today, and *if* we decide to go in search of the book later, we will take you with us.'

However, I made a mental note to check the boot of the motorcar before I drove off this morning, just in case.

There are any number of disguises available to a person wishing to make enquiries in the countryside. A laden wagon and bad shoes are necessary for itinerant smiths or sellers, but short of that, it is a matter of small, key flourishes. A pair of strong binoculars transforms any set of tweeds into the garments of a devout birdwatcher. A ridiculous hat, a well-used Ordnance map, and a voracious appetite mark one as a committed rambler.

However, we did not think the Darleys the kind of people known to move among the eccentrics, which left out ramblers and birdwatchers.

'I'm afraid it's horses, Holmes.'

I had a riding outfit folded away in a cedar chest, and Holmes had portions of the necessary clothing, but in the end, he had to make a quick trip down the Turl for proper riding trousers. As he was waiting, Miss Pidgeon and I cast around for the other essential part of our outfit: horseflesh.

When Holmes rang to say that his trousers had been provided and donned, I checked the car boot, then circled through Oxford, pulling to the side along the High so Holmes could jump in, before continuing across Magdalene Bridge and out through Headington. I wound along country lanes and villages to the stables kept by one of the late don's former students, where we found a lot of fat horses in the care of three thin sisters.

We chose our mounts first by their lack of distinctive appearance, and second by the recommendations of the sisters. We let them saddle the beasts, but earned their approval by double-checking the girths ourselves before mounting up. We headed north, Holmes' saddlebags bulging unbecomingly with Ordnance Survey maps.

It had been too long since I had been on a horse. My hip sockets always forgot how very wide horses' backs were, and my legs how much work it was to perch in the stirrups for hours on end. We had the sense to stop well before Darley Holt to fall from the saddles and stagger around for a while, returning the circulation to our limbs. The horses looked askance at this behaviour, but it did mean that when we remounted and rode the last ten minutes, we were able to drop from our saddles with the proper degree of insouciance.

We did not need to stay for luncheon at the public house, once we had the information we needed – that new friend of ours, Lady Darley: she had a house around here, didn't she? And where might that be, precisely? – but the smells from the kitchen would have been tempting even without the exercise, and the beef pie was almost worth the effort of getting to it.

We rode on, our aches nicely anaesthetised by drink. Between the maps and the local informants, we found the manor house without much problem.

It seemed small for an earl's estate, although as we came nearer, the truth of the matter emerged: what looked like a simple Georgian block from the front actually had a pair of wings extending out the back, one side substantial, the other less so. It was two storeys high, with possibly a third tucked under the roof slates. The front door was graced by a grand portico with tiny upper-floor balconies on either side. Both balconies had French doors; between them, a wide arched window topped the portico like a tea cosy. Fortunately, the Victorian improvements had ended with those unsuccessful architectural fillips, so the house merely came across as slightly abashed, rather than actively shamefaced.

Vines crept up iron trellises on either side of the portico; a lawn suitable for garden parties stretched out alongside; in the distance, a few acres of woodland rose up, marked on the map as Darley Grove. A trio of ancient beeches partially blocked the stables, but as we rode on, the low buildings came into view. They appeared to be stables and kennels, with nearly as much square footage as the house's ground floor. Walls and out-buildings hinted at a sizeable kitchen garden behind the house, but fields rolled out on all sides: the estate of a fox-hunting man.

Although perhaps not at the moment. Holmes climbed down and bent over his horse's front hoof as if in search of a stone, while we listened intently, but in vain, for evidence of hounds. We continued up the lane that wrapped around the house and its paddocks. This time, he dismounted and handed me the reins, to walk along the road behind me and stand as if relieving himself. In fact, we both listened and, this time, breathed in the air moving down from the house.

Birds sang; lambs bleated; the odours of spring lay all around.

But we could catch neither the smell nor the sound of dogs.

'They do still have horses,' I noted.

'The viscount and Lady Darley did go for a ride in Hong Kong,' Holmes recalled.

Idly, I reflected on the change of titles: Viscount Darley was now the Earl of Darley, but what about his stepmother? The countess – Darley's wife – old Darley, that is – wasn't she now the 'dowager'? Perhaps that depended on whether or not Tommy had married. I imagined that Charlotte, Lady Darley, would wince at the word 'dowager.'

A figure came out of the stables block with a bucket. He crossed the gravel yard to the back door, which he pushed open but did not enter. A few seconds later, a woman came to take the bucket, standing for a time in conversation. She then closed the door. The man returned to the stables.

'What do you think?' I asked Holmes.

He shook his head. 'It looks too quiet for them to be in residence. But if even one of them was home, or if they drove up while you were in the yard, you'd be trapped.'

'I'd just have to take off cross-country. That, after all, is what this animal is for.'

He cast a dubious eye at the fields. 'Rather tall hedges.'

They did look a lot higher than the low shrubbery I had urged the mare over on the ride up, and there were three, four – five of them between yard and road. 'I'll just have to hang on,' I replied, and whipped out the final piece of my disguise: a tube of scarlet lipstick.

Holmes corrected a slip with his pocket-handkerchief (horseback not being an ideal place for the application of make-up). I buttoned my spectacles into a pocket, then reined my mare around in the direction we had come in, kicking the beast into a trot. Holmes continued leading his horse along the road, since it was better to claim incipient lameness than to park one's horse in the middle of a lane for all the world to wonder at.

I jogged along, slowing to a walk as we turned into the drive. Weeds sprouted through half a mile of gravel. Fields turned to lawn near the house, and my mount's ears went forward, confirming that there were others of her kind in the stables ahead of us. Opposite the front door, the stables came more clearly into view, one wing of it given over to a more modern form of transport: motorcars. One of the three spaces was empty. I hoped devoutly that both residents were inside it, until evening at least.

The house was quiet, without the endless strains of Tommy's gramophone, but a glance in the sitting-room windows showed furniture, not dust-covers. The Darleys were either in residence, or not away for long. The mare tossed her head, and I made my grip on the reins go loose.

'Not yet,' I murmured at her ears. 'If I want you to make a break for it, you'll know.'

No head leant from a window; no surprised voice called a greeting to an old shipboard acquaintance. I made it to the yard between house and stables, where I paused, wondering whether housemaid or groom would be a more likely conversationalist.

My choice was made for me when the man I had seen earlier came out of a stall, pulling off his soft cap to reveal a tonsure of greying hair.

"Elp you, miss?'

I donned a full-blown upper-class drawl and tried not to squint myopically at him from beneath the brim of my helmet. 'Yaiss, I was out for a ride when I saw this place and it occurred to me that I'd seen a photo of it, in a friend's rooms – in college, you know? This is the Darley place, isn't it?'

'That it be, miss.'

'Oh, jolly good! I shall enquire at the house.'

'Sorry, miss, but the Darleys baint 'ere. They be gone, visitin' friends. Leicester, I b'lieve t'was.' I drank in the creamy Oxfordshire accent, so rich in rhotics and lacking in initial H's and final G's. My smile seemed to make him nervous; his hat began to revolve in his hands.

I came to myself and raised my chin again, that I might look down my nose at the rustic. My smile merely polite now, I asked him more about the Darleys, leading the man in a casual conversation about their friends, their horseflesh, their habits, the household staff. When I had as much information as I thought I could extract without rousing his suspicions, I made one last query concerning their expected return, and put on a look of disappointment at the news that they were not expected until the weekend.

'That's too, too bad. Oh well, another time. Thanks so, and cheerio!' I yanked the horse around and urged her forward before he could venture any questions in turn.

But I was not quite quick enough. 'Miss? Miss, who shall I tell 'em was by?'

'Susan,' I called over my shoulder, and drove my heels into the mare's ribs. She was startled into a canter, nearly dumping me to the gravel, but we cleared the drive without Tommy's sports car (Surely he would drive a sports car?) flying at me down the lane. I posted briskly along until I had caught Holmes up, then let the mare slow to an amble.

'Why has this country never adopted Western saddles?' I complained.

'Because English women prefer their backsides muscular?'

I laughed aloud. 'There is that. The Darleys appear to be staying here,' I told him, 'but they're away until the weekend. As the butler told Billy, in Leicestershire.'

'I was relieved when you did not come flying across the fields.'

'Not as relieved as I. I also think the poor fellow was well distracted by the lipstick. When he tells Tommy – sorry, I just can't think of him as "Lord Darley" – when he tells them there was a visitor, all he'll be able to say is that there was a young woman named Susan who had bright lipstick.'

He handed up the handkerchief that he had applied to my mouth earlier. When I returned it, the linen looked as if it had been used to mop a severed artery. He folded it cautiously into a pocket, then worked his left boot into its stirrup.

'He did not recognise the horse?' he asked, gathering the reins.

'He looked, but his gaze did not sharpen.'

'Good.'

'Something else.' I frowned, trying to pull together vague impressions. 'I think – his country accent was a bit distracting, but I *think* he doesn't like the Darleys much.'

'Doesn't respect them, you mean?'

'That's it. A certain . . . laconic flatness to some of his remarks. And although the place appears to be fully staffed, there were weeds growing in the drive and the windows wanted a scrub.'

'Interesting.' He shook his horse into a walk.

Servants don't need to like their employers – in some ways, it's easier if they don't – but a lack of respect undermines the entire machinery. For a gardener to let the weeds grow and the housekeeper to lose her pride – and for a grey-haired stableman to allow his disdain to leak out before a self-proclaimed friend of the family – their feelings had to be pretty close to contempt.

Interesting, indeed.

We disembarked from the saddles that afternoon with all the enthusiasm of geriatrics. I leant on the mare, trying to straighten my spine (I wish I could say that I was more successful at this than Holmes, twice my age) while making casual and appreciative conversation with the sisters. Helping to groom the beasts restored a degree of flexibility, but still, we walked away with the uncertain gait of a newly landed Atlantic passenger. Both of us stifled groans as we folded into my motor.

'Oh, for a Japanese bath!' I said.

'Capital idea,' he said.

Unfortunately, my own bathtub was not big enough for two. More through self-interest than a concern for my husband's spine, I made a suggestion. 'Holmes, what about if I drop you at the Turkish baths on Merton Street? A long steam and a good pummel will set you up nicely for an evening of burglary.'

'An idyllic proposal, Russell. However, I fear you shall be returning to Oxford without me.'

'Why? What do you have in mind?'

'That public house on the main road, six miles from Darley Holt. If the staff of a household are displeased, they talk over their beers.'

I sighed, resigning myself to the aches in my limbs and the smell of horse in my skin. 'I'll come, too, Holmes.'

'No. We can't have Miss Sato casting about the streets of Oxford. In any event, your presence would stifle the topics I intend to pursue.'

In the end, I did not argue too hard.

CHAPTER THIRTY-FOUR

What comes in between
A man and his father's house?
Traces of the past.

IRONICALLY, WHEN I WALKED through my front door, Haruki was in better shape than I. My muscles seemed to have petrified on the drive back.

'You are injured! What happened?'

'Not injured, just sore. Riding horses is an activity one needs to do often in order to do at all. I'll be fine after a bath and a drink. But I need to speak with Miss Pidgeon first. I'll be right back.'

Miss Pidgeon's reaction to my state was less overt than Haruki's, but for her, the raised eyebrows were extreme. 'Yes, I know,' I told her. 'I won't come in, but I wondered if you might possibly have time for a little job?'

One of the other advantages of having Miss Pidgeon so immediately to hand was her willingness to perform the odd task for me. I paid her, despite her protest, knowing that money was tight in her half of our little compound. I did try not to take advantage of her, although she claimed not to mind grocery-shopping and queue-standing. Still, her favourite tasks were those that involved the shelves of libraries.

Today's job would be to her liking: a quick trip to the Oxford Town Hall. When I explained what was needed, she gave a brisk nod. 'That is in fact highly convenient. I was just remembering that I needed to bicycle down to the lending library this afternoon. I can easily stop by the records office while I am there.'

I gave her solemn thanks, and watched her catch up her hat and an empty book bag.

Miss Pidgeon was not a terribly accomplished liar. But her bicycle tyres were crossing the gravel before my own kitchen door shut behind me.

Haruki was no more convinced by my claims of well-being than I had been by hers. She stood at the foot of the stairs watching me pull myself up by the handrail, but it was true: heat and a large brandy loosened muscles. An hour later, I pattered down the stairs again, conscious of a howling empty pit within.

'I'm starving. Do you want anything?'

Bread, cheese, pickle and a slab of leftover beef pie vanished from my plate, followed by a bowl of bean soup (both the latter thanks to Miss Pidgeon), some biscuits with more cheese, and a handful of dried fruit. Haruki ate a bowl of cold rice with green tea poured over it.

I piled my dishes in the sink. As I was filling the kettle, Miss Pidgeon's homely face went past the garden window. I gestured her inside – although as was her habit, she knocked before reaching for the knob.

'That was fast,' I said – the file in her hand and the look on her face told me she'd been successful, despite the hour.

'It was just on the edges, but yes, the house was there.'

She laid the file on the table and turned to go. 'Wait, do have a cup of tea, Miss Pidgeon,' I said.

But no, she had dinner to put on, or a cat to feed, or something.

What was the equivalent of 'house-proud' when it came to the job of being a good neighbour?

I allowed her to slip away, then bent to see what she had brought me.

'What is that?' Haruki asked.

'Well, Holmes and I saw the Darley house from the outside, but it occurred to me that if we could locate a valuation or survey of some kind in the local records office, it might give a description of the rooms. I would go down to Somerset House, but I don't really have time for another trip to London, and I thought Miss Pidgeon might not mind having a quick word with her friends at the Town Hall. And look what she's found.' I laid a page in front of my guest: a drawing of the house, both its main storeys, each room bearing a neat label.

The soft spring evening light faded over Oxford while Haruki and I pored over the house plan. Later, as the ground-floor lights in the houses around us began to shut off and the upstairs lights took their place, we chose clothing appropriate for a country house break-in. She had the basics, although she requested a coat that she could button over the sling. The result looked like a joke, but she said it was comfortable. I filled a rucksack with dark clothing for Holmes, spare torch batteries, a length of rope, and the like. While I waited for the pot of strong coffee to brew, I studied my companion's child-sized hands.

With that arm, letting her inside the house would be risky: even someone capable of walking the Marconi wires on a ship might find it difficult to scramble from an upper-storey window without a full complement of functional limbs. Still, if she remained on the ground floor, she should be able to work a window-latch and drop out from there.

'I don't have any gloves that will fit you,' I said.

'It is not cold.'

'I was thinking of fingerprints. I could paint your fingers with shellac, but that's both confining and uncomfortable. Or you could take great care to wipe down anything you touch.'

'Fingerprints will not be a problem,' she said.

I opened my mouth to remind her of how she'd underestimated the University's constables. Then I decided against it. 'See that you do,' I told her. 'I have no wish for Holmes to spend his waning years behind bars.'

I poured the coffee into a flask, shoved it and a packet of sandwiches into the rucksack, and looked around my tidy scholar's house, wondering if this would be the last time I stood here.

I tried not to think about what had happened the last time we'd gone after the Darleys.

The pub was closed. The headlamps played across its front as the wheels left the road's metalled surface. The rear passenger door opened, and Holmes dropped inside, stinking of beer, tobacco, and stale sweat. The lingering traces of horse about him seemed almost fresh by comparison.

Wordlessly, I handed him the flask and sandwiches. With equal silence, he pushed the two counter-agents to ethanol down his throat. After a time, he capped the flask and I pointed out the pile of his clothing. His boots went away across the weed-choked gravel, then returned a few minutes later, diverting to the far back to stuff his old garments in among the tyre-irons.

The male person who re-joined us was considerably less oppressive.

'The local community believe that Thomas and Lady Darley are rather more intimate than one might expect of a young man and his stepmother,' he reported.

'But – they could scarcely bear to look at each other!' The moment the protest left my mouth I heard its absurdity: there can be more than one reason for two people to avoid one another's gaze. 'Oh,' I said.

'Indeed.'

'Well, that would certainly explain the weeds and the windows.'

Haruki spoke up. 'Do you mean they are having an affair?'

'The Darley footman's sister is married to the innkeeper's younger brother,' Holmes said. 'The footman likes to gossip, and country folk are happy to pass talk around.'

'Do you suppose . . .' Haruki's voice trailed away.

'That they were involved while his father was alive?' I finished for her. 'If not actively, they may have been considering it. They did take great care not to be seen together much.'

'I thought they simply did not get along.'

'Sons and second wives often do not,' I agreed.

'Shall we go?' Holmes asked.

'Look at this first,' I said. I gave him the sketch of the house and a torch to view it by.

'This is not your handwriting,' he noted.

'Miss Pidgeon went down to the Town Hall for me, and got lucky.'

'Ah,' he said. 'Your Irregular.'

I laughed. 'She would be secretly delighted at the title. Now, it's possible that the Darleys keep the book, or even just the document, with them wherever they go, but that's not likely. If it's locked up in the London house, we'll make other plans. But if it's here, Haruki and I agree that it's in a safe. And a safe is most likely either in the ground-floor room marked "office", or upstairs in his dressing room. If you're right, that Tommy has taken over his father's life along with his father's wife, he's probably moved into his rooms as well.' The two main bedrooms and their dressing rooms were next to each other, allowing free passage between them without risking the eyes of guests or servants.

Not that one can keep private activities from servants for long.

'Lady Darley may have a jewel safe as well,' Holmes pointed out.

Great: two safes to open. Maybe three. 'Are your hands steady enough for safe-cracking?' I asked.

'They will be, yes.' I hoped that was so. I could open a combination mechanism, but I lacked his vast experience, and frankly, his cool nerves. Hunching over a dial while listening for servants was not my idea of entertainment.

As I drove, he and I discussed our plan of attack, occasionally tossing a question at Haruki. I found the access lane across from the house that we had spotted from horseback that morning, its surface chewed by the hooves of livestock and the tracks and tyres of farm machinery. Holmes jumped out to open its gate. I shot through into the field and behind the stand of trees, shutting off the headlamps. Black clamped down. The engine's cooling noises seemed very noisy in the stillness, and Haruki and I moved quietly as we climbed from the motor, letting the doors click shut.

The moonlight was thin. We followed Holmes' shielded torch across the rutted soil to the gate, working its latch shut lest some farmer's herd take a stroll. In the silent night, we stumbled along uneven ground towards the road.

Rather, two of us stumbled. Haruki had eyes like a cat. She seemed to pay little attention to the torchlight, yet her feet met the uneven ground as if it was midday. She did not even seem much bothered by having one arm strapped to her side.

We lesser mortals made it to the metalled surface without planting our faces in the mud, then continued more quickly up the road and down the drive to the Darley house. Altogether, a walk that might have taken six or seven minutes in daylight had only taken twice that.

Country houses generally had substantial locks on the front door, designed for giving reassurance to the family, and more practical locks on those doors used for the comings and goings of servants throughout the day. We circled to the back, and were inside within minutes.

The lurid gleam from Holmes' torch reassured us that no scullery maid slept before the fire. We moved on into the house. Miss Pidgeon's work proved invaluable, allowing us to anticipate what we would find around each corner. We first established that the ground floor was unoccupied, then went through the gun room, which contained enough armament for a revolt – everything but an automatic pistol. We re-locked the gun-room door, explored the office enough to see that it had no safe, then left our small companion to search the remainder of the ground floor while Holmes and I headed upstairs.

At the foot of the formal stairway we paused. The hands of the grandfather clock showed two minutes to midnight; weeds and unwashed windows cautioned that no one would have rushed to repair a creak in the stairs. So we waited for the clock's hands to click forward, then trotted up the stairs with its gong to hide any underfoot creaks.

The house was a squared U, its left-hand wing (here on the upper storey, the guest rooms) somewhat longer than the right, which housed the servants. The flat bottom of the U, downstairs a drawing room and the office, up here held the suites of the house's master and mistress (appropriate terms, here). These rooms faced the drive, while the guest and servants' wings looked out onto garden and stable yard, respectively. A long corridor hugged the inner wall of the U, with paintings and doors on one side and windows to a formal courtyard garden on the other. A short length of side-corridor across from the stairway ended in the big arched window over the portico, making the U of hallway more of a squat Y. This truncated corridor separated the main bedrooms to our left from the guest rooms to the right. We turned left.

Six rooms lay along this section of the house: two suites, each with bedroom, dressing room, and a bath and lavatory. Having established that they were empty, we then stuck our heads in all the other doors on the first floor, other than the baize marking the servants' wing, but all the beds were empty.

Holmes started on Tommy's quarters while I headed for Lady Darley's perfumed bower, trying not to sneeze. Her bed was wide and soft, its coverlet a riot of embroidered Chinese flowers. The walls were covered in pale blue watered silk, with long curtains of a slightly darker shade. A glance behind the curtains showed a pair of French doors and their diminutive balcony.

Her jewel safe was in the dressing room. It was a steel monstrosity that Holmes could have stood in without having to stoop – probably designed to store the household plate when the family was away, rather than just tiaras and necklaces. I eyed the mechanism, and went in search of my husband.

Tommy's safe was much smaller, and the mechanism simpler – Holmes had the door open already. I looked in over his shoulder, and realised that 'Lord Darley's safe' would have been a more accurate description.

'So Tommy did take over more than the title,' I murmured.

The steel box held the possessions that Darley the Younger would wish to keep from the eyes of servants every bit as much as his father had. I was prepared for the pornographic photographs, having been through Lord Darley's rooms before, and there was little need to hold the reels of film to the light to guess what was on them. But the files were the clincher: the Prince Regent of Japan had not been Darley's only victim.

Many of the files were old, their letters and photographs so outdated as to be useless as a source of blackmail in these free-and-easy times: few would pay to be saved from a mild embarrassment. Holmes left those where he found them, although he did tuck two envelopes and a file into his shirt-front, their contents having political revelations whose stir would be further-reaching.

He also removed two letters in foreign writing, one of them in Arabic (which he read) and the other in Bulgarian (which he did not).

There was a gun here, as there had been beside Thomas Darley's bed, but both were revolvers, not automatic pistols. No Bashō. No Hokusai. No Japanese books at all, other than a racy little thing featuring Samurai and geishas in unlikely positions that I was tempted to steal until I pictured Mrs Hudson's reaction.

'Anything?' said a voice behind us, causing me to drop the book and Holmes to crack his head on the door.

'You're supposed to be downstairs!' I hissed.

'There is nothing down there,' Haruki said. 'I thought I could be of some use up here.'

'If we need to get out fast, you'll never manage with that arm.'

'What, from one storey up? I could jump that far with *no* arms.' I frowned at her left arm, but having seen her on the ship's wires, it was hard to argue. 'What have you found?'

Nothing, was what we had found. Holmes rose. 'That dial stood on nineteen,' he told me, and walked through to Lady Darley's rooms. I arranged the files and erotica as they had been, closed the door, turned the dial to 19, and went to see how Holmes was getting on.

Haruki sat on her heels beside him, holding the torch while Holmes, eyes closed, focused all his attention on the play of the dial beneath his fingers. Her face was serene, patient, as it had been that day in the Prince Regent's garden. As her father's face had been, three days before . . .

She was such an enigma. She looked like a child; she was far too trusting, she had rushed unthinking into an unknown place, and paid the price. Yet where someone her age ought to be chewing her fingernails, here she was waiting for this relative stranger to do an unlikely job. I wished her father were there, to ask. I wished her father were there, to see her, trim and confident with one arm in a sling.

The steel behemoth gave a small sigh, and Holmes reached for the handle. Haruki rocked smoothly back and stood, thumbing the shield off her torch so we could look within.

We gaped in astonishment. The vast space was almost empty. A couple of leather and silver devices whose purpose I did not want to know; a dozen jeweller's cases containing diamond necklaces, diamond tiaras and a diamond bandeau; decorative boxes that held an assortment of rings, earrings, bracelets, and lesser necklaces, and that was all.

We examined every box, searching for false compartments. There were none. At the end, we shut the door and turned as one to look at the dim outlines of bed, settee, decorative table, and a pair of waist-high Chinese urns on either side of the curtains, with the French windows overlooking the Oxfordshire countryside.

We spread out to search. Holmes went over to the twin urns, Haruki began opening drawers, and I – I reluctantly turned my light to the bed, then its table. In its drawer lay a lace-trimmed handkerchief, a velvet eye mask with elastic band, a tube of lavender-scented hand crème, and a pair of cotton gloves that reeked of lavender. Next came a small silk bag with a decorative button which, when I opened it, contained pretty much what I had expected. Below that was a small Morocco-leather notebook with a tiny silver pen on a ribbon. This I picked up eagerly, only to find many of the pages torn away, and the remaining ones covered with housekeeping memoranda and notes for future shopping expeditions: *Stockings. Mrs T's hat – feather? Send furs. Guest room linens?*

Unless the countess used some diabolically clever code, these were just notes.

The little notebook had concealed another volume, this one an illustrated edition of the Burton *Kama Sutra*. Very thoroughly illustrated – but as I glanced through them, my amusement faded. I looked more closely, turning one page, then another, mirth turning to something nearer shock. On the surface, they were simply randy pictures, fit companions to the hearty and cheerful coupling of Mr Burton's text. Then the eye caught an unexpected shape, an odd expression, and the pictures turned . . . nasty. Graphic and brutal and more about pain than procreation, the images were appalling. They made me want to scrub my eyeballs.

I flipped shut the cover, taking an involuntary step back. Could Lady Darley . . . ? Was it possible to look at those images and not see . . . what I saw? And if that was possible, if she was in fact innocent enough to see nothing but a nice, sexy, exotic romp, who could have been cruel enough to play that kind of a joke on her?

Gingerly, unwilling to pick that volume up again, I edged it aside with the tip of my finger, finding an ivory comb, a tiny tube of something called 'Eye Rejuvenator', and the decorative Bible I had seen in Japan.

Grateful that I had not been confronted by a stash of bed-toys (and wondering if I was being prudish), I closed the drawer and went to help Haruki check behind the other drawers.

At the end, we stood near the door and looked back at the room. 'Do you want to move the furniture to look under the carpet?' I asked Holmes.

He shook his head. 'It wouldn't be in a place requiring more than one man to uncover. That bed would need four strong footmen. It must be somewhere else.'

'What about the room marked "library"? Close enough to the bedrooms to feel safe, but separate.'

Blackmailers had a tactile response to their key possessions: they liked their stolen diaries or photographs close to hand, for the same reason that girls hid love letters amongst their lingerie: to gloat and caress them. Practical reasons might separate an extortionist from the source of his power, but ideally, he – or she – wanted the physical reminder close at hand.

As we walked down the carpeted corridor, the clock at the foot of the stairs rang two.

The door to the room marked 'library' opened not off the main corridor, but from its subsidiary leg. To our left were a pair of doors. The first was covered with light brown baize: a glance showed narrow, uncarpeted stairs descending to the kitchen realm. The second door was painted wood, behind which lay a shallow storage room packed to bursting with steamer trunks, hatboxes, valises, and the like.

Separated from these doors by the width of a corridor and the great arched window, a single, far grander wooden door opened into a book-lined room. Physically it was the start of the guest room wing, but the placement of its door and the sumptuous fittings said that this was not a room for guests. Heavy curtains in a rich shade of orange hid the other set of French doors and their balcony. Logs and kindling lay in the marble fireplace, ready for a match. Bottles and glasses clustered on a sleek sideboard next to a gramophone. Three comfortable chairs and a wide settee were arranged on a modern orange and green carpet in front of the fire. The closest thing to library furniture was a spindle-legged gilt writing desk against one wall; most of its top was taken up by two small porcelain busts and a hideous little ormolu clock.

The room might have been designed originally as a place to read, but that was not its chief purpose now. The books were too uniform and decorative, the lighting too poor. In a public house, this would be the snug. There was even a latch on the door, lest a maid walk in at some inopportune moment.

'How do they think they can keep their affair secret?' I wondered aloud.

'A year has gone by, since Darley's death. Perhaps they intend to move to Paris. Or New York.'

'They could never raise their heads in Society.'

'This is 1925,' Holmes pointed out. 'If one has money, one forms one's own Society.'

'Not if one wishes to attend Palace functions.'

His voice went hard. 'No Darley has been invited to the Palace since 1914.'

Yes, I thought: he would have seen to that much, before returning to his German spy case in America.

Haruki had begun to methodically examine the room's furnishings, tipping back paintings, running her good hand along the seams of the settee, pulling open the drawers on the writing desk. Each time she finished with something, she made a show of cleaning it with her linen handkerchief. She was humouring us, clearly disbelieving in the danger of fingerprints.

Didn't matter, so long as she wiped things down.

We spent an hour searching that room, treading on each other's toes all the while. Every book, every picture, every inch of the mantelpiece. At the end, I clawed my fingers through my hair. 'There's nothing here.'

Haruki dropped onto the settee, cradling her arm. She looked pale. Holmes was grey with fatigue. He would probably kill for a cigarette. We all needed to eat something. And the clock had sounded three: before long, the servants would begin to stir.

'Are we yet satisfied that it's not here?' I asked. 'Shall we try the London house next?'

Neither of them replied. We were all gazing off into the preceding hours, trying to see what we might have missed. Holmes and I ought to check the downstairs – although, having watched Haruki search, she seemed as competent as I when it came to mistrusting surfaces.

Failure, again. The first time, Lord Darley had outsmarted us, unlikely as that seemed, sticking his copy of the Bashō to the underside of a dining table. This time, we had looked at all such places, and found nothing. The library had given me such high hopes: not only close at hand, the room was so personal, it would feel like a haven to someone wishing to hide a valuable piece of criminality. The room had even been made over by its current residents: the rest of the house had paintings and decorations accumulated by previous generations, but here the wallpaper was fresh, the paintings *au courant*, even *avant-garde*. The gramophone on the sideboard was new, as were the records – many of them dance numbers, which explained the room's patch of bare boards rather than carpet to the walls.

It was a distinctive room. One could imagine the lovers choosing the pieces, comparing swatches of orange curtain fabric to the orange in the painting across the room. And the paintings: four of them, by different artists – not, I was glad to see, including Damian Adler. To find the work of Holmes' son here would be intolerable.

But the style was not unlike Damian's: powerful, clear, modern. One of them was by a Spaniard whose work I had seen somewhere, a biting mockery of accepted virtues. Its figure in a City suit bore a slight resemblance to Lord Darley, although the crucified man sneering down at him had the pencil moustache and slicked hair of a jazz singer – looking not at all like Tommy, so the piece had probably not been commissioned.

Holmes stirred. 'I shall take a look at the rooms designated "guest bedrooms" on Miss Pidgeon's map,' he said. 'Russell, would you please make certain we have left no fingerprints?'

I grunted, absently. Something about the paintings was prodding at the back of my mind. 'Do these pictures make you think of something?' I asked Holmes.

He looked from the crucified jazz singer to the huge and undeniably phallic snake curled lovingly around a trio of kittens, to the cityscape with the brilliant green sky, and shook his head. 'They make me think we should ban the sale of oil paint for a generation.'

I looked at Haruki, but she just shook her head. What was

it? Something that Holmes' eye did not see, but mine did . . .

'Jesus!' I said.

Holmes raised his eyebrow, but I was not cursing. I looked at him, feeling the grin grow on my face. 'I know where the book is.'

Chapter Thirty-Five

A woman of flesh,
A girl made from tempered steel,
A man caught between.

WE STOOD BESIDE LADY Darley's bed, an unshielded torch shining into the drawer.

'Lord Darley attended church services on the ship,' I said. 'His wife preferred a day's riding. She has none of the paraphernalia of religion in her rooms – not so much as a gold cross on a chain. She is having an affair with her husband's son, may have committed adultery with him, and has paintings mocking religion in the room she created with her lover. Yet she keeps a Bible in the table beside her bed, beneath dirty books and, well, things.'

I did not doubt what I would find. I pulled the Bible out from under the cotton gloves, the notebook, the *Kama Sutra*, and the rest, thumbing back the ornate silver latch. Inside lay the frontispiece, as it had earlier. I had even admired the binding that kept a book's internal pages flat, rather than splaying to follow the cover.

This time, I turned back the pages themselves. And there, at the beginning of 2 Kings, a rectangle had been sliced through the remaining pages. Inside it, fitting the hole precisely, nestled a book I had seen before, yet never laid eyes on.

I let Haruki work the Bashō from its nest.

One could see its age. Bourke the Younger had done a superb job on his fake, but if one actually looked at this one, one could feel the number of hands that had opened it in its eighty-odd years of life, the royal – nay, divine – eyes that had lingered over it.

To have it in the drawer with that . . . other thing was an obscenity.

Haruki made to slip it behind her sling, then hesitated, and held the book out to me. 'Will you look for the document, please, Mary?'

I laid down my torch and accepted the volume that could topple an empire. Taking the knife from its sheath in my left boot, I slipped its point between the layers of the cover, using slow prising motions to keep the sharp steel from slicing through fibres. When the two halves were apart, I held out the book, spine-side up. Holmes raised the torch's beam for her. Haruki's childlike fingers eased between the layers, to emerge with a bit of paper folded into quarters. She started to drop the book onto the bed, then caught herself, handing it to me instead. She undid the folds, her eyes travelling down the first line of characters – and then closing, in a moment of relief.

She let the page fall back into its tight folds without reading to its end, then inserted the letter into the cover, slid the book into its case, and finally tucked the whole thing into her sling. Except that her hand came away still carrying it – no: not the Emperor's book, but Bourke's copy. One of them.

'That's the one Darley had in Tokyo?' The one that deceived the Prince Regent. The one Sato had died to give him.

She smiled.

Of course it was. As if she might have been able to get at the other, stored safely on the Bodleian's shelves. Far too safely. For the first time, it hit me: How on earth were we going to trade the real one for theirs? And on its heels, a second question: Or would Haruki have her own thoughts, as to whose was the rightful claim?

She laid the false Hokusai in the Bible, and the Bible in the drawer. I arranged the *Kama Sutra*, the notebook, and the rest back where they had started. The drawer closed on this peculiar mix of holiness and sin, and as if to signal its import, a quick flare of light flashed through the room. Startled, I looked into Holmes' face, realised that I could see it – then realised what that meant.

'A car!' He was already in motion, around the bed to the balcony, peering through a gap of the curtains. Haruki and I stood breathless, waiting . . . Then the ripple of laughter came, followed by the slam of a car door.

'The guest rooms,' Holmes ordered. We scurried from the bedroom and down the corridor, past the short leg of hallway and around the bend into the guest wing. Haruki and I stopped there, although Holmes continued on, opening the furthest door and disappearing inside. I heard the faint sound of a window cracking open, and he returned, having ensured our escape route.

We clustered at the bend to listen.

Noise echoed from below, voices and the thump of a door closing. The voices grew more distinct, rising up the stairs. Eventually, sound became words.

'– that Annabelle would want to marry him?' Tommy's voice, the same pompous drawl I had spent weeks hearing on the *Thomas Carlyle*. 'He hasn't tuppence to his name.'

'He is quite pretty.'

'And she's a dog. But a rich dog.'

She laughed. 'You're a bad man, Tommy.'

'That's why you love me.'

'What were you and Anthony talking . . .' Her words became abruptly indistinct, although we could still hear the cadence of speech: they had gone into one of the bedrooms. Haruki stepped away, slipping past my grabbing hand. Halfway down the corridor she paused to listen. But the words were still unclear, so she, damn her wounded hide, then strode off down the carpeting to press her ear against Lady Darley's door.

'Holmes, this is impossible,' I hissed.

It was also a touch ridiculous, two people cowering in the darkness while the third stood blatantly under the stairway lights. The Darleys were heading to bed: how much helpful information were they likely to let slip around their toothbrushes? That only happened in detective stories.

He agreed. We crept forward on the thick carpet towards the muffled voices. At the doors, his hand reached out for Haruki's good shoulder, but before he could turn her around and propel her towards the staircase, Tommy's voice came, shockingly close.

'I'm going to have a drink. Come with me?'

The rattle of the doorknob no doubt hid the reply, but we did not wait for it. The voice sparked an undignified sprint down the corridor, Haruki at the fore.

Except that, instead of making for the dim safety of the guest wing, she turned abruptly left, into the truncated corridor with the big window at the end. I, with Holmes at my back, veered after her.

She grabbed the door to the storage room and stepped inside. No room for us, no time to yank her out. I reached for the baize door ('*What did you think of that bubbly they served? He can put me in the way of a few cases, if we–*') but Holmes scooped me up and shoved me towards the library. Madness – but no time to argue, just duck inside and thread a path through the furniture while

Holmes eased the door shut, then followed me across the room to the French doors that I had ready, unlatched and open. He passed through the orange curtains, then tugged them together but for a crack before shutting the glass doors.

'What the hell was she thinking?' I whispered furiously. 'And why didn't you let me go down the servants' stairs?'

'They might ring for the butler. As for Miss Sato, she no doubt wanted to listen in.'

'What is she, a child?'

Then the library lights went on. We sank to the balcony's tiled floor, and prepared to wait out the lovers while they had their drink and went back to their rooms.

I hoped they wouldn't dawdle: it was cold out here.

Holmes' arrangement of the curtains had granted us a narrow slice of the room. Tommy had put on weight in the last year – he looked more like his father than ever.

The new earl laid a match to the fire, then poured a drink, walking over to study the mocking crucifixion for a minute before turning towards the door. 'There you are. That's a jolly robe on you. What would you like?' he asked. 'Shall I ring for Baker?'

'No, don't wake him, unless you want ice. Although it's bad they didn't notice us coming in.' She, on the other hand, was looking extremely well. Widowhood clearly suited Lady Darley – widowhood and an illicit affair. Her 'jolly' robe was a very effective piece of the dressmaker's art: a sumptuous garment of dark red silk that looked about to slither to the floor under its own weight, with a neckline arranged to draw attention to womanly breasts. Her hair, too, seemed designed to tantalise, with pins holding its richness in precarious balance. She even sat down with a seductive wriggle that

I did not think was unconscious, and raised large brown eyes at the young man before the fire. 'I told you the servants were getting irresponsible. Is there any of that Chartreuse left? The bottle that mad friend of yours gave us?'

'Should be a little – yes, here.'

'Just a mouthful. That's good. Aah.' She sat in the chair closest to the fire, her face towards us. Tommy stood with his back to the fire, gazing down at her.

'Tired?' he asked.

'Long drive.'

'I know. But isn't it nicer to be back here, rather than stay another night up in bloody Leicestershire?'

'It's nice wherever you are, my dear.' Some faint shade of meaning in her voice caught my ear, although there was nothing untoward in her face: gentle smile on her full lips, eyes crinkled in a show of affection.

'I'm not sure about Baker, but I think we really ought to clear out the staff of the London house. They're getting on my nerves, a little.'

'Couldn't we retain the cook?' she asked.

'Clean sweep might be better.'

'Whatever you say.' There it was again: did she sound just the least bit . . . condescending? If so, it disappeared in the next sentence. 'Your barrister friend seemed a bit more optimistic, tonight.'

'He did, didn't he? We might not have to move to America, after all. Though it would be a pity not to have it in a church.'

'Damn the Church,' she said, and he laughed.

'The laws of consanguinity,' I breathed into my husband's ear. English civil law might possibly be persuaded that Lady Darley had never been Tommy's stepmother, since he was an adult before his

346

father married her, thus raising no bar against their marriage – but the Church of England would never agree.

Again, I wondered at that faint dismissive edge to her voice. One did not generally patronise a man one was in love with.

They talked for a while: a show they'd seen in London; gossip he'd heard about the actress and the theatre's owner; a statue that he wanted to buy and she did not. My hands went numb.

At last, he moved, setting his empty glass on the mantelpiece and walking around to the back of her chair. He bent to nuzzle his face in his lover's neck. She tilted her head, encouraging his mouth to travel down. Several minutes passed, and matters were on the edge of becoming uncomfortable for a pair of onlookers when Tommy straightened and stood away, holding his hand out to the sitting woman. 'Come to bed.'

She stretched out an arm to her glass, down to the last half-inch – then jerked at some motion behind the young man. He whirled around to the back of her chair, and the two of them stared towards the library door, the sides of both faces taut with alarm.

'Who the bloody hell are you?' he demanded.

'Tommy, that's – it's the Japanese girl. From the boat – and the party.' Holmes' iron grip stopped me from rising to crash through the doorway. 'Wait,' he whispered.

Quivering with reaction, I obeyed.

Standing in the doorway, demure as a child and one arm in a sling, Haruki Sato looked like the most harmless thing in the world.

CHAPTER THIRTY-SIX

Bashō's words, burning.
The burn of a knife on flesh.
A young man who burns . . .

'WHAT THE DEVIL ARE *you* doing here?' Tommy demanded.

Lady Darley spoke at the same instant. 'How did you get in?'

Haruki answered her first. 'The front door was not locked.'

'Of course it was locked! We always lock it.' But her pretty hands gathered the neck of the silk she wore, as if in defence.

'Perhaps your servants always lock it for you.'

'Tommy did tonight.'

'Perhaps the lock is broken.'

In the face of Haruki's calm insistence, one could see doubt creep onto the woman's face. Still: 'It was locked, but never mind. What are you doing here?'

'I wish to speak with you about my father,' she said.

Tommy intervened. 'Your father? Why should we know him? I'm going to ring for—'

'My father died with yours.'

'He—' The young earl had been turning towards the bell pull beside the fireplace, but at her words, he jerked around, his face going from shock to rage as the implication hit. 'Your father was that drunken bastard of a wine waiter? Why didn't you say – Christ! You little bitch, I ought to—' He changed direction, hands clenched as he stalked around the chairs.

'Tommy!' Lady Darley's sharp voice brought him to a halt, then immediately modulated into cajoling. 'Maybe we should let her explain? We can always telephone the police afterwards.'

'Darling, this person's father was that clumsy idiot who tripped and knocked my Papa . . .'

His words ran dry, as a son's loss grappled with the lover's gain.

'I know, dear, I heard the child. Perhaps she's here to apologise for the man's stupidity.'

Haruki betrayed no reaction to the Darley insults. *Get the job done.* Sato had lived by the motto. He had given his dignity for it, and his public honour. And ultimately, his life. 'I am not here to apologise. My father, too, died that night.'

'If he hadn't, I'd have seen him hanged for it, damn his eyes.'

'And now *you* are Lord Darley.'

This time he did hit her – one stride forward then an open-handed blow that sent her staggering against the bookshelves. She had not even tried to avoid it, this woman who could throw him across the room – snap his neck if she wished – merely cringed enough that his blow landed, not on her face, but against hard skull.

He cursed and shook his fingers, then seized the nape of her neck and propelled her towards the settee.

The countess's expression had not changed at this eruption of violence. She sat back in her chair to study the uninvited guest. 'Very well. You are not here to apologise. Why are you here?'

'As I said,' Haruki told her. 'I wish to speak about my father. And also about a stolen book.'

Sudden electricity crackled through the room: I almost expected to see hair rising.

Lady Darley reacted first, snapping to her feet. 'Tommy, where's the gun?'

'Where it always is.'

Beside his bed: we'd seen it in the search.

She flung herself out of the room while Tommy loomed over the invader, ready to tackle her. Haruki merely studied the crackling fire. Her toes, I noticed, barely touched the floor.

Lady Darley came back, carrying both pistol and Bible. She laid the ornate volume on the low table, and resumed her chair. It was not the first time she'd handled a gun.

Tommy flipped back the cover. He stopped. 'It's still there.'

'No,' Lady Darley said. 'That is one of Mr Bourke's.'

Pages tore as he ripped the book from its nest. He frantically clawed the book out of its slipcase, flipping through it, then taking it to the lamp to look more closely. 'Are you sure?'

'Yes.'

He threw it down and stared at Haruki. 'Where is it? You bloody bitch, I'm going to—' Again, Holmes' hand held me back. Tommy pounced on the gun, Lady Darley's grip tightening for a moment before she let him take it.

'Tommy!' The crack of Charlotte Darley's voice brought him to a halt. The weapon was three feet away from Haruki: I'd seen her in action on the dojo floor, but that distance made grabbing difficult. 'Let me take a look at that sling she's wearing.'

The knife the countess drew from the writing desk was designed to separate uncut book pages: plenty sharp enough to separate skin. She stepped between Tommy and Haruki, pausing with the blade against the small woman's neck . . . then continued on, sliding it between the sling and the arm. She sawed. The sling fell away. She sawed again, and the sleeve parted, revealing the neat wrappings I had put there in Oxford. The third time, her motions against the gauze must have prompted a reaction, inaudible across the room.

'Hurts, does it?' The older woman pressed firmly against the arm, and this time, the gasp was clear.

The pain was unnecessary. The rich brown hair bent down over the arm, so close I thought the woman was about to taste the blood – and, in one of those odd connexions the brain produces under stress, I suddenly knew that the toys in the bedside table were used not on her, but by her.

However, she drew away without an open display of barbarism, tossing aside the knife before she reached into the body of the sling.

She slid the book from its cover to examine it, then slid it back into its case – and hauled off to hit Haruki across the face with it, snapping her head around. When she sat down again, there was a cruel smile on her lips – a smile that Tommy, standing behind her with the gun, did not see.

'Is that the copy?' he demanded.

'No, see how pretty it is? This is the original.'

The countess fitted the book into the Bible's hidden compartment, closed the cover, and gave it an approving pat. Then she took the project that Bourke the Younger had laboured over so long, pulled it from its slipcase, and tossed both onto the flames. The pages unfurled, an accordion banner of ink and colour spreading over the logs. The fire paused, then began to lick at its edges. She picked up her near-empty glass, then, and turned back to the intruder. 'So. Why did you want the book?'

'It belongs to the Emperor of Japan.'

'Prince Hirohito gave it to King George,' she pointed out.

'His Highness did not know what he was giving.'

'A book.'

'A document. But you did not look for that, did you?'

Lady Darley's gloating look faltered. The Chartreuse splashed across the table as she lunged for the Bible. Its silver corners dug a long scratch in the polished wood, and she made a little cry of frustration as its latch defied her crimson nails.

But at last she had it. Tommy's attention had lapsed, and now would be the time for Haruki – but she made no move, merely sat swinging her legs, watching Lady Darley pull out the book, yank it from its case, rip open the back edge of its cover . . .

And confirm that the document was inside.

The face she turned on Haruki made me wonder why I had ever thought the woman beautiful. 'It's still there. Tommy, keep your eye on her, for heaven's sake. And do sit down. We may be here for a while.'

God, I hoped not. The servants were going to find us here, frozen onto the balcony like a pair of crouching gargoyles. But Tommy reluctantly decided his lover was right, and dropped into a chair with his back to us.

'Tell me why I shouldn't let Tommy shoot you right now? It wouldn't be difficult to explain. Tommy and I came home. Found you here. You threatened us. You had a knife – that knife.' She nodded at the abandoned page-cutter on the table.

'My corpse might be awkward to explain. Especially after cutting away my sleeve and bandages.'

'I am very good at explaining.'

'I believe it. On the other hand, I will quietly go away, if you only answer my question.'

'You expect us to—' Tommy bristled, but the countess spoke over him.

'What question is that?'

'Darling, you don't—'

'Let her speak, sweetheart,' the countess said, then added, 'Please?'

'We can't let her go!'

'Why not? We have the book. We have the letter. Without those, what can she say? A young woman, consumed by grief over her father's death, blames the English people she sees as responsible. She'll either get a prison sentence for breaking in and threatening us, or be deported. Either way, she's harmless.'

'What if she saw the . . . other things.'

'You think she got into *that* safe? Look at her, Tommy. She's a child.'

We all looked at her. A tiny figure with a bleeding arm and the face of an adolescent: absurd, to picture her as a safe-cracker.

I began to see why Sato had dispatched his daughter to learn the ways of the West: a weapon that disarming could be formidable.

So make your move, I urged silently, *before we freeze – or the sun comes up to turn us to stone.*

'What is your question?' Lady Darley asked Haruki.

'One question, my Lady. Was it your husband who came up with the rather complex plan that centred around the Emperor's book? Or was it you?'

The answer to that would explain all the other cases in Tommy's safe as well – although Haruki was not about to admit that she had seen those.

I thought the countess was not going to reply. So long a silence passed that Tommy shifted in his chair, although the two women merely gazed at each other, motionless.

'Tommy, would you please telephone to that nice friend of your father's on the Oxford police force? Tell him we have caught an Oriental breaking into our house, and would like him to make a quiet arrest.'

'I'll ring down to Baker first. Bloody servants, I can't think why none of them have heard—'

'No, don't wake them. Just the police. Please, Tommy dear. The number is in my book, in the top drawer, under "Gable".'

He located the book, fumbled it open. He actually laid the gun on the desktop to make the call. The person who answered was not the pet policeman, but between Tommy's name and the aristocracy in his voice, the man clearly agreed to wake the Inspector and send him out immediately.

Tommy took the gun back to his seat.

Lady Darley spoke. 'You will be arrested, young lady, and I will see to it that you are deported. You will go home, and you will permit me to conclude my business with your Prince. *Our* business,' she amended, darting an artificial little smile across the table at her lover. 'If you do not, if you attempt to raise a protest concerning the book, it will be your word against ours. The courts will treat you harshly. You will risk an international incident, which would carry its own consequences once you are back in Japan. An international incident that could well spill over onto the honour of your beloved Emperor.'

Well, I thought, the woman had certainly figured out what mattered to a citizen of the Land of the Rising Sun.

'One answer,' Haruki bargained, 'then I go.'

'One answer, then the police take you away,' the countess corrected her.

'Charlotte, why say anything?' Tommy protested. 'Let me ring for Baker. He and the footman can sit on her until your Inspector Gable arrives.'

But the woman wanted to tell her prisoner the truth, for the same reason she had run the knife blade down the half-healed wound: to cause pain. She wanted Haruki to walk away aching with the knowledge of who was responsible. Knowing there was nothing that could be done about it.

'I first met the gentleman who would become my husband, Lord Darley – Tommy's father, James – some years ago, through a friend in Paris. James had an agreement with the fellow, that whenever he came across some particularly juicy bit of scandal, he would put Émile onto it, and in turn Émile would drop a few guineas in his hand. The upkeep on a place like this, his social responsibilities, the occasional game of cards or flutter on the ponies – life can be quite expensive, for a gentleman.

'Émile and I had a similar arrangement, although my tips were generally about the women – and frankly, more valuable. When James and I first met, we were both married, but I liked him well enough. Émile died during the War, as did my first husband. James's wife died a few years later. He and I happened to meet again, three years ago. We found that we still enjoyed the other's company. The following spring – this was 1923 – he proposed. It was, in truth, as much a business arrangement as anything else.' She gave her husband's son what was intended to seem, and apparently was accepted as, a shy and apologetic smile. I shuddered, although probably it was from the cold. Holmes wrapped his arm around me, as we pressed close for one another's warmth.

'I did not, as many thought, marry James for his money. Since the War, I had established quite a number of lucrative ventures, all on my own. One of those harmless sources of income was to connect certain wealthy art-lovers with a gentleman who often got his hands on some very high quality art reproductions – even, occasionally, the originals.'

'A "fence", I believe they are called,' Haruki offered.

'A *provider*. It was through this gentleman that I heard of the Emperor's book, and particularly of its hidden document. I was intrigued, and borrowed the document to have it translated. Even then, I was not certain as to the precise meaning, but I suspected that it was important.

'This was happening around the time that James proposed. I accepted, and in the course of merging our houses, we also merged our . . . ventures. I don't remember which of us it was who thought to include Japan on our world itinerary, but we agreed, it would be the ideal opportunity to offer the book to its owner. Although as I suspect you are aware, the book did not include the document.'

Time was passing, soon the stars would begin to fade in the sky – and although my body craved the sun's warmth, it would be a disaster. Holmes was aware of it, too: I could feel his growing uneasiness.

'Thank you,' Haruki said. Then her gaze shifted, to the young man with the gun. 'And you, young Lord Darley: are you satisfied with this answer?'

The countess looked suddenly wary. 'Tommy, sweetheart, I would like to get to bed before—'

Haruki talked over her, speaking still to Tommy. 'Your father died. We all believed he was the blackmailer. Well, we knew he was *a* blackmailer – a young woman named Wilma Roland gave her life to prove it. But how convenient for you, not only that his papers lived on, but that his widow knew precisely what to do with them. I imagine the papers were kept in his safe, not in hers. Am I right?'

'Servants go into the big one,' he said. 'Charlotte's maid—'

'Tommy,' the coaxing voice began.

Again Haruki cut her off. 'But all the papers were kept *there*, even for projects that belonged to your father's wife. Am I correct?'

'It's more convenient, to have them all in one place.'

'For her, certainly. If the Japanese police had arrested your father, and if the English police had come here to investigate, would they have found any evidence at all that he had not acted on his own?'

Tommy ignored his lover's protests, even without the prisoner's help. 'That means nothing.'

'Doesn't it? What if the police came to arrest you now? Would they find any evidence at all in the safe – that safe in *your* room – to tell them that Lady Darley knew anything at all about your crimes?'

'Of course they would!'

'Tommy!'

'I mean, there've been times when she . . . did things.'

'Which of you shot the fence, Bart Collins?'

'I never—'

'The Bourkes may be irreplaceable, far too valuable to shoot, but which of you spread the dismembered rabbit around the Bourke workshop by way of a warning?'

No response.

'Also, a Japanese translator by the name of Rai Hirakawa was taken from the river in London, a few days after Mr Collins was shot.' The name tickled the back of my mind . . . where? In Sussex: the newspapers. An inquest. 'I imagine that Lady Darley took care to be busy in some public place at the time he died. Attending a party, having her hair done.'

'I—'

Haruki continued. 'Another guess, since I seem to be having such luck with them. I would guess that your lover found her husband a little too civilised. That he was willing to commit blackmail, but she could not urge him into actual murder. For that she required someone a little more . . . "malleable", is, I think, the word. Did she seduce you before you left England? Or was it on the voyage over? Certainly you had cuckolded your father before you boarded the *Thomas Carlyle*: why else never meet her eyes on the ship? And having seduced your body, she then took her time on the home voyage to seduce your morals. Letting you know how exciting she found it when you were . . . ruthless. As your father never was.'

After a long and electric moment, Tommy's head turned to look at the countess. I expect he was unaware that his hand followed his gaze – but she was not. She flicked an uneasy glance at the revolver, then restored her smile. 'Tommy, darling, you can see what she's doing, can't you? Trying to drive a wedge between us? I love you, Tommy. You know that. I've given you . . . everything.'

'Lady Darley, how did your first husband die?'

The countess kept her pleading eyes on the young man. 'I told you, he died in the War.'

'Yes, but in battle? Or was his body found in a Paris alleyway?'

Where the hell did Haruki get her information? She wasn't inventing it – the words hit the older woman like a body blow, her wide eyes coming off her lover at last. 'No! It was . . . he died on the Front. So many did.'

'Many did, true. But not him. And if Lord Darley – James Darley, that is – had not died a year ago falling from the roof of the Imperial Hotel, when would he have died? Would he have made it all the way home again, or might he have encountered a fatal accident somewhere along the way?' The black eyes returned to Tommy. 'Lord Darley, Charlotte Bridgeford married your father not because she wished a partner, but because she required a shield.

A "scapegoat". I suggest that she intends the same for you.'

Lady Darley did not quite dare to attack her, not with the gun still in her lover's hand. Instead, she tossed her lovely hair, which had somehow come down around her shoulders. She laughed. 'Oh, Tommy, this really is extraordinary. Ring Gable again and ask how long before we can get this creature out of our lives. You'll see that . . . that . . . Oh, what is it *now*?'

The countess's exhortations were pulled apart by a series of odd moves by Haruki: first she swivelled in her chair to look at the gilt desk behind her, then straightened to lean back on the settee. She propped one foot on the table, then the other, ankles crossed. Her fingers locked across her stomach, her mouth tucked into a secret little smile.

'What?' demanded Lady Darley. 'What are you smirking at?'

'Merely the hour.'

'It's four o'clock in the morning. Why the devil does it matter?'

'You are about to have visitors,' Haruki said.

As if in tardy confirmation, the clock downstairs chimed. The sound stopped, faded, and merged into a distant approaching murmur.

A car on the road – and a play of lights as it turned down the drive.

Chapter Thirty-Seven

Hawthorn: birds nesting.
Nakasendo: monkey's fur.
Two uses of moss.

WORDLESSLY, HOLMES WRENCHED HIMSELF upright using the balcony railing, then tugged me to my feet, pushing me in the direction of the portico roof.

I clambered across the gap, then scurried, bent double, across the dim light from the arched window – nearly sprawling on my face as I tripped on something. I pushed into the vines growing up the trellis, as Holmes did the same on his side. The narrow strip of light across the balcony abruptly became a flood as the orange curtains jerked apart. Tommy's silhouette moved across the tiles where we had been seconds before. He looked down at the drive.

His voice was quite clear. 'This will be Inspector Gable. Here, you take the gun in case she decides to make a break for it. Shall I put the book away?'

'No, just put it on a shelf – it's the one thing the girl won't talk about.' The car stopped directly before the portico. The scrape of a door latch was followed by feet on gravel, crunching across to the steps and up the landing to the door. The bell rang, followed by the hollow demands of a knocker.

If the servants slept through this, they had been drugged.

However, Tommy reached the downstairs door before any servant could. 'Good morning, Inspec – oh, sorry. I was expecting Gable. He sent you in his place, did he?' The jovial beginning followed by marked uneasiness told me all I needed to know about Inspector Gable.

'I don't know anything about that, sir,' said a man with working-class Oxford tones beneath the accents of education. 'My name is Ambrose. This is Constable Harwood. I have come to investigate a report of criminal activities taking place inside this house.'

'Well, yes, although I'm not sure that there's much investigation required. This girl broke in, little Japanese thing, not dangerous I'd guess but somewhat nervous-making, nonetheless, and . . .'

His voice faded as he stepped back to allow Ambrose and his man to enter. With the voices inside, there was little danger of being overheard. 'What do you want to do?' I whispered to my large and all-too-nearly-visible husband.

'I propose that we take our leave of this circus before we are spotted. Miss Sato appears to have made plans that do not involve us. In any event, we can be of more assistance to her cause from the outside of a gaol cell than from within.'

'Agreed.'

Inside, the three men reached the top of the stairway, continuing down the short length of corridor. Their voices were strikingly clear. As I ventured a peek around the vines, I noticed that one segment of the big arched window had been left unlatched, and was slightly open: another sign of careless housemaids. Tommy's pronounced drawl informed the Inspector about how he and Lady Darley had driven back from Leicester after a party (casually dropping the names of a few august fellow guests) and were having a nightcap in the library when . . .

The voice became muffled as the men entered the library. Holmes and I prepared to make our departure down the trellises – and then came the other voice.

'Good morning, Miss Sato,' said Ambrose. 'I trust we hit the time about right?'

Holmes and I froze into place.

'Thank you, Inspector, you are quite on time. This is Charlotte, Lady Darley and Thomas, Lord Darley. I believe you will find some items of interest in the safe in Lord Darley's dressing room. The combination is 12; 2; 19. I believe that is the date of the former Lady Darley's death.'

'Lord Darley, Lady Darley, you are under arrest for the – watch out, she's got – oh, good. Miss Sato, I'll take that weapon, if you please. Constable, please keep control of Lady Darley.'

It was at this point that the other members of the household belatedly trailed up from their beds: butler, footman, housekeeper, and two or three maids, roused by the tumult at the door. Tommy did his manly best to summon them to action but, given a choice between a large constable and their disliked employer, none cared to risk physical intervention.

Ambrose sent the servants downstairs to await him in the kitchen, then said something I could not quite hear. Tommy's voice, however, rose clearly through the small gap in the window nearby.

'My good man,' he began to bluster, 'surely you can see this . . . *person* is an intruder? She broke into my house, she *threatened* Lady Darley, and if she knows the combination to the safe there's no doubt she's stolen us bli—'

'Tommy, for God's sake, shut your mouth!' the countess snarled in a fury, but it was too late.

'Burglary, is it?' Ambrose asked, sounding quite cheerful at the prospect. 'Perhaps my constable and I ought to have a look. Would you all be so good as to assist us? Yes, you too, my Lady.'

Tommy had fallen silent, no doubt perceiving that he had made a mistake, although very possibly not knowing precisely where. But the countess knew. As Ambrose and his constable began to shepherd the three of them out of the library, she first cajoled, then protested, then began coldly to declare that the Inspector had no reason to remain here, this was a purely domestic dispute, that it was all a misunderstanding, and that if he insisted on remaining in the house, she would have his job.

Her voice, rising with every step closer to the bedrooms, faded once they stepped inside. Lights went on in adjoining rooms.

Bemused, I looked at my husband's dim outline. 'What a very interesting development.'

'Russell, we must leave. First, however . . .'

He stepped across to the balcony and pulled open the French doors. I peeped around the edge of the arched window again, to make certain the constable wasn't standing there, then crossed the portico in Holmes' wake – reaching down first to see what had tripped me.

It lay immediately under the section of window that was standing ajar. As if someone had tossed it out – or silently stretched down an arm with it while her compatriots crouched ten feet away.

A narrow rectangle some eight inches tall, wrapped in waterproof paper, the ends neatly tucked in. There was just enough light for me to read the oversized printing on the cover:

Please exchange the book, not the letter.
Also, please wait one week.

I ripped it open.

'Holmes!' He was just shutting the French doors. He looked at my hands. I looked at his. The contents were identical.

'How many of these dratted books are there?' I asked.

Holmes shoved his copy in his shirt-front and stepped onto the trellises; I scrambled to follow.

We made it away from the house without being discovered, by police or servants. On the other hand, we then were forced to spend a very long time buried in some very uncomfortable hedgerows, watching a house in which very little happened. The sky grew light, stable hands came and went, two birds lined their nest in the hawthorn above our heads. Shortly after dawn, two more police cars came up the drive, each carrying a uniformed constable and an officer. All four went in the front door. No one came out.

When the sun was high enough to thaw my fingers, I laid my warm sweater on the grass and arranged the two books on top. The woven surface underneath and thick white hawthorn blossom overhead made me imagine for an instant that I was kneeling for a hanami, setting out a picnic beneath flowering trees. The picnic itself would have been most welcome: cold vinegared rice; chewing my way through a plate of octopus. I'd even drink the sake, were that the only – I shook myself free from the memories and returned to the problem at hand.

'Could Bourke have made *three* copies, and lied to us?' I asked Holmes. 'Or could someone other than Bourke have made one?' Two? A dozen?

'I believe you'll find that one of these is the Bodleian's copy.'

I was shocked. 'That's not possible!'

'No?'

'No one can steal from the Bodleian. I mean, *I* could figure out a way probably, but a stranger? How would she even find the thing?'

'An intriguing question, I agree.'

'So which one is it?'

He raised an eyebrow at the two books, then went back to watching the house.

I picked up the one Holmes had taken from the Bible, and looked, as the countess had done, to see if the document was still there. But unlike her, I then cautiously worked it out, gingerly unfolding it, hoping it would not instantly shatter into four ragged rectangles.

It was blank. Oh, yes, it was old, its folds heavily compressed by apparent decades within its hiding boards, but unless the document had been written in invisible ink, this was a decoy.

I turned to the copy that Haruki had placed on the portico roof, wrapped in dark brown waterproof paper. (And where on earth had she got that?) It, too, had a folded piece of very old-looking paper inside the parting of the cover – only this one was not blank.

The page seemed to hold several lines of spidery Japanese calligraphy, although since this one, too, threatened to fall apart along its fold-lines, I let it close without stretching it flat. I slid it back into the rooftop copy, where Haruki had left it.

So, which one of these was which? I could only hope that the true Hokusai was not a drift of crumbling ash in the Darley fireplace.

I opened the copy I'd tripped over on the roof – call it A – to a random page. I then found the same illustration in the other – call it B, the one Holmes had retrieved from the Bible – and squinted critically from one to the other. B was the more impressive, its colours more beautiful. A was more subdued, the overall effect a fraction plainer. However, A was the one that tempted the hand, made one want to caress the gorgeous illustrations. I found the page showing the Mojiro-joku post station, and studied first one monkey-rock, then the other. B was more beautiful; A was more alive.

I laid Copy A back on its dark brown waterproof wrapping.

'If one of these is the Bodleian's copy,' I said, 'although I'm not saying it is, since it will make Thomas Bodley turn in his grave and Mr Parsons take to his prematurely, then what she pulled off with the Darleys was a shell game. Say she brought in two copies under that ridiculously large coat of mine she insisted on wearing: the Bodleian's, and the Prince Regent's. Remember, Bourke said that one was better than the other – and that was the one he gave the Bodleian? Haruki brought both of them here. While we were freezing our toes off on the balcony, she went back to Lady Darley's bedroom, traded the Prince's copy – call that Copy C – for the original – call that A – that was in the Bible, and wrapped the original in the waterproof paper. She slipped it onto the portico roof while we were distracted by the Darleys, and slid the better copy – copy B, which she stole from the Bodleian – into her sling for the countess to find.

'Copy C went onto the fire. That left what Lady Darley believed was the original, but was in fact this very pretty copy B.' I tapped a thoughtful finger on the book Holmes had rescued. 'Drawing the woman's attention to its hidden document was a risk, but if one only looks at the edges of the two folded pages, they look identical. Leaving the original out on the roof was another risk. But clearly, Haruki couldn't take a chance on keeping the document on her person, not if she had already arranged for the police to come. And if we didn't happen to see the book there, I suppose she would either have got a message to us, or retrieved it herself. Are you asleep?' I asked, becoming aware that I had been musing aloud for some time now.

'The branches are too sharp for that,' he said.

I flattened the brown paper and read again the words she had written there, with what looked like the grease-pen I kept in my desk. 'She wants us to exchange the Darley original for the Bodleian's fake, minus the document. Or if you're right, replace their missing fake with the original they should have had in the first place.'

'That should make for an interesting exercise.'

My heart quailed at the idea of being caught in the act. To never be welcomed inside those hallowed doors again? Unthinkable. 'Maybe I could just post it to them.'

'In any event, Russell, you have seven days to plan your attack.'

'Yes, waiting a week. But, the "Also, please wait one week". Wait a week before returning this to the Bodleian? Or before we break her out of the Oxford prison?'

He just shook his head and reached for his cigarettes.

I wished I smoked. It might take my mind off how hungry, thirsty, and tired I was. I prayed that the motorcar was well enough concealed: if the police had found it, it was going to be a long walk home.

Half an hour later, the front door came open. Lady Darley stepped out, Tommy at her heels. 'Oh, no,' I breathed. Those two plausible aristocrats had convinced Inspector Ambrose . . . but no: one of the officers and his constable were following close behind. And the men appeared alert rather than abashed. They put the Darleys into the back seat of the last motorcar to arrive. The two remaining constables came out, carrying crates, loading them into Ambrose's motor. One constable took up a position beside it; the other went back inside. The two men who had escorted the Darleys drove off with them.

Five minutes later, a section of the arched window opened. Haruki bent to peer down at the roof, then looked out as if she could see us, a quarter mile away. Her head pulled back, and the window closed. But when the front door came open again a few minutes later and she stepped out, Ambrose's hand was on Haruki's good elbow. Then the sun glinted from her wrists: handcuffs. 'Oh, damn.'

Ambrose placed her in the back seat of the other motor. He stood for a moment, talking to her, then shut the car door. The other inspector climbed in, the other constable got behind the wheel, and off went Haruki Sato to the Oxford gaol.

Ambrose himself drove away minutes later in the motor laden with crates, leaving a single constable on the doorstep of Darley House.

Holmes and I roused our aching bones, and went to see if my own Morris was in the field across the road. And if it wasn't, to find a comfortable place where we could lie down and die.

The motor was there, thank heavens and the unsuspicious gaze of the Oxford police department. I drove slowly through the spring morning, listening to the light snores from the back, knowing that this would be the last sleep Holmes permitted himself today.

Safe behind my door, we bathed, Holmes shaved, we ate. When he had reached the tobacco stage, we laid our two books on the table before us, and we talked.

Chapter Thirty-Eight

Ivy crowds the sides
Of the Divinity School,
Oxford's beating heart.

'How could she get a book out of the Bodleian?' I fretted. 'How would you have done so?'

'I wouldn't. I have a reader's card, and they all know me, but even I would think twice about stealing something under their noses. The Bodley's had three hundred years to learn how to spot a thief.'

'But if you did?'

I ran a hand through my hair. 'I suppose I'd hunt for a librarian vulnerable to bribe or threat. Short of that, I'd carry a book in, put in a request for the Hokusai, and pray hard that Haruki had the sense to put a book – any book at all – in the Hokusai cover box when she took it out.'

'Might she have done the same?'

'What, bribe a librarian?'

'Replace the book with one she'd brought.'

My eyebrows climbed. 'You think she got a reader's card?'

'You might enquire.'

'Indeed I might. And sooner rather than later. The other question

I have is, how does she know so much? Lady Darley's first husband; that translator, what was his name? Hirakawa? Are we *sure* she's not one of Mycroft's?' It was intended as a joke, but it fell rather flat.

'Miss Sato looks to have been here a bit longer than she admitted to you. And, she has made full use of her father's network of extended family and "ears".'

'If we hadn't been so almighty occupied, this past year . . .' We might have made enquiries about Lord Darley and his new wife. We might have followed the trail of the Emperor's book back to 1921, when it went into King George's hands. We might have done all kinds of things, if we had not come back to England last June and been thrown instantly into one case, then another, and a third . . .

He crushed out his postprandial cigarette. 'I shall go and have a word with Miss Sato's friend and arresting officer, Inspector Ambrose.'

'Will you ask to see her?'

'That will depend on what the good Inspector has to tell me.'

No, there had been no reader's card issued to the name Sato. None issued to any small Japanese person, male or female, in recent weeks.

I was sorely tempted to request the Bashō volume, so I could be certain if it was actually missing from its paperboard case, but the dangers of bringing a loss to the Librarian's attention – and worse, bringing my own interest in the book to his attention – were too great. I went back out into the Schools Quadrangle, and tried to study the familiar walls with a stranger's eyes. Schola Moralis Philosophiae; the mismatched but amiable columns of the Tower of the Five Orders; windows all around me, behind which, for three hundred years, intense and gifted minds had been set alight by the printed page.

This place was my home like none other. If that tiny young woman had breached its defences, I wanted to figure out how. I could, of course, ask her, when next we met (be that behind the walls of the prison, or in freedom), but if the past twenty-four hours had taught me anything, it was that Haruki Sato had lied to me.

For how long?

I examined the Quadrangle walls, and saw a dozen places where a nimble-footed acrobat could jimmy a window and slip inside. Lies, and the stories she had told me . . .

My own mind, as I stood there surrounded by a million pages of human thought and knowledge, began to glow, then slowly to burn.

This entire case was about books, beginning with the one in my hands when, thirteen months before, Haruki and I had met on the deck of the *Thomas Carlyle*. Our first conversation had been of poetry. Lady Darley later spoke of William Shakespeare and Matthew Arnold. And at the centre of it all, Bashō's folding-out story of a Nakasendo journey.

Stories.

Something touched my elbow. I looked down into the worried face of a sub-librarian, saying some words. I nodded and gave him a few words in return, then I turned and left the Quad before he could break any further into my thoughts. I went out through the passageway between the Schools of Natural Philosophy and Music into Radcliffe Square, turning right: down Brasenose Lane, up the Turl, and back along Broad Street. There I paused to look up at the walls of the Divinity School. It had been festooned with ivy, when first I saw it during the War. Were it still, I might have suspected earlier.

I continued the circuit, down Catte to Radcliffe Square again. There I nodded to myself, having confirmed what I'd thought, before doubling back through the Schools Quad to follow Parks Road towards the north end of town.

I had once walked into a lamp post in this city, when my eyes were taken up with a book, and I suppose this day, too, I must have had any number of near-misses. I had a vague sense of blaring horns and alarmed expressions on the faces of strangers, but my mind was too busy weaving a story out of a year's worth of threads to pay them any attention.

I made it to my front door without mishap. Some time later, I looked down in surprise at the cup in my hand. My mouth tasted of tea, my eyes were half-blind from standing in the sun.

I looked around. Holmes was sitting at my kitchen table, a newspaper spread out before him and a bemused look on his face.

'Hello,' I said.

'Are you quite well, Russell?'

'I'm not sure.' I took another sip from my cup. For some reason, it was tepid. I pulled the cosy off the pot and topped up the cup with a remarkably powerful-looking brew, and sat down. 'What did Inspector Ambrose have to say?'

Holmes looked at me for a moment, one eyebrow raised, before deciding to humour my question. 'She came to him ten days ago with a story he found—'

'Wait: ten days ago?'

'The Tuesday of last week.'

'Go ahead.'

'She told him a story that at first he found hard to credit, of a local earl who ran a nice line in blackmail. His impulse was to show her the door, but she had letters, from three high-ranking individuals, requesting that the reader tender any assistance possible to Miss Haruki Sato.'

'There wasn't a letter from the Prince, surely?'

'No. But one was from the Japanese ambassador to America. She spent the better part of the day in the Inspector's office. At the end, he was convinced that she might be speaking the truth, and furthermore, that the plan she presented him was workable.'

'She came with a plan ready-made,' I said, not a question.

'She did. The specific details came later, but he agreed to her basic request: that she be permitted to pursue the evidence in her own way. Then, at a time to be arranged, the Inspector would arrive at the Darley house with at least one constable, a man who would not be intimidated by the thought of putting darbies on a nob, as it were. At that point, she would be able to provide him with the evidence he required for prosecution.'

'I should like to meet this Inspector Ambrose,' I reflected.

'She – or rather, her extended "family" – must have looked long and hard to locate someone who would not only listen to the outrageous claims of a small Oriental female, but would then cooperate with her in a plan of action. Inspector Ambrose comes from a family of devout trades unionists, and although he is Labour rather than Socialist, he seems of a remarkably bolshevist nature.'

In other words, a man both positioned and primed to raise an uproar at any attempt to give the Darleys a quiet aristocratic pass. Whether he would do so remained to be seen.

'And do you feel the prosecution of the Darleys will actually go ahead?'

He smiled. 'I had the distinct impression that Ambrose relished the feathers that have begun to fly at all levels of law enforcement in London. It took him some time to locate an expert in how one went about arresting a peer. And some of the papers he took from that safe name regular guests at Sandringham and Balmoral. Were it not for the uncomfortable evidence, Ambrose would be on his way to walk a beat in the Upper Hebrides.'

'And Haruki?'

'She is both the case's weakest point and its greatest strength. Her "attempted burglary" is the reason Ambrose came to Darley House in the first place. Because he was arresting her, he was required to examine the premises closely to see what she had stolen. In the course of the search, he happened to uncover evidence of crimes far greater than a break-in.

'To dismiss the burglary case against her could undermine the greater case. She will be charged with trespass and a handful of other crimes. Ambrose tells me that she not only agrees, she insists on it. He also tells me that there will be no denying that both Darleys knew of the contents of that safe. Their fingerprints are all over the inside. Hers, too.'

'Really?' Overlooking fingerprints seemed the mistake of an amateur.

'It would appear that Lady Darley's jewels were kept in and among the file-boxes containing letters and photographs. Making it difficult for her to claim she had not been in Tommy's safe.'

'But—' I stopped, then felt a slow smile grow on my face. 'Miss Sato was a busy girl, while Tommy and his stepmother were talking in the library.'

'Yes.'

'Well, I suppose we should be grateful it's only gaol, and not a broken neck. Did you see her?'

'I did not. And it being the weekend tomorrow, I doubt we shall be granted a visitation until Monday. Now, would you like to tell me – What is it? Why are you laughing?'

'"Get the job done."' I sat back in my chair, filled with rueful admiration. '"Our most important skills are those of deception."'

'I beg your pardon?'

'You and I have been played, Holmes. Like a pair of fish. From the moment she told me she came from a family of acrobats. "We use the tools we have", she said. Or as her father put it, "Get the job done", no matter the cost to your life, your pride, your freedom.' I shook my head. 'If only she'd told us the truth from the beginning, this might all have been avoided.' Or not. But without the chance . . .

'How?'

'I realised something, at the Bodleian this morning. You know how one small fact can tip everything on its head?'

'The world rests on tiny things,' he agreed.

'In this case, it's the absence of blood.'

'Ah.' He sat back, taking out his tobacco.

'Haruki Sato told us a story – a story, then its sequel. Designed for us, specifically crafted to entice two clever English detectives to enter the circle of another Englishman, and help retrieve a book. From the moment she made a friendly remark to me as I sat on the deck reading, she was getting a sense of who we were, whether we were sufficiently clever for her purposes, how she might win us over. The only slip she made was to let us see her on the high wire: if we'd really thought about it, that skill might have put us on the alert earlier, made us question her claim that she was not herself trained in the family traditions. Though I wouldn't even bet she hadn't calculated that particular "slip" to the last degree.

'She knew about us before she boarded the *Thomas Carlyle*. Not everything, but enough to get her started. The irony of it is, you and I would have helped her anyway, even if she and her father had been completely honest about their goals. But they couldn't be certain about that. So they told us a story.

'And – a double irony, especially bitter – the story came to a very traditional Japanese end last spring, with almost no help from us. We were just a back-up plan that turned out to be unnecessary, since the Emperor's hidden servant managed to get inside, and give his life for his master, preserving the future and avenging the past.

'If the Prince Regent had looked closely enough at the book then and there, we might actually have been of some use. But by the time he noticed the substitution, the Darleys were far beyond their reach.

'So, the entire charade began again. Only now the stakes were substantially higher, and Haruki no longer had the experience of her father to draw from.

'So she returned to the tools that had served her well the first time: Sherlock Holmes and Mary Russell. She did her own investigations, traced the book from King George to the Darleys. Then she went sideways, as we should have done, making enquiries into the history of Lady Darley.

'As you said, she appears to have been in England more than the few days she told me. She must have been very busy, putting together her information – and her story. I came back and she was here to greet me, standing in my kitchen with blood pouring down her arm.' I met my husband's eyes. 'That young woman could have scaled the Bodleian during the dead of night in an ice storm. What is more, none of the iron fences show the least sign of blood.'

It took a moment for the meaning to penetrate; when it did, even he drew back, appalled. 'She did that to herself?'

What courage it had taken, to savage her own arm.

'And I'd thought *she* was the too-trusting innocent. Just as I thought she got hurt because she came to Oxford without knowing the lay of the land – that she was ignorant of how the Bodleian worked and who Bulldogs were, and paid a hard price for that ignorance. But in fact, her arm was injured precisely *because* she knew how things worked. She'd known how *I* worked from the start, when she told me about coming from a family of acrobats and saw my polite scepticism. She also knew that I would be an extremely efficient . . . "tool", here in Oxford, if only she could overcome that mistrust. Once she had set me in motion, she could keep me in the dark, exaggerating her fever, letting me believe I was carrying out matters in my own way – leaving her free to slip out the back and buy waterproof paper, see her Inspector, do whatever she needed. All she had to do was pay that initial price.'

She'd known precisely how to manipulate me. Knew I would consider it unthinkable that any sane person would do that to herself. So I did not think it – neither of us did. And with her flesh she bought my – our – blind belief. *Get the job done.*

The room was silent. Holmes came to the end of his cigarette, and pressed it thoughtfully in the ashtray. 'I do not think,' he said, 'that she knew what her father intended, that night on the Imperial roof.'

'Not consciously, no. But afterwards? She must have looked back at every moment, studied it all, and realised how thoroughly her father had kept his plan from her as well as from us. None of us would have agreed to his death, so none of us knew. And when she came here, she followed his example. You and I would not have agreed to her arrest, so she said nothing.' I grimaced. 'Every person who looked at Haruki Sato saw a girl with a charming smile – including us! We never even considered that she might be a person who could rip open her own flesh, just to come in under my guard.'

'Madness,' he said.

'A tragedy. We'd have helped her, without question. You'd have jumped at the chance to catch James Darley.'

'But not to kill him.'

'Yes. We let them know that we would draw that line, didn't we?'

'I also expect Miss Sato needed to feel in command of the operation, to the end. That is the problem with bringing in partners: it limits one's freedom of action.'

'Still, she did trust us at the end, with the document.' She must have hesitated over the decision, I thought. It was nice to know that we had proved a marginally more desirable alternative than simply burning the thing. I drew a deep breath, and looked into Holmes' grey eyes. 'Do you think . . . did she come here with the intention of following in her father's path? Killing the Darleys, and herself?'

'I think it very possible.'

Neither of us looked away. Both of us were thinking of the woman's abilities, and the fact that at the moment, but for a few locks, she had the Darleys very close to hand.

CHAPTER THIRTY-NINE

Temple of the Book:
A Fool's errands all around:
Gallows lie below.

GIVE ME A WEEK, she had asked. In the end, it only took her five days. The Darleys were arrested on Friday morning, ushered into the dank and draughty confines of His Majesty's Prison, Oxford, a part of the castle complex dating back to the eleventh century. The Empress Matilda had escaped over the frozen Thames, but then, she had a great deal of help from within.

Apparently, the two Darleys did not.

On Monday, I returned to the Bodleian and filled out the request slips for a number of books that had nothing whatsoever to do with Japanese art. When I walked back out through the Schools Quad, I was covered with drying sweat and tingling with nerves, but the Bashō – in its naked silken slipcase – was sitting on a high shelf in Mr Parsons' office, waiting to puzzle the poor man when he came across it. I could only hope his wrath at finding an empty paperboard case on the shelves (or – catastrophe! – a case containing the wrong book) did not result in a sub-librarian losing his job, or his head. Or worse, cause Mr Parsons to believe that he was becoming absent-minded . . .

Wednesday morning, the Earl of Darley and Charlotte, Lady Darley (quite alive and filled with imperious fury) were formally charged with a long list of crimes. The four intervening days, I later learnt, had seen a whirlwind of consternation as far up as the Palace: how could one conduct the trial of a peer charged with blackmail, and not make public the specifics of the evidence?

But Ambrose hung tough. Haruki had either been lucky, or chosen the point of her wedge with great care. Probably both.

I added that to the list of questions I intended to ask her.

Finally, on Wednesday afternoon, the post brought notification from the prison that we would be permitted a half-hour of visitation on Thursday morning, to speak with prisoner Haruki Sato.

Holmes had been in London, adding his weight to the prosecution, but he caught a late train back to Oxford. He had questions of his own.

I woke that night, for no discernible reason. Some tiny noise . . .

I slipped out of bed and went down the stairs.

Moonlight came through the sitting room windows. The book that Holmes had pulled from Lady Darley's Bible was sitting openly on my desk, as it had been since Friday. *All those books*, I reflected. Bashō's poems, the Bard's plays, a countess's empty Bible. And now this one, a lovely fake with a history of its own. I slid it from its case and turned back the front cover.

The document I had left sitting inside it was gone.

In its place was a folded square of the paper from my desk. As I picked it up, a few tiny spots of brightness fluttered out. I switched on the desk lamp to see: three cherry blossoms, perfect and white against the dark wood. On the page were two English sentences in her trim writing, followed by three rows of descending Japanese characters, then the poem's English translation:

380

My very first word of you warned that I should take great care, because you and your husband were English shinobi. If in the future the Sato family may be of any service to you, I would consider it a sign that you forgive my betrayal of your friendship.

In a castle keep
The prisoner sees the moon.
Freedom lies just . . . there.

For the first time in days, I felt my face relax into a smile. I returned the blossoms to the paper, the paper to the book, and the book into the slipcase young Mr Bourke had so ingeniously crafted. I checked the doors and windows – locked, all of them – then went back upstairs. No need to rise early; no cause to brood over an assassination of Darleys, or to agonise over how we might prise a friend out of the English justice system. Upon her noble face there would be *no note how dread an army hath enrounded her*; in the background no war-engines, no awareness of gallows in a courtyard below.

'What was it?' My house: my right to investigate untoward noises. But that did not mean Sherlock Holmes slept through them.

I climbed back into my warm bed and pulled the blankets up around my ears.

'Nothing, my dear Holmes. Nothing more than a little touch of Haruki in the night.'

ACKNOWLEDGEMENTS

For the ladies (and gents) of the Capitola Book Cafe, for twenty-one years of Laurie King celebrations: my thanks are laid at your feet.

My love to Linda Allen, the agent who got me here.

Thanks are also due, a thousand times over, to my publishers, Allison & Busby, who make my books stronger, less nonsensical, more beautiful – and available, to people like you who might want to read them.

Special thanks to Kate Miciak, Libby McGuire, Jennifer Hershey, Kim Hovey, Scott Shannon, Sharon Propson, Kelly Chian, Carlos Beltrán – and welcome, Julia Maguire. I owe you guys everything.

To Mr Masashi Okamoto and the staff of Japan's excellent Nara Hotel, who took in three very lost travellers and made them welcome.

With thanks to Michelle Geissbuhler, and her alter ego 'Wilma Roland,' for joining in the fun during the 2013 spring campaign.

To Commodore Everette Hoard of the *Queen Mary*, Long

Beach, who answered many odd questions about cruise liners.

To Evelyn Thompson, for setting this foreigner straight on matters Japanese, and Jean Lukens, ever ready to put pen to paper for the sake of illustrating Laurie King.

To Liz McCarthy of the Bodleian Library, with thanks for the archival boxes, and apologies for the misdeeds of certain characters herein.

And just to be clear: no books were stolen from Bodley in the making of this book, just as no misdeeds have ever been known to happen in Tokyo's peerless Imperial Hotel, in any of its manifestations.

Clearly, any errors that remain in the book were despite the best efforts of these good people.